SECRETS *of a*
SOAP OPERA

Diva

ALSO BY VICTORIA ROWELL

The Women Who Raised Me: A Memoir

SECRETS *of a* SOAP OPERA

Diva

A NOVEL

VICTORIA ROWELL

ATRIA PAPERBACK

New York   London   Toronto   Sydney

ATRIA PAPERBACK
A Division of Simon & Schuster, Inc.
1230 Avenue of the Americas
New York, NY 10020

First Atria Paperback edition May 2010

ATRIA PAPERBACK and colophon are trademarks of Simon & Schuster, Inc.

For information about special discounts for bulk purchases,
please contact Simon & Schuster Special Sales at 1-866-506-1949
or business@simonandschuster.com.

The Simon & Schuster Speakers Bureau can bring authors to your live event. For more information or to book an event contact the Simon & Schuster Speakers Bureau at 1-866-248-3049 or visit our website at www.simonspeakers.com.

Designed by Suet Chong

Manufactured in the United States of America

1   2   3   4   5   6   7   8   9   10

Library of Congress Cataloging-in-Publication Data
Rowell, Victoria.
   Secrets of a soap opera diva : a novel / Victoria Rowell.—1st Atria pbk. ed.
      p. cm.
1. Television actors and actresses—Fiction.
2. Television soap operas—Fiction. I. Title.
PS3618.O876S43 2010
813'.6—dc22   2009038948

ISBN 978-1-4391-6442-6
ISBN 978-1-4391-6484-6 (ebook)

William J. Bell
March 6, 1927–April 29, 2005

Creator and executive producer of the soap operas The Young and the Restless *and* The Bold and the Beautiful *was an extraordinary man of infinite courage and creativity, inspiring the daytime drama industry to be more than a soap opera. Once a comedy writer in Chicago, Bill's passion for writing was as infectious as his humor. He mentored in his own legendary way and it was a privilege to be in his wake, breathing and sometimes dancing life into his words as the popular Drucilla Barber Winters for more than a decade on the number one daytime drama,* The Young and the Restless. *I will forever hold dear his notes, photographs, and our time spent in Malibu with his wife, Lee, or in my own backyard in Hollywood. But above all I will cherish our SECRET. Bill gave new meaning to the Socrates quote, "The best dancer is also the best warrior."*

Calysta Jeffries is like a chocolate-covered spider—calculating, delicious, and spellbinding. She can do no wrong in front of the camera and that's all I care about.

—AUGUSTUS BARRINGER SR.

Author's Note

What a privilege it has been performing for a global audience as an actress for more than two decades.

Suspending disbelief, true soap opera devotees in the millions escape for one hour a day into the fictional swirl of their favorite daytime drama, five days a week, two hundred and sixty episodes a year. For generations, soaps are shared like a prized heirloom, passed down to children and grandchildren alike.

In England it's *Coronation Street* and *EastEnders,* Brazil tunes into *Of Body and Soul,* one of India's many sudsers is *Kumkum.* The Caribbean is glued to the number one soap opera in America, *The Young and the Restless,* airing three times daily.

Many die-hard fans go so far as to schedule college classes, while others rearrange lunch breaks, doctor appointments, and business meetings around their favorite daytime drama so as not to miss one second of nail-biting cliff-hanger suspense. Fans around the world would defend this: "It's a way to put real life on hold, unplug, and unwind."

As if soap writers intuitively know the despair and dreams of those watching, a single episode can uplift spirits while shedding light on serious topics ranging from foster care, illiteracy, and breast cancer to AIDS. A soap opera and its cast of characters have the incandescent ability to transcend language and cultural barriers, addressing millions of viewers around the world in a single sitting.

Though we can't accurately measure the global phenomenon of soap opera culture, one thing is certain, the "stories" allow grown men and women to laugh one minute and cry the next without apology.

I've read thousands and thousands of letters over the years from fans who shared how they learned to speak English watching a soap opera, or coped with isolation when suffering from chronic debilitating illnesses.

Elders reported how their beloved sudser didn't just keep them company; by engaging in one of their favorite pastimes, they felt they were keeping up with extended family members on the tube.

The imprisoned, those confined to hospital beds, and those without a bed at all proved they had one thing in common—knowing they could depend on the companionship of a soap opera, hence making it not just a daytime drama but rather a lifeline.

To soap opera fans around the world, from Africa, Greece, India, Poland, France, Germany, Japan, Brazil, Romania, the Caribbean, and Israel to Italy, Australia, Indonesia, and parts in between, Thank you with a capital T for your loyalty over the years.

Warmly,

Victoria

SECRETS *of a*
SOAP OPERA
Diva

Like Thoroughbreds at the Kentucky Derby . . .
so are the bubblers at the Sudsy Awards

Ever noticed how horses act once the shot rings out at Churchill Downs? Those Thoroughbreds show more restraint than the average bubbler, aka fame-obsessed soap star, once their soap is announced winner for Best Daytime Drama Series at the Sudsy Awards. Most soap stars are so desperate to make the leap from the daytime plantation to the promised land of prime time and feature film they lose all sense of decorum when truckin' toward the stage.

I'm not saying, er typing, any names, but a particular aging actress went so far as to knee an adorable thirteen-year-old child actor in his still-developing nether regions to get her usual spot next to the executive producer onstage. If you don't believe moi, look at the 2008 Daytime Sudsys on YouTube. A fan recorded it with her Handycam!

In desperate hopes that some *CSI, Mad Men,* or even *Dancing with the Stars* producer might "discover" them, soap stars can't resist the opportunity of having their freshly Botoxed mugs exposed during an hour of prime-time television.

This year, however, it isn't the award for best show that has people buzzing on the soapvine or around watercoolers. It's the bubbler battle for Best Lead Actress in a Daytime Serial that has sudser fans and industry insiders alike talking.

I predict gold-plated statuettes will roll, right along with a few heads, if Calysta Jeffries doesn't finally take home the Sudsy for her role as fan favorite

Ruby Stargazer on *The Rich and the Ruthless* after tonight's live broadcast from the Kodak Theatre in Hollywood.

Inside sources reveal the feisty actress has been threatening to quit her soap if she doesn't win this year. Would Calysta Jeffries really do that to *R&R*'s creator Augustus Barringer, who basically plucked her from Obscurity-ville and made her a star all those years ago? I guess we'll find out tonight.

Log on to SecretsofaSoapOperaDiva.com right after the telecast for all the juicy behind-the-scenes dish.

The Diva

CHAPTER 1

The Sudsy Awards

The night belongs to you, kid," said soap opera mogul Augustus O. Barringer, squeezing my hand. The legendary creator and head writer of my sudser, *The Rich and the Ruthless*, the number-one-rated daytime drama in America and around the world, watched weekly by more than a hundred million fans, said, "I can feel it."

"You really think so, Mr. Barringer?" I asked anxiously.

"Mark my words."

The long, boring technical awards were still under way with a svelte Valerie Bertinelli presiding. We were seated in the second row, smack dab behind Oprah's fabulous head of hair, which only served to remind me of how I had nailed an audition for a movie the talk-show icon had produced, snagging the coveted role opposite one of her favorite actresses as her sister. Naturally, being so excited I told the world, later finding out from my lazy agent, Weezi Abramowitz, who called me in Greece where I was soaking up fun and sun before filming, that I'd been stripped of the part. O's people decided it wasn't such great casting after all, replacing me with an out-of-towner. From that moment on, my vacation was wrecked. I drank myself silly with ouzo from Santorini to the Acropolis. Thank God it was only a nagging recurring dream.

Jolted by flashing paparazzi, the cast of *The View*—Barbara, Whoopi, Joy, Sherri, and the Republican—paraded by, air-kissing their way into front-row seats next to Rachael, Dr. Phil, Tyra, Regis, and Kelly.

Since the financial collapse, the whole daytime industry was on its ear. The soap opera spectacular's producer, Dick Allen, being on a shoestring budget, agreed to merge with game shows, talk shows, the Internet, and cable TV, resulting in the universe of daytime programming gathering under one roof to pat themselves on the back at the Fortieth Annual Daytime Sudsy Awards, held at the Kodak Theatre in the heart of Hollywood.

After fifteen years of false alarms, I was finally poised to win the coveted Sudsy—the Pulitzer Prize, the MacArthur Genius Grant, the Guggenheim of daytime drama—for my unforgettable portrayal of firebrand Ruby Stargazer on television's most popular soap opera, *The Rich and the Ruthless.*

"Calysta, you look amazing," said Shannen Lassiter, a costar and rare friend from the show, seated next to me.

Shannen played Dr. Justine Lashaway, sexy resident colonoscopy specialist, pediatrician, gynecologist, neurologist, popular obstetrician, podiatrist, and occasional veterinarian for the fictional citizens of suburban Whitehaven, Montana, on *R&R.*

Shannen's character was perpetually in a three-way tryst that relentlessly included Phillip McQueen (ex–Otis DuFail, *Our Lives to Contend,* now Barrett Fink, *The Rich and the Ruthless),* a Pierce Brosnan wannabe. A diva in his own right and theater scholar from Pepperell University in Maine, he was once the legendary better half of daytime's hottest gay super-couple and winner of the coveted Sudsy Crier of the Year Award earlier that evening. The gold-dipped statuette rested on his wife Pinkey's plump lap.

"Thanks, Shannen." My Rolfed-Boot-Camp-Pilates-Workout body was poured into a stunning strapless peach b. Michael gown emphasizing my derriere, décolletage, and clavicles. My soap critic pal Mitch Morelli had arranged for Jacques St. Jacques, jeweler to the stars, to drape me in half a million dollars' worth of dazzling borrowed diamonds for the evening. The only drawback was the jeweler's henchmen following me everywhere.

Shannen would also no doubt make the Best Dressed lists in all the magazines, looking radiant in a ruffled emerald green Moschino Couture, her hair with a teased Brigitte Bardot bump at the crown of her head.

Mr. Barringer had defied strict orders from his doctors and wife, Katherine, by coming to the Sudsy Awards on what was surely going to be a night we'd never forget. After growing weary of seeing me overlooked year after year, Augustus had come out of semi-retirement specifically to pen a Sudsy-Award-winning storyline for his protégée.

Ruby Stargazer's beloved daughter, Jade, the product of a crossover dalliance with Thrust Addington, who starred on *The Daring and the Damned,* Augustus Barringer's number two soap, was kidnapped by Ruby's archnemesis, deranged scientist Uranus Winterberry.

And in case you missed that episode, let me tell you, I peed all over that scene, I truly did, delivering the monologue of a lifetime as armed gunmen held me at bay while Uranus Winterberry ordered Jade dropped into an active volcano. Not to toot my own horn or anything, but it was one for the soap opera record books. Matter of fact, I won a Silver Star in *Soap Suds Digest* that week!

Even my jealous costars secretly agreed over mojitos at a pre-Sudsy luncheon at the Barringer Bel Air compound earlier in the week that I wouldn't be leaving the Kodak Theatre without a Sudsy in hand, though most of them did whatever they could to prevent it from happening.

"I'll see you in the pressroom and I'm taking out a full-page ad in *Variety*, Calysta," Augustus said proudly. "You are to *The Rich and the Ruthless* what De Beers is to diamonds."

"Ugh, it's disgusting the way he gushes over her," huffed Alison Fairchild Roberts, the sour, aging leading lady on *The Rich and the Ruthless,* to her husband, *R&R*'s greedy co-executive producer Randall Roberts. She was wrapped head to toe in pleated gold lamé with a hideous matching cape, resembling Nacho Libre on acid. Mercifully, she left the turban at home and had her hair in a "Pebbles" updo. I must say the costume made a great reflector on the red carpet. Alison and Randall were seated in the row behind us, bookended by Drew and contestants from the show *The Biggest Loser.*

"The last thing I need is for Augustus to hear you bad-mouthing Calysta on her big night. I'll never hear the end of it!" Randall said.

It was no secret among *The Rich and the Ruthless* cast and crew that Augustus favored me. Many speculated that it was more than a professional relationship, and I let them gossip themselves to death. Whatever was between Augustus and me, you can best believe I'd be taking it to my grave.

From the moment I auditioned for Mr. B in 1994, for a role I hadn't been right for, we both knew we had more than a soap opera between us. In two words, we clicked. Augustus quickly created a new role, that of feisty Ruby Stargazer, tailored for me after I confided a bit about my background. Our bond was forever sealed. And on the day I signed my first three-year contract, Augustus shared his favorite Brian Tracy quote with me: "All the people and situations of your life have only the meaning you give them . . . and, when you change your thinking, you change your life, sometimes in seconds." Mr. B quickly became the paternal figure I'd never had, making more than sure that my needs were met on and off the set. I never could've afforded the down payment for my Malibu home if it weren't for him.

The only way to repay him was through hard work. So I decided not to take my growing concerns about *R&R* to the titan. I understood how his from-another-era thinking made him oblivious to change.

I picked my battles and those I battled with, namely, Edith Norman, president of daytime television for the World Broadcast Company network, and her co-conspirator, Randall Roberts. Unfortunately, I could watch molasses go uphill in the dead of winter faster than I could get them to change any of their antiquated ways.

"You do realize if Calysta wins tonight she'll be even more full of herself," Alison shot to her husband, pursing her thin lips.

"Shh," Randall snapped, holding his manicured index up for emphasis.

"Don't shush me. It's bad enough Obama won. I can only imagine—"

"Keep your voice down," Randall scolded.

I spied the conniving pair in my Dior compact as I powdered my nose and checked my lipstick, preparing for my close-up.

Shannen looked back, scanning to the last row, where her scowling husband, Roger Cabott, washed-up hardscrabble lead actor on *Obsessions*, the campy half-hour supernatural soap, dead last in the Nielsens, was seated with his lackluster cast. Married or not, all soap stars were ordered by their networks to sit with their own shows.

Shannen smiled, waving hopefully, her Verdura pavé diamond cuff reflecting the buttery chandelier lighting. Roger looked at his younger wife before glowering forward.

"What a gorgeous bracelet," I remarked, snapping my compact shut, sliding it into my Jimmy Choo evening clutch.

"Roger gave it to me when we were first married and he was making lots of money on *Our Lives to Contend*. I've kept it in the vault, but I think this will be the last time I'll be seen wearing it," she said, wistfully tearing up. "It's a mortgage payment."

Shannen met her Svengali-like husband years ago at a Hugh Hefner party, where she'd been serving as a hostess. Secretly, I wondered if she sometimes regretted not choosing the star quarterback of the Baltimore Ravens, signed to a "fifty million dollars over six years" contract, who'd been infatuated with her.

"Girl, don't cry, you're gonna mess up your makeup."

A powder-room break later, the conspicuous Jacques St. Jacques henchmen in tow, fearing I'd gnawed off a diamond or two in the stall, Shannen and I teetered back down the aisle on four-inch Christian Louboutins and Giuseppe Zanottis, where I spotted the other two black actresses in daytime and waved. Though my feet were screaming for mercy, I knew suffering for fashion was a diva *must* and pretended they belonged to someone else, grateful for the magic of adrenaline, fame, and a potential Sudsy Award. I vamped on.

Of course we took the long way back to our seats, tap-dancing in front of Ellen, giving her a wink and an overexaggerated smile, hoping she'd invite us on her show. She was still looking for George Clooney, rumored to be a surprise Sudsy presenter and a closeted soap fan of Susan Lucci.

The plush vermilion chairs were a refuge for our tortured, pinched pigs.

"I swear, Calysta, I thought Roger was going to haul off and clobber me, I've never seen him so mad. He called us 'self-obsessed morons' and complained that our 'stupid show' gets to sit front-row center almost every year, while he has to sit 'damn near the lobby with the friggin' fans.' Plus everyone knows *Obsessions* is getting canceled."

The Rich and the Ruthless, number one for the past fourteen seasons, always got prime real estate. We bubblers took full advantage too, nestling our tightened and lifted derrieres into plenty of camera chairs. But what we detested almost as much as being on the "D" list with Hollywood casting directors was taking on the additional expense of a limousine whether we were nominated or not. The WBC network was too strapped and too cheap to pick up the tab. I decided to be my own chauffeur and kept the five hundred smackers in my bailed-out bank account.

Coked-out, oversexed teen heartthrob Toby Gorman, a Brad Pitt lookalike, climbed onstage clad in a double-breasted John Varvatos slim suit. Toby played the on-again, off-again love interest of my TV daughter, Jade, on *R&R*. Southern belle Josie Lynn Walraven, leading lady on the low-rated sudser *Obsessions*, wobbled onstage with him to announce the Sudsy Award for Best Lead Actress in a Daytime Serial.

Cameras zeroed in on all five nominated actresses: Judith Simmons, doe-eyed lead actress on *Our Lives to Contend*, nominated for seventeen Sudsys, winning eight; underappreciated soap legend Shelly Montenegro, the catty, drag-queen-esque gay icon on *The Daring and the Damned*; Lesley Francine, who to much fanfare had reprised her legendary role as America's soap opera sweetheart for six weeks on *Medical Clinic*; scenery chewer Emmy Abernathy, a three-time Sudsy winner as Gina Chiccetelli on *The Rich and the Ruthless;* and finally me, Calysta Jeffries, the favorite to win for my portrayal of Ruby Stargazer.

Too excited to breathe and feeling butterflies in my stomach, I closed my eyes laden with two pairs of false eyelashes, trying to think positive thoughts. *Here goes everything.*

"And the Sudsy goes to," Josie drawled for effect. She was actually from Hoboken, New Jersey. "Emmy Abernathy for Gina Chiccetelli, *The Rich and the Ruthless!*"

The room erupted in a mixture of applause and shocked gasps as the voice-over commentator announced, "This is Emmy Abernathy's fourth Sudsy win."

The haunting theme music for *The Rich and the Ruthless* played softly in the background.

I sat there transfixed, in shock again, my eyelashes feeling twice their weight, teeth gleaming, yet on the inside something irrevocably broken.

Leaning in, Augustus said, "I'm so sorry." *R&R*'s creator had to appear gracious, so he stood up in his elegant Armani suit, along with his wife, Katherine, daughter, Veronica, and son, Auggie Jr., to greet Emmy before she passed.

"Congratulations, Emmy."

"Oh my *gawd* thank you, Mr. Barringer," Emmy exclaimed as Augustus kissed her on the cheek. The press whore accidentally-on-purpose stepped on my toe with her big-ass 10½ foot as she made her way up the steps to the stage. Wearing a cheap crimson see-thru dress so tight it looked like an Oscar Mayer weiner casing, and no panties as usual, Emmy enthusiastically waved and blew kisses to the mezzanine.

Phillip McQueen whispered disgustedly to a bored Pinkey, "That's what I call putting perfume on a pig."

Roughly grabbing the Sudsy from a stoned Toby, Emmy proceeded to the microphone.

"I never expected to win *again*."

Breathe, girl, I told myself, suppressing the urge to stick my finger down my throat.

"I don't even have a speech prepared."

Seconds later Emmy plucked a crumpled piece of paper from her hoisted cleavage and read, "Oh my *gawd* this is *truly* amazing. First, I just want to thank L. Ron Hubbard. And I have to pause to say I *cannot* believe here I am once again on the *same stage* that stars like Helen Mirren, Hilary Swank, and, you know . . . um, the first African American to win, Halle Berry, all accepted *their* Oscars. Oh, *wow*, and they like all begin with 'H'! And before I forget I want to do a shout-out to all my *homies* in Bed-Stuy-do-or-die. *Holler!* Now, I would like to say thank you to all the fabulous women I had the honor of being nominated with. No, you didn't win, I did, but that doesn't mean you guys aren't really, really good actresses too in your own right, especially my costar and dear, *dear* friend, Calysta Jeffries! God bless Emmy Abernathy!"

Narcissistic Emmy had no idea she'd just blessed herself. I struggled to maintain my composure, as the camera zoomed in close enough to count my nostril hairs.

"Calysta, this award, my award, is for you too. Thanks for being such a phenomenal screen partner this past year. You were in *every* one of the scenes I submitted for Sudsy consideration. I seriously wouldn't have been able to snag another one of these babies without you. You really raised the bar."

Shannen cupped her hand over her mouth and asked, "Didn't you tell me your Grandma Jones said liars run the risk of being struck by lightning?"

"Yeah, that's why there's nothin' but silicone and cheese up there," I replied out the side of my mouth.

Edith Norman and everyone at *The Rich and the Ruthless* knew how Emmy really felt about me. She'd been furious when she learned she'd be sharing tube time with someone she secretly envied more than de-spised. Girlfriend had to be on her game to play with me.

There were two things Emmy and I had in common, unhappy child-hoods and a soap opera. She was a tough New Yorker, daughter of a crack addict, who fought like hell for everything she wanted, and so did I. Truth be told, I actually got a kick out of acting with the muffin-eatin' heifer. But after the word "Cut" all bets were off.

A *RICH AND THE RUTHLESS* OFFICE FLASHBACK . . .

"There's no way I'm working with that freak," Emmy said.

She'd stormed to Randall's office seconds after reading the first script.

"She's some kinda psycho robot, man. She never flubs a line and knows ev-eryone else's too! And have you noticed how she just has to win every scene? It's creepy." Emmy shuddered. "I'd rather work with that cow Alison."

If philandering was an Olympic sport, Randall Roberts would take the gold every time.

"Isn't there anything you can do, Snuggle Bunny?" Emmy asked, stroking *Randall's head and sitting in his ample lap, stretched out by beer and Chinese take-out.*

"Sorry, Emmy, it's a done deal. Augustus wants the storyline, but since you're already here, you think we could squeeze in a quickie?"

BACK TO THE SUDSYS ALREADY IN PROGRESS . . .

"I'm not joking up here, people," Emmy continued with her back-handed praise also known as a *compli-dis.* "Working with Calysta Jeffries is like taking an intense five-day-a-week acting workshop. She's *such* a mentor. Let's hear it for Calysta Jeffries!"

To thunderous applause, disguising my contempt, I rose to the occasion, blowing kisses and mouthing Thank yous into the camera for millions of viewers at home and around the world. If Emmy thought she was going to make an ass out of me on prime-time television, she had another think comin'.

Raging on until two in the morning, a steady stream of inebriated bi-coastal bubblers partied on to pulsing music and animated industry chatter at the lavish *Rich and the Ruthless* post-Sudsy Awards shindig at the legendary paparazzi-filled Roosevelt Hotel.

Navigating overstuffed furniture and humongous melting *R&R* ice sculptures, popular gossip columnist Mitch Morelli finally caught up with me.

"I think it's a goddamn shame you didn't win tonight, Calysta," he bluntly stated. "This was *your* year, and this toxic industry knows it!"

My every instinct told me to say what I'd said for the last fifteen. That Emmy or someone else had the better reel, or that it was an honor just to be nominated, but something inside me couldn't, no, wouldn't let me lie about the network's scandalous secrets one second longer:

the block voting, the notorious sexual campaigning, and the money-hungry power struggle between the Barringers and the WBC.

"Damn right it was my year, Mitch! But considering how certain vicious bubble-troublemakers who call themselves peers vote for who-ever campaigns with Starbucks and Krispy Kremes as opposed to *actors* who turn in solid performances, I'll never win, 'cause, honey, I don't do doughnuts. You can print that, every last word!"

UH-OH SPAGHETTIOS, Sudsy lovers. On-set spies tell The Diva there is trouble a-brewing on the set of daytime's numero uno soap, *The Rich and the Ruthless.*

Calysta Jeffries, who all but had the Sudsy in the dish, once again lost out to her costar Emmy Abernathy, and boy oh boy, was Miss Calysta p.o.'d! Here's what she said to *Cliffhanger Weekly*'s soap columnist Mitch Morelli:

"But considering how certain vicious bubble-troublemakers who call themselves peers vote for whoever campaigns with Starbucks and Krispy Kremes as opposed to actors who turn in solid performances, I'll never win, 'cause honey, I don't do doughnuts . . ."

Those sound like fighting words to moi! Wow, who knew Krispy Kremes were such a good career investment? A little birdie tells me execs at WBC and *The Rich and the Ruthless* are not too happy with Miss C. Be sure to keep checking back to SecretsofaSoapOperaDiva.com as this explosive news and dirt develops!

The Diva

CHAPTER 2

"Never Trust Anyone Who's Had a Happy Childhood," the Saying Goes

*W*ell, don't just stand there leaving me in suspense, Thelma, what's the child's name, for heaven's sake?"

"She goes by Calysta and is a natural for sure. Just like that feisty actress on my soap, Yesterday, Today and Maybe Tomorrow."

"Calysta what? She must have a last name."

"Well, all right, her real name is Beulah Espinetta Jones, lives right here in Greenwood, but no one's supposed to know according to the director. She's half black and from where I sit at the piano during rehearsals, quite attractive, and talented too."

Grandma Jones could hardly believe her ears as the two pale society ladies chattered away in their Delta drawl. Having licked her last stamp, she jotted down the details before leaving the post office.

Later that evening, the only black person in the audience, she nervously sat in *the last row of an improvised theater in Carrollton, intensely watching me act up a storm.*

During the curtain calls she made her way to the back of the building and asked for me.

"I'm sorry, ma'am, but you must be mistaken, there ain't nobody in this here production named Beulah Jones," the stage manager responded.

Giggling and puffing on a shared clove cigarette, I heard, "Beulah!"

A buzz kill for sure; I didn't need to turn around to know who it was. I exhaled the smoke through my nostrils like a defeated dragon, dropping the butt and grinding it beneath my sneaker.

We rode home in deafening silence in Pride-All Taxi Service. The frozen expression on Grandma Jones's face made her chin dimple like a pocked orange skin.

Arriving at the front door, exasperated, she searched her bottomless black pocketbook, her painted fingernails scratching the polyester lining for the key. And as she opened it she looked dead at me, saying, "You not too grown 'n' I ain't too old, now you get you a switch 'fore you come in, and don't be steppin' on my strawberry patch either. No dilly-dallyin'."

After washing my mouth out with soap, Grandma found the hidden strength all women possess, no matter how old, to whup any lick of disobedience or theatrical fantasy out of me.

Not daring to look up past her knee-highs, I cried out, "Grandma, please stop! I promise never to do it again."

She continued swingin' with her J. C. Penney coat still on, a hard staccato rhythm in her voice as if in a trance, saying, "Only-freaks-and-strange-folk-want-to-be-on-stage-and-TV-and-you-let-that-boy-kiss-you-all-over-your-mouth-for-everyone-to-see-if-I-evah-catch-you-hitch-hikin'-or-actin'-up-on-a-stage-again-so-help-me . . ."

As I lay in a cold sweat, the merciless ringing of my telephone rescued me.

"Ms. Jeffries?" asked my answering service.

"Huh? I'm sleepin'."

"I'm sorry to disturb you, ma'am, but your agent is on the line."

"For crissake, what does he want? Never mind, put him through," I slurred wearily with a splitting hangover, gulping down a bottle of Evian next to my bed.

Weezi—my agent, manager, publicist, legal counsel, confidant, financial adviser, and escort—barked into the phone, "What the hell are you trying to do to us?"

Never signing a contract, we were each other's first clients, during the lean years, ever since I stepped foot in New York City a zillion years ago.

He always managed to irritate the hell out of me, like the time I met him for lunch at Chateau Marmont, a favorite Hollywood haunt for A-list movie stars. Weezi insisted on introducing me to De Niro, never mind that he didn't know the man, who was minding his own business, incognito at a neighboring table. Putting on a thicker than usual New York City accent, Weezi shamelessly asked, "Yo Bob, how ya doin'? Loved ya in *Raging Bull,* ma' man. My client Calysta here is quite the actress on the number one sudsah, *The Rich and the Ruthless.* I'm sure ya hearda' it."

What came next trumped all. Weezi brazenly slipped his business card onto De Niro's table, a glossy picture of himself on the back.

Cringing, I wanted to evaporate. The A-lister took another sip of espresso before peering over his shades, saying, "I don't do soaps," and walked off leaving Weezi's card and a half-eaten biscotti.

As much as I swore I was firing Weezi after that embarrassing episode, like thousands of times before, I knew I wouldn't, 'cause pastures just ain't greener on the other side. I tolerated him the way he tolerated me, one day at a time.

"Huh?" I asked groggily, forgetting I'd tucked myself in with a bottle of Moët and a tin of Godiva. I attempted to hold the phone to my throbbing head, CNN's Nancy Grace blaring in the background.

"Those quotes you gave Morelli," Weezi reminded me. "You've caused a goddamn firestorm. The network is pissed and so is the show!"

"Oh . . . that?" Hadn't thought much about my conversation with Mitch until that very moment. "Maybe I went a little overboard, I was fired up. It'll blow over."

"A *little* overboard? Your stunt is being talked about all over the place. *Cliffhanger Weekly, Soap Suds Digest,* SecretsofaSoapOperaDiva.com, *Daytime Confidential* . . . you name it. And not just soap press, *Access Hollywood,* Nelson Branco, even Perez!"

"Wow, Perez? I finally made it."

"This isn't funny and it ain't good," Weezi griped. "The network's scrambling. A reporter from *Black Enterprise* has already requested an interview with you and the WBC's head of diversity, Josephine Mansoor, concerning alleged unfair practices on your soap."

"Oh boy," I said, sitting up, clearing hair out of my eyes.

"You've caused quite the commotion."

"And that's a bad thing? You know how many times I've been up for that doggone Sudsy. If it sheds some light on this screwed-up, narrow-minded industry, good."

"Calysta . . ."

"Thanks for the wake-up call, I have thirty-three pages today."

"You mean thirteen."

"No, I mean what I said, thirty-three. If only I got paid by the page like that diva in Britain."

"Calysta . . ."

"I know, keep dreaming. Later, Weezi."

I hung up and dialed Grandma Jones.

"Hey baby," she replied on the second ring as usual. "What's wrong?"

"How'd you know?"

"It's six thirty in the morning out there in Hollywoodland and you're supposed to be gettin' ready to tape my *story.*"

"Grandma, I swear the devil's at my heels. I have *had* it!"

"What happen' this time? And before you start, Beulah, I hope you didn't go 'n' pop that Gina Chiccetelli in the lip even though I don't like how she's been tryin' to take your man again."

"Grandma, first of all, that's her storyline, second, she's paid to be a floozy. And third, no, I didn't go 'n' pop Gina in the lip. It's worse than that."

"Beulah, ain't nothin' God and your grandma can't fix; now you tell me with a quickness what's goin' on out there!"

I hated my birth name, Beulah Espinetta, with a passion. I changed it the moment I boarded the train from Greenwood to New York City with blurred stars in my eyes, twenty years earlier.

"I didn't win the Sudsy again, Grandma."

"Is that all?" She dismissed me. "Sugah, that's yesterday's news. Been knowin' since last night, but wasn't gonna bring it up 'cause I know how you let that mess bring you down. But you sure did hold your own, Beulah, I don't care what anybody says. Made me just as proud, the way you held up your head even though you didn't win and kept right on smilin', blowin' kisses into the camera and everything, and I know that was just for me. You gave new meanin' to 'Folks push you back only as far as you let 'em.' Made *all* of Greenwood feel good, sure did."

"What?"

"Chile, I had the whole neighborhood over here. You coulda' canceled Christmas. Couldn't tell a soul you wasn't gonna win that Sudsy. No sah-ree. Sister Whilemina made fried chicken and greens, Miss Bessie made mac and cheese, and I made my monkey bread and a Sock-It-To-Me cake that wouldn't quit. Tongues was lickin' brains, baby . . . lickin' brains. Plus I made my special Manischewitz punch with bananas to wash everything down real good."

It was bad enough that I'd lost, but to find out the whole town was watching!

"Chile, folks was yellin' at the television somethin' fierce when those imps gave the Sudsy to that Gina Chiccetelli. She can't act her way out a brown paper bag nohow. Doggone shame you didn't win that trophy."

"You can say that again, Grandma. Emmy's got four Sudsys to my *none*. One thing's for sure, she's been doin' a lot more than actin' all these years."

"Ms. Jones, tell Calysta she was snatched like *all get out* last night!" a voice yelled in the background.

"Shush your mouth! What'd I say 'bout talkin' like that in my house," Grandma scolded. "Back in the day I'da washed your mouth out with soap."

"I ain't said nothin' Beulah ain't never heard before."

"Pipe down and button up," Grandma commanded. "That girl and her fresh mouth, always running like a bell clapper."

"Who's that?" I asked.

"Miss Whilemina's fast granddaughter Eartheletta. Got herself in a little trouble so she's visitin' from Chicago for a few weeks thinkin' she grown. Now listen to me, Beulah, never mind all that foolishness out there, I raised you right and you'll get yours the old-fashioned way. Besides, you done won eleven NAACP Image Awards."

"Yes, Grandma, and I'm very proud of that," I replied, knowing I couldn't begin to explain Hollywood politics. Though the prestigious Image Awards were star-studded, and the NAACP was steeped with rich political and theatrical history as far back as the 1915 protest against D. W. Griffith's *Birth of a Nation,* the painful absence of qualified brown people before and behind the lens still remained and affected everything from soap operas to feature films. The camera didn't lie, and it was still out of focus.

"And how many times can Gina Chiccetelli . . . I mean Emmy Abernathy say she's been on the cover of *Jet* or *Ebony*? Shoot, I have two scrapbooks full of your clippin's for safekeepin'. Winnin' an Image Award is one heck of a prize, baby, you right up there with all the big shots, and

Harry Belafonte still looks good, used to be sweet on him. I'm lookin' at that Image Award you sent me right now. I have it smack dab in the middle of the kitchen table with the salt and peppa' shakers so *no one* can miss it when they come visit. Now, I know there's one award missin', and I bet you even keepin' a space for it, but don't you worry, somethin' bigger is comin' down the pike. I can feel it. Been prayin' for it to happen for ya."

"Thanks, Grandma. Just wish the haters would stop the madness and vote fair."

"Babygirl, you know that ain't gonna happen 'cause you'd win. And if you win they'd think you too big for your britches and had too much power, and if *you* had too much power you'd change some things, and they can't have that. Beulah, what have I told you? When you leave this earth, awards ain't gonna matter one iota. 'A man's life consisteth not in the abundance of the things which he possesseth . . .' That's Luke 12:15. 'For what shall it profit a man, if he shall gain the whole world, and lose his soul?' That's Mark 8:36. Now don't you go concernin' yourself with all that other foolishness. Who gives a good kitty what those simpletons on the *story* think? You and I both know you can act up a storm and so do your fans. You're *favored* and can't no one take that from you."

Grandma Jones's friend Miss Odile, a member of the Church of the Solid Rock choir, told me when I was a little girl that I had something wild behind my onyx eyes that folks just couldn't put their finger on, that I was intelligent beyond my years and beyond book smarts. I had learned the hard way and by listening to the whispers between the lines of life. My inner compass always in overdrive, I read people comin' and goin', by using what was oftentimes frowned upon, "the knowing," my intuition, my lifeline. Regrettably, I stopped listening to it as I got older, trading my psychic wealth in for a different kind of fortune.

"Now stop running up your phone bill and go to work and make that money. Lord knows that remodel must be costin' you a pretty penny. Sure wish I could see it."

Grandma Jones had never been on a plane in her life. Furthermore, she was certain California was going to slide into the Pacific Ocean when the next earthquake struck. I didn't spend too much time thinking about her prediction, but Grandma Jones was spot-on about my kitchen remodel. Like everyone else in Hell-A, I was dealing with a pirating gangster, also known as a general contractor. I nicknamed him Jack the %#&*ing Rip-Off. The project was already six months overdue.

"Okay, Grandma, I better get to work."

"And tell my grandbaby I said she needs to write to me more."

"I'll tell her tonight," I promised. "She's in New York for two weeks with Dwayne, visiting his family. And Grandma, I almost forgot, are you taking your high blood pressure medicine?"

"No, it makes me feel funny. I went back to boilin' the bush with a little parsley and my stewed prunes. I feel just fine now."

"Grandma, you know what the doctor said—"

"Yeah, I know what he said, but that don't make him right. Doctors these days have a pill for everything, and I'll be doggone if I'm gonna make somebody rich off my itty bitty Social Security. Listen, Beulah, you know I love you to bits and sure wish you'd go back to church. I'll keep prayin' for that end."

"I love you, Grandma."

We hung up.

Grandma Jones was my rock. I'd never known my mother, Maddie Mae. She'd died giving birth to me, a mere child herself at sixteen. Aside from Ivy, Grandma Jones was the only real family I had.

In that moment, I desperately wished I could go back home for no other reason but to rest my head on Grandma's talcum-powdered chest.

CHAPTER 3

Cotton Capital of the World

FLASHBACK—CIRCA 1990

*B*efore excommunicating myself from the tambourine-shaking Church of the Solid Rock childhood I grew up in, I needed to take care of some unfinished family business.

In the short summer months, Grandma Jones shared her secret escape, her tired old soap opera, Yesterday, Today and Maybe Tomorrow, while massaging comfort into my dusty scalp. As she lounged in overalls that could walk themselves, I scanned our front room from between her knees. It was a cluttered hodgepodge of personal treasures and furniture that she would never let go of, a collage of religious items and funeral fans, plastic fruit and silk flowers. Oval-framed photographs, including one of her deceased husband, Orville, hung in the center of long-dead *relatives against dulled wallpaper, their gloomy expressions peeking out from behind bubbled glasses.*

I'd better not make a sound or else. Anyone who knew Grandma Jones knew to strictly adhere to her rules when her "stories" were on: "Don't call, don't talk and definitely don't visit!"

Witnessing yet another soap-a-licious sex scene, I drifted, remembering one warm afternoon under a wide blooming dogwood, raining dainty white petals on my face.

"Thanks for bringing me a cola, Keithie."

"It ain't for drinkin'," he dryly replied, clumsily unbuttoning my dress.

Naïvely I asked, "W-w-ell, if it ain't for drinkin', what's it for?"

"Just in case."

I didn't know diddly-squat about contraception, but I did learn soft drinks could be used for more than quenching ordinary thirst.

There were two things Grandma never missed, church and her "stories." She had a unique way of breathing requiring her whole body to conspire to do so: inflating her Mahalia Jackson–size bosom like a big helium balloon, holding her breath for several seconds before exhaling. The rhythm suddenly stopped and so did her braiding. Alarmed, I scrambled to my feet and leaned in. Relieved, I felt the shallowest exhale of baking soda breath, informing me that Grandma Jones was still alive.

I tiptoed across the creaking floorboards, turned down the volume, and just two channels away found an oasis in a vintage movie already in progress. Though the reception was poor, I made out the glamorous women doing exactly what I secretly wanted to do. Everything crystallized as I raptly watched the dazzling ladies parade around in pretty crinoline dresses, listening to their fancy talk.

Grandma believed the devil's work was concealed in TV, with the exception of her "stories" of course, so she forbid me to watch anything she didn't approve of first. But this was my chance to take a bite out of forbidden fruit while she catnapped, and boy, was it sweet.

As soon as she began to stir, I switched back to her "love in the afternoon," jettisoning out, organ music playing as credits rolled.

Next I heard, "Mother Hubbard, I missed my stories again! Beulah, why didn't you wake me up? Shooot!"

Without fail after her meltdown, Grandma got on the phone getting the scoop.

"Shush your mouth, Whil, you don't say, tell me my girl Calysta lived. Whachoomean, next week? Can't stand those cliff-hangers, make us all wait till Monday to find out if somebody lived or died. Who? Thought that old buzzard got hit by a bus last year or some such foolishness. A ghost? If they keep writin' wishy-washy and bringin' folks back from the dead I'ma stop watchin'."

My earliest theatrical memories were eavesdropping, listening to the vivid stories told by Miss Odile. In cinematic detail, she shared the wicked adventures of her sister, Minnie Red, living in New York City doing the devil's work, while Grandma Jones listened.

"Sakes alive, Minnie's up north struttin' on that stage big as day, performing half naked with them opera folks, when she could be right here in Greenwood as the musical director of our church choir, T'h!"

As I stood in the cut of our damp pantry listening, all the glittery descriptions of Minnie Red up north sounded anything but sinful to me. She was where the real divas dwelled. She had the right idea gettin' the heck outta Greenwood. I'd only wished it were me protected by the supernatural force field of a stage.

That night I closed my eyes and ran away to join the opera folks in cloudland. You couldn't tell me I didn't belong either, proudly garbed in a medieval helmet, curled ram antlers growing from my head toward the heavens with lots and lots of bushy red synthetic extensions trailing past my ample backside, cosmically priming me for Hollywood.

Dreaming on, in miles of diaphanous chiffon, suspended above the enormous brightly lit expanse, attached to a series of cables, I weightlessly winged it from stage right to stage left to the shrill of a rotund prima donna.

"O sublime fantasy, lasting castle-builder, keep me birdlike, away from my countrified earthbound existence in the Cotton Capital of the World . . ."

Suddenly the songbird ceased to sing, a deafening silence replacing her like a bad understudy. My heart raced. Everything stopped—that is, almost everything. Tragically, I had run out of stage and cable. Wingless, I perilously plummeted into the black vortex of an orchestra pit. That's where the damn dream abruptly ended. Knowing then as I surely know now, it was only the beginning of lights, camera, calamity, and claws.

MEGASHOCKER! Toby Gorman of *The Rich and the Ruthless* is in the news again, kids, and it ain't for a Sudsy Award. Performing a lewd act and exposing himself in public is the official charge. Gorman's lawyer had this to say about his client: "Toby is young and acted under the influence. He's really a sweet kid!" Supportive members of *R&R*'s cast packed the Los Angeles courtroom, and of course, Phillip McQueen and Alison Fairchild Roberts broke down in tears after the sentence was read. But really, it wouldn't be the first time a soap star had made scandalous headlines and for far worse.

The Diva

CHAPTER 4

Bigtooth Maple

My life took a dramatic turn one ordinary Saturday afternoon at the tender age of seventeen. It began the way it always did, dreadfully, cleaning an inheritance I knew I'd never claim. Somethin' was gonna happen, oh yes, I predicted things all the time and was usually right. Scared some folks half to death too.

Running late and pedaling double-time, I'd forgotten to tie up my braids, unraveling the way an old lie was about to. Couldn't risk the chunky church ladies tattlin' on me. They all thought a girl runnin' around with loose hair meant flirt'n and conceit and that was a sin. So I turned my rusty bike around and headed home quick in a hurry.

Rolling up on the lawn flushed, with the taste of salty perspiration in my mouth, I ran toward the back screen door. But before I opened it I stopped dead in *my tracks, hearing familiar voices coming from the woodshed. I sank down in the clover and crabgrass and crawled closer.*

Peering through dusty windowpanes, amid bunches of drying homegrown herbs I saw the obstructed profiles of Grandma Jones and Pastor Chester Winslow, the white town preacher.

I was able to make out every other word over the drumbeat of my heart, but what I saw filled in the blanks.

"How's . . . television work . . . and how's my . . . ?"

Never looking up, she replied with a nod.

He kept talking, I strained to hear. Then something happened that shook me to the core, something that was clearly routine. He handed over an envelope crammed full of cash.

". . . takin' real . . . care of my little . . ."

Feeling sick, I collapsed to the ground, under the stinging truth that Winslow plundered the plate every Sunday. He took up two collections and now I knew why.

"The second collection is for a very special cause."

Everyone in the congregation wondered what that "special cause" might be.

"Shake it down 'n' roll it ovah. If you've got five give ten, if you got ten give twenty, but good God Almighty whatever you do, don't let me hear loose change hit my dish."

The holy looter walked out our shed, his monstrous two-tone Cadillac kickin' up dust as Grandma shuffled back into the house with the weight of guilty knowledge on her shoulders.

Back on my bike, riding it like the dickens, I took a shortcut, a narrow path sliced through the woods, fragrant with wild blueberries, beating Winslow by a nick.

Oblivious, I charged out of a service room, looping an apron around my neck, a bobby pin between my teeth.

"Whoa, slow down, Beulah, where's the fire?" he asked as he hung his straw hat in the vestibule. "My goodness, I don't think I've evah seen you in such dis-a-rray or in a rush to work."

Caught off guard, a mountain of tousled hair piled on top of my sweaty head, I stood there, stuck in quicksand until he asked, "How'd you get those grass stains?"

Glancing down to see the evidence of spying earlier, I removed the bobby pin from my mouth and answered, "I w-was . . ." I stuttered, feeling perspiration trickle down my back.

"Never mind, Beulah. Why don't you take that rat's nest down so pastor can see just how long all that thick hair is. Reminds me of your mother. Promise I won't say a word to your grandma." He chuckled, staring at me as if reliving his pitchy past.

"No! I mean I have a lot of work to do today."

Startled, he snapped himself back and responded, "Yes, well get my tea ready and make it snappy."

I scurried into the kitchen, sharpening my teeth on a bold plan.

Along with unmistakable traits from my father, I inherited my mother's face, soul, and the task of cleaning Winslow's house.

If the truth be told, I wasn't the only child sired by him. Under the pretense of offering spiritual guidance and bereavement counseling, he preyed on innocence and took advantage of trust. The jackleg preacher had a long history of enlightening with more than just words, lifting the downtrodden with one hand while helping himself to the collection plate and the young sanctuary sisters with the other.

I came to understand that my grudge would have to be patient, and no one saw my fury comin'. At seventeen, I'd already worked for Winslow for three long, bitter years.

Like clockwork, I removed the beautifully appointed Limoges tea service I'd washed countless times from the china closet I'd dusted just as many, folded the monogrammed serviette I had starched and pressed, and placed it on the silver tray I hated polishing. Winslow received tea every Saturday afternoon after penning his Sunday sermon.

"Beulah, where's my tea, I'd like to have it while I'm still alive." He snickered as though he'd said something funny.

From beneath grizzled eyebrows, he followed my every move as I set down the tray in his mothball-scented office.

The nauseating request "Why don't you stay?" came every Saturday afternoon and I declined with the same worn-out answer as I poured.

"Sorry, pastor, I have chores at home."

Maybe the repulsive coot wanted to confess, but it was too doggone late and a truth I already knew.

Eyes narrowing to a sinister ice blue, he dismissively flicked the back of his spotted hand with a sugar cube pinched between his abnormally long fingers, resembling falcon's talons that always had Friday night's catch gucked in 'em.

I walked out of his office, down the long hallway, the same way I walked in, through the front door, unscathed with my panties on.

I never looked back.

CHAPTER 5

Shedding a Shady Past Quicker Than a Crepe Myrtle Could Shed Its Bark

As we strolled arm in arm just like we did every Sunday for eight o'clock service, Grandma Jones noted, "What an outstanding morning, Beulah."

"Yes, ma'am. Sure is."

No sooner did she say that, she asked, "What the devil could all the fuss be about?" noticing folks carryin' on something terrible in the hazy sunshine. It was pure pandemonium outside the Church of the Solid Rock.

"Sister Jones, Sister Jones," Deacon Cyrus cried out, frantically half-limping down the nasturtium-lined walkway, waving his handkerchief. "Pastor Wins . . . Pastor Wins . . . Pastor Winslow's on Main Street!"

Grandma tightened her grip on my arm.

"When pastor didn't show up this morning, Sister Odile done run over to his house and found him dead at his desk, mercy . . ."

He'd need a truckload of that, I thought as I pretended to be consumed with grief.

Grandma Jones had to be led under a shady bigtooth maple where my childhood friend Seritta, pregnant with her first, cooled her with a recycled fan featuring a shepherding Jesus on one side and an ad for Pecks Funeral Home & Life Insurance on the other.

It was church all day and then some, one week later. Following the repast, nightfall blanketed Greenwood as we returned home. Exhausted, I slipped into my nightie then headed to Grandma's bedroom but found it empty. I checked the kitchen—sometimes she made herself a hot toddy before retiring, swishing back the dread of the day—but she wasn't there either.

Set against a silhouette of pecan trees laced with kudzu vines, she stood like shiny black marble, silvery moonlight illuminating Grandma's dark blue skin.

In a raspy whisper, she commanded, "Come 'ere, chile."

Barefoot, I stepped off the uneven porch, cutting into muggy night air with uncertainty; an exaggerated symphony of stridulating cicadas and the intermittent twinkling of fireflies ushered me closer.

In a flash, Grandma backhanded me square across my face. Had it comin', just didn't know when.

"Didn't have the courage to do it myself," was all Grandma said. She reached up, cradling my stinging face in her knotted hands, saying, "You gotta go."

With the ghost of Maddie Mae between us, Grandma tucked me in that unforgettable night, her eyes swollen with grief.

"Love you, Beulah."

I held my breath for several seconds.

"Didn't always say it but that don't mean it wadn't always there."

As much as I tried to hold on to my anger and tears, everything broke inside for me and my grandmother.

Pulling her handmade crazy quilt over me like a protective shield, she said, "Sleep, Beulah, you're gonna need your strength. Ask for forgiveness and whatever you do, promise you'll nevah, evah talk about what happen'."

"Promise."

Before turning off the light she reached into her robe pocket and pulled out a key, placing it on a chest of drawers. "Tomorrah, go down to the cella'. Behin' the stair is a piece of old wood level with the dirt with a heavy rock on top. In that hole is everything I been savin' for you. I'ma have you go up north 'n' stay awhile. A friend of a friend's gonna keep an eye on ya."

I had no idea Grandma Jones knew a soul outside Greenwood, with the exception of Minnie Red in New York. I hoped it would be her.

"And don't be openin' that box till you pull outta Greenwood, ya hear?"

"Yes, ma'am."

She closed the door.

I fell asleep to her weepy singsong redemption.

Before the rooster's call I knew something wasn't right. I flew down the stairs, tearing through the house, and found Grandma slumped on the couch with an open Bible on her lap. I was never so petrified, standing in disbelief for the longest before approaching her. A homemade bookmark at her feet read: Romans 6:9, "Death no longer has dominion . . ."

"Nooo, come back, Grandma! It's all my fault. Don't leave me here all alone . . ."

Startled awake, Grandma Jones exclaimed, "What in the devil are you carryin' on about, Beulah?" knocking me backward. "And why are you down there on the floor lookin' like zip-in-distress an' actin' like you got no sense? What time is it anyway? Musta' dozed off. Couldn't get a lick a sleep last night for nothin'."

"Grandma, last night—" I began.

"What about it?" she cut in, daring me to remember. "Yesterday never happened, Today's a new deal, and Tomorrow's your future. Now get those clothes pressed and no cat faces on my shirts."

And that's the way it went.

After a short investigation, it was determined that Pastor Winslow died of a massive heart attack, and the church ladies were all too concerned about my departure. Next came the Greenwood Inquisition from a corpulent Miss Whilemina, puffed up like an overstuffed hen, cornering me at church that next Sunday.

"Beulah, where you gonna go, chile?" she asked, fogging up her glasses, magically pulling a crumpled Kleenex she'd tucked under her twinset sleeve. "And who's gonna take care of you? Remember you're only seventeen. Your grandmother sure ain't got no money to be sendin' you up north to that sinful place, New York City. Look what happened to so-and-so . . . I forget her name, but it wasn't good. Nothin' but Satan's temptations waitin' for you," she said, shaking her wigged head, a church hat perched on top, accented with an oversize gold begonia.

Little did Miss Whilemina know, New York City was exactly what I needed to spread my wings and dive into a new me.

"I'm gonna stay with my . . . um, make-believe cousin DeeDee before I go out to California," I replied.

"DeeDee? I ain't never heard nothin' about no DeeDee before and I been knowin' your grandma all her life. You sure you tellin' me the truth, Beulah?"

As sure as the nose on my face, I wanted to say, but responded, "Yes, ma'am, I'm sure."

I was finally heading toward a future where nobody knew me. I could start fresh. It had to be better than what I was leaving behind.

After a tearful send-off by Grandma Jones, her prayer circle, Seritta, and the rest, Deacon Cyrus droned on forever, bringing up Winslow's "Home Going Service," a longwinded sermon about hell and damnation, and a drill of the Ten Commandments before delivering me to the red brick train station. He gave me a parting hug that lasted a smidge too long, so I stepped on his left foot, rumored to have been afflicted with a nasty case of gout.

Shedding my shady past quicker than a crepe myrtle could shed its bark, I boarded, heading for Grand Central Station. The first jolt was strong. The second, final.

As the train gained momentum, Smokebush and Oleander blurring together, I stretched out my legs on the upper bunk feelin' kinda grown. After a treat of Grandma's applesauce cake, I looked down at the metal box resting beside me. Before turning the key, I took a deep breath, then pulled the stubborn lid open.

On top, there were two photographs of my mother I'd never seen before. No more than five years old, she was sitting on Grandma Jones's lap, both of them looking *serene, without smiles. In the other, she was holding Easter eggs in her Sunday best.*

Gently placing the photos to the side, I poured a string of pearls out of a satchel, in mint condition. Next, wrapped in plastic and newspaper, secured with hardened rubber bands, was a stack of cash: three thousand, six hundred and forty-two dollars in small bills! Wow! I'd never seen that much green before in one place but I didn't have to think long to know where the blood money had come from.

At the very bottom, a sealed yellowing envelope. I sliced it open with my pocketknife. There were two documents, one my birth certificate that stated Maddie Mae Jones, Mother—Father, Unknown. I took my time unfolding the other, a letter, spreading it out on my lap. It read:

Sweet, sweet Beulah, by now you are of age. Love you more than all the stars. Wanted you to have somethin' when you left Money Road, a little of your mamma and me to remember us by. God Bless, Grandma Jones.

A tear spilled, bleeding the blue ink into the white. I read it over and over before placing all my new treasures in my purse. I peeled off a twenty-dollar bill and added it to what I had pinned inside my bra.

Still seeing them as an unwanted reminder of my father, I sliced off ten inches of my plaits, opened the narrow window next to my bunk, and tossed the locks into the wind, watching them dance away like two drunken schoolgirls.

The monotonous rhythm of the train wheels relaxed me as I looked out across acres and acres of cotton fields, knowing spirits were waving with pricked hands, whispering, "Don't forget, Beulah."

Under the Mississippi sky, ablaze with a blanket of stars, I perilously hung hope onto the tip of one of Orion's pointy fingers, embarking on an odyssey that would ultimately bring me more than Erica Kane fame.

When I arrived at Grand Central Station a day and a half later with optimism in my heart, Minnie Red met me at the station just as I predicted, and man, can I say glam-o-rous! Her hair was done. *Brows all arches and whatnot, dressed to the nines! I felt like a country bumpkin in my tired outfit.*

"How was your trip, Beulah?" she asked in a fake accent somewhere between London and Greenwood. She had some white man on her arm.

"Fine."

My great expectation that she'd show me the ropes was short-lived. After a week and five hundred dollars lighter, I was on my own. I didn't waste time acclimating to my new environment, making the residential YWCA my new home.

Struggling in the Big Apple slinging hash that first year was no fun, but Grandma had taught me how to hold on to a penny. Then I met smooth-talkin' Ian Grady, also known as "trouble," and I admit, I moved way too fast with the ex-boxer, getting a quickie marriage license at City Hall before our daughter, Ivy, was born in the spring of '93.

Picking husbands wouldn't be one of my strengths. As swiftly as we tied the knot, I untied it and got a Mexican divorce by mail after Ian was carted off to Rikers for the umpteenth time for petty theft and a potpourri of other charges. I tore out of New York City for the Golden State with Ivy on my hip like my hair was on fire.

LATE-BREAKING NEWS, hot off the press, kids. Soap stars are getting swatted like flies. As reported last week, *R&R* is starting to pass out pink slips faster than I can say "81% off on *Cliffhanger Weekly* for a six-month subscription." I guess it's not surprising, since *Our Lives to Contend, Medical Clinic,* and *The Daring and the Damned* all axed at least two of their major stars last year in an effort to save money. And trust me, honey, the dominoes have only begun to fall. So much for champagne wishes and caviar dreams . . . back to tuna and beer.

The Diva

CHAPTER 6

Forty Acres and Recurring?

*E*choes of Grandma Jones's voice continued buzzing in my head two espressos and several Tylenol later. Still suffering from a colossal hangover, I was trying to get rid of a stubborn sheet crease across my cheek, which I managed to camouflage with a "shut it down" Patricia Underwood brim.

Gingerly tipping through my forever-under-construction kitchen toward the garage for work, I heard my BlackBerry playing Rachelle Ferrell's latest hit signaling an incoming call. Honestly, I still didn't completely understand how to work the damn thing, although my sixteen-year-old computer-savvy daughter, Ivy, had shown me countless times.

"Hello," I whispered into the device. Anything louder would have set me back several migraines.

"Good morning, Calysta, this is Edith Norman," she announced in a piercing voice.

Edith Norman? Why's the president of daytime television for the WBC calling me?

"Hey Edith, how's tricks?"

"Excuse me?"

"Uh, never mind. How are things?"

"Not very well, I'm afraid. I know you have an early call time, but I'd like you to stop by my office first."

"Um, sure, can you tell me what this is about?"

"I think you know."

The phone went dead and I thought of a horoscope clipping I kept in my wallet: "A test will come on how quickly you can overcome disappointment. Be careful with your words and listen closely to others, they may ask you to give something for nothing."

The sole of my Ong shoe pressed the gas pedal and I began the long trek from my palm-tree-lined driveway in Malibu Canyon to *The Rich and the Ruthless* set on the WBC lot in Burbank. I hit the CD button and was jolted by the sounds of someone calling himself Soulja Boy, quickly replacing Ivy's disc with the soothing voice of Lizz Wright.

My stomach tightened as I vroomed my Jag down the 101 freeway thinking, *Can't let thunderpants Edith see me sweat. Forget her. There ain't no way in hell I'm about to let some uptight suit put the fear of unemployment in my spirit. Gotta be about the business and hold it down. They need me more than I need them.*

I'd better keep my inner Beulah at bay. I had way too much riding on my soap career to go into Edith's office with an attitude.

Ivy's private school tuition, my mortgage, and taking care of Grandma Jones and, heck, half the town back home in Mississippi depended on my income from *The Rich and the Ruthless*. Since she retired as a cleaning lady at the Greenwood Country Club, there was no way Grandma could survive on what little she received from Social Security. My paycheck made it possible for her to live comfortably, not to mention making payments on a subprime loan to keep my friend Seritta's property from going into foreclosure, plus a little extra cash to supplement her food stamps, and sad to say, bailout money for a few others.

Seritta had stood out among so many faceless Greenwood elementary and high school classmates. She was always tall for her age, but what most impressed me about my friend was her loyalty, defending me when someone wanted to start some mess in the playground.

"I'ma beat you up after school, Beulah," said Jadasia Pickens, the school bully. "LL always thinkin' you better than everybody else with your light skin and long hair."

With her eye line coming to the middle button of Seritta's blouse, Jadasia stood there, trying to figure out how to save face and ass at the same time.

After guiding my Jag up to the WBC security gate, I flashed my *R&R* ID while humming Chaka Khan's remix of "I'm Every Woman" with a renewed sense of empowerment.

"Morning, Ms. Jeffries," greeted the guard. "You sure are *wearin'* that hat."

"Why thank you, Jay," I said, looking over my vintage cat-eyes. "You know I'm never caught without one."

"Sorry you didn't win the Sudsy last night," he added. "Everyone and their mamma was pullin' for you."

"That means a lot to me, Jay," I said with stiff gratitude. "Be sure to thank everybody for their support and tell 'em there's always next year," I lied as my gut, my thong, and anything else that could twisted themselves into a pretzel.

"Sure will, Ms. Jeffries, sure will."

My face dropped faster than the S&P 500 the second I passed the security gate. Miraculously, I managed to find a parking spot.

"This has got to be a good omen," I said aloud as I squeezed my two-seater between an obnoxious custom-painted orange Hummer and a silver Ferrari.

I glided through the metal detector located at the Artists' Entrance and into the building. There had been a threat against Edith's life the year before and a soap stalker on the prowl for Emmy Abernathy.

"Have a good one, Ms. Jeffries," the guards said in unison from their desk.

"You too, fellas," I flirtatiously replied with a wink, stepping onto the elevator.

"Damn shame she didn't win the Sudsy, she's the only reason I watch that corny soap."

"Me too, man."

Exiting four floors later, I began my *Waiting to Exhale* journey down the long hallway to the executive offices, lined with more than thirty years of framed cast photos from *The Rich and the Ruthless*.

With the poise of a classically trained ballerina, and my patrician nose (a genetic imprint from my lecherous father) held high above my bee-stung lips (a nod to my mother), I stopped short of the *R&R* etched glass doors, leveling my eyes at the latest cast photo.

I was standing in the back row with jive-ass Ethan Walker cheesing as usual; next to us were a bitter Dell Williams, who played the recurring character of Queenie the maid for the entire run of the show; Pepe, the Finks' constantly recast Mexican gardener; veteran bubbler Wilson Turner, *R&R*'s favorite go-to plumber, judge, cop, drug dealer, and preacher; and Jade (like Beyoncé, Prince, and Drake, she went by one name), who played herself, Jade, my valley girl daughter who wanted the world to know she was a quarter Persian, a quarter Sicilian, a quarter Creole, one-sixteenth Osage Indian, and the rest she didn't want to talk about, including being bulimic. It wasn't entirely the ingénue's fault; the blue eye shadow, matching contact lenses, blond highlights, and staying a size zero were encouraged by Edith and the rest of the gang.

Next year I'll be in the front row, I vowed before bouncing through the *Star Trek*-ish double doors.

"I'm here to see Edith," I informed the chubby secretary. "She's expecting me."

"Thank you," she replied. She was a pleasant, pale woman with a shock of red hair pinned up with lime green butterfly barrettes. She pressed the intercom button. "Ms. Norman, Calysta Jeffries is here to see you."

"Thank you, Fern. Send her in."

"I just love you on the show and I was really rooting for you last night, Ms. Jeffries," Fern gushed as I attempted to walk past.

"Thank you."

"My aunt Midge loves you too. She lives in Des Moines, Iowa, never misses an episode of *The Rich and the Ruthless.*"

"That's wonderful," I replied, stopping to momentarily regard Fern with a warm smile. "I'm glad you and your aunt enjoy the soap."

"Oh my, do we ever." Fern giggled. "Now tell me, just between us girls, did you know who your baby's daddy was?"

"Excuse me?"

"Your *baby*, you know, Kip, you had him last November. The stillborn? You weren't sure if he was Dove Jordan's baby or if Whittaker Kincaid, the Moroccan arms dealer, was the dad?"

I contemplated explaining to Fern that I was Calysta Jeffries, not Ruby Stargazer, a fictional character on a soap opera, but I didn't want to bring on another migraine or disappoint a fan, so I decided it wasn't worth it.

"Ruby's always known Whittaker was the father," I assured her, leaning over to whisper, "but I can never tell Dove."

"I knew it." Fern gasped, grateful for the inside scoop. "I made a bet with all the women in my bowling league that Whittaker was the father all along."

"Well, I better go in."

"Have a nice day, Ms. Stargazer, I mean, Ms. Jeffries."

I opened the door to find not only Edith but Randall Roberts, Felicia Silverstein, co-head writer of *The Rich and the Ruthless,* and Daniel Needleman, the show's nerdy publicist. They were all seated around a conference table that looked to have been inspired by Arthurian legend.

"Good morning, everyone," I greeted, laid out in a fierce beige Comme des Garçons suit.

"Come in, Calysta," Edith said. "We've been expecting you."

"Had I known it was a party I would have brought champagne!"

Daniel pulled out a chair and I flashed him a smile before taking it, facing Edith. Pointedly looking at Randall, I said, "What a gentleman. Some folks could learn a lot from you, Daniel. So, what's going on that I had to miss rehearsal?"

"Never mind the rehearsal," Edith began. "There are more pressing things."

"Oh?"

"As you know, *The Rich and the Ruthless* and the network, per our joint operating agreement, have an Out clause in your contract that allows us the opportunity to reevaluate your performance on the show every thirteen weeks."

"Yes, of course I'm aware of that, but considering I signed a three-year contract just two months ago, I'm sure that isn't on any of your radars," I stated confidently.

"Actually, we've decided to exercise the Out clause," Edith returned.

The words hung in the air, locked by smugness and condescension.

"What?"

"We're putting you on hiatus," Edith continued.

"Hiatus?"

"Yes, for the foreseeable future Ruby Stargazer is being back-burnered," Randall finished.

"You can't be serious?"

"You heard right," he said, not hiding his smirk.

"What is this, some kind of punishment for speaking out in the press last night?"

"Of course not," Edith said. "Frankly, the decision was made weeks ago."

"Yeah, right, I smell stink all over this."

"Although I must admit," Edith began, "the blatant disrespect you showed for the network, *The Rich and the Ruthless,* and the Barringer family by providing that tabloid reporter with those slanderous remarks really did drive home the point that you're unhappy here with the *R&R* family, and as much as we love you, it was high time we reconsidered our association."

"Family? Love? Are you actually using those two words in the same sentence with *The Rich and the Ruthless*? Who are you trying to kid, Edith? There's more love between Angelina and her dad than on this soap."

"Calm down, Calysta."

"No, you calm down, Edith. I may not know the ins and outs of corporate America to the extent that you do or the long-term chokehold the financial collapse must have on the show, but one thing I do know is that I bring home your target audience in the *millions*, not to mention advertising dollars and press, and you want to 'reconsider your association with *me*'? *R&R* was on cancellation watch when I joined and in less than six months we were the number one soap in the country and have remained there! I fought like hell to bring about diversity in front of and behind the camera even though every qualified professional I presented was unilaterally rejected, with one exception, Kimesha Nosegay. You-all remember her, don't you?"

"Oh brother, here we go again," Randall moaned. "Can we stay on topic?"

"I couldn't be more on topic if I tried. A single black mother fresh out of an Inglewood salon, she did more than stuff hair under a wig, lacquer it with Final Net, then claim victory at the Sudsys for Best Hair. Never once did she show disrespect, even though the idiot in charge of the hair department insisted on segregating her due to Emmy's incessant complaining, 'It smells when Kimesha presses Calysta's hair with those medieval combs, even Ethan and Jade think so.'"

Ethan was the ultimate brown-noser. He shifted like the scent of shit in the wind if it meant saving his own ass.

"Stop exaggerating, Calysta," Randall admonished.

"It's no exaggeration. Did you know Kimesha was *so* incredibly competent even Katherine and Veronica Barringer hired her for private affairs? Then *poof*, just like that she disappeared."

"I know nothing about that."

"Sure you do, Edith. You paid Kimesha pennies to tighten your weaves in the privacy of your own home in Pasadena."

"I have had about as much as I'm—"

"I'm not done," I snapped. "As much as you pay Danny Boy here to keep it out of the press, this soap is *huge* in black households, yet there's barely a black storyline on the page let alone anyone of color on the stage. If the fans only knew how I've had to pull tooth-and-nail to get the basics, while you-all scandalously line your pockets with sponsorship dollars, cheese for the camera, and collect yet another NAACP Image Award, which clearly you don't display in your offices, only the Sudsys. Diversity my butt, Josephine Mansoor is asleep at the wheel."

"If I give *you* special attention everyone will want—"

"Excuse me, Edith? Did you say *special*? Don't have a soul on the show to do my special hair, dress my special behind, or write my special lines. Who do you think's doin' it all—a ghost?"

Edith squirmed.

"Do you honestly believe the viewers are tuning in to watch Phillip McQueen cry over another one of Queenie's sticky buns? If you're unsure just check SecretsofaSoapOperaDiva.com."

"Calysta, *shut up*," Edith barked, like my name was Sally Hemings. "I'm sorry, I didn't mean to say that."

Knowing she did, I wanted to say, "Bitch, *shut* don't go up," but kept the verbiage on the Anglo tip.

Everyone sat there, looking like they were stuck on stupid, and they were. Maybe, just maybe, the truth was finally crystallizing on the noses and eyelashes of the guilty like an early Mississippi frost.

Barely audible, a taciturn Daniel Needleman, who should've been drivin' a Mister Softee truck, spoke for the first time. "Miss Jeffries, we appreciate all your many efforts to assist with marketing *The Rich and the Ruthless*," the publicist began.

"Save it, Daniel. You don't have to thank me for doing *your* job. I know you were too busy making arrangements for *other* actors representing *R&R* at the Nymphette Awards in Monte Carlo, or was it the sixty-third *Cliffhanger Weekly* cover shoot for Alison? What's that pat line you give my manager year after year? Oh yes, 'Brown doesn't sell.'"

Daniel dropped his head.

"Edith, now you see firsthand the *ego* we've had to endure all these years," Felicia said with a sneer.

"Ego? How 'bout your *envy*? You've got some nerve, Silverstein, coppin' an attitude with zero ink in your pen game. Didn't you win a Sudsy last year off a storyline *I* wrote and submitted to you on the downlow just so the black cast had *some* airtime? And didn't I have to tell you UES meant Upper East Side? You thought 'all up in my grille' had to do with burgers."

Busted.

"You've had it in for me since day one. Couldn't stand that Augustus respected my opinion and consulted with me on a regulah about your tired asinine plots. *I* rewrote my storyline so my character didn't have an incestuous lesbian affair with her daughter. Or how 'bout the time you wanted me shackled as a runaway slave in a dream sequence, 'Ruby Stargazer channels her ancestors,' a weak attempt to honor Black

History Month. Remember that one? I gave this show a gift, on a silver platter. And did it for free because I *cared* and knew who was watchin' at home."

"As usual, your attitude and allegations are offensive, incomprehensible, and befuddling!" Felicia admonished.

"No, as usual I'm callin' it the way it is. And I'll tell you what's befuddlin'. You-all building a core black viewership off of fifteen years of *my* blood, sweat, and tears, and a *grip* off of pornographic ads showin' black chicks caressing detergent like it was a dick, about to have an orgasm—"

"Ohmygawd!" Felicia gasped.

"—and now you're ready to cut *me* a deal worth forty acres and recurring? Sorry, ain't gonna happen 'cause Calysta don't *coon*."

"That *word* . . . did you hear what she said, Edith?" Felicia asked in tears. "Do something!"

"Calysta, you're making chicken salad out of chicken fingers—I mean, feathers," Edith scoffed.

"Guess I should be flattered you tried incorporating another one of my rewrites from last week's show into your everyday conversation."

Flushed, Edith flexed her jaw.

"Augustus created a monster in you," sighed Randall. "When I think of all the times I defended you when others wanted you out."

"That's rich. Randall, my knight in shining snakeskin."

I couldn't help but stare at his new wiry hair plugs. It was rumored his last transplant was monkey hair and had to be removed following a severe allergic reaction. These were no better.

I began laughing hysterically at the craziness of caring too damn much.

"This is no laughing matter," Edith coldly interjected. "And the network doesn't share your sense of humor about the situation."

"I'd like to know what Augustus has to say about all this," I stated with a stone-cold straight face.

"He can't help you this time, Calysta," Randall warned. "Auggie's health is in a precarious state. He's in no position to make decisions about his soaps."

"He's still senior executive producer and head writer," I reminded them.

"In name only," Randall declared. "Augustus coming back to write your storyline this past year was basically his swan song. Pity it didn't win you the Sudsy."

"Yeah, I'm sure it breaks your heart."

"You'll be hearing about this soon enough, so I might as well tell you now," he began.

"Hear about what?"

"Augustus signed over control to Auggie Jr. and Veronica, naturally Katherine—"

"Ah," Edith interrupted, "what Randall is trying to say is that he'll have creative control of *The Rich and the Ruthless* . . . eventually."

A terrifying sense of disbelief washed over me.

"Poor Auggie," Randall continued. "He just isn't the man he once was. It's really sad."

"I'll tell you what's sad: that a shameless, bottom-feeding imposter like you has somehow managed to snow the Barringer family into believing you're a competent producer. And let me just say this: no matter how sick Augustus Barringer may be, he will always be ten times the man you wish you were."

"Think whatever you want, Calysta," he replied carefully. "It won't change the fact that it's only a matter of time before I have final say over who's under contract on *The Rich and the Ruthless*. I support the network's decision to terminate yours *one hundred percent*."

Augustus couldn't know about this. Even on his deathbed he never would've tolerated my being treated this way.

"We'd love to have you make the occasional guest appearance, on a recurring basis, but that of course is entirely up to you," Edith suggested.

"How generous," I mocked. "What? Unwrap Ruby Stargazer like a holiday ornament for Christmas episodes and Sweeps stunts to counsel her rapidly aging daughter about her sexually transmitted diseases? No thanks, I'll pass."

"Since you asked," Felicia spoke up, "the plan is to introduce a younger generation of characters through Ruby."

"Let me guess, using the old *growth serum* again?"

"We're aging Jade to twenty-one."

"And you wonder why soaps are the laughingstock of the entertainment industry? You people are certifiable!"

"I don't think *you,* of all people, want to go there," Felicia said.

"You know what . . . ?" I stood up, pushing the swivel chair out from under me, moving around the table in her direction.

Randall stepped in between us, a nefarious grin spreading across his splotchy face, knowing he had me where he wanted me.

"Calysta, have a seat." We stared each other down until his cell phone vibrated. "Excuse me, everyone, I have to take this call," he said, slithering to a corner.

Omni-eyed, I took in the assembled player haters and said, "To hell with this—I'm out." Snatching up my metallic Miu Miu handbag, I headed for the door.

As I was about to walk out Daniel Needleman asked, "Ms. Jeffries, what are you going to tell the media? The show would appreciate the courtesy of having time to prepare a brief statement."

"You mean like the courtesy I've been extended here today? Be sure to check out the next issue of *Cliffhanger Weekly.* It'll be a page-turner."

"Calysta, be reasonable," Edith implored. "Don't continue on this whole 'unfair practice' bandwagon regarding the Sudsy Award voting and all the other things. It makes you look bitter. The voting procedures for all the WBC daytime programs are scrupulous. Evidently the majority of the voters simply didn't feel your performance was worthy of a

Sudsy this year, or for the past fourteen for that matter. I'm sure it wasn't personal."

"Of course not."

"And I'm sorry you spent your own money on hats and gloves and nonsense like that thinking the fans cared about what you wore on the show. We told you from the beginning they're not interested in your fashion eccentricities. Besides, hats are old-fashioned. As for hair and makeup, the soap offered you a trunk of wigs in various styles and colors; however, you made the decision to go gawd knows where to have some kind of *process* done at your own expense."

"For your information, Edith, the fans *do* care, and since we're listing, I suppose I shouldn't take it personal that you've never sent me on a location shoot."

"I'm sure I don't know what you're talking about," she countered.

"Yeah you do."

"Location shoots are based upon storyline and the demographic we are desperately seeking, especially in this uncertain financial climate."

This was Edith's way of saying the show was promoting the white actors. While the soap's brass plumped up their Nielsen and Madison Avenue ratings on the backs of black households, black soap stars were oh-so-underpaid, rarely benefiting from the audience they pulled in and secured. Yep, *R&R mined* for gold and stole it in plain sight but couldn't *mine* me. Not for sale.

"I'm sorry if you feel you were slighted, Calysta," Edith added.

"Next you're gonna ask why can't I be more like Dell? In an apron, never speakin' out, ending up with a broken spirit. Or like Jade. Sorry, 'tragic mulatto' just isn't a role you'll *ever* get to see me play."

"You're off topic again," Felicia taunted.

"Yes, Calysta, let's stay focused. To suggest that your ethnic background or anyone else's has influenced the roles or tenure on our soap is ridiculous. The WBC and *The Rich and the Ruthless* have always been strong supporters of fairness and diversity. Alluding to a disparity based upon race at the WBC is categorically untrue. I must insist you refrain from making such libelous statements or our legal department will be forced to take necessary action," a steely Edith warned.

"You can't expect me to buy into this bull any more than your using intimidation will keep me quiet."

"Let's get back on track to why we called this meeting in the first place, shall we?" chimed in Randall. "Sorry for the interruption, my friend's running a workshop at Sundance and needed some advice."

"We'll need your decision, Calysta, in the next twenty-four hours," Edith said.

"You must be half crazy if you think for one second that after all these years on this soap, I'd accept recurring. Furthermore, there's no way in hell I'd play a supporting role to that valley girl Jade and a bunch of models learning how to act on my watch."

"Pick your poison," Randall said. "As Edith stated earlier, whether or not you choose to accept the terms we've offered is entirely up to you."

"That's right, if you decide not to accept recurring, there will be no turning back," Edith finished.

"What's that supposed to mean?" I asked.

"If I could just put in my two cents?" the publicist nervously interjected, turning to Edith and Randall. "The fans would never accept a recast of Ruby Stargazer. They just wouldn't."

"You know, for the first time since this meeting got started someone has actually said something that makes some sense. It's about more than recasting another dispensable tanned actress in Hollywood. And speaking of tanned, I know you-all darken and lighten my skin in post-production to satisfy advertisers."

"That's preposterous," Edith said.

"There she goes again." Randall yawned.

"Save it. If you'd cast a black family, y'all wouldn't have to do it on the cheap, using me like your own digitally correct Paint-By-Numbers kit.

Just hire some chocolate up in here and stop the madness! And Daniel's right, if you recast Ruby Stargazer, fans *will* turn the dial, and you can take that to the bank."

"That's precisely why if you don't accept the offer we've generously presented, we'll have no choice but to kill Ruby off," Randall said.

Looking through each of them as if they were glass, I retorted, "Please, not even the people in this room are *that* crazy. You haven't re-covered from the one million viewers you lost after Derrick Taylor left the show for *Pathological Murders*. Without Ruby Stargazer the soap dies a slow death. Now *you* pick your poison."

"My, you do think highly of yourself, don't you?" Edith asked, rising, plucking her tortoiseshell glasses off the tip of her nose, using her Betsey Johnson skirt to polish off a smudge. She walked over to face me with her pinched expression and beady eyes.

I couldn't help but think, if only Nigel Cooperman, Edith Norman's predecessor, hadn't left. He had loved me from the start, even writing up a secret holding deal to ensure I stayed with the network. Sadly, he and his family suffered great damage to their Brentwood home in the 6.7 magnitude of the '94 earthquake, his wife becoming so distraught they quickly moved cross-country to New York, where Nigel now helmed *Sesame Street*.

"Let me make this perfectly clear," Edith warned me. "As talented and popular as you may be, you've made it hard at times for me to re-member why I let Augustus hire you in the first place. Your costars and even some of the crew hate working with you."

"Could it be because I don't take crap off lazy dumbbells?"

Ignoring me, she continued, "I have in my hand a short list of actors and three crew members who signed a petition to have you removed from the show *before* the Sudsy Awards. Even Ethan Walker signed it."

"So?" I said, rolling my eyes. "That doesn't surprise me."

"So, on top of that, you show an alarming disregard for authority. As I said before, we'll need a decision in the next twenty-four hours."

"Oh, you can have it now."

"Why don't you take some time to think about it?" Daniel suggested.

"Go polish some more apples, Danny. What's there to think about? Kill Ruby Stargazer off; I quit," I declared, tossing my script on the table before walking out.

"Good-bye, Ms. Jeffries," Fern called after me.

"It's never good-bye, Fern, just so long. And tell your bowling league and your aunt in Iowa hello from Ruby Stargazer."

"Oh, I most certainly will," Fern exclaimed. "They'll be so thrilled!"

Edith, Randall, Felicia, and Daniel peeked out, taking in the exchange along with the rest of the staff.

"Fabulous," I said with a granite smile, extracting mirrored shades from my purse. "Oh, and Fern, after you've told them Ruby Stargazer said hello . . ."

"Yes, Ms. Jeffries?"

"Tell 'em your bitch of a boss smoked her."

CHAPTER 7

"D" for Difficult

here's no way in hell I'm going back, Weezi, and that's final!" I was having a full-blown indulge-a-thon, slumped on my down-feathered sofa, eating pecan and praline ice cream while glued to a Claudette Colbert marathon on Turner Classic Movies. Hadn't moved from that spot since truckin' home from the WBC studios eight hours earlier.

"You don't have a choice," Weezi explained over the phone. "You *must* tape your final scenes or you're gonna be in a world of trouble."

"What kind of trouble? They're the ones who pushed *me* off the show. They wanna dump me off a boat somewhere off the coast of guess where?"

"Where?"

"Africa! How lame is that? Those racist slimeballs. Why should I go back and help them destroy my character?"

"Because you're still under contract, that's why, and the last thing we both want is for you to be back on your rump in an infomercial demonstrating at three a.m. how to tighten your maximus, minimus, and medius using the Butt-Blaster: Firm the Flab Forever gizmo. If you don't go back it'll kill your chances of booking another soap. Plus the show could sue you for breach of contract."

"This is really rich," I began, knowing Weezi's objective was to keep me where I was, his sole meal ticket paying him nine thousand dollars a month in commissions. "Edith and her gang can shake me quicker than a bad habit, but you can't shake them for nothin'. What's wrong? Afraid to rock the boat for fear you'll lose your gravy train?"

"C'mon, Calysta, don't talk like that, look how far we've come together. You know I'd do anything for you. Think about your future. You can handle one more week of those nitwits with your eyes closed. Hell, you've been doing it for fifteen years, what's one more week?"

"Why don't you come down to the set and find out," I snapped.

"I would if I could but I have to check on a new client. She's only eighteen and working on that new Russell Crowe film. She's having trouble remembering her lines."

"Gee, Weezi, I wish I could feel sorry for her but—"

"Just one more week, kiddo, you can do it," he encouraged. "Try to think of the money you earn from this day on as dough for your daughter's trust fund or that kitchen remodel."

"Wow, thanks for the free financial planning, Weezi. God knows, less deserving people on *R&R* get double what I make and they're reading off goddamn cue cards!"

"All right already, who said life was fair? Not everyone's as smart as you. You'll have every producer in daytime begging to give you a contract if you would just be a good girl and finish out your last week without any drama."

"Weezi, do you realize if you weren't such a complacent slug you could be pulling double the commission out my—"

"Look, I've got an important meeting at the Polo Lounge and I'm just itchin' to use my new pink card. You know what they say, a good meal lubricates business."

"Is that what they say? Didn't know."

"You've got two choices: A, you can go into work all half-cocked and wreck your career, or B, you can show up at the soap and kick butt knowing the entire industry will be watching. If you finish without any problems the soap galaxy will be your oyster; otherwise, you'll be branded too *difficult* to work with."

There it was, the dreaded "D" word. I imagined myself in a yellow Big Bird costume with a cutout for my face, on the set of *Sesame Street*.

"Hi kids! It's me, your old friend Calysta! The letter for today is 'D' for difficult. You see, when men in Hollywood speak out about incompetent producers or asinine writers or in general fight for their rights, they are called words that begin with 'P' like passionate and 'C' like courageous, but when women, especially women who are 'B' for brown, speak out they are called the bad, bad 'D' word, difficult. Spell it out with me, d-i-f-f-i-c-u-l-t!"

"If you just play the game, I know I can get you on *Obsessions*," Weezi said, jolting me out of my daydream.

"Let's stop the b.s., shall we? You might have watched *The Rich and the Ruthless* once the whole fifteen years I was on the air. By the way, I found out you called Daniel Needleman and asked, and I quote, 'Is *The Rich and the Ruthless* actually the number one soap opera in daytime?' News flash, it's been number one since I joined. But before you go offering up my *aging, difficult, colored* hide to the worst show in the history of daytime television, you might want to check and see how much longer *Obsessions* is gonna be on the air. It's being canceled next week!"

"Oh, really?"

"Yes, really. And maybe I don't want to be on another sudser; have you ever considered that? If you would maybe break a sweat trying to find me a steady gig in prime time or a breakout indie role, I wouldn't have to deal with soaps anymore."

"Calysta, be realistic, there aren't a lot of opportunities in prime time and film for women over thirty-five. Especially women of color, unless you wanna do a reality show."

"No shit, Sherlock. Tell me somethin' I *don't* know. I'll go in and finish up the week, but that's it." *Click.*

BLIND ITEM: What daytime diva, recently forced off her soap, came in to tape her swan song scenes only to discover her security privileges were revoked? That's right, kids, soap ID badge #J25320 snatched! Read it and weep.

This soap superstar was literally kicked to the curb and had to park outside along the street! Heavens to soapsuds, what's love in the afternoon coming to? As if that wasn't humiliating enough, the producers sent out a tween *intern* to escort the famed bubbler to and from the set! What, did they think she was going to make off with those tacky knockoffs? Thank gawd the fashionista had the good sense to start bringing in her own bangin' threads. Shame, shame!

The Diva

CHAPTER 8

Access Denied

I turned my black-on-black Volvo SUV (my Jag was in the shop for a tuneup) onto the WBC lot, stopping at the guard gate, rolling down the window as I approached.

"Morning, Jay."

"Morning, Ms. Jeffries," he replied with nervousness in his voice.

"Oh my gawd, it's Ruby Stargazer!" yelled dozens of enthusiastic fans outside the gate. The game show contestants had been waiting since the wee hours of the morning in hopes of landing a seat on *Deal of the Century*, the popular lead-in game show to *The Rich and the Ruthless* on the WBC television network.

"How y'all doin'?" I yelled back to the crowd.

"We're doing great now that we've seen you, Ruby. We love you!"

called back an exuberant fan standing with a group in matching red T-shirts with THE WILLIAMS FAMILY FROM ST. LOUIS emblazoned on them. "Keep representin', Ruby!"

I beamed, grateful for the much-needed ego boost.

"Big crowd this morning," I said, returning my attention to Jay.

"Yes, ma'am. Sure is."

"How's Thalia and the kids?"

"Everyone's doing fine . . . doing fine."

"Wonderful," I replied, waiting for him to raise the gate. "Well, I better get goin'. You have a good day."

"Ah, Ms. Jeffries . . ."

"Yes? Is there a problem?"

"I'm sorry, ma'am, your security access has been denied."

"Stop jokin' and let me through."

"No, I'm serious. Ms. Norman sent a memo stating you had to park outside the gate this week."

"Really." A horn sounded behind me.

"I'm sorry, ma'am."

"No, you're just doin' your job, Jay," I said through clenched teeth.

Gripping the steering wheel and pissed, I shifted my SUV into reverse, sending it squealing back, burning rubber out into the street, nearly colliding with Emmy's candy apple red convertible Porsche.

"Hey, watch it, sistah. Now that you're about to be unemployed and all, I'd hate to have to sue you for dingin' my ride with that soccer mom mobile," Emmy cackled in her leather "To Catch A Thief" driving gloves, looking over her jeweled Bvlgari sunglasses, gunning her engine up to the gate.

"Ohmagod, look, it's Gina Chiccetelli, everyone!" screamed the fans. "Gina, Gina, can you look this way?" as they aimed their disposable cameras at her.

On cue, Emmy's designer Pomapoo raised her tiny head and pedicured paws, posing for them, teeth bared. Unprovoked, two months prior, the vicious three-pound six-ounce mutt bit an extra. Emmy settled out of court but was ordered to muzzle her precious pooch if she wanted it on the WBC lot.

Ignoring the still-screaming fans, Emma flashed her badge and glided onto the lot, her vanity plates reading R&R STAR.

After parking along the curb, a country mile from the WBC gate, I climbed out and began searching for loose change.

"Here, Miss Stargazer," said a young passing fan in full dress blues balancing a tray of coffee, offering me a handful of quarters.

"Thank you, um, Tom," I replied, eyeing his oversize yellow name tag. "I know I have change in this purse somewhere."

"That's all right. It's on me," he said. "When I go back next week for my second tour of duty I'm gonna tell everyone how I helped out my favorite soap star!"

I smiled my gratitude at the young soldier, sensing he wouldn't be coming home. As he walked away, I fought back tears, retrieving my hatbox and makeup kit from the backseat.

No crying, I mentally admonished. *Think about the fans in the crowd. They came all this way to forget about their troubles and to suspend reality on that silly game show. Never expected to see you too. So suck it up. And I mean suck it up right now. Nobody wants to see a sniveling soap star.*

I flashed a smile as I signed autographs, shook hands, and posed for pictures. The *R&R* cast and crew had begun arriving for work, noticing me on foot.

"What the hell?" Daniel Needleman mouthed through the window of his Lexus.

Holding my chin up, I trudged back up to the security gate, hot. A pubescent man was now standing with Jay. He couldn't have been more than nineteen.

"Ms. Jeffries, this is Perry," Jay introduced.

"Okay," I replied with an impatient tone.

"He's a new intern at *The Rich and the Ruthless*."

"It's an honor to meet you, Ms. Jeffries," he said. "You're my mom's favorite and I've been watching you since I was four."

"Thank you, Perry. Listen, I would love to autograph a picture for your mom, but can you catch me later? As you can see, I'm having a rough morn—"

"I don't think you understand, Ms. Jeffries," Jay said. "Perry is here to escort you onto the set."

Just then the game show audience erupted into the biggest reception yet.

"Come again? Speak louder! I can't hear you with all that racket behind me."

"Perry is here to escort you onto the set!" Jay shouted.

"Um, yeah, Mr. Roberts told me I was to shadow you at all times when you weren't taping this week," the pimply intern stuttered.

"It's okay, Jay, I'll escort Ms. Jeffries to the set," came the instantly recognizable, sexy voice of Derrick Taylor, my former leading man, on and off stage. We had been the most popular black super-couple in daytime. Derrick had left his wildly popular role as Dove Jordan on *The Rich and the Ruthless* two years earlier for the WBC prime-time series *Pathological Murders,* and more than a million viewers left with him.

My heart skipping a beat, I turned around to see my old flame pulling up beside me in his custom Rolls-Royce Phantom Drophead convertible.

"What's going on, sexy?" he asked with a grin that revealed his twin trademark dimples. Derrick employed his good looks like a well-used passport.

A smile broke across my face.

The intern stood in disbelief, seeing Derrick Taylor, the eight-pack-sporting soap-star-turned-prime-time-vigilante-action-hero up close.

"Mr. Taylor, I have specific orders," Jay said tensely. "I could get in trouble."

"Chill, anybody gives you trouble, tell 'em to come see Derrick Taylor," he said with a cocksure attitude. "Calysta, get yo fine ass in this car, we're holdin' up traffic."

He didn't have to ask me twice. Undone as I was, I managed to vamp my way around the polished Rolls and slide into heaven.

Smelling of Armani's Acqua di Gio cologne, Derrick leaned over to lay his firm lips on my cheek. And like Pavlov's dog, I had a reaction that remained concealed.

"Derrick, you're a lifesaver. Some girls get a prince on a white horse; I get a brutha in a bullet gray Phantom."

"What can I say? I'm always happy to help a damsel in distress."

We shared a laugh before I looked away. Derrick parked.

"So, shortie, what's going on? You have a flat or somethin'?"

"It's a long story."

"You know your new leading man, Ethan—" Derrick began.

"Please don't call him that," I interrupted. "He's a bad replacement."

"Remember when the dork left me that stalker message on my voice-mail?"

"Who could forget?"

"It was wack. 'Man you got the crib, the ride, and the women I want and now you got my show. Good luck you bastard.'"

"What a loser," I clucked. "He's still braggin' about that *Pathological Murders* audition to anyone who'll listen. Ain't nobody tryin' to hire his bubbler butt outside of daytime. You might consider getting a restraining order," I suggested as we maliciously snickered together.

"I've been hearin' all kinds of crazy mess about you leaving the show. Is it true, babe?"

"Yeah, it's true," I said, disguising my pain. "And I'll tell you what else is true."

"What's that?"

"I truly miss you on the set, D. These people get crazier by the day, tryin' to minimize the tracks we laid down for this damn sudser and doin' it *without* the same paper."

"Word. Ain't that nothin'? *Believe,* with Edith 'n' the Barringers, *dollar's king.* They still ain't ready to invest in big brown but *trust . . .* they will. In the meantime you gotta be lookin' out for number one. You still cute 'n' got time on your side. Remember, black . . ."

". . . don't crack. I feel you on that," I replied. "I shoulda left when your behin' did. Heard daytime only has a few more years."

Derrick had declined to return to the number one soap during his last round of contract negotiations, when despite his titanic stature as daytime's most popular actor, *The Rich and the Ruthless* refused to offer the soap god the same northern-million-dollar salaries offered to popular white leading actors. The WBC, not wanting to lose Derrick, a Nielsen ratings magnet, offered the hunky leading man a series regular spot on the primetime procedural *Pathological Murders.* He more than cleaned up.

"So where's the exotic location shoot this year?" Derrick teased. "Flying anywhere nice in the honeymoon jet?"

Laughing briefly, I thought of my many trips on the Vinn Hansen private plane. Pretending to be at cruising altitude, the grounded jet consisted of a seventy-two-inch-radius wall, four portals, and four seats.

"Man, I got as far as Pittsburgh. Cheapskate Randall had the temerity to piggyback my personal appearance at a mall in the hood with no air-conditioning. Bootlegged the gig, turning it into a location shoot."

"Ooh, that's rough, Calysta."

"I swear it was over a hundred degrees in that damn building. Sweated my hair out lookin' *busted* for three whole days." I shuddered. "I don't understand why I stuck around this place for so long."

"Because you love it."

"Huh?"

"Maybe not all the cast or the crap, but you love playing Ruby Stargazer, and more than that, you love your fans. Hell, most actors see daytime as a stepping-stone to prime time. But you would've been perfectly happy sticking it out for the long haul if those idiots only knew how to treat a *sistah* of substance."

He was right. Most soap stars wanted to be on prime time, prime-time stars wanted to be movie stars, movie stars wanted to be rock stars, rock stars and wrestlers wanted to be politicians, politicians wanted to be in Hollywood, and all I wanted was to be Ruby Stargazer on *The Rich and the Ruthless* for the rest of my life.

"So what are you gonna do?" Derrick asked, as he rolled the car up to the Artists' Entrance.

"Hell if I know. You-all hiring over at your show?"

"You know if they were you'd be the first honey I'd call."

"Yeah right; you know you want some spicy young thang to play your love interest."

"They don't get any spicier than you, mamma. By the way, I kinda miss those plastic palm trees that the soap borrowed from *Deal of the Century* for our tropical destination shoot."

"Liar," I said with a half smile.

Derrick got out and went around to open the door for me.

"Holy crap, is that who I think it is?" one of the extras asked a fellow day player as they passed by.

Derrick cheesed for the girls while I shook my head.

"Boy, you never quit."

"Fo sho," Derrick said, grinning. "Can't nobody match my swag!" He took my hand. "On the serious tip, it's gonna be all right, babe, 'cause you're one of the most talented, beautiful women I've ever had the plea-sure of working with on and off the set." He winked. "And you know what else? We're both Taurus: sexy, sweet, and stubborn. Remember what our motto used to be over some Hennessy?"

At first I pretended I didn't, knowing Derrick had it tattooed on his right bicep.

"Oh yeah, *Never Blend In.*"

"That's the ticket," he said, raising the sleeve of his skintight T-shirt. "Stand your ground, girl, and don't give up a blink. Put your game face on and no matter what, don't break your cool. I ain't even worried about-cha. Be honest, you know you love makin' coin."

Laughing, Derrick pulled me in, locking his seductive bedroom eyes on mine and saying with devilish charm, "Call me if you need anything, and I do mean anything."

His Phantom sped across the lot.

Seeing Willie Turner's Impala Caprice approaching was an immediate downer, reminding me exactly why I was rescued in the first place. Couldn't believe that shmuck Randall had the audacity to send an intern to escort me to the set.

Wasn't enough that he and his ant farm had managed to drive me to quit, now they were out for humiliation.

"They're messin' with the wrong woman today!" I said under my breath.

CHAPTER 9

"Nothing . . . Absolutely Nothing"

W ho's your naughty Snuggle Bunny?" Randall asked Emmy mid-thrust in his corner office.

"*Goo* are."

"Louder," he demanded in a growling whisper, spanking the bubblette, causing her to wince.

"*Goo* are," she repeated, garbled words coming from the corner of her mouth, face smashed against a pile of *R&R* scripts on his desk. "*Goo are my gaughty, gaughty guggle gunny.*"

"That's right," he grunted. They were having a celebratory romp in honor of Calysta quitting the soap.

Randall had taken two Viagras just for the occasion, which had become routine despite doctors' warnings.

Only six weeks earlier, he'd been rushed to Cedars-Sinai Hospital suffering from Viagra-induced heart arrhythmia after washing the pills down with merlot before a quick after-hours tryst with Emmy, not realizing red wine and the penile enhancer don't mix. Later that night, Alison found her hubby slumped over on their black toilet in the master bathroom clutching his flabby chest.

Randall continued to have his Viagra shipped in bulk from Mexico, delivered to an undisclosed P.O. box in Watts. Naturally, he kept a healthy stash in his office desk, because he and Alison hadn't had anything even close to fellatio since *Everybody Loves Raymond* went off the air.

He momentarily fixated on a real-life nightmare: Alison bolting naked from their bed, stomping toward the kitchen, her entire body feeling as though it were being roasted over a spit, standing in front of their open Sub-Zero fighting merciless sweats, also known as "the change of life." Randall had crept up behind the ugly spectacle, disbelieving that his trophy wife was now reduced to a menopausal mess.

"Are you all right, Alison?" he asked as he put his hand on her clammy shoulder.

Screaming bloody murder she whipped around, spewing, "I was until you practically mauled me, you idiot, scaring me half to death. I came down for a Fudgsicle to cool off. And by the way, you fell asleep again."

Since then, Randall had felt less blameworthy and allowed himself guilty pleasures. For instance Emmy, bent over his desk.

Unlucky at love, Emmy had learned a long time ago to grit her teeth and suck it up, quite literally, to get what she wanted. And what she wanted was a clear shot at the leading lady slot on *The Rich and the Ruthless,* stopping at nothing to get what she set her sights on.

She knew that Edith Norman was famous for forcing network producers to put their aging leading ladies out to pasture to chow down on cud once they turned the undesirable, leprous ages of thirty-five to

fifty. Clinging to daytime like an *African Queen* barnacle, Alison Fairchild Roberts was waaaay past the *sell by* date.

With an actress's window of opportunity so narrow in Hollywood,
Emmy thought nothing of allowing Randall to occasionally plow her
like an overgrown cornfield if that's what it would take to get him to
anoint her America's Next Queen Bee of *R&R*.

Always calculating, she moaned between thrusts and thoughts, "*Oh,
phow-guggle-gunny-gou're-guch-a-guckin'-monster,*" slappin' pride on Randall's face.

Emmy had an easier time relating to a storyline that had her character, Gina Chiccetelli, as the long-lost daughter of a Martian than to
the role of a woman sexually satisfied by anatomically deprived Randall
Roberts.

A million miles away, she mulled over her options, not wanting
to risk having her ace in the hole get sentimental about sending his
dicey-wifey off to Destination Nowhere, so she picked up where she
left off, adjusting her recently Botoxed face still plastered against a stack
of scripts to throw in a few extra bonus strokes, "Oh, phow, phow,
*phow*wwww!"

Meg Ryan couldn't have faked it better.

Randall collapsed on her back, his hairy, sweat-soaked body greasing
against hers like Crisco in a hot skillet. Emmy cringed, sliding out from
under him, pulling down her Zac Posen dress.

"That was un-freaking-believable!" Randall exclaimed, falling back
into his chair, catching his breath as he squeezed a dollop of Purell between his fat palms. The producer's heart was pumping so fast he thought
it might explode.

Maybe next time just one Viagra? he thought, placing the anti-bacterial
back on his desk.

Unlocking her jaw with a series of facial contortions, Emmy replied,
"Snuggle Bunny, about Calysta . . ."

"What about her?" he asked, tucking his shirt back into his trousers.

"I don't know, I guess I'm a little worried," she admitted. "Are you *positive* she's leaving the show?"

"Pussycat, how many times do I have to tell you, she's O-U-T, out. We offered her recurring and she turned it down. End of story. Ding, dong, the bitch is dead!"

"Yeah well, I'll believe it when she drives off the lot for the last time with her hatboxes, hair extensions, and straightening combs." Emmy snorted. "It didn't work the last time we tried to get her to quit, ya know!"

"Yeah, but the difference was Augustus was still in charge," Randall reminded her. "In the past, whenever she tied her little red g-string into a knot, her godfather was always there to talk her down from the ledge, but not this time."

"How do you know she wears a red g-string?" Emmy challenged.

"Huh?"

His mind darted back to a few weeks earlier, when he had snuck into Calysta's dressing room while she was on-set. Snooping around, he found his Holy Grail: a lacy red thong dangling from Calysta's bathroom doorknob.

Inhaling it, he whispered, "Who's your daddy now?" while masturbating, before stuffing the g-string into his pocket and making a quick exit.

"Uh . . . just a figure of speech," Randall replied, fingering Calysta's g-string in his pocket.

"Mm-hm," Emmy said, unconvinced.

"Ms. Jeffries, you can't go in there!" Randall heard as the door to his office was flung open.

"Watch me lookin' good doin' it," I said, entering, Randall's secretary Anita hot on my heels. "An intern to escort me?"

"What do you think you're doing, Calysta?" Randall demanded.

"I tried to stop her, Mr. Roberts."

"It's all right, Anita."

"Yes, sir," she said, cursing in Spanish under her breath, closing the door.

I gave the guilty pair a slanted look before sitting down on his leather sofa, coolly crossing my legs.

"What do we have here?" I asked.

"Nothing, absolutely nothing!" Randall said defensively.

"Humph, sure sound jumpy for somebody doin' 'nothing, absolutely nothing.'"

"For crissakes, Calysta." Emmy sighed. "We're talking about my storyline. Jeesh, what do you think we're doing, banging each other's brains out on the couch?"

"No question you've been bangin' somethin'. Why don't you make yourself useful and open a window. There's an unmistakable tartness in the air," I said, moving to a chair.

"Sticks and stones may break my bones but Randall's making me a di-rec-tor," Emmy sang.

"You a lie," I said, redirecting my attention to Randall. "I've been on this soap for how long? And you're lettin' *her* direct?"

"What can I say, she's earned the show four Sudsys, Calysta. *The Rich and the Ruthless* has always rewarded high achievement."

Emmy flashed a satisfied grin.

"And what do you call my eleven NAACP Image Awards over the past fifteen years?"

Emmy sucked her teeth and rolled her eyes, saying, "Oh *those*," dismissively. "They don't count."

"Emmy . . ." Randall warned, standing. The last thing he wanted was Al Sharpton on his doorstep. "This meeting is over!"

"I wonder how Alison would see this 'creative meeting'?" I baited.

"Oh wow, you're like really reaching," Emmy snapped. "Alison's a friend of mine."

"Yeah sure, just like we're BFFs, right?"

"You know what? I've tried to be your friend, Calysta, but you just won't let anybody in. It's that wall you have built up around that little heart of yours. I really feel sorry for you. I'm sure your tough childhood in Mississippi had something to do with it, but when are you gonna let someone in?"

Applauding, I said, "You actually managed to pull that monologue off without one cue card."

"All right, that's enough, you two," Randall said, taking his seat again as his phone beeped.

"Mr. Roberts, sorry to interrupt, but your wife is on line one," Anita announced.

"Tell her I'm in the middle of a meeting and I'll call her back."

"She said it was urgent, sir."

"Tell Alison I'll call her back!" Roberts yelled.

"I'll go, Randy," Emmy offered. "Three's a crowd . . . besides, this is her last week on *The Rich and the Ruthless* and I have all the time in the world to discuss *my* future . . . on the show," she added with a wink.

I resisted the urge to say anything as she passed, reeking of her signature fragrance, Paris Hilton's Can Can.

"Right, we'll finish this another time, Emmy," Randall insisted, clearing his throat while straightening his Hermès tie.

"Whatever you say, Randy, you're the boss. Oh, Calysta, some parting advice: be sure to roll over your 401(k), or better yet liquidate. You're gonna need the cash. I'm afraid there's no government bailout for aging actresses. Retirement's a bitch."

"Good-bye, Emmy," Randall said.

"Could ya hit that magic button between your legs and let me out?" she asked with skanky innuendo.

"Uh sure," he said, flustered, pressing the control under his shoe as Emmy sauntered out.

"Flat-ass bitch," I said.

"That's totally uncalled for, Calysta," Randall scolded. "You really need an attitude adjustment."

"That what you were givin' Deep Throat? An attitude adjustment?"

"I'm not going to dignify that with a response."

"We both know the only reason that trailer trash knows exactly where your 'magic button' is, is because she's performed *fumer le cigare* too many times for anyone, including you, to count."

"Your opinion means less than nothing to me," Randall began. "But you should be forewarned, if you even think about going around spreading malicious gossip and lies about Emmy and me—"

"Oh please. I could give a good kitty what you do with that hussy. I came up here to ask why you think I need a damn *intern* to escort me to the set of my show."

"*Your* show?" Randall laughed. "Let's get something straight, you're part of the cast like everybody else. Everyone's a star on *The Rich and the Ruthless* and you're all treated equal. And for the record, this is *my* show. Had you figured that out earlier, things could have been a lot different."

"By 'figuring it out,' do you mean giving in to your sleazy advances?" I retorted. "No thanks, I'd rather take a Timex on my way out. I know what you're trying to do, Randall. You ain't slick."

"And what exactly is that, besides trying to keep this sudser afloat?" Randall sighed. "As for the intern, Edith and I agreed it was best."

"For who? Humph, Edith." I smirked. "I'll just bet the two of you burned the midnight oil on this one."

"I have to ask you to leave," he said, his voice brittle.

"If you think you're gonna drive me to go Angry Black Woman and pull out an Afro puff my last week of taping you're gonna be disappointed, because I plan to leave *R&R* with my dignity intact. So bring it, do your worst. Now, I have a rehearsal to get to and with all the roadblocks you-all set up this morning I hope I haven't missed it. And uh, can you hit that 'magic button,' not the one between your legs, the one on your desk to tell your German shepherd Anita to heel. Next time she barks, I'll bite."

Charging behind me, Randall shouted, "Why can't you be like all the other actresses on this show?"

"Because I'm not," I responded, never turning around, disappearing through the glass doors.

"Frigging nut job," Randall muttered under his breath, all the staff watching as he returned to his office. "What are you all staring at? Go back to work!"

Snatching up the phone, he dialed Edith's extension.

"Hello, Edith Norman's office, president of daytime televi—"

"Fern, put me through."

"Yes, Mr. Roberts."

"I was just about to call you," Edith said, watching the air show on one of her three flat screens. "Tell me you have good news."

"It worked like a charm," he lied.

"Excellent! We've got to focus on painting Calysta as Soap Opera Enemy Number One to convince the fans and all of daytime that she's a menace to our production and unemployable. *She's* unbalanced, not the show or the network," Edith said conspiratorially. "The fans have been going absolutely ape shit since SecretsofaSoapOperaDiva.com broke the news that she's leaving. It's ridiculous. Don't these people have lives? Keep up the pressure, Randall. Calysta has to quit the show in a rage for my plan to work. Once she's gone, the ratings will temporarily suffer, which will make the Barringers think long and hard about Augustus's stance against selling his shows to the network, especially with his precarious health and the state of the economy. Not even a family as loaded as the Barringers can afford to keep producing soaps that are rapidly hemorrhaging sponsors and viewers. It defies logic that Augustus wouldn't simply take our offer and live out the rest of his days with his precious Kitty in the South of France."

Randall quickly agreed. "But that makes too much sense for that workaholic."

"Augustus has relied much too heavily on black viewing households. We have to go after a more, shall we say, Red State audience if our soaps are going to survive."

"Works for me."

"WBC stock has tumbled dismally from last year's high of fifty-seven dollars a share to three dollars and fifty cents. I've lost my ass on investing in this network. If things don't turn around soon I'm going to be looking into the eyes of a loan shark."

The fact that Edith Norman still had her job ranked with Doug Flutie's "Hail Mary" pass. She continued, "Let's go over why I need your pathetic soap opera to stay at number one. *The Rich and the Ruthless* and *The Daring and the Damned* give the WBC its seed money to shoot the network's prime-time pilot shows. And I need to keep the coffers full in order to keep my job."

"A reliable source tells me that Veronica Barringer was spotted at Bonhams & Butterfields auction house after hours, hawking one of the family's prized paintings," Randall reported.

"Delicious dirt," Edith squealed.

"It's only a matter of time before Auggie Jr. sells the soaps to the network."

"Then I can finally rebuild *The Rich and the Ruthless* and *The Daring and the Damned* the way I want to, attracting more of those *Twilight* teen viewers instead of their grandmothers still watching the re-re-re-runs of *Diagnosis Murder*."

"Don't you mean *we* can finally rebuild the soaps?" Randall corrected. "Don't forget our arrangement, Edith; once we get the Barringers to sell, you're making me Senior Executive Producer of *R&R,* right?"

"I haven't forgotten," Edith coldly replied. "Just do your part and make sure Augustus's little pet diva Calysta acts out in such a horrendous way I can justify never hiring her back. I want that bitch and any other actor who thinks they can step out of line to realize no one gets away with making Edith Norman look bad; no one."

Long before Edith was named President of Daytime Television for the WBC, she'd made an attempt at an acting career. Augustus had cast her as the long-lost half-sister of the wildly popular Rory Lovekin, played by Alison Fairchild Roberts on *The Rich and the Ruthless*. While Edith had managed to nail the part at the audition, she froze up once she was in front of the camera.

After weeks of production delays and botched dialogue, even *with* the help of cue cards, Augustus called Edith into his office to inform her, "I'm sorry kid, you're just not cut out for this."

Devastating.

Shortly after signing what she thought would be a three-year contract, she'd purchased a posh condo and a fancy car, both of which were repossessed by the bank.

Humiliating.

She went back to waiting tables, occasionally taking in work as a masseuse. One of her regular clients happened to be Executive Producer of the hit prime-time sitcom *Shirley, You So Crazy*. He offered her a job as a production assistant and she offered him a Happy Ending.

The *Shirley* gig led to various prime-time episodics. Edith's big break came when she was named an Associate Producer for one of the WBC's prime-time soaps during its first season.

By the time the wildly successful show was canceled, twelve seasons later, Edith had moved up to show runner, heralded as "The Woman Who Saved the WBC." This led to several high-profile prime-time projects, all of which flopped.

Attempting to make good on their investment and avoid paying an expensive severance package if they fired her, the WBC gave Edith the position of President of Daytime Television. The network figured they could utilize her expertise to make their daytime soaps, which had been struggling since the first O.J. Simpson trial, a booming success. The move effectively made Edith Norman Augustus's boss.

From day one in her new position Edith had done everything in her power to take control of the Barringer empire, determined to make Augustus pay for ruining her dreams of becoming the next Meryl Streep, though she would have settled for Rhea Perlman.

Like a spider, Edith licked with her feet. She thought she might finally get the chance she'd been waiting for with Augustus's declining health, leaving at the helm his ambivalent son, Auggie Jr., who'd been trying for years to persuade his stubborn father to sell the soaps.

She malevolently reminisced about a recent call Auggie made from her office to his dad in the hospital.

"But Dad, we could make a bundle if we sell outright to the WBC . . . forget about licensing!" he had reasoned.

"I already make a bundle," Augustus replied. "How many times do I have to tell you, success is not a miracle? I have given you the reins of our family dynasty on a silver platter and all you can do is look for ways to give it away. The answer is no, and that's the way it's going to stay!"

MEOW, MEOW. An inside source on the set of *The Rich and the Ruthless* texted moi with news of quite the catfight in the wardrobe room this morning.

Apparently Lead Cat-ress Alison Fairchild Roberts wasn't exactly purring when she found out another soap tigress would be donning the legendary wedding dress she wore a kabillion years ago for her first of seven soap opera weddings to Wolfe Hudson's character Vidal Vinn Hansen.

The tigress in question, Calysta Jeffries, was equally ticked at the very thought of having to wear Roberts's tacky taffeta hand-me-down.

You mean to tell me daytime's number one soap has resorted to recycling wedding dresses? LMAO. Sounds like somebody better line up a few more detergent sponsors!

The Diva

CHAPTER 10

Wardrobe Malfunction

fter leaving Randall's office, I beelined it to the wardrobe department to meet with *R&R*'s Nazi wardrobe mistress, Penelope Wilcox. I needed to discuss my wedding gown for Ruby Stargazer's upcoming nuptials and honeymoon scenes. Even though I was on my way off the soap, I intended to go out with sizzle and style, a no-expense-spared fashionista bang.

Shannen and I jokingly referred to Penelope as the Pattern Cutter behind her back. With a swamp brown, cobweb-looking beehive, she ruled over the wardrobe department with iron pinking shears.

"Hi, Penelope, got a second?"

"Not now, I'm very busy letting out Alison's DKNY pantsuit for next week's Fink Enterprises boardroom scenes," a jittery Penelope snapped, on her fourth cup of coffee. "She's put on a few more pounds, poor thing, menopause. Alison's going to be featured on MTV Romania," she added, never looking up. "Oh, by the way, bring in your Patricia Underwood cloche and your Kai Milla dress tomorrow. We're reshooting a scene from last week before you leave the show."

"Not the scene where everyone clapped. The one the cameramen hooted and whistled and bought me drinks at Formosa Café afterward for. Not that scene?"

Everyone knew green-eyed Alison Fairchild Roberts never hesitated to phone up her henchman husband, demanding he target certain actresses for their stellar performances, making them do a scene over and over and over until it sucked. If that evil shrew could keep a daytime diva from getting a Sudsy, she was guilty as sin.

"Calysta, I don't have time to watch a soap. I barely have time to read scripts, let alone dress a cast with weight problems."

"Friggin' unbelievable."

"What's that?"

"I said, I'll come back later this afternoon to discuss my dress."

"What dress?"

"Uh, my wedding dress? You do realize we're shooting those scenes this week?"

"Oh . . . that, right, they must've forgotten to tell you—"

"Tell me what?"

"You won't be getting a new dress," Penelope replied. "No budget. Sorry."

"Are you serious? No budget for Ruby Stargazer's *wedding dress*?"

"Yep, Mr. Roberts sent out a memo to crack down on frivolous spending."

"And you consider my wedding dress 'frivolous spending,' yet you find more than enough money to take Phillip McQueen out to lunch, then to Rodeo Drive with his portable color palette, searching for threads that 'complement his skin tone' and 'bring out the robin's egg blue in his eyes'? I know you've grown accustomed to relying on me schleppin'

in most of my own wardrobe, but sorry, not this time. I don't happen
to have a couture Jane Wilson-Marquis wedding gown hangin' in my
closet."

"Oh relax, will you!" She sighed, slamming down her pinking shears,
and grabbing a fistful of keys, skittered across the linoleum floor to un-
lock a huge metal door bolted like Fort Knox. It swung open. An oversize fan whirring in the corner struggled to circulate the stinky ether,
kicking up floor-to-ceiling funk from costumes dating back to more
than thirty years ago.

"I already have the perfect wedding dress for you. Wait right here and
don't touch anything," she ordered.

Did she really think I wanted the two dozen recycled Spanx shapers
hanging over the dryer? Or was it Maeve's Halloween sweater? Oh I
know, it must be Alison's shoulder-padded apple green tweed jacket with
the magenta-dyed rabbit collar.

The Pattern Cutter disappeared into racks and racks of sequins and
feathers, returning like Moses parting the Red Sea moments later with
an ivory hot mess, bouffant leg-o'-mutton sleeves and faux pearl embroi-
dery across the breastplate. The train wrapped around her arm looked
to be the length of two football fields and was attached to a crown of
rhinestones, giving new meaning to "gluegunning."

"See, now won't this be absolutely perfect? As for shoes, before you
ask, we have the Lucite or the flesh-colored Capezio heels."

Speechless; my eyes widened as I took hold of the flammable fabric
for a closer look at the monstrous confection.

"Be careful, it's vintage," Penelope warned.

"Did I miss something in the script? Are Ruby and Dove having a
seventies theme wedding?"

"Don't be ridiculous, this is a superlative dress. It took more than
eighty yards of imported silk-faced poly-satin and taffeta, the expertise
of two dozen seamstresses, and more than six hundred hours to produce. You'll look, how do you say . . . *bangin'*."

"Uh, it's six sizes too big."

"So, I'll have Thomasina take it in a bit."

"Why does this dress look familiar?"

"Yoo-hoo, Penelope, are you finished yet?" interrupted the nasal shriek of Alison Fairchild Roberts.

She was standing at the door, looking like yesterday, with her hands on her hips in a gold-monogrammed white terry cloth robe, a towel turban wrapped around her head.

Alison's nose was upturned, not because she was born that way or because she was the ultimate snob, but because of a botched rhinoplasty that also had the undesirable side effect of leaving her forever sounding like Miss Piggy on helium.

"I'm sorry, Alison, as you can see my work has been rudely interrupted. I haven't quite finished letting out your slacks, but I'll have them ready by the end of the day," a cowering Penelope promised.

"No worries. But make it snappy, don't forget we have a Tsumori Chisato fitting for my next *Cliffhanger Weekly* cover shoot."

"Uh, didn't you say Alison wouldn't be needing that pantsuit till next week?" I reminded Penelope. "I would think *my* wedding dress for scenes in a couple of days would take top priority."

"Oh yeah," squeaked Alison. "Ruby Stargazer is getting married this week, huh? Right before getting whacked on her honeymoon. *Bummer.*"

If there was one actress I despised more than Emmy it was that *Valley of the Dolls* train wreck Alison. As *R&R*'s first breakout star and one of only four original cast members left from the soap's 1972 premiere (the others being Wolfe, Dell, and Maeve, who played Alison's mother), Alison hadn't exactly been pleased when I joined the sudser. I quickly gave her a run for the distinction of being one of daytime's most popular actresses.

Before Alison could come up with another dig, she spotted her dress on Penelope's cutting table.

"Hey, what's my Givenchy-inspired wedding gown doing here?" she asked as she rushed over to snatch it up. "Penelope, you told me it was part of an exclusive costume display at the American Federation of Television and Radio Artists."

"*Your* wedding dress?" I asked incredulously.

"Yes, the first time I wore the dress was in 1976 when my character, Rory, married Vidal, that was the year of the bicentennial," she marveled. "Then after our divorce in 1980 we remarried in 1984, me symbolically wearing the same dress. We went on location to Tortola. Now *those* were soap opera weddings to *remember.* You wouldn't know anything about that, though, would you, Calysta, since *supporting* actors don't get to go on location shoots?"

"Whoa, whoa, whoa, Penelope, you were going to put me in the same dress Alison wore when Nancy Reagan was running the country?"

"I was going to have it dyed peony pink, Calysta. Jeesh, we're not going for a virginal bride here."

"Are you crazy?" Alison demanded. "No one else is wearing my dress!"

"All right, calm down," Penelope said, gathering more of the taffeta. "*Of course* I was going to ask for your permission first."

"Which you most certainly would *not* have gotten," Alison snapped, pulling more of the fabric toward her. "This dress is sacred. How do you think my legions of fans would react seeing *her* in it?"

"They'd probably wonder why the hell my size four figure was in your tent."

"You miserable—"

"Alison, please let go," the Pattern Cutter begged, pulling in the opposite direction.

"I will not! I'm taking my dress with me for safekeeping!"

"It's property of Barringer Dramatic Series. Be reasonable."

"*No,* you goddamn traitor!"

"*Alison!*"

I stepped back and stared in bug-eyed bewilderment at the bizarre fiasco unraveling.

As the two tussled over the taffeta, Alison's turban and robe came undone, revealing her wet, overbleached tresses and saggy ass.

Maybe I've been too hard on Randall. Nah, they deserve each other.

After a loud rip signaling the dress was torn, Alison squealed, "Oh my gawd. Look what you did!" as she pulled her robe shut.

"Me?" the Pattern Cutter exclaimed in shock.

"Penelope, you're in *so* much trouble. You've ruined a masterpiece! Wait until I tell my husband. And as for you, Calysta, I can hardly wait until you're finally off *R&R*. Randall and I are planning one *helluva* party the day you fall off that goddamn boat."

Alison flung the remains of the ripped dress in Penelope's face before storming out, leaving the Pattern Cutter convulsing in tears.

Wow, I thought as I slipped out to prepare for my scenes, *these wack-a-doodles are crazier than I thought.*

CHAPTER 11

Nipplegate

The Rich and the Ruthless had never hired an African American writer in its thirty-seven-year run. I was forever rewriting my scenes for the production, and they loved it. Who wouldn't? It was free! Randall and Edith knew I was passionate about my work, all of it. They got me on the cheap and looked the other way while someone else got credit for it. My scripts were always covered with penciled-in rewrites and personal notes.

Fans always wrote in asking, "Calysta, who writes those feisty lines for you?"

"*Me* do it," I'd write back.

FADE IN:

Int. Jordan/Stargazer apartment—day

(*Ruby Stargazer walks into the living room past the kitchenette with a basket of laundry to fold to find Dove staring out of a window—a suitcase at his feet*)

RUBY

Ten thousand shares of Fink stock for ~~your thoughts.~~ *what's tickin in your clock.* ∧

DOVE

(*Turns to Ruby, then looks away*)

I didn't hear you. How long have you been standing there?

RUBY

Long enough to realize you're serious about ~~leaving.~~ *bouncin'.* ∧

DOVE

Ruby . . .

RUBY

(*Cross to Dove*)

~~No~~ *Hush* Dove, don't say ~~anything.~~ *a doggone thing* ∧ Just listen. I know I made a ~~mistake~~ *a mess of things* ∧ . . .

"*Cut!*" boomed Randall, sitting in the control booth next to Julius, who was eating popcorn, one of three rotating directors. "Calysta, I can see the outline of your nipples through your sweater. I told you to wear those Nipples-No-More," he shouted over the loudspeaker. With a live feed throughout the WBC studios, anyone could watch and listen to us taping and they always were.

"The glue from those patches gives my silver dollars a rash."

"What?"

"My areolas? Maybe if you didn't keep the set so damn cold it wouldn't be a problem."

The set was kept at what felt like two degrees above freezing at all times, supposedly to keep us all alert and perky. It felt like a meat locker. On second thought, that's what it was.

"Since you're on a Nipplegate bender again, Randall, why is it that you don't make any of the guys wear the Nipples-No-More? Ethan's are twice the size of mine and have piercings," I retorted. I'd bet Derrick and his costar were laughing hysterically back in his custom double-banger trailer, the duplex of actor housing, across the lot.

"Very funny," Randall said stiffly as he dialed.

"Hello, wardrobe," Penelope warily answered.

"Get those nipple busters down here stat!"

"Sorry, Randall, we ran out. You said we didn't have it in the bud—"

He hung up.

I said, "Can we get back to work? We have eighty-two pages to tape, and that doesn't include the scenes we have to do because of Maeve's bronchitis."

A reluctant Randall nodded in agreement.

"Okay, let's pick it up from your line, Calysta," the director said.

I took my place, nipples and all.

RUBY

Hush

~~No~~ Dove, don't say ~~anything~~ *a doggone thing*. Just listen.

I know I made a ~~big mistake~~ *mess of things* going behind your back ~~to try~~ *actin' shady tryin* to win you Fink Enterprises, but baby I did it

for you.

DOVE

That doesn't excuse all the damage you caused.

RUBY

(Ruby grabs Dove's arm/goes to her knees)

I said I'm
I'm so sorry, Dove. Please forgive me. Don't make me beg. If only

I could turn back the clock. You're the only
You know there ain't no other man for me
man I'll always love, you have to believe that.
a little scratch in the groove
Now, Let's not let this get in the way of us getting
hitched.
married.

DOVE

(Pulling Ruby up to her feet)

What? Are you serious?

RUBY

a heart attack.
As serious as that tornado that ripped through White-

haven last year trapping us in the Fink wine cellar

during their annual Christmas party.

DOVE

Ruby, I . . . I don't know what to say. This is highly

irregular.

RUBY

Dove baby, *just say yes, sweetheart.* I want to be your

woman again.

(Cue organ music)

Will Edith Norman finally hire a new writing team and get rid of that hack Felicia Silverstein? I've got a great idea! How 'bout the cutting-edge number one daytime soap opera hiring a few top-drawer minority writers? I hate that word "minority," it sounds so, er, racist and condescending. But you know, black, Hispanic, Indian, Asian, oh you get it, actual "color" television. To my knowledge, there's like three black scribes in all of soap operaland. It's just my opinion but isn't it time for CHANGE?

The Diva

CHAPTER 12

Who's Writing This Crap?

*F*rom the bed in his private hospital suite, Augustus Barringer yelled, "Sonofabitch, who's writing this crap! And what happened to the lighting?" He was watching an episode of *The Rich and the Ruthless*.

"Daddy, you have to stay calm," Veronica Barringer, his debutante daughter, warned. "You can't risk your blood pressure going up."

"How the hell do you expect me to stay calm when someone's writing b.s. like that on one of my shows? I want you to get Felicia on the phone now!"

Veronica sighed. She knew allowing her father to watch episodes of his struggling flagship show was a bad idea, but her mother had insisted, "Television is a defining aspect of your father's life." Katherine

Barringer reasoned, "If we take that away from him, we might as well start digging his grave now."

"Daddy, I'll speak to Felicia as soon as I get back to L.A.," Veronica promised. "Right now I'm focused on you getting better."

"Never mind that. I've got a team of overpriced doctors and your mother to worry about that. I need you to jet back to Los Angeles and head up writer duties on *R&R* and oversee *The Daring and the Damned* until I get out of this damn bed and back on my feet. Should've hired you out of college, Ronnie, and fired Felicia the day she suggested we stop using real fur on the show after she came back from that goddamned PETA fund-raiser."

"Daddy, you've gotta be kidding, I've only dabbled in writing. A few articles a year in *Artforum*, that's it."

"Look, I didn't donate all that money to Syracuse and get you into the Newhouse School for nothing."

"But there's no way I can manage writing scripts *and* oversee story content for both shows! Besides, I'm not going anywhere until we figure out what's been causing these strokes. The shows will survive."

"You'll do what I tell you to do. And whaddya mean there's no way you can manage both shows? Hell, I wrote both soaps for years and the only vacation I ever had was open heart surgery. You kids today have no ambition."

Any other time, Veronica would have launched into a heated discussion with her father about how the soap world had changed, but instead she decided to let him have the last word.

"God knows your brother isn't capable."

Veronica's older brother, Auggie Jr., who had been blessed with more than most in the hunk department, oversaw the business aspects of *The Rich and the Ruthless* and *The Daring and the Damned,* acting as co-executive producer alongside Randall Roberts during Augustus's absence. That is, when his golf game and partying allowed him the spare time.

"How's your father doing?" an elegant Katherine asked in her trademark brahmin voice, walking in chicly dressed in Escada.

"Everything's fine, Mother," Veronica said with uncertainty in her tone.

"The hell it is," Augustus bellowed. "*R&R* is disintegrating into an *Obsessions* circus, thanks to Felicia's barbaric writing, and our son and Randall are just sitting by letting it happen! Next thing you know, *The Rich and the Ruthless* will be *The Lost and the Forgotten*. And what's this business about Randall wanting a pay increase? That bum's already overpaid. Is he out of his mind?!"

"Augustus, dear," Katherine said soothingly. "There will be plenty of time to worry about everything once we get you well."

She leaned over to kiss her husband on the forehead.

"I suppose you're right," he replied, his wife's relaxed tone calming him down. "So when can I go home anyway?"

"The doctor said he would be in to talk to us about your test results sometime this morning," Katherine assured him.

The three of them had been at Johns Hopkins Hospital in Baltimore, one of the world's most prestigious medical centers for neurological studies, for more than two weeks. Augustus had begun suffering from mini-strokes the previous year.

"Have you heard back from Randall about Calysta?" Augustus asked.

Veronica had hoped her father would have forgotten about the sticky situation with Calysta. Augustus had been livid when he learned one of his most popular stars and a personal favorite had allegedly chosen to leave the show.

"No, Daddy, Randall hasn't called back. But he assured me that he was doing whatever he could to convince Calysta to change her mind and stay on the show. I told him you said to give her whatever she wants, including a raise."

"And has Edith made any of those changes we discussed at our last meeting with Josephine Mansoor? Diversifying the show a little and getting rid of the deadwood? And what about those eye-popping losses we had last quarter?" Sitting up on his own strength, he added, "I mean it, Ronnie: with the soaring costs to run our shows, not one more bonus for those lazy crooks."

"We have this under control, darling," Katherine reassured him, concerned for her husband's health but knowing the fatherly bond between him and his protégée was sacrosanct.

"I know, Kitty, but I'm ashamed to admit I've never hired a black writer on *The Rich and the Ruthless* in all thirty-seven years. And Queenie's been in that wig so long I thought that was her own hair and there's nothing right about that. Once again the fans know precisely the direction *R&R* needs to go in and perhaps *now* is the time to modernize before we lose what audience we still have."

"Now, Daddy, I think you're going a little overboard here. Edith thinks it's best if we wait until you're home before any big changes are made."

"Fine, but if Felicia writes one more godawful scene I'm ripping out every wire I'm hooked up to and crawling back to the studio. Do I make myself clear?"

"Perfectly. But please calm down before—"

Just then a no-nonsense Jamaican nurse barreled into the room with another huge bouquet of flowers, asking, "Mr. Barringer, is d'ere a problem? I could 'ear your voice clear down d' hall," as she set the elaborate arrangement by the window. "If you get any mo' flowers, I'ma 'ave to put 'em on d' floor." She sucked her back teeth. "You're 'posed t' be restin' but if you're goin' to get all excited 'avin guests in d' room I'ma 'ave to ask your folks to leave."

"We understand," said Kitty. "It won't happen again."

"Doctor's orders, Mrs. Barringer, not mine. *Rich and d' Rut'less* is my *faaa-v'rite* story ya know. Love to go home 'n' watch it wit' a bowl of curried goat and relax. Shows t'ree times a day in Jamaica," the nurse added with a chuckle.

"That's nice," Katherine said, nodding.

"Do you t'ink I can get a couple of d'ose autographed pictures from Ruby and Vidal?" she asked.

"Sure," Veronica replied.

"T'ank you. Now please keep it down," she said, exiting with a gracious smile.

Augustus loudly whispered, "Tell everybody I'm *sick,* not *dead.* No more flowers. Donate the money to that orphanage Hollygrove or Save the Whales. Now, listen, if we don't start recognizing that our core audience looks like the woman who just walked out of this damn room we're—"

"Now, Auggie, let's not get excited again," cautioned Katherine. "Remember what the nurse just said."

"Okay, okay, but we can't afford to lose Calysta too. Derrick Taylor took over a million fans with him when he walked," Augustus lamented, resting his head back into his pillow and looking up at the ceiling. "If I knew then what I know now, I'da paid Derrick what he asked for, and what I was paying Wolfe. Calysta's a straight shooter, she'll tell me what the devil's been going on. Get her on the phone, Veronica."

"She most certainly will not," Katherine vowed. "If an actor wants to leave our show, there is nothing we can do to stop that from happening. Please rest, dear."

"But Kitty, you know Calysta isn't just any actor. I don't believe for one second she'd quit without talking to me first."

"Good morning," said the neurologist, Dr. Gould.

"What's good about it? What's the word, doc? When can I get the hell outta here and back to running my business?" Augustus asked impatiently.

"Well, Mr. Barringer, the good news is you can go home fairly soon. Maybe as early as two weeks."

"Two weeks?" asked Augustus.

"Isn't that too soon?" Katherine inquired.

"That's too long, doc," Augustus complained. "Between two shows that's twenty episodes I can't afford *not* to be a part of."

"Mr. Barringer, I wish I could tell you—"

Like her father, Veronica cut to the chase. "Dr. Gould, what's the bad news?"

"I'm afraid treating your father is going to be more complicated than we had anticipated."

"What do you mean?" Katherine asked.

"Given Mr. Barringer's age, his carotid endarterectomy nine years ago, plus his history of high blood pressure, further surgery would be risky."

"What are his other options?" Veronica asked.

"There is medication that can be prescribed, however there can be significant side effects."

"Look, I don't want to hear about any side effects because I'm not taking your blasted drugs. My head's my bread and butter," Augustus replied. "And I can't create stories for two goddamn soap operas if you all are treating me like a lab rat."

"Mr. Barringer, there is one other alternative."

"What's that?"

"We could simply monitor you and see if the attacks increase in intensity."

"So basically what you're telling me is I've got a ticking time bomb in my head and there's not a damn thing you can do about it?"

"No sir, I'm not saying that at all. There's a good chance that you may never have a major stroke."

"But there's also a chance that he could," Katherine said quietly, the realization hitting her.

Augustus knew the score and so did his doctor. Each episode had been worse than the previous one.

He looked up at Kitty and Veronica and on their faces found love and strained concern.

"Would you both give me a moment?"

"But Daddy—"

"I've worked my whole life and for what?"

"But—"

"I need some time to think."

"It's all right, dear, we'll be back in an hour."

Katherine gave Veronica a knowing look. They both kissed him and left.

No one understood Augustus better than his wife.

Outside his door, Veronica whispered to her mother, "Mom, I think Dad's right. I should head back to California and find out what's going on."

"That's a good idea, sweetheart, but why not text your brother first. Perhaps he can shed some light on things. I'll be sure to keep you posted on your father's progress. Promise."

"I'll *call* him instead," Veronica insisted.

Inside the room, Dr. Gould said, "Mr. Barringer, please let me know if you have any questions."

"Yeah, sure, doc," Augustus said, watching him leave.

I've got to protect my family business, he thought. *But how?*

He was certain those he entrusted with his number one flagship sudser were sinking it faster than viewers could change the channel to Univision's *Al Diablo con los Guapos* (To Hell with the Handsome).

After their last volatile discussion about selling their soaps to Edith Norman and the network if anything ever happened to Augustus, Auggie Jr. had assured his father he wouldn't bring up the sensitive topic again.

I can't leave that to chance, Augustus reasoned, reaching for the bedside phone, dialing his high-powered attorney's office in Century City.

"Mason, it's Augustus."

"Hello," he replied. "How are you feeling?"

"Never mind all that. I need you to get on the first plane to Baltimore."

"Is everything all right?"

"It will be," Augustus swore. "Just as soon as I make some changes to my will."

One of the first things soap fans ask bubblers is "What's it like to do love scenes with So-and-So?" In the minds of our fans, the very thought of getting paid to bump, grind, and grunt, simulating love scenes with impossibly beautiful soap gods and goddesses, must be the closest thing to paradise on earth, right? Uh yeah . . . not so much.

Now don't get The Diva wrong, I've had plenty of fun during coitus with a few soap stars over the years, especially a young tenderoni with a body that wouldn't quit and the libido to match. Shhh! Don't tell.

Then there are other bubblers, the ones with the breath of a mastodon without water for a week, climbing into bed on-set still smelling of the actor or actress they'd just finished, um, running lines with in their dressing rooms.

Trust me, darlings, there is a distinct disparity between *love in the afternoon* and real life. Too bad it takes some bubblers much too long to know the difference.

The Diva

CHAPTER 13

What's Love Got to Do with It?

aving read somewhere, "Music is the wine that fills the cup of silence," I had Miles's *Bitches Brew* playin' in the background. I knew the next two hours were going to be sheer heaven.

If there was one thing I hated, it was a lazy, selfish lover, and Derrick was far from that. I never had to take the lead. Always ready to put my pleasure before his own and light my fire, he was willing to give me as much as I could take.

Careful to pick my paramours, I refrained from a bad trait that occasionally crept in, being overly possessive, sometimes turning me into an Alex Forrest stalker.

After taking a hot bath and moisturizing with Crème de la Mer lotion, I lit lavender candles on my nightstand and sprinkled rose petals on my California king.

I nervously waited in my black satin Valentino peignoir, wondering how much my body had changed since our last rendezvous two years prior.

Hearing his Phantom roar up, I felt my adrenaline surge as I bolted for the door. Heart pounding, I let him ring the bell three times before I opened it.

There he was, my soap opera perfect bull, all six foot two of him, insanely handsome with his Gucci silk shirt half-unbuttoned showing off his eight-pack, a bottle of champagne in his fist.

"Got here fast," I greeted him.

"Said it was important," he replied, kicking the door shut, his masculine arms wrapping around my waist, molding my body into his.

Derrick laid a smoldering French on me for what seemed like an eternity. Feeling his *l'érection,* my instant recall kicked in, remembering what a generous lover he was.

"How 'bout we head upstairs, cut the lights, 'n' do more than kiss?" he said right out.

Dizzy, I said, "You read my mind."

Effortlessly, he swept me up as I locked my arms around his thick neck, stroking his curly hairline, inhaling his spicy cologne.

Derrick took in the ambience of my bedroom and said, "Nice," while gently placing me on the bed and unbuttoning the rest of his shirt. And I wasted no time unbuckling his belt.

My fiery, well-endowed lover couldn't wait to get started. Removing my negligee, revealing my youthful 36-24-38, Derrick crooned, "Baby, you got the kind of liquid body that makes a man sweat."

I have to agree with that proverb, "Age is just a question of mind over matter. If you don't mind, it don't matter." My last lover couldn't keep up, though younger, and was bewitched as much as he was amazed by my sensuality and unexpected bedroom acrobatics. But not Derrick, he just indulged.

"Damn, girl, what you been doin' keepin' that body so tight?"

"A little Kundalini now and then," I said. As we slowly glided our soap-a-licious bodies between the Egyptian cotton sheets, I gave Derrick an all-access pass.

"Yeah, I'ma lay some Hip Woo Wong on you to*night*."

"No freaky-deaky, okay, Derrick? It's been a minute."

"I gotchu, no worries," he said with a mischievous grin. "I'll hit that sweet spot just the way you like it, nice and slow. Just lay there and be the Nefertiti you are."

Being a Taurean, Derrick hadn't forgotten one lick of what I liked.

I loved the weight of his sculpted body, his penetrating eyes locked on mine before he buried his face in my cleavage.

Temperatures rising, the flowmaster's powerful, hot tongue traced slowly and deliberately downward, canvassing my quivering torso beyond my Brazilian, devouring me. I lost all sense of control, honey pouring between my thighs, intense pleasure covering my face, eyes rolling back, savoring every moment as I moaned, "Don't stop . . ."

"Just gettin' started," he whispered in his molasses voice, workin' my body in reverse, seductively adding, "Time for the main course," wiping his mouth with the back of his hand.

"Derrick, I can't, I can't . . . "

"Good. I like it when I leave you breathless."

He wasted no time, separating my toned thighs with one of his own, arching my back, and sliding his thunderous arm under my hips, lifting them.

With the influence of Venus ruling, Derrick thrust further as we moved in unison increasing our rhythm, my sculpted legs locked around his broad back clearly indicating we had done this before. Not caring if my neighbors heard, I screamed a lick from an oldies favorite, *"You arrre my starship, come take me out tonight . . . ,"* before exploding into silky ecstasy. This was exactly what I needed before all the b.s. tomorrow.

I was set to begin taping the big Wedding of the Century scenes on *The Rich and the Ruthless* and knew Randall, Emmy, and the rest of the haters were plotting to do whatever they could to make my exit as memorable as possible. At least now I'd go to work perfectly relaxed.

With the whir of a ceiling fan above us, we floated in rapturous delight, basking in the afterglow two hours later in each other's arms.

"Daaamn, that was off the grid. You sure know howda put it on a brutha," Derrick exhaled. "How 'bout I get that bubbly and fire them jets back up?"

Shy of commitment after two failed marriages, I began searching for an escape.

"Listen, D, I have an early call tomorrow," I said, sitting up, feeling claustrophobic. "I mean, I 'preciate you hookin' a sistah up and all, but . . ."

"Girl, you trippin'." He dismissed me, flexing his arms folded behind his head. "Jus' needed someone to take your mind off all that drama on the soap, release the tension. I know how it is. Too much pressure make a pipe burst. It's all good."

Derrick's nonchalance stung me. Secretly, I hoped he'd want to get something started again, only I didn't want to be the one who appeared white-on-rice clingy or eager to go back down Memory Lane. It had ended badly the last time, when I discovered he was simultaneously dating two models and in retaliation tagged his Trans Am rims with pink glitter spray paint and graffiti'd "2-TIMER" on his windshield. Luckily, there were other disgruntled love interests so he never figured out who had exacted her revenge.

Girl, just tell the brother how you really feel. Stop pretending to be Miss Independent when all you really want is to rest against the security of Derrick's delicious chest for eternity.

Ready to finally spill my guts, I began, "Derrick, honey, I—"

"Hold up, I ain't tryin' to marry ya or nothin'. Busy and able as I am, might not be so lucky next time catchin' me."

Derrick was right. I could take a catnap during my lunch break onset tomorrow.

In an immediate about-face I reasoned, "Yeah, you right, boo, I was trippin', but I'm so thirsty I could spit dust. How 'bout I look good waitin' here on those bubbles you said you were gonna get?"

"Be right back."

While Derrick got the Clicquot, I thought, as clairvoyant as I sometimes could be, I couldn't begin to predict what would happen on the set of *The Rich and the Ruthless,* and at that moment I didn't care. With D'Angelo's "How Does It Feel" playing in the background, all that seemed to matter was Act II with Derrick. Everything else would have to wait in the wings.

CHAPTER 14

The Pinkeye Blues

*O*n little sleep, I woke the next morning remarkably rested, ready to take on the world. In other words, fortified to head into *R&R* with unflappable purpose. Before leaving Derrick asleep in my bed, I kissed his salty lips, a lasting memory from our steamy tryst the night before. Glancing down to see his enormous *l'érection* I thought, shaking my head, *What a waste*, before whispering, *"Je t'aime*, Derrick."

His show was on a two-week hiatus and I knew he would have no problem showing himself out. More important, I knew he wouldn't go rifling through my medicine cabinet and drawers like I regrettably had at his pad in the past. Why do we girls do that, knowing we're gonna find something we wish we hadn't?

The first person I ran into on the set was buppie actor Ethan Walker.

After Derrick quit *R&R,* producers hastily decided to bring back their favorite go-to plumber, judge, cop, drug dealer, and preacher, veteran bubbler Wilson Turner, as my interim love interest. Wilson was formerly with *Yesterday, Today, and Maybe Tomorrow,* a canceled soap from a bazillion years ago.

If it weren't for Grandma Jones being so over the moon about her senior citizen heartthrob's return, I don't think I could have endured the girdle, the Tab, the Bumps No More, or the Old Spice cologne. Not to mention the coal black Afro toupee he religiously wore, cut to topiary perfection, glued carefully against his gray fringe.

I'd assumed casting might have considered someone younger than a senior citizen, silly me. Luckily, the fans hated the pairing. Enter Ethan Walker.

"How's it going, Calysta?" he garrulously asked on the go, dressed in Sean John sweats and a Clippers fitted cap, attempting to hide yet another nasty case of pinkeye.

"It's going," I replied. "Wanna run lines?"

"Sure, cool, right after I check my fan mail. My bin is overflowing, dude. Meet you in your room, say fifteen?" The elevator doors closed.

"Sure, fine, fifteen," I shouted to the stainless steel. "Pompous ass," I muttered as I walked toward my dressing room. "They must be half crazy if they think I'm gonna kiss his contagious butt today."

"Talking to yourself, Calysta? You're a girl after my own heart," said Maeve Fielding, shuffling up next to me in slippers, robe, and sunglasses. "Did you hear Beyoncé is starring in a new movie about Etta James?" she mumbled, noshing on scrambled eggs from the commissary.

I pretended not to know. "Really?"

Maeve was one of those people who felt the only things they could talk to me about were black entertainers and, of course, Nelson Mandela. Yes, I'd met people like her before, but Maeve took it to a whole 'nother level.

"Yeah, I loved Etta, but one of my all-time favorite blues singers was

Bessie Smith, now *that* was a singer and a half. Listen, Calysta, would you follow me to my dressing room? I could really use your help. Alison is hogging the new hairstylist again. Randall is insisting she change her hairdo for the third time today."

Reluctantly I said, "Sure, Maeve," knowing exactly what she needed my help with.

Walking past her plastic ficus tree decorated with one lone Christmas bulb, she peeled off her kerchief, dropping the paper plate into the trash, oldies music playing in the background as she growled, "Damn scrambled eggs are always cold."

Forty bright vanity lightbulbs betrayed the icon's prunish face as she sat down in her director's chair, stamped Lady Leslie Lovekin on the back. Makeup was not her friend. Each wrinkle illuminated, her Clara Bow lips gripped yet another cigarette.

"That's Tommy Dorsey and His Clambake Seven, you know. Bet you never heard of them," she announced, tossing the metal lighter onto the vanity.

"Bet you're right."

She took in a long drag, swaying to the tune before exhaling, smoke curling toward a struggling air vent plugged with dun-colored Kotex. Maeve's dressing room quickly went from semi-smoke-free to a suffocating carcinogenic hell. Pushing mounds of makeup to the side, she reached across and snapped off two pieces of medical tape, attaching them at her temples.

"I bet you can sing, Calysta," she said, looking at herself in the mirror. "Seems like all you colored—I mean," she went on, enunciating carefully with the cigarette in the corner of her mouth, "African American people can carry a tune."

Clamping the petite metal clip to the thumbnail adhesive, she stretched the flesh-toned lanyard over the crown of her head, asking me to secure it with my finger as she continued to pull it across her wig cap, attaching it to the other side, giving herself an instant face-lift.

I'd helped Maeve before with her freakish stage trick. But hey, who was I to judge? Times were tough for everybody and no one had "extra" for nip/tucks these days.

"Yep," she continued, pulling on her wig, "I even saw Billie Holiday perform in New York City, she was—"

Cutting her off, I said, taking shallow breaths, "Listen, Maeve, I'd really love to hear more and I'm a big fan of everyone you've mentioned, but I gotta do my hair and makeup and run lines."

"Oh okay. I gotta be honest, I'm dreading your wedding. I hate being a glorified extra in those damn scenes. All those long boring hours, and the overtime stinks to high heaven. Anyway, thanks, Calysta."

As I opened her door I said, "The movie Beyoncé starred in is *Cadillac Records* and it's *been* out on DVD."

"Already?"

"Yeah, the studios tend to do that after a year or so. And Maeve, did you know that Carol Channing was black?"

"Where did you hear that? That's the funniest thing I've ever heard."

"It's true. It made national news. My Grandma Jones always believed Dinah Shore and Ava Gardner belonged to our club too. You know what they always say, 'Check the cuticles.' See you on-set." I fled, leaving Maeve staring down at her fingers.

Sixty seconds later, I dumped my makeup kit into the dressing room sink. After starting to apply foundation to my neck and face I suddenly stopped, taking in the reflection behind me, flooded with memories of room 21J fifteen years earlier.

"What's up with the Africa poster and the leopard couch?" I'd asked a college intern.

"Oh, Mr. Roberts told us to put this stuff in here."

"I moved from New York, not the Congo, for crissakes. Might as well kept goin' with palm wine and Kola nuts."

Now in the refuge of my warm Jamaica pink dressing room, tastefully decorated by moi, its atmosphere one of sophistication and calm, with an inconspicuous herbalist staff in the corner and photos of Ivy and Grandma Jones throughout, I prided over a framed *Cliffhanger Weekly* cover boasting Derrick and myself, the only soap cover anyone of color ever got.

My landline rang.

"Calysta?" an *R&R* office staffer asked.

"Yes."

"I have a call for you from a Zylissa. Says she knows you."

"Put her through," I said with a sigh.

"Calysta?"

"That's me."

"Hey girl, whatchu up to?"

"Gettin' ready for a scene. How 'bout yourself?"

"Hmph, gettin' ready to get evicted if I don't book this dumb Valtrex commercial, I know that much. I'm so tired of auditioning. I didn't get *any* play during pilot season either. I coulda' peed all over a role if one existed."

"I know, but you can't give up now."

"Who says? If I could find me a sugar daddy like Kara did I sure would. Yeah honey, he's like in his seventies or somethin' and gives her whatever she wants."

"Yeah, but what does she have to give him? Never mind, I don't *even* want to think about it."

"Pays her rent, got her teeth fixed, she drivin' a new Mercedes, got diamonds, shops on Rodeo not Rod-e-o, and he takes her to Europe on business all the time. And for that, I think I'd find me a way to give my sugar daddy whatevah he wanted. 'Cause right about now, these casting directors are cookin' my last grit and I ain't about to go back to Americus, Georgia."

"Don't talk like that, Zylissa."

"They're never gonna cast me in Hollywood, and you know why.

Same reason I can't get arrested on your Creole-lovin' soap as a damn day player. They either go for shallow or *LL*. Ain't even thinkin' 'bout my deep chocolate ass, my gapped tooth, my dreads, my dream, my truth, my *me*. I get to the callbacks, then the callbacks for the callbacks, meanwhile I'm tryin' like hell to hold on to my killa performance and they already done picked long hair, light skin . . . as usual. Those phony-ass-kissin' producers with their big Chiclet-capped teeth smilin' back at me like I got the dang job, knowin' I ain't got shit."

Near tears, she said, "All I want to do is act, Calysta, and sink my Chi-town theater experience into somethin'. I jus' wanna work. I swear they only bring me in to fill up that sign-in sheet and make their sorry casting office look busy."

"I know, Zylissa. I know, but you can't wait on the phone to ring. Check out Whoopi. Or CCH and Latifah. Even Mo'Nique. They're *always* creatin' their own stuff 'cause they know they have to. They're in a movie or producin' one, writin' a series, and in their downtime they're doin' a play or writin' books. Look how many auditions it took *me* before I even got *this* gig."

"Yeah, you right, but Calysta, you be the exception to the rule, girl. Even though you in that *LL* package you just as darkskinned as you please on the inside. Everything about you is chocolate. I ain't nevah seen someone lookin' like you workin' as hard for the money."

Laughing, I said, "You so crazy."

"You think I'm jokin', I'm serious."

"Remember in NYC when Weezi booked me on that crazy music video that went all night?"

"Who could forget? Up twenty-four hours for zip."

"But be honest, Zylissa, it's how we met and we *did* have fun, and we *did* meet Hammer."

"Sure did. Girl, don't make me laugh."

"Where is he, anyway?"

"Mmm-mmm, preachin' or somethin'."

"Tell you what, I'll front your rent, but this is the last time. You still owe me from last year. I ain't forgettin'."

"Don't take this the wrong way, Calysta, 'cause you know I love ya, but girl, you're tighter than Dick's hatband. You be squeezin' a penny so tight Abe be sittin' on his *own* lap."

"Very funny. Stop by the set tomorrow for the check."

"A check? I ain't got no bank account. I don't even have a cell no more. I'm callin' you from a pay phone and had to take a bus to that."

"What happened to your ride?"

"Got a boot on it. Didn't have insurance any old way and could barely afford gas, so good riddance, repossess the friggin' leased ride. I even called my ex-boo Seaweed last night just so I could get some free food. I'm sorry, Calysta, but I need cash and I need it now."

"Okay, okay, come at lunch and don't be late like always. And don't throw me under the bus and sneak upstairs to casting saying I sent you, like last time. That really pissed me off; I took all kinds of heat. You know I gave them your picture and résumé four times."

The loudspeaker broke in: "Calysta, you're needed on-set in ten minutes for item twelve, page sixty-nine, Ruby and Dove's bedroom."

"Ten minutes?" It wasn't uncustomary for our show to shoot out of sequence, but man, was it a pain in the neck.

"Did you say be there in ten minutes, Calysta?"

"No, I mean—never mind. Gotta go, Zylissa. Twelve sharp."

"Cool beans, can I get some lunch in the commissary?"

"Yeah, go 'head. Later."

"Calysta, five minutes for item twelve, page sixty-nine, Ruby and Dove's bedroom," repeated the stage manager.

After racing down the stairs to the honeymoon set, a taping schedule in hand, I asked, "What's going on? My scenes don't tape for at least another hour."

"Not anymore. Randall moved them up. Emmy has a callback for *Big Love* so we're taping out of order."

"But I'm not ready. Besides, Ethan's drooling over his fan mail, we haven't had a chance to rehearse. And tell Randall he's got conjunctivitis again, I'm not going near his face."

"Tell him yourself. And he wants you to wear your hair up, Alison's wearing hers down today."

A blinking red tally light signaled that Randall and Edith were up to their old tricks again, taping my every move, watching on their office monitors.

If the duo managed to throw me off my A-game during my last days on the show, the press would roast me alive for "sour grapes."

I coolly replied, "I'll be back and ready to tape in five."

I'm gonna turn in the best performances of my Rich and Ruthless *career, I* vowed as I marched back to my dressing room. *They're gonna be so spectacular, so breathtaking, so awe-inspiringly fierce, that fans and critics alike will never forget them.*

CHAPTER 15

A Pachyderm in the Room

*A*ll right, people, let's do this," the stage manager said.

"Where the hell is Ethan?" Julius boomed.

"I think he's still in wardrobe," Ben Singh, the production assistant, answered.

"Don't think, find out!"

Ben rushed off, cursing under his breath in Hindi. The East Indian couldn't believe he was paying back a hundred thousand dollars in student loans to NYU Tisch to chase after wayward soap stars.

Running down the hall, he crashed into Fern and quickly asked, "Did you remember to fill out the paperwork for the Kangaroo Awards for Emmy and Alison and pack their fan mail bins?"

"Yes!" an exasperated Fern answered, rushing into the elevator cradling Edith's lunch—Arby's take-out and a Fresca.

"Good," Ben muttered, walking away, "I don't think I could survive another vicious fan mail tantrum from those stupid bimbettes. Why is it *my* fault the majority of their mail comes from prison inmates? I can't wait to get back to Bollywood, what was I thinking?"

I waited on-set in a turquoise Manoush negligee from my personal collection, not wanting to run the risk of having the Pattern Cutter put me in one of Emmy's cheap Hustler teddies.

A winded Penelope struggled to keep up, trailing behind Ethan's billowing trademark peacock-embroidered silk set robe.

"See you after these scenes, Penelope, for my wedding gown fitting," I called to the pickled costume designer.

She dismissed me with a look as Ethan blindly tossed his robe at her.

"What the hell?"

The buppie bubbler in his Kid 'n Played out haircut was standing over me, a Cheshire Cat grin on his face, wearing only a thong made in the shape of an elephant's face, his infinitesimal boyhood loosely nestled in the limp trunk.

"Bitchin', huh?" he asked.

Silence.

"Ethan, what the hell do you think you're doing?" Julius scolded.

"Ah, c'mon, Jules. What's the big deal?"

"Trust me, not much," I quipped. "It's bad enough I have to deal with your damn pinkeye, now you expect to climb into bed with me wearing that *thing*? Nobody wants to see that madness."

"I do!" Emmy excitedly interjected, standing on the fringe rubbing her thigh, salivating at the sight of Ethan's elephant package. "Oh . . . did I say that out loud? Lighten up, Calysta, it's not like it's gonna bite ya. From what I've heard you could use—"

"What happened to a closed set?"

"Don't be so serious," Ethan chided. "Emmy's right, have a sense of humor. Besides, Randall said it would be fun."

"Oh, yeah? Then tell him to slap on one of his wigs and do the damn scene himself."

"All right, what's the holdup?" Randall rushed onto the set, unprofessionally assuming director's duties—again.

"Where's Julius, he's directing this episode, right?" I inquired.

"Calysta, don't make waves. What's going on?"

"You know damn well what's going on. And thanks for changing the schedule without any notice."

"Yeah, thanks, Randy," Emmy interrupted, boldly walking onto my set with her yelping miniature *chien* in the crook of her arm. "I think I booked the part on *Big Love*."

Randall and Ethan adlibbed congratulations.

"Puh-leeze," I mocked.

"They've already called my agent for my measurements. Even though when I first got there, after *all* that rehearsing I did with Ivana, casting said, 'We're just doing the last scene,' which means they've already found who they're lookin' for, those bastards. But clearly, I was so on top of my game I knocked the competition right off the wire!" she squealed. "Oh, and Ethan, I hope I helped out last night, rehearsing those Ruby Stargazer lines with ya," she said, laced with seedy innuendo.

"Yeah, thanks, Emmy. You're the best!"

"Good luck," she teased, trotting off.

"No wonder you have pinkeye. You better hope that's all you got from that skank," I remarked.

"Oh, Calysta, you can't be this upset about a thong, a little eye infection, and a schedule change," Randall said.

"You won't be satisfied till I storm off this set, will you? Well, I have news for you-all, you're wasting your time 'cause it ain't gonna happen."

"Honestly, you're making chicken salad out of chicken feathers."

"Wow, you too?"

"Huh?"

"Never mind."

As Phillip sashayed over to the Fink Manor set, he hissed, "Are you ever going to finish your scene, Calysta? My gawd it's been like ten minutes already. MPD must be a bitch."

"What did you say, punk?"

"He said nothing, Calysta, absolutely nothing," said Randall.

"Would that be the same *nothing, absolutely nothing* when I walked into your office and found you and—"

"Don't go there," he warned.

"Then get off the damn set so I can do my job."

Randall glared, skulking into a corner outta joint.

"All right, let's get back to item twelve, page sixty-nine. Ready to shoot, guys?" Julius asked.

Pulling back cranberry polyester sheets, I answered, "Yep, I'm not here to waste any more of my time or Augustus's money. Come on, Ethan, grab your trunk and hop in. We got a job to do."

"Five, four, three, two, *go!*"

                              RUBY

Oh, Dove, my love . . .

                              DOVE

Ruby, darling, don't speak. I've been waiting all my

life for this moment . . .

Randall glanced over at a prying Alison. He hadn't seen his wife since yesterday when they'd had a huge fight over Edith again. He'd spent the night on his office couch, not alone.

"We have to step up our efforts," Randall whispered.

"*Our* efforts? *You* need to get some courage between your legs or borrow some, instead of wasting it on the extras," Edith chided into the phone. "I heard about last night's escapade," she went on, glancing at her Movado. "Our *uppity* antebellum diva is proving to be a tough nut to crack and all you can do is bitch, bawl, and moan? Time is running out, Randall! You have until the end of the week to prove what a loose cannon Calysta is or the deal's off," Edith fumed, slamming the phone in his ear.

I've got to figure out how to paint Calysta as the big black stain on our pedigree show, Randall told himself. *And I've got to do it fast.*

                             RUBY

Oh, Dove . . .

                             DOVE

Ruby . . .

                             RUBY

Dove . . .

Is a daytime producer stepping out on his soap diva wife with a network exec? Numerous inside sources have revealed that top-secret meetings are taking place between Randall Roberts, co-executive producer of *The Rich and the Ruthless,* and WBC executive barracuda Edith Norman. Now to be fair, these two budget crunchers could just be rubbing their, um, "heads" together about how to stop the ratings hemorrhage that has transpired since yours truly revealed the wildly popular Ruby Stargazer was being killed off, but we hear Randall's wife, Alison Fairchild Roberts (Rory Lovekin, *The Rich and the Ruthless*), doesn't believe Randall and Edith's clandestine meetings are so innocent!

The Diva

CHAPTER 16

It's All About the Upper Lip

After an aborted peace offering the moment Randall entered Alison's Liberace lair, she couldn't wait to tattle about the Pattern Cutter.

"That incompetent, tasteless twit Penelope; she *ruined* my wedding dress!" she screeched.

"Your wedding dress?" Randall asked. "What the hell was she doing with that old thing? Alteration work again for free? Come to think of it, that's not a bad idea, you and me *renewing our vows* on television. We'd get a ton of press out of it."

"Not the dress I wore when *we* got married in Maui, you idiot. The *important* one when my character, Rory Lovekin, tied the knot with Vidal Vinn Hansen in St. Croix."

Randall bit his tongue. Only a self-absorbed bubblette would ever equate the wedding dress her fictional character wore on a soap opera to memories of her own real-life nuptials, and his wife was the queen of self-absorption.

"I thought that dress was in some costume display," he replied.

"Well, it's not. That bitch Keira Knightley's costume from *The Duchess* beat me out. Mine is in shreds in that Colleen Atwood–wannabe's den of fashion faux pas. Can you believe she was actually going to let that *beast* Calysta Jeffries wear it for her *joke* of a soap opera wedding? I tried to rescue the dress and Penelope attacked me in wardrobe. Tore it to shreds right before my eyes while Calysta did *nothing, absolutely nothing* to help. It was all so traumatic. Look, I have a bruise on my arm," Alison blubbered.

"There, there, my pet," Randall soothed with a hug.

Going Sybil, her fake sobs instantly ceasing, Alison said, "Take your skivey hands off me. You think I don't know what you've been up to? It's all over the studio."

"Darling, you're overreacting. What's this all about?"

"Don't play dumb with me," Alison warned, steeling herself. "I know you're screwing her. I can smell that she-wolf on your top lip."

Randall felt a sinking sensation in the pit of his stomach as he hastily curled his lip up to his nose.

"Let's keep our voices down, you know Emmy listens through the vents."

"What do I care about Emmy? I'm *talking* about your affair with that man-eating shrew Edith Norman."

"Edith?" Randall was both confused and relieved. "You can't be serious?"

"*Dead* serious. I'm not stupid. I feel all those jealous losers in hair and makeup staring at me. Do you have any idea how many times I've overheard them gossiping about us while I'm reading the *Enquirer* in the chair? They all think I'm clueless to you banging every broad behind my back! And guess what? I've known for years! *That's* acting.

But what the hell was I supposed to do, Randall, huh? Get a divorce? Not on your life. Not after all I've done to keep this sham of a marriage intact. And if you *do* manage to leave me alive I'll fight you tooth and nail for everything. I dragged you out of the WBC mailroom when I was twenty-one and now I'm fifty-eight and if you think you're going to trade me in for a new model like one of your Corvettes, think again! You're stuck with these girls." She pointed to her pendulous breasts as she stood there completely naked, winding tighter. "And you better sleep with one eye open, buddy, otherwise you run the risk of me hunting you down and filleting your dick like thinly sliced sashimi."

Randall felt his balls shrink to the size of two chickpeas.

"You've humiliated me for the *last* time!" she cried, tearing one of her gold-framed *Cliffhanger Weekly* covers off the wall and hurling it at his head.

"Are you insane?" he asked, ducking just in time.

She reached for another, and then a third.

Even a shameless hound dog like Randall Roberts wouldn't touch cankled Edith Norman with her flat chest and frizzed-out pageboy, if Gertrude Stein herself rose from the dead to tell him the network exec had *uterus didelphys*.

"Alison, stop! I have *not* had sex with Edith Norman, my gawd, give me *some* credit."

"You're such a bad liar, Randall." She hyperventilated, pulling on a pair of Spanx. "I read all about your little tryst on SecretsofaSoapOpera-Diva.com."

"Oh come on. You don't believe that stupid gossip blog?"

"If it's so stupid, why all the private meetings, huh? I hear you frequent her office more than the guy who waxes her back."

With his balls in a vise, Randall offered an olive branch, helping Alison with her robe. He knew it was time to come clean. Well, almost.

"Listen, Alison, it's *not* what you think."

"I think you don't want to push me too far," the distressed diva ranted, ruminating about how quickly she could get her hands on their Bank of America safety deposit box filled to the gills with skimmed cash, compliments of Augustus Barringer.

"Alison, just hear me out. But you can't breathe a word of it to anyone, not even your hairstylist. And *definitely* not the other actors on the show."

"Oh please, as if I even take the time to talk to any of those idiots once the director yells Cut," she dismissed. "Who am I gonna tell?"

"I've been meeting with Edith because the network is interested in buying the Barringer soaps."

"Oh for crissakes, that's old news. And it's not gonna happen as long as Augustus is alive."

"Exactly. From the looks of things, he won't be a factor for much longer."

"What do you mean? I know he gave temporary control of the soaps to his bratty kids, but that's just until he gets better, right?"

"He isn't going to get better, Alison."

A shiver shot up her spine as she slowly sat.

"Doctors can't figure out what's causing the strokes he's been having and fear a major one is around the corner."

Alison and Augustus had had their ups and downs over the years and she'd never forgiven him for allowing Calysta to do film projects like *The Refined Politician* with Danny Glover and *Dumb Bell* with Beau Bridges, while preventing her from starring in *The Cellist* with Robin Williams. Though still holding a grudge, she couldn't begin to imagine a world without Augustus Barringer in it.

"There has to be something they can do?" she asked. "I mean come on, the Barringers have more money than the Vatican. Surely, they can find some sort of specialist?"

"They're doing everything in their power," Randall asserted. "But let's face it; Augustus isn't the youngest rooster in the barnyard."

"Don't be so insensitive. I know we haven't always gotten along, but we owe him for our careers, our fortune, and our mansions in Hawaii and Holmby Hills."

"That's why I intend to honor his legacy by doing what he never could."

"I don't follow."

"Augustus is a genius when it comes to storytelling. There aren't many writers in daytime who can compete. Maybe Agnes Nixon. But as a current businessman, he's always been shortsighted."

"Go on."

"Augustus could've sold his shows to WBC a decade ago and made a killing, but he was too stubborn to give up creative control. Something tells me his wife and children won't feel as passionate about keeping *The Rich and the Ruthless* and *The Daring and the Damned* in the family."

"My gawd, Randall, that's cruel, you're talking about the man like he's already in the grave."

"Oh don't go all soft on me, Alison. More than likely, Augustus won't be recovering from this. Even if he does, the damage the strokes have already done won't allow him to keep running one show, let alone two. On a lighter note, we both know that Auggie has absolutely *no* interest in running the family business, and up until recently we'd see Veronica and Katherine Barringer even less, a fan club thingy here, an awards ceremony there, and that godawful company Christmas party. We're finally poised to grab the brass ring and I'll do whatever it takes to make that happen for us."

"Where exactly does Edith Norman fit into all this?" Alison asked, washing a pill down with a bottle of Save the Glaciers water.

"She's assured me that if I convince Auggie Jr. and the rest of our gravy train to sell *R&R* and *D&D* to the network, she'll make me Senior Executive Producer of *The Rich and the Ruthless*."

The look of pity for poor, ailing Augustus left Alison's eyes, replaced with a pair of sparkling green dollar signs.

"Senior EP?" she repeated, rushing over and wrapping her arms around Randall. "Do you have any idea how much *moolah* that means? We'll make *millions*."

"*Now* do you see why I had to be so secretive? We have a lot riding on this venture."

"Oh Randy," Alison purred, moving in closer, playing with her flip, surveying the broken glass. "You're right, I did overreact, bloody menopause. I'm sorry, Snuggle Bunny, that I doubted you. Do whatever Edith needs you to do to get control of these goddamn soaps, then I can finally get rid of that old windbag Maeve and pesky tramps like Emmy and Shannen, once and for all."

CHAPTER 17

Everything's Under Control

*V*eronica Barringer hit Redial on her iPhone for the third time.

"Pick up the phone, Auggie," she huffed, sitting in the lobby of the private waiting area of Thurgood Marshall Airport.

"Auggie here, talk to me."

"Where the hell have you been?" Veronica exclaimed. "I've been trying to reach you since yesterday! Things are really bad."

"What's wrong? Is Dad . . . ?"

". . . dead? No, you moron. And you'd know that if you were here."

"Oh come on, Ronnie, not you too," he moaned. "Mom's already given me enough grief. All of us can't be in Baltimore. Who's gonna run the company?"

"Funny you should mention that. What's the word on Calysta? Have you spoken with her? Dad's ready to climb out of his hospital bed and crawl back to Los Angeles to prevent her from quitting the soap."

"Dad knows about Calysta? Who the hell let that happen?"

"His nurse brought in a copy of *Soap Suds Digest* and she was the 'Ruby Stargazer Falls Overboard' feature story."

Auggie was hoping Calysta would've taped her final episode and been off *The Rich and the Ruthless* before Augustus was any the wiser. He didn't personally have a problem with the bubbler, but his co-executive producer Randall Roberts did, and Auggie relied on him way too much to handle the day-to-day drudgery of running *R&R* to not support him. He didn't like playing referee between the two, since that might mean coming into work on days he'd rather be downhill skiing in Dubai, golfing in Scotland, or racing in Monte Carlo.

"Tell Dad we tried everything we could to get Calysta to stay, but she insists that she's ready to move on and try new things."

"Auggie, Dad may not be at his optimum right now, but his b.s. meter is functioning just fine. He's not going to buy that load of bull any more than I do. We have to get a handle on our family business," Veronica said pointedly. "We're still feeling the ripple effect of the market and we can't afford to keep losing money hand over fist. And do I need to remind you we sold one of our paintings?"

"Look, Ronnie, I'm doing the best I can to keep things running smoothly here, all right?"

"Have you even been to the set?"

"Of course I have, I'm there right now."

"*Fore!*" yelled out a golfer.

"Three, two, one, *go!*" Auggie covered. He'd been doing more than twenty-seven holes of golf, ensconced with two young babes at the majestic Desert Princess Country Club in Palm Springs.

"Auggie, where are you?"

"Huh?"

"You heard me." She paused. "Are you golfing?"

"Are you deaf? You just heard me count down the show."

"Seven or the nine iron?" asked the caddy to high-pitched laughter in the background.

"Hey Tiger, my body henna is so sexy, wait'll you see," giggled Ginger, peeling down her lowriders.

"Yeah, wicked sugar scrub," agreed Sparkle. "My skin's as soft as a baby's *ass*."

"Who's that?" Veronica questioned.

"Who do you think? It's Shannen and Emmy in a scene. I'm on the set, for crissakes. Look, I've got to get back to work. Give Mom and Dad a hug for me, and tell them I've got everything under control."

Outside of the triple-cha-ching overtime, if there's one thing bubblers hate more than any other it's taping a soap opera wedding storyline or any mega-event, be it a costume ball, gala fund-raiser, Christmas party, you name it.

While the audience eats those scenes up because they get all its favorites into one room, dressed to the nines in the latest glitz and glam, they're torture for the average narcissistic soap star.

The taping schedules for those scenes usually go well into the next day, and soap divas and drama kings who literally pass each other in the hall and parking lot daily without speaking are forced to intermingle for hours at a time, doubling up in dressing rooms because of all the extras and special guest stars.

The only people who enjoy soap opera wedding arcs are the bubblers playing the bride and groom. That's their big moment to shine and a chance to add valuable footage to their Sudsy reel in hopes of a gold-dipped statuette. This week, the oh-so-friendly cast of *The Rich and the Ruthless* have been taping Ruby Stargazer's Soap Opera Wedding of the Century storyline, and honey, let me tell you, there's some drama going on over there in Burbank!

Inside sources have informed The Diva that that rascal co-executive producer Randall Roberts has actually encouraged certain members of the cast and crew to in effect drive Calysta Jeffries batty during her last week of taping. Roberts wants to make sure the actress never sets foot on his set again. Will Calysta crack under the pressure? If she does, you know I'll tell you all about it.

The Diva

CHAPTER 18

Nice Day for a Soap Opera Wedding

THE RICH AND THE RUTHLESS MEMO:

If you didn't call in your edits by 5:00 p.m. yesterday—tough! NO CHANGES ON SET! Actors will share dressing rooms for the Dove/Ruby wedding. Suck it up, and don't bring in your pets. Everybody know your lines and let's try to get this puppy in the can by 11:00 tonight. Finally, DO NOT remove the price tags from your wardrobe. Penelope will be returning the garments to Neiman Marcus following taping the show. Shhh . . .

Thank you,
Randall Roberts,
Co-Executive Producer

PROLOGUE

SCENE ONE

FADE IN:

Int. Fink Manor—bedroom—day

(Actors will repeat the first page of dialogue and match the blocking exactly from yesterday. Ruby Stargazer is in one of the eighteen guest bedrooms of the sprawling Fink Manor preparing for her wedding. A silk-grosgrain-ascotted Barrett Fink, not a hair out of place, shows up without knocking to escort her down the aisle. Barrett's first line of dialogue is heard over the end of the last scene showing Uranus Winterberry lurking in the misty background. Make sure we have exaggerated fog)

BARRETT

I don't think I've ever seen a more lovely bride.

RUBY

(Sees Barrett in vanity mirror. Turns to face him)
Barrett, you startled me! Is it time?

BARRETT

(Tapping his watch)
Almost, kid. You know who I've been thinking about today?

RUBY

Who?

BARRETT

Queenie; if only she could see what a beautiful young
lady and bride you turned out to be! Damn that Uranus Winterberry for running her down while she was
out grocery shopping with that unmarked car after she
found out Queenie was the only witness to her impreg-
nating Gina knocked out from an overdose of cough medicine with that turkey baster!

RUBY

(Begins to tear up and plucks a tissue)

I've been missing Mamma today as well.

"Wait, wait, wait, Julius, for crissakes!" Phillip McQueen screamed, breaking from character. "Open the boom, Cisco."

"Stop tape . . . stop tape," called the stage manager.

"What's wrong, Phillip?" asked an annoyed Julius.

"I thought we were trying to expedite," Phillip whined. "We need to get through these lines so we all get home at a decent hour, this is ridiculous repeating yesterday's material."

"You didn't seem to think it was so ridiculous when I had to repeat myself a half dozen times for your pitiful return to the show, clawing from six feet under, buried alive, finally agreeing to new contract terms. And everybody knows you're the one who called Mitch Morelli to leak your deal to the press."

"Bitch."

"Double bi'aaatch."

"Phillip, you're in the zone right now. Can we get back to work before your tears dry up? I hate when you use that damn menthol contraption for artificial crying," said Julius.

Exasperation washed over Phillip's crimson face, a face that conspicuously had too much M-A-C makeup layered on it.

"You know the deal," placated the director over the loudspeaker. "It's for the fans that missed yesterday's episode."

Smiling to myself, I watched a furious Phillip prance back to his mark, a miniature sandbag with a pink "X" embroidered on it compliments of the Pattern Cutter.

"Let's pick it up," commanded the stage manager. "Five, four, three, two, *go!*"

BARRETT

(Stepping into the bedroom/crossing to a window)

You know? What I wouldn't give . . .

RUBY

Go on?

BARRETT

. . . for one of Queenie's sticky buns right now?

RUBY

Ah, Mamma's sticky buns. There wasn't a problem in the world she couldn't solve while slaving over your Viking stove baking those confections of love.

BARRETT

(Turns to Ruby)

My old man loved Queenie's sticky buns.

RUBY

Didn't he though? God knows I could use some of Mamma's reassuring sugar right about now myself. I miss her so.

BARRETT

(Pulls a handkerchief from his lapel pocket and wipes his tears)

She's with us in spirit, Ruby. You would've made old Queenie proud today.

RUBY

You think so?

BARRETT

(Walks over to Ruby and puts his hands on her shoulders)

I know so. Look at you, who would've thought the once mute, illiterate teen, jazz dancer, turned preacher's wife, turned talk-show host, turned international spy could've convinced Dad to take you in, later turn-ing out to be Queenie's long-lost daughter? *I* person-ally never could've imagined you in *my* mansion about to marry a captain of Fink industry in my employ, Dove Jordan. Stand up, Ruby, and let me take a look at that dress *I* bought for you.

RUBY

I guess my transformation has been pretty miraculous, huh?

(Ruby Stargazer twirls in her wedding dress as a montage flashback of her fifteen-year run on the show plays with Celine Dion's "Because You Loved Me" in the background)

BARRETT

You've come a long way, Ruby Stargazer.

RUBY

(We need to see a lot of tears here as Ruby stops

twirling. She may be slightly dizzy)

Yes I have, ~~and if it weren't for you and your~~ *and the sooner I jump that broom, the*

sooner I can shake this Whitehaven wedding cake dress

~~father, I wouldn't be able to go downstairs and~~

and get my party on!

~~get married. I don't think there is any way~~

~~that a poor soul like me, a once mute, illiterate teen,~~

~~jazz dancer, turned preacher's wife, turned talk show~~

~~host, turned international spy could ever thank you~~

~~enough.~~

"For crissakes, Calysta, don't say that," Phillip fumed, breaking the imaginary fourth wall.

"Don't say what?"

"That line about jumping brooms and *partying*," he hissed. "It isn't in the script and mucks up my timing."

"Here we go again with the *acting police*. Why are you such a nitpicking *yawn*? Just say the words so we can move on."

"*Cut!*" Julius yelled. "Now what?"

"Said somethin' that's not in the script. Phillip's having another meltdown."

"Be right there," an unraveling Julius said.

"It's called *improvising*, Phillip, *embellishing, gilding the lily*? Adds *flayvah* and it's what makes a scene sing and Ruby Stargazer who she is, *real*. You might try it sometime instead of obsessively goin' by every *if, and,* and *but* in your pretentious script binder. This ain't Shakespeare, pal."

"Who the hell do you think you are?"

Method acting could be such a good thing but bubblers like Phillip McQueen gave it a bad reputation. He had no problem suspending reality when it came to being *Mahstah* of fictitious Fink Manor, which consisted of two interchangeable 15 x 15 rooms boasting mirrors and beaux art appointments, faux-painted plywood walls, a stairway to nowhere, an oversize chandelier, a *huge* bucolic estate backdrop dotted with grazing horses in the distance, and of course a loyal maid named Queenie. The pompous actor had everything he needed to go back, say, four hundred years.

Equally as alarming was how excited Jade and Ethan got over the occasional scene written for them in the Fink big house.

"Calysta, did you hear the news? Our wedding is going to be at Fink Manor!" Ethan had exclaimed, nearly wetting himself, as if it were Versailles.

I had looked at the Uncle Tom and thought, *When is he going to wake up?*

Perhaps I was hypersensitive to the display, hailing from Mississippi, but that couldn't be a bad thing.

"Listen you cross-eyed yokel, I know exactly who *I* am and who you're *not* and that's a few things. If I were you, I'd force quit now before I give *Daytime Confidential* the exclusive they've been sniffin' around for."

"Excuse me?"

"Oh, so now your incendiary ass is deaf?"

"Okay, okay, guys, we have guests on the set. Cool it," Julius warned, joining us.

"She keeps changing the lines," Phillip complained. "I'm just trying to get some artistic clarity here."

"McQueen is being anal *as usual*."

"Calysta, would you please not change what's written? You know how sensitive Phillip is about the script and tag lines. You also know the rules, if you don't get your changes in before five o'clock you're SOL. Now let's finish this damn scene. The soap is on an ultratight budget, we have a boatload of work to do before lunch, and the producers don't have time for friggin' bickering!"

"*Fine,*" I retorted. "Next time, King Lear should find a few minutes to rehearse this poetic magic instead of posturing in the mirror with a can of hair spray and a mascara wand."

Phillip had selectively forgotten that I'd pitched him to my actress-turned-prime-time-casting-director friend Boston Ferrar, years earlier when things were placid on *R&R.* Don't get me wrong, I definitely had my reservations from the get-go, but everyone faked the funk. Boston was under the gun and needed to quickly recast an actor who'd come down with a nasty case of adult chicken pox. She was in search of a leading man on a popular David Kelley series for six episodes.

Stupidity being the voice of reason, agentless McQueen telephoned casting, saying, "The role is simply too small." That was the last time I ever recommended an actor for anything. McQueen was aiming high after all, he liked being a big minnow in a small pond and he got his wish, Top Frog.

From my first day on the *R&R* set, Augustus had encouraged me to flesh out the soul of Ruby Stargazer over many a dinner and gin and tonic. His instincts were razor sharp and our hard work was validated when fan mail and reviews poured in from all over the country and around the world. Fans thanked *The Rich and the Ruthless* creator for finally putting a relatable crossover character of color *on* his show and *in* a meaty role.

Conversely, I still couldn't smash through the glass sudser ceiling. And the second Augustus relinquished control, Edith and her crew, including a paid-off reporter with a bad attitude, worked overtime, chipping away.

I reminded myself, *Twenty-four hours, and then I'm scot-free like Celie in Purple, just one more freakin' day.*

CHAPTER 19

That's Right, Mother . . .
I Found Your Diary

ith soft harp music playing in the background, Maeve Fielding, the salty tough-as-nails octogenarian who played matri-
arch Lady Leslie Lovekin on *The Rich and the Ruthless,* said, "I hate these
goddamn all-day weddings."

Barely able to blink from her homemade face-lift, Maeve, along with
the rest of the cast, was seated on the Wedding of the Century set, waiting for Ruby Stargazer to make her appearance, descending the enormous sweeping staircase and gliding down the rose-petal-lined aisle in
the Fink Manor living room.

Maeve turned the hands of time back three decades, recalling Alison
in her first, now infamous scene on *The Rich and the Ruthless,* so popular
to this day it's a top-rated clip on YouTube. Maeve's character tried to
reason with her rebellious teenage daughter Rory Lovekin, played by

Alison Fairchild Roberts, attempting to talk her out of her harebrained scheme to trap Barrett Fink into marriage with another spawn.

LESLIE

What you're doing is wrong, Rory. Can't you understand that?

RORY

What can I say, Mother, I've learned from the best. I'm tired of being poor. You squandered the family fortune forever ago and we can't continue to live off of your title, a title you manipulated your way into after poisoning Father's beloved first wife with arsenic. That's right, Mother! I found your diary. The only people in Whitehaven who make it are the rich and the ruthless, people like the Finks, and I want to be one of them!

(Cue organ music as Rory throws herself across her canopy bed)

Following take after take, Maeve—who'd been kicked out of Old St. Vincent's convent in Girardeau, Missouri, a gazillion years ago for beating up another nun, had run off to join Hollywood's nostalgic Golden Age, and had married three times (rumored to have murdered her last two husbands)—had had enough of the ingénue's snot hanging from her nose.

Unscripted, she'd grabbed Alison by her ponytail, cussing her out, "Listen, you little bitch, you have the acting skills of a lobotomized chihuahua," before storming off the set. All caught on tape. Hating each other ever since, the thespians never showed it in public.

"So Maeve, did you hear—"

"No, I didn't hear and I don't care."

"Randall and I may be going to Cannes this year. And I'm auditioning for *Dancing with the Stars* next week." Alison gloated, seated next to her in a Madras dress, digging out her blush and compact from a makeup kit.

"I haven't watched that show since those boobs picked Cloris Leachman over me. How dare they? I used to be a hoofer and I coulda' danced circles around that broad."

"I could just faint, I've been dieting all week for my audition," Alison continued.

"I can't wait to faint in this goddamned wedding scene so I can crawl the hell back to my dressing room, take off this freakin' suit, and beeline it to the airport." The legendary soap star was scheduled to appear the next day on *Celebrity Poker* in Las Vegas.

"Oh, Maeve, stop complaining, it's a mystery that Felicia still insists on writing for your character after that pathetic on-camera gastro-bypass storyline fiasco. That was really desperate."

"No more desperate than your last extreme acid peel, which kept you out of work for two weeks."

"In case you didn't know, our target demo is women eighteen to forty-nine, not seventy-five to a hundred and two . . . and since no one else will tell you, you've got *grandma* caked in the corners of your mouth."

"She-devil," Maeve hissed.

"That's quite enough from both of you," boomed Wolfe Hudson, the dashing, sophisticated Danish-born leading man, seated behind them next to his new love interest Dr. Justine Lashaway, played by the sexy, much younger Shannen Lassiter. "These are Calysta's last scenes and you boobs are already making it difficult enough for her. And take off those hideous slippers and put your heels on, Alison, so that ve can shoot this shit. I have an important meeting with James Cameron tonight."

"Figures you would defend that lunatic," she shot back.

"Hey, Alison, keep your opinion to yourself," Shannen exclaimed. "Calysta's my friend."

"Poor you." She dismissed her before saying pointedly to Wolfe, "The two of you are cut from the same cloth."

"How right you are. Consummate professionals. I only regret I never had the pleasure of sharing a storyline or two vith her. If you hadn't had the forethought of marrying the producer, you vould have been playing an aging Sleeping Beauty at Disneyland years ago."

Alison had turned around to give Wolfe a piece of her mind when she zeroed in on Phillip and me standing at the threshold of the lavish living room to swelling violins playing Beethoven's Concerto in D Major, a full-size portrait of Barrett Fink in the background. Flattering filtered light illuminated Jade, Ethan, and Wilson Turner (now the preacher) all in place. Naturally there were no other family members for the black cast; it was assumed we raised ourselves in the wild.

Costumed in Sonia Rykiel, Emmy was oblivious, wildly texting in her seat, "Hey Snuggle Bunny, are you watching? Get ready. XOXOXO."

The room was decorated with lit candles, white roses, peonies, and a smattering of extras, including arbitrary bad child actors stiffly saying their one line like wooden soldiers, beamed in by stage mothers hoping for a *National Velvet* breakthrough.

If there was anything a Barringer production didn't skimp on it was candles, flowers, and real champagne for a wedding, budget or no.

With everyone on their tired, swollen feet, Alison arched her eyebrow and said, "Damn, the bitch looks absolutely fabulous."

Clad in her unwearable secondhand wedding dress the Pattern Cutter had stitched together partially, I found out later, with one of her tablecloths, I was, critics argued, the most radiant bride *The Rich and the Ruthless* had ever seen. My hair, upswept in a regal Audrey Hepburn–inspired do courtesy of my emergency glam squad from Inglewood, was adorned with those dewdrop Czechoslovakian hand-blown crystal beads. Only I rocked the baubles like nobody's business.

As Phillip escorted me down the aisle, I caught Wolfe's eye as he mouthed, "Knock 'em dead." I beamed, heading toward my soap opera wedding crescendo. He was my favorite person on the show besides Shannen.

"Calysta certainly looks better than you did stuffed in that marshmallow monstrosity all those years ago," Maeve whispered to her TV daughter.

Alison sat in the throes of stunned silence, bitterly realizing none of their conspiracy was working out the way they'd hoped.

CHAPTER 20

The Martini

FADE IN:

Int. Fink Manor—Living room—day

   (Scene in progress, Barrett Fink gives Ruby over to Dove Jordan to be married. Reverend Atticus stands before them. Ruby's daughter, Jade, is the maid of honor)

REVEREND ATTICUS

Who gives this woman to be joined in the bonds of Holy Matrimony?

   (Catch reaction shots of actors' happy tears if there are any)

BARRETT

(Proud, emotional)

I do. Good luck, kiddo. Dove, you'd better treat her right or you'll answer to me. And remember I can find you easily since you work for me.

(The crowd laughs)

DOVE

You got it, boss.

(Ruby and Dove kiss)

Over the last two years, Ethan had thoroughly ruined the popular character Derrick made famous, instantly transforming him into a minstrel, complete with spoons and tap-dancing to the Virginia Reel. He delivered the lines exactly as written, but for once, at least for *our* Wedding of the Century, I wished he would rail against Felicia Silverstein's blatant attempts to keep the black characters on the show in a perpetual place of servitude.

DOVE

(Looking deep into Ruby's eyes)

You look beautiful, my darling.

RUBY

(Flirtatiously)

Yeah, you clean up pretty nice yourself.

~~And you look like a prince.~~

REVEREND ATTICUS

Who has the rings?

JADE

Oh WOW, like I TOTALLY forgot them.

RUBY

(Agitated but not mean)

What?

JADE

Mom, I am SO sorry. Just a second, Reverend Atticus, I will like TOTALLY go get them.

BARRETT

It's all right, everyone. Just a momentary delay. Organist, why don't you play something . . . weddinglike in the interim?

DOVE

Thanks, Barrett. I don't know what I'd do without you, man. What a colossal save.

JADE

(Rushes down the aisle about to exit when villainess Uranus Winterberry enters)

Oh my gawd! Uranus Winterberry. You're . . . you're supposed to be dead!

URANUS

Hello, Jade, rumors of my death have been greatly exaggerated. My, my, my, where has the time gone? You've grown since I almost dropped you into that active volcano in Montserrat.

(All actors react with horrified adlibs. Make sure the extras keep their mouths shut or we'll have to pay them)

RUBY

Uranus Winterberry! I swear, if you touch my baby—

(*Ruby reaches into her cleavage and pulls out a box cutter. Vidal protects Justine and Rory. Leslie faints. Gina Chiccetelli tries to revive Leslie. Dove and Barrett are behind Ruby. Lots of screaming and action shots from our stars*)

URANUS

(*Grabs Jade and pulls out a gun*)

Not so fast, Stargazer.

RUBY

Drop the gun, Uranus. This beef is between you and me. Leave my daughter out of it.

JADE

Mommy, Like HELP or something!

URANUS

Mommy dearest can't help you this time, sweetie.

RUBY

I'm not going to ask you twice, Uranus.

URANUS

I would say the person wielding the Derringer decides who gets to call the shots, wouldn't you?

(*Gun-toting Uranus throws her head back in villainous laughter*)

RUBY

(Drops the box cutter)

All right. I'll do whatever you want.

URANUS

That's more like it and exactly what I needed to hear.
I'll make an even trade, YOU for Jade.

DOVE

(Stepping forward)

Ruby, don't do it.

URANUS

Shut up and step back, bozo, if you don't wanna get
wacked.

RUBY

Uranus, let's settle this score once and for all.

(Fade out to commercial 3)

"Ugh." Those insipid lines replayed in my head as I undid the hook-and-eyes to my bodice, watching Nancy Grace while I nursed my knee with an ice pack in my dressing room. I'd strained it during my fight scene on the roof of Fink Manor. *R&R* had been too cheap to hire a stuntwoman.

Felicia tried so hard to keep Dove as Ruby Stargazer's "one true love" after Derrick left the show. Her small myopic brain thought the fans would buy into anyone brown. *Wrong.* Everyone knew Derrick's Dove Jordan was the real love of Ruby Stargazer's life and no replacement was ever going to work.

I played the oldest trick in the book, resisting Ethan on camera in hopes the producers would fire him. It was no secret I missed the amaz-ing chemistry I felt with Derrick.

"What does it matter now anyway?" I sighed aloud. "I'm leaving the show; who cares who Ruby's true love is?"

"Hey, Calysta," Shannen said, walking in.

We were temporarily sharing my dressing room because of all the ex-tras and full cast, plus special accommodations that *should* have been for Grammy Award–winning guest artist John Legend, after much begging by Weezi to Edith on my behalf to spice up the soap and boost sagging ratings. Come to find out the WBC never came up with the money, so instead they hired R&B duo K-Ci and JoJo.

"Oh, hey," I said, grateful for the interruption. "How's the gang be-havin'?"

"It's pretty quiet, to tell you the truth. Emmy's hiding out in her dressing room, guess she's afraid of running into Bonnie."

Bonnie Blackburn had played the role of Uranus Winterberry, the most dastardly villainess in the history of *The Rich and the Ruthless,* on and off for the past twenty years. The network paid her a queen's ransom to return for Ruby's final storyline.

"Do you remember Bonnie's last stint on the show when Uranus Winterberry became involved in that torrid lesbian love affair with Em-my's character?" Shannen asked.

"Who could forget? The affair soon spilled over into real life and onto all the tabloids. They couldn't keep their hands off each other and didn't care who saw their girl-on-girl lip locks, even at the annual fan club luncheon, now that was *crazy.*"

"Why do you think it suddenly ended?"

"Girl, where were you, under a rock? That gossip was all up and down the soapvine. It ended because Emmy found Bonnie in bed with another woman. She swore off Bonnie but Bonnie wasn't about to let *chica* go, so things got a little aggressive on the set. Emmy actually hired a bodyguard for protection. Talk about *lipstick drama.*"

"Is it true Augustus threatened to fire both of them if they didn't stop the madness?"

"Yep. Emmy ended up quitting for a year in protest, but nobody cared. She moved to Memphis and tried to get a country western singing contract but it was a bust. She begged for her job back on *R&R*."

"Wow."

"Wow, what?"

"I'm gonna miss all this. Who am I gonna talk to after you leave?"

"You'll be fine," I assured her.

"Yeah, but it won't be the same without you."

"You got that right." I laughed. "And here's something else I'm right about, you're gonna be America's next big soap star if this industry lasts long enough. Don't let this bitter bunch steal your thunder, and whatever you do don't get stuck, you have what it takes to do other projects. Keep your day job but stay hungry and keep your options open or else your fruit will die on the vine."

"Yes, ma'am," Shannen agreed, wiping away a tear.

"Okay, cast, I know you're tired but this is the Martini shot. Five minutes . . . five minutes until we're back," announced the stage manager. "Calysta, Wolfe, Ethan, Jade, Emmy, Shannen, Phillip, Maeve, Wilson, get your touchups and be camera ready for scene forty-seven in the Fink Ballroom. And to all the extras, I know it's been a long day and you've had to occupy your time, but please put away your dominoes, cards, knitting, and crossword puzzles before you come to set."

We stood up wearily.

"Shannen, would you be a love and help me fasten up this Rory Lovekin Original?"

"I'd be honored."

"Careful, it's vintage."

"No . . . it's a masterpiece."

We laughed so hard we cried.

"Let's get to set and kick butt before Julius has a coronary."

CHAPTER 21

Sudser Showdown

FADE IN:

Int. ballroom—night

Scene in progress

(Dove and Ruby are having their first dance as husband and wife. Followed by animated well-wishers spilling out onto the lanterned portico)

DOVE

Have I ever told you what an incredible woman you are?

RUBY

Yes . . . but tell me again.

DOVE

I can't for the life of me figure out what I did to deserve such an incredible woman. The way you raced to
the roof of Fink Manor to save Jade's life was nothing
short of heroic. I feel so safe in your arms.

RUBY

All in a day's work.
~~I'd do anything for my child.~~

DOVE

I can't believe, after all these years, Uranus Winterberry is finally dead and we're finally married.

RUBY

(*A flashback to the Fink Manor rooftop where Ruby is*
standing over Uranus's body)
Dead as a doornail. I made sure of that. I kicked her butt
~~I can't believe it either. Where did I find the~~
into tomorrow.
~~strength?~~

DOVE

Now we can live happily ever after.

GINA

(*Appearing out of nowhere, sidles up next to Dove*
and Ruby)
Well, well, well, if it isn't the happy couple. Mr. and
Mrs. Dove Jordan.

DOVE

(*Aghast*)
What are you doing here, Gina? You were not invited.

GINA

(Goading)

Oh come now, Dove, you didn't think I'd miss out on Cupid's arrow miraculously finding another sucker's heart? The idea, blessing you with another shot at marriage, tying the knot at none other than Fink Manor. How could you have possibly thought I'd miss out on witnessing your nuptials and the chance to wish the happy couple bon voyage?

DOVE

You are blatantly disregarding the restraining order my attorney levied against you for falsely accusing me of sexual harassment and for hiring a hit man to as-sassinate me.

GINA

(Tossing her head back laughing)

Threaten your life? Don't flatter yourself. That rubbish was thrown out of court yesterday. Overwhelming evidence proved I had nothing to do with that Russian hit man.

RUBY

Don't make me call security.

GINA

(Brushing Ruby's threat aside)

Let me guess, you don't want your new hubby to be in the same room with his ex-lover?

RUBY

(Facing off)

Besides being certifiable, you're a nasty drunk, Gina.

Dove came clean about your ~~little sordid~~ funky affair eons

ago. We're past that. Move on.

GINA

I bet you wouldn't be past it if I told you I was

pregnant with his baby.

(Cue organ music)

RUBY

Sorry to burst your bubble, but Dove told me last night,

and I've decided to support him one hundred percent in

being a father to that child, after a paternity test.

Face it, Gina, Dove and I are married and there's not a

damn thing you can do to ever come between us again.

GINA

Oh spare me, Ruby. You don't love Dove. You're just a

golden-igger.

The extras gasped.

"*Cut!*" screamed an unraveling Julius, taking a swig of Johnnie Walker from his flask. Rubbing his eyes, looking at multiple screens in the control booth, he asked the rest of the crew, "Did she say what I think she just said?"

Everyone looked back deadpan, not wanting to get involved.

"Emmy, what the hell did you just say?"

"My line, what'd you think I said?"

"You ain't slick. It's like sayin' Schwarzenegger's name with a slant and a smile."

"I don't think she was calling you anything," Ethan said, taking her side.

"Let's pick it up, same place," Julius said.

                              GINA

Oh spare me, Ruby. You don't love Dove. You're just a

gold-digger.

                              DOVE

That's enough, Gina.

                              RUBY

No, let her hang herself. It's her last pathetic at-

tempt to try to win you back.

                              GINA

I wouldn't have him now if he were the last man on

earth. I don't do sloppy seconds. But you can bet he'll

find someone else to bed soon enough. A man like Dove

Jordan can't be satisfied by one woman, can you, Dove?

Do you really think he'll be faithful while you're

globetrotting around the world playing super spy?

                              RUBY

Oh, about that. I have a new *gig* right here in White-

haven. Dove's appointed me Chief of Security at Fink

Enterprises.

GINA

What? Barrett promised me that job. What am I supposed
to do?

RUBY

What else? Be my assistant.

"Okay, this scene is *so* not working for me," Emmy huffed.

"*Cut!*" Julius yelled, on the verge of a nervous breakdown. "Emmy, what's the problem? And where's Maeve? She's supposed to be in the background."

"Uh, Maeve left the building. She thought she was through," the stage manager said.

"That's what she always says," replied the pissed-off director. "It's always that or her 'bronchitis' flaring up."

"Something's missing in this scene, it's flat," Emmy said. "I need to be doing something with my hands. Someone get me a glass of sparkling water, ASAP!"

"What for?" I asked.

"Mind your own beeswax, sistah. You make your movie and I'll make mine. I know *you* of all people aren't questioning a little improvisation."

"Whatever floats your boat," I replied as a flute of Perrier flew in for the bossy bubblette.

"Okay, where can we pick it up from?" she asked Julius.

"Take it from 'Barrett promised me that job.' In five, four, three, two, *go*."

GINA

Barrett promised me that job. What am I supposed to
do?

RUBY

What else? Be my assistant.

Unscripted, Emmy took a healthy swig of water off camera, then brazenly spewed it in my face, bursting into a fit of hysterical toothy laughter. I waited for the brass to do something, but they didn't, at least not right away. Doing the opposite of what was expected, I stood in that *peace which passes all understanding* kind of stillness that tends to scare folks. As the vile sludge slid off my rouged cheek and onto the hand-me-down wedding dress, I finally heard, *"Cut!"*

Peripherally, I spied Alison, Phillip, and a few others intensely watching.

"Open the boom, Cisco."

"What is it, Calysta?"

"You have to ask? Obviously I need to wash this hate off."

"You can't do that, Calysta!" shouted Emmy. "You need to stay exactly the way you are for *continuity*."

"And you *need* to shut your mouth. The only reason you still have teeth is 'cause I have a daughter to raise and a mortgage to pay."

"Calysta, we don't have time for all this, Emmy's right," Julius agreed. "It's just a little water."

"Water, my eye. It's *spit*," I corrected, fighting to repress my growing emotions yet knowing the Mississippi spirits were taking hold, and the bull was about to go ballistic.

"You *people* always get so sensitive over nothing," Emmy taunted me with a snicker.

"You think it's funny?" I said, refocusing my fury on the harlot as a mist of perspiration spread above my upper lip.

"Obviously you've never heard of a *spit take*."

My chest tightened, and a small voice, no doubt inspired by Weezi, begged me to push through. *Don't let them win, make it to the finish line.* But his voice was unilaterally silenced by Beulah Espinetta Jones.

I know you ain't about to stand there and let that white girl get away with spittin' on you. You forgettin' what Grandma Jones told you 'bout her great-grandmother havin' her bottom lip pinned to her shirt for lookin' up at some so-called mistress of the Big House and how 'bout the time . . .

I glared at Emmy, who was obviously delighted by her little stunt, and slowly unclipped my earrings.

"What are you doing, you freak?" she nervously asked backing up. "Nobody likes you here, you know. I personally hate you."

I said nothing as I stalked her every step, kicking off my lava lamp Lucite heels.

"What's going on that's got you watching the show?" Randall asked his wife as he emerged from her bathroom zipping up his pants.

"I think your crazy plan finally worked. Take a look at the monitor," she responded. "Calysta just took off her earrings and her pumps. What do you think that means?"

"Oh shit," said Wilson Turner, still in his preacher's robe. He knew all too well what it meant when a black woman took off her hoops and heels.

"What do you think you're gonna do?" Emmy asked snidely.

"This," I replied, rocking back on my haunches, balling up my fist, and punching her in the face.

"Oh my gawd! She hit me!"

Before a stunned Emmy could get away, I grabbed the back of her bleached hair, spun her around, and slapped the taste of *today* out of her mouth and into *tomorrow*, wrapping my fingers around her neck.

"Help . . . Phillip, Randall . . . ! Calysta's trying to kill me!"

Phillip, coward that he was, scurried off-set the moment his name was mentioned.

Emmy struggled to grab my do but couldn't get a grip thanks to my

Inglewood glam squad; they'd sealed it to last for at least a week with the new and improved Stay-Forever platform hair lacquer hair spray.

"Ohmagod," Alison cheered, singing, "Calysta's snaa-apped, Calysta's snaa-apped!"

"Emmy!" Randall exclaimed, rushing out the door for the set.

"Wait, where are you going? Let's watch this catfight together," Alison said suggestively, disrobing again.

"I better break it up before someone gets hurt."

Attempting to rescue Emmy, Randall and Ethan were soon dragged down into a pile of crinoline and triple-tiered butter crème frosting. The bottom two layers were Styrofoam.

Taking an enormous fistful of cake, I stuffed it into Emmy's mouth, saying, "Here, bitch, how's that for improvising? Try to spit that out at me."

"That's enough," Randall said, pulling me off and tossing me to the side.

"Oh my gawd, your face!" he said in horror. Declawed, Emmy was cowering on the floor in the fetal position, smeared head to toe with icing.

"Someone call an ambulance!" Randall ordered.

"I'm bleeeeeeeeeding, Snuggle Bunny. Calysta tried to kill me."

"It's going to be all right," he assured her. "Ethan, carry her over to the couch."

"Snuggle Bunny?" Alison asked herself as she continued watching the fiasco from her monitor.

*   *   *

"Randall sure was willing to go out there and risk a clawing to protect that tramp Emmy," Edith cackled to Auggie Jr., who was sitting in her office. "I wonder if he would've been so ready to respond if his wife were the one out there being mauled? In a small way, I kinda feel sorry for her."

"Yeah. I gotta real big lump in my throat," Auggie said sarcastically. "Who cares? They're all idiots." He yawned.

"I've already called Calysta's rep," Edith said with an evil grin.

"Who can we axe next?" a salivating Auggie asked. "Let's rake out all the riffraff, except for Shannen, I like her."

"The highest paid, of course, or cut the bubblers' salary down by half."

"Can we do that?"

"Where else are they going to go?"

"Way cool!"

"By the way, your sister was on the set yesterday asking a lot of questions, which I found odd."

"Aw, she's just getting antsy 'cause she's worried about Dad. Don't worry. I know how to handle Veronica."

From her dressing room, Alison could tell by the look of compassion her husband had on his face for Emmy that it was more than a producer/ actor relationship. She had seen that look too many times before.

Edith isn't the one Randall is having an affair with, it's that tramp Emmy, Alison thought.

Back on set Randall declared, "Calysta, your behavior is outrageous."

"*My* behavior? That heifer called me a nigga' and spat on me."

"What I saw was an actress trying to enhance a scene before you viciously attacked her. I'm sure Edith's already called your rep. Clear out your dressing room and get off the WBC premises immediately! You're done here, Calysta."

"What are you talking about? You ain't got no power." I dismissed him, smoothing my wedding dress and slipping my heels back on. "Fight or no fight, *one monkey don't stop the show.* I still have two more scenes to do and after that? Trust, I'll be more than happy to get up outta here. That bitch," I said, pointing at Emmy, "is just a scratch in the groove."

"You won't be taping those scenes," Randall said confidently as he rocked Emmy in his arms. She was still trembling like a wet cat. "We want you off this set and off the WBC lot at once or we'll have WBC security throw you off!"

"That won't be necessary," I replied.

The sick smile forming on Emmy's malevolent face read, *Mission accomplished.*

As I stormed off the set for what was likely the last time, the cast and crew stared. A grip pulling cable said, "Hang in there, Calysta, you deserve better."

Out the sides of their mouths, the cameramen growled. "Nice left hook."

"Yeah, you gave her one for a lot of us."

"Thanks guys."

They'd been promised a show and I'd more than delivered one, fifteen years in the making.

Meanwhile, Edith, in her office, urgently texted Randall:

"Brilliant! Emmy just earned herself another Sudsy! Destroy all tape w/her spitting ASAP. Have her loop any dialogue we lose. Use Calysta's pitiful reaction as the tag. Remember divided we fail. And good work making Calysta redo her scene from last wk. You wore that loudmouth down to pulp. Have to say, the original was friggin amazing. Too bad the fans will never see it."

A memo was already taped to my dressing room door when I reached it.

VACATE AT ONCE!
YOUR SERVICES ARE NO LONGER NEEDED ON *THE RICH AND THE RUTHLESS.*
Edith Norman,
Sr. VP of Daytime Programming

I ripped it off, slammed the door, and slid to the carpet; tears of pent-up frustration and bittersweet victory streamed down my face.

Needing a friend, I dialed Derrick.

"Yo, sexy, wassup?"

"Everything's a mess. I finally beat that bitch up."

"Which one?"

"Emmy."

"Listen, babe, sometimes you think things are bein' done to ya when they're bein' done for ya. Try to look at this as an opportunity to spread them lovely velvet wings of yours and fly. Remember what you told me your Grandma Jones said when I was rasslin' with them fools when they didn't wanna pay me right? 'There ain't no testimony without a test.'"

"I remember."

"Now get ready, I'm on my way. And don't worry 'bout your car either, we'll get it tomorrow. I'm gonna scoop you up and we're gonna talk about your future over some Slippery Shrimp at Yang Chow's and put a smile on that pretty face, and then I'm gonna take you over to Club Seven-forty."

The first time Derrick took me to Club 740 I'd had no idea where I was going.

"Sit back and relax, I've got a surprise for ya," he'd said.

Driving down a gritty street peppered with food vendors and crackheads inhabiting cardboard boxes, we pulled up to a valet sign, a splashy "Seven Forty" painted on the façade of the building.

"Good evening, Mr. Taylor." The brawny bouncer greeted us as we glided

through the red velvet stanchions, past the rowdy snaking line of partygoers waiting to get in.

Once Derrick and I were through the door we never stopped drinking or dancing to the pounding hip-hop beat of Bobby Valentino. Derrick was the type that always attracted a crowd, whipping off his shirt, driving everybody wild, and I mean everybody, before going into his freestyle; so smooth, graceful even. The only problem was, some diva who was done, done, done, and on the fringe pressed up against my man and I had to tell Miss Thang to back it up.

Batting her lashes, she asked, "Aren't you Ruby Stargazer?"

Hearing her baritone, I asked, "But I thought you were a . . . ?"

"No, diva, I'm a boy, but tonight I'm a girl just like you. I ain't after your man, all I wanna do is dance. So do you think we can share and get this party started?"

Grandma Jones was right, I thought, coming out of the memory. Only freaks and strange folk wanted to be on stage and TV.

I was finally free of *The Rich and the Ruthless*. Not that I knew exactly what that meant. But as sure as the sirens I heard in the background, the second act of my life and career had to get better.

SIX MONTHS LATER

BLIND ITEM: Which daytime exec and her partner-in-crime executive producer are set to do the unthinkable, recasting one of their most beloved heroines? When the daytime diva who created the legendary role first announced she was leaving the soap, they both swore a recast was absurd. Apparently slumping ratings, a financial tsunami, and a disgruntled leading man sick of being paired with reality-show rejects has them thinking otherwise. Will this soap actually be stupid enough to go there? Talk about jumping the shark! Keep checking back for more updates at Secretsofa-SoapOperaDiva.com!

The Diva

CHAPTER 22

Girl, When You Coming Back to the Stories?

*W*hoever came up with the advice "Never go to the grocery store hungry" was a smart, smart man. Wait a minute, who am I kidding? It *had* to have been a woman. Guys don't worry about tracking calories or counting carbs. A heavyset man could still land a hot girl-friend or wife. If you don't believe me just look at every network sitcom green-lit since 1998. Scarfing down three monster burgers in a sitting, dudes have no problem burning it all off with an afternoon game of golf and a secret rendezvous in the rough.

Meanwhile, it took me Pritikin, The Hollywood Diet, and most effective The Eleven-Day Lemon-Cayenne-Pepper-Garlic-Honey Cleanse/Fast, plus three full decathlon sessions with Anvar, my demanding Swedish trainer, to work off just one extra piece of Sweet Lady Jane chocolate cake at my friend Bill's baby shower.

I reluctantly put down the pint of ice cream I'd been contemplating and guided my shopping cart, which I clearly didn't need, in the direction of the produce section to the piped-in elevator music. If I was ever going to fit into the size-four Carolina Herrera gown I'd been eyeing for the premiere of Jamie and Brad's new movie—I'd gone up two sizes since leaving the soap—I'd better leave the sweets alone and stick to organic fruits and veggies.

I'd stopped off at Whole Foods to pick up a few things on the way to Ivy's lacrosse game. The plan was get in and get out before heading to my daughter's elite private school in Santa Monica.

Pushing my cart up to a towering Red Blush grapefruit display, I began the ritual Grandma Jones had taught me. First, I squeezed the succulent orb, scrutinizing its skin for the right color and texture, finally inhaling it to detect any whiff of decay. This might seem over-the-top for the purchase of a simple grapefruit, but honey, if this was all *you* were gonna eat all day you'd make your *pamplemousse* your best meal too.

Out of the corner of my eye, I saw a pleasant-looking black woman staring at me from her motorized shopping cart. Her hair was styled in a lacquered French twist with a swoop. She was wearing a peach St. John knit pantsuit with fringed cuffs and matching pumps.

Realizing I'd caught her staring, she quickly looked away, only to resume a few seconds later.

I glided over to the blueberries and pomegranates. Been consuming way too much sugar and was desperate for antioxidants.

"Excuse me?" came a voice from behind.

I turned to find the same woman, close enough to warrant breaking out the keychain pepper spray Derrick had given me.

"Yes?" I asked looking down at her, knowing full well what would follow.

"Aren't you . . ."

Here it comes, I thought, smiling.

"No"—the woman changed her mind—"it can't be. You look so

much *darker* on the stories and *thicker* too. Besides, Ruby Stargazer would never be doin' her own shoppin'."

"It's me," I confirmed, putting the woman out of her misery.

"*Lord* have mercy, Ruby it *is* you," the woman exclaimed, grabbing her heart-shaped mocha brown face in her hands.

"Yep."

"Ruby Stargazer," the woman gushed. "You're my biggest fan." A few shoppers began to stare at the spectacle.

"Come again?"

"I mean I'm *your* biggest fan," the woman corrected. "I just love you on *The Rich and the Ruthless.*"

"Why thank you."

"Girl, when you coming back to the stories? It just ain't the same without you. You know you represent."

There it was, the question that had followed me everywhere I went since my character Ruby Stargazer slipped off the honeymoon yacht and descended to her watery grave six months earlier.

When those fools on R&R *learn how to treat people,* I wanted to respond, but decided against it. I didn't want to ruin the fan's moment.

"I'm not sure," I demurred. "No one on *R&R* has thrown Ruby a life preserver yet."

"Makes no sense to me and my sisters." The woman sighed, furrowing her eyebrows and sucking her back teeth. "T'h, you were the only reason we watched *The Rich and the Ruthless.* Cried like a baby when you fell off that boat. Shoot, it was bad enough when they replaced Dove Jordan with that other actor, but when they tried to replace you, I just about had a fit. Said that's enough and went back to watching that *other* story. You know, the one with Angie and Jesse."

"Love them," I replied.

"Mmm-hmmm, yeah, they brought 'em back after twenty years, chile. You know Jesse died *on-screen* in Angie's arms and we all saw the body. They haven't found yours yet."

"They haven't?" I asked, playing along. I was well aware that Ruby Stargazer's final scenes were played out by a last-minute recast from some reality show and Ruby was only presumed dead.

"Nope, we all believe you've dog-paddled your way back to land, rescued by a rare tribe that's crowned you their African queen."

"Wow, that's good. Have you ever considered writing? We could use you."

The fan bashfully smiled saying, "No. I'm just a receptionist and catch the stories on my lunch break."

During my tenure on *R&R*, I rarely watched the air shows, reason being it drove me crazy seeing boom shots, entire walls reverberating when a door shut, or worse, Emmy Abernathy's eyes frantically reading off cue cards. Since I'd sped off the WBC lot for the last time, especially since Phillip and Emmy threatened to leave the show if I returned, *R&R* had a Season Pass on my TiVo. I had become obsessed with knowing what Edith and Randall planned to do with my character.

"Wow, wouldn't that be something if Ruby was still out there," I said. "Well, it was nice meeting you . . ."

"Now Ruby, they *did* find traces of your DNA on a track from your weave off the coast of them Seychelles Islands where you and Dove went on your honeymoon."

I grimaced. That asinine excuse for a plot point had been Felicia's vicious way of still punishing me.

"Listen," I began, "I'd love to talk to you some more . . . what did you say your name was?"

"Etta. Etta Jean Paisley," she proudly said, extending her hand.

"Nice to meet you, Etta," I replied, taking it.

"The pleasure's been all mine. Wait till I tell my sisters an' 'em that I met Ruby Stargazer in the supermarket."

"You do that, Etta. So long," I said, waving as I slowly walked backward, building distance.

"Wait, Ruby!" Etta vroomed forward toward the Chiquita display. "Before you go, could you do me a big favor?"

"What's that?"

"Would you sign a few autographs for me?"

"Uh, sure, but I don't have anything to write with."

"That's okay; here you go." Etta Jean whipped out a pen, handing it up to me along with a grocery pad that had been resting beside coupons in the basket attached to her cart.

"Who should I make this out to?"

"First one's to Apollinaire," she instructed. "She's my oldest sister who lives out in St. Louis, never misses an episode. Oh, and can you add 'Your sister Etta Jean is amazing'?"

> *To Apollinaire,*
>
> *Thanks for watching* The Rich and the Ruthless . . . *Etta Jean is amazing!*
>
> *Blessings,*
> *Calysta Jeffries*

"Here you go. Who's next?"

"Oh . . ." Etta paused, scrunching her face in disappointment.

"Is something wrong?"

"I was just wondering . . ."

"Wondering what?"

"Could you sign them as Ruby Stargazer?"

No matter what else I did in my career, Ruby Stargazer would always be more famous than Calysta Jeffries or any other role I played.

Always grateful to a fan, I rewrote the autograph to Etta's sister Apollinaire in St. Louis, and one to Lovey in El Dorado, Arkansas, to her specifications. Then Etta called her mother, Metra, holding her cell phone to my ear so I could say hello while finishing the final autograph to Etta herself, all signed, "Ruby Stargazer."

Making my way up to the checkout counter, I looked over to the magazine rack out of habit at the tabloids. The usual suspects were front-page news. Just a little farther down on the rack I got a kick out of counting how many "Is Ruby Stargazer Returning from the Dead?" headlines I could find on the cover of the soap rags.

If I had a nickel for every *Cliffhanger Weekly* and *Soap Suds Digest* cover that had my face plastered on it since I'd been fired from *R&R* I'd be Bill Gates rich. The same magazine editors who repeatedly told the soap's publicist and Weezi for fifteen years, "Brown just doesn't sell our mags," were now capitalizing on my popularity and the massive outcry for my return.

The soap rags also irresponsibly sent panic across American checkout counters, posturing me "in negotiations" for an imminent return, just so fans would continue to tune in and buy their sudser tabloids. And I knew *R&R* paid them handsomely to keep stoking that fire.

There I was again, airbrushed to perfection on the glossy cover of the latest issue of *Soap Suds Digest.* The caption read: "Mega-Shocker News: Will Ruby Stargazer Return from Her Watery Grave?"

My eyes scanned over to *Cliffhanger Weekly.* The headline read: "Breaking News: Is Calysta Jeffries Being Recast?"

My heart picked up a few beats.

"How are you today, ma'am?" asked the cashier.

"Fine," I replied, hoping I was doing an adequate job of masking the anxiety attack I was experiencing.

Attempting to calm my nerves, I threw the copy of *Cliffhanger Weekly* facedown onto the conveyor belt along with my packages of blueberries and pomegranate seeds.

"Paper or plastic?" the bag boy asked.

"Ah, paper, please."

As the cashier handed me my receipt, the sexy young bag boy, resembling hip-hop sensation Mario, flirtatiously asked me, "Do you need a carryout?"

Since I never looked my age, it wasn't uncustomary for younger men to make passes. I wanted to say, *Sweetie you can carry me anywhere you want to*, but behaved.

"Love one."

After a few minutes of searching, I retrieved my Jag keys from my 2007 D&G jacket. Times were tight and I shopped my closet like a Filene's Basement closeout sale. Naturally it was in excellent condition.

I tipped the scrumptious bag boy a fiver after he shut the trunk. "Thank you, ma'am." He beamed. "My grandma loves *The Rich and the Ruthless*."

I instantly wanted my money back; the thrill was gone.

I climbed into my sports car with the rolled *Cliffhanger Weekly* in my fist, anxious to find out about the potential recast of my signature role. Couldn't believe Edith and Randall would be stupid enough to go there. *R&R*'s online viewers had cyber-tarred and feathered Yancy St. Martin, the *So You Wanna Be a Supermodel* winner who'd replaced me during Ruby's honeymoon death scenes.

Before I could flip open to the magazine's first page, I was interrupted by Eldar's "Nature Boy" ringtone.

"Hello?"

"Calysta, where in the hell are you?" my ex-husband Dwayne Jeffries aggressively shouted into my ear.

"Who do you think you are asking me where I am? Last time I checked I hadn't been your wife in over six years."

"Did you forget Ivy has a major lacrosse game tonight? It starts in thirty minutes."

"No, I didn't forget. But did you forget I'm the one who juggles a real job and pays the tuition while you're out juggling two or three video hoes a week? You show up for one of Ivy's events on time and come off as a hero. Pathetic."

"The fact of the matter is, our daughter's in her first playoff game and her mother is nowhere to be found," he replied smugly.

Dwayne met me when Ivy was just five years old. I had appeared on his low-rated daytime talk show to promote *The Rich and the Ruthless*.

At first I thought he was charming, the sex was mezza mezz, and he had nice teeth. It turned out he was arrogant, argumentative, a freak in bed, and the teeth were veneers. However, he and Ivy had formed an undeniable bond. We married and Dwayne became a paternal figure in her life, even after we split up.

"You know what, get off my back. Tell Ivy I'll be there as soon as I can."

Pressing the End button and putting my key in the ignition, I knew I'd have to read about the Ruby Stargazer recast later if I was going to make it to Santa Monica in time to catch at least some of my daughter's game.

I pulled out of the parking lot and headed for the Pacific Coast Highway. As I sped along, my thoughts kept drifting to the magazine sitting next to me. I wanted to tear it open so bad and read about the recast.

Come on, Calysta, get real, this is only a soap tabloid, it's not Rolling Stone. *How many times has the magazine touted my return to daytime in the last six months, turning out to be totally false? I don't know why people bother picking up these stupid rags.*

It was probably all just a silly rumor created on one of those anonymous soap blogs.

Something up ahead was stalling traffic. Probably another mudslide or a wreck.

No matter how long I lived in Southern California, it never ceased to amaze me how traffic could crawl to a complete stop over roadkill, road rage, or rubbernecking.

Frustrated, I grabbed the mag and quickly thumbed through it.

WBC President of Daytime Television Edith Norman and Randall Roberts, Co-Executive Producer of *The Rich and the Ruthless,* are reportedly moving ahead with plans to bring back the wildly popular heroine Ruby Stargazer in time for February Sweeps, in honor of Black History Month and the WBC's new diversity rollout led by Josephine Mansoor, hiring more young African Americans due to a firestorm of ongoing criticism. There has been no official word as to whether or not the sudser has approached Calysta Jeffries to reprise the role, but according to respected soap reporter Mitch Morelli the character of Ruby Stargazer is likely to be recast.

I reached for my BlackBerry and auto-dialed Shannen, putting the phone on speaker, not noticing that traffic had begun moving again. The driver of the SUV behind me honked, startling me.

"Dammit," I spat, accidentally dropping the rag.

"Hello, Calysta?"

"Hey," I replied, straining to sound cheerful while reaching between my legs.

"Something wrong?"

"Nah, just calling to catch up," I replied, forcing nonchalance. "What's the latest on the soapvine? Anyone else been let go?"

"Yeah, they fired poor Willie Turner again, and rumor has it the Pattern Cutter could be next," she squealed. "But that said, things are worse than ever. Alison got her way as usual. Randall hired another hairstylist and Felicia stopped writing scenes for Wolfe and me and brought in a twenty-two-year-old Latin hunk to pair me with named Javier de L'Vasquez, who was a breakout star on the Mexican telenovela *Mi Amor, Mi Odio.*"

"What's wrong with that?"

"He's playing the new Pepe."

"Oh. Well, if nothing else, the soap's consistent," I replied. "Always open season for recasting the minorities."

"Yeah well, Roger's pissed."

"Roger? Thought you guys were separated?"

"We were but he threatened to commit suicide. Anyway, sharing scenes with Wolfe was one thing, because Roger didn't see him as a threat, but the moment he caught a bedroom scene of Javier and me online he went bat-shit crazy. Javier is Mark Consuelos–Mario Lopez *gorgeous,* by the way."

"Yeah, but you coulda done all right stayin' in that storyline with Wolfe. He's still rated the sexiest and most popular actor in daytime. Don't forget how that silver fox heroically carried you up two flights of stairs out of a burning building like it was nothin' last year when you were knocked unconscious by that psycho Rory Lovekin, connecting a two-by-four to your skull like she was Jose Canseco on steroids."

"I know, who could forget? And that was the problem," Shannen firmly stated. "Alison got her prickly panties in a bunch the moment I had chemistry with Wolfe and we definitely had plenty of that. She knows the only thing that keeps her on the air is their super-couple status fueling her popularity."

"And don't forget she married that undie-snatcher Randall Roberts," I said acidly. "Girl, I don't know how you're still doing it. I am *so* much happier now that I'm away from all that poison," I lied.

I was itching to ask Shannen about the Ruby Stargazer recast rumors but didn't want it to seem as if that was the only reason I had called.

"It's *much* worse since Mr. Barringer recently had a turn for the worse," Shannen reported.

"What!"

"Auggie Jr. is still Co-Executive Producer, but he's basically never at the set. He's letting that ignoramus Randall do whatever he wants. Oh and you'll never believe, Veronica Barringer's been hanging around the set lately. How weird is that? Calysta, are you there?"

"Uhh, yeah," I replied, half paying attention. I was in disbelief that I hadn't been informed of how ill Augustus actually was.

"You haven't asked about the recast."

I was relieved she'd brought it up so I didn't have to seem desperate.

"What recast?" I pretended not to know.

"Hate to tell you, Calysta, but there's serious talk of replacing you and Ethan is first in line making recommendations."

"Figures . . . Shannen?"

"I'm still here. When you left, you told me you never wanted to know if they decided to recast, and here I am bringing it up. I'm sorry."

"I've changed my mind. Tell me everything," I said as I reached into my handbag for my stash of Xanax, quickly retrieving a couple of pills, swallowing them dry.

"All right." She sighed. "The word on the set is yes, they are secretly *testing* actresses to play Ruby Stargazer this week, and they're going for a big name."

"Like who?"

"I have no idea. Edith and the *R&R* brass are being really tight-lipped."

My exit off the 10 freeway was still a good twenty minutes away from the Westside Waldorf School. I was feeling calmer, but my head began to swim as I haphazardly straddled two lanes, almost sideswiping an Escalade, causing the Filipino driver to flip me the bird.

Sorry, I mouthed to the driver.

"Calysta, you all right?"

"Yeah, yeah, drivin'," I slurred. "Shan, you're such a good friend, I-gotta-go-better-get-off-the-phone-don't-wanna-get-a-ticket."

"Okay, please call me later," a worried Shannen said as she hung up.

I threw the phone into the passenger seat and blasted the music.

A big-name actress . . . those bastards.

I darted into the carpool lane and floored it.

I gotta get to Ivy's game.

Crossing four lanes in seconds, I headed up the off-ramp. The traffic light changed to red just as I skated under it, narrowly missing an oncoming cement truck. I looked back to see the driver shaking his fist and no doubt yelling obscenities. By the time I looked forward a school bus full of children had stopped in front of me.

Slamming on the brakes, skidding sideways, I screamed, *"Oh, shit!"* Everything seemed to happen in slow motion and the last thing I remembered was crashing my Jag full speed into a light pole.

Disgraced Soap Diva Crashes Car in Drugged Out Stupor!

BREAKING NEWS: Former *Rich and Ruthless* siren Calysta Jeffries crashed her vintage Jaguar into a streetlight in Santa Monica, blocks from her teenage daughter's school. The award-winning actress, who up until six months ago played Ruby Stargazer on the soap, is said to be laid up in serious condition, according to her spokesperson Weezi Abramowitz. Inside sources say alcohol and drugs may have been a factor. Ever since Jeffries was fired from the #1 WBC soap shortly after her shocking on-set brawl with Sudsy Awardee and costar Emmy Abernathy she's been abusing the mood enhancers. It's so sad what this industry can turn people into. Keep checking back as this tragic story develops!

The Diva

CHAPTER 23

Under the Influence

"W hen I grow up I'ma be a GREAT BIG STAR!" I exclaimed, throwing my arms open wide for emphasis.

"You are?" asked Miss Whilemina, visiting from next door. She came over every afternoon in time to watch the "stories" with Grandma Jones.

"I sure am. I'm gonna be an actress on TV!"

"Well I'll just say. Do me a favor, chile, and remember me here in Greenwood, Mississippi, when you make all that big-time money, okay?"

"Okay," I promised. "I'm gone be the biggest star EVER!"

"Beulah Espinetta Jones, get your skinny behind in that kitchen and stop talking all that Who-Shot-John before I get the strap," Grandma Jones warned from her usual place on the sunken-in sofa, a dishrag over one shoulder and a picture of a flaxen-haired, blue-eyed Jesus hanging above her. "How many times do I have to tell you, all that show business carryin' on is for freaks and strange folk?"

"But—"

"Don't you but me, Beulah. You better look like doin' those dishes if you know what's good for you."

"Yes ma'am," I said, shoulders slumped in defeat.

"I mean you better wash those dishes good too, you know how yolk sticks. And dump that swill bucket in the compost pile while you're at it," Grandma Jones called out during a commercial break, Miss Whilemina nestled next to her unwrapping tinfoil containing a dozen hot wings, anticipating picking up where they left off on their favorite soap, Yesterday, Today and Maybe Tomorrow. "And wipe those dishes dry and put 'em away before you go outside and weed my herb garden. Ya hear? Beulah? Beulah Espinetta, don't make me get off this couch!"

"Yes ma'am. I hear you, I hear you, I hear you . . ."

"Mom, wake up!" a familiar voice called out, as hands were gently rocking me. "You're dreaming."

I opened my swollen eyes to find Ivy's concerned face looking down at me.

"What?" I asked groggily, my head pounding. "Where's Grandma Jones?"

"In Mississippi, where else would she be?"

I slowly realized I wasn't in Greenwood anymore. Everything was so hazy, so white, so sterile. And where was all my Barbara Barry furniture?

"What's goin' on?" I panicked, as I unsuccessfully tried to sit up. "Ouch! Where am I?"

"Lay still, Mom." Ivy gently guided me back.

"You're at St. John's," answered a pissed Dwayne. His voice made me wince.

"What?"

"You've been here for the past forty-eight hours," he continued. "Ever since you wrapped your car around a light pole."

Nothing Dwayne said was registering. I remembered getting groceries . . .

How'd I get from pomegranate seeds to a hospital bed? I'd read something in a tabloid that involved Randall Roberts . . . what was it?

The details were fuzzy, but one thing I knew for certain, as with most of the showbiz calamities of my adult life, trifling Randall Roberts somehow played a part.

"Was anyone else hurt?"

"Luckily no," Dwayne coldly informed me. "Considering how impaired you were it could have been disastrous."

"Impaired? What are you talking about?"

"No mystery here, Calysta. You were driving while under the influence. You better thank God you only have a coupla' cracked ribs and didn't kill yourself or someone else."

"What? No, I mean I wasn't impaired!"

"Dwayne, take it easy, Mom's just been in an accident."

"I . . . I remember having a split of champagne before going to the market, and that certainly wasn't enough to make me crash my car."

"They found alprazolam in your system," Dwayne said.

"Alpa-what-um?" Ivy asked.

"I'm sorry you have to find out about your mother this way, honey, but—"

"Shut up, Dwayne."

"It's Xanax," he persisted. "They found a bottle spilled out all over the passenger seat of your mother's car."

"Okay, okay, *crucify me.* Yes, I occasionally take a Xanax for my panic attacks, which you contribute to, but what does that have to do with—"

"You know you're not supposed to drink and drive, much less mix it with pills."

"Well thank you, C. Everett *whatshisface.*"

"Who?" Ivy asked.

"Your mother doesn't know what she's talking about. It's Dr. Regina

Benjamin, new surgeon general. Saw it in *Jet*." Dwayne's real inspiration
for the subscription was "Beauty of the Week."

"My head—"

"Mom! I'll get the nurse?"

"Yeah baby, need something for the pain."

"Okay, be right back."

"That's *not* going to happen, I will not allow our daughter to enable
your druggin'," Dwayne pontificated, blocking Ivy's exit. "And furthermore, Ivy will be staying with me for the foreseeable future."

"You're out of your cotton-pickin' mind."

Maternal adrenaline temporarily numbing my agony, I pressed the
button on my automated bed to sit up. "I'm the primary parent."

"Not anymore you're not," Dwayne said arrogantly, unfolding an
official-looking document. "Don't strain yourself trying to read it. It's a
court order giving me temporary custody."

"You can't be serious?"

"Do I look like I'm joking?"

"I get into a little fender bender and now you're snatching my
child!"

"If I hadn't been quick on my feet, Child Protective Services would've
been all over me and you like a wetsuit."

"Guys, Mom, Dad, stop fighting."

"You're right, honey, pass me my BlackBerry. It's in my purse. I need
to call Sly."

"He's already in the waiting room." Dwayne sneered. "He called yesterday and asked me to let him know when you regained consciousness.
The accident's been on *Wendy Williams* 'Hot Topics' for the past two
days. She keeps rerunning you being cut out of your car with the 'Jaws
of Life.' See what an embarrassing mess you've made?"

"And how much did you get for the story, Dwayne? Ivy, go get
Sly."

"But Mom, you should rest. Can't you do this later?"

"Just get him, baby."

Ivy stared Dwayne down with a "don't mess with me" attitude heading out the door.

Taking advantage of her absence, Dwayne continued, "This wasn't just some 'fender bender,' Calysta. What if Ivy had been in the car with you?"

"I know you're *not* gonna stand in my face and spin this to make me look like some kind of unfit dope fiend mother!"

"Calysta, you can't even take care of yourself right now, let alone a teenager. You act as if life is one big soap opera."

"For someone who's always ready to call me a hack and put me down for makin' a livin' off of daytime, you sure don't mind collectin' that soap opera alimony, do you? If you think I'm gonna sit back and let you take Ivy without a fight you got another thing comin', brotha'. I wouldn't put it past you to be goin' after custody just so you can suck more money out of me in the name of child support. You'll be hearing from Sly first thing tomorrow, you can best believe *that*."

"I predict your attorney will have more pressing things on his agenda. Like keeping his client out of jail."

"Everyone told me it was a mistake to trust you to adopt Ivy in the first place, but I was hardheaded."

"Always living in the past, chasin' shadows . . . whatever, Calysta, I'll just chalk up all your yammering to those chemicals swimming around in your toxic brain. As for Ivy, biology notwithstanding, she's my daughter too and my first priority. I'll do whatever it takes to protect her."

"Get the hell out!" I screamed as Sly and Weezi entered, Ivy rushing to my bedside.

Dwayne caught the door, saying, "We'll be back tomorrow *if* you've come to your senses. C'mon, Ivy. This is no place for you."

"Just ignore him, Mom," Ivy whispered into my ear as she gave me a kiss.

"Love you, babygirl," I tearfully said. "Promise to make it up to you."

She reluctantly walked out with Dwayne.

"How's it going, Calysta?" Sly asked. "Never trusted that man."

"Yeah, I tried to tell her he was a scumbag."

"Weezi, what are you doin' here?"

"Thought it was a good idea to come for moral support. You know how much I care about you."

I looked at him sideways. Weezi was there for all the wrong reasons.

"Sly, how could you let this happen?"

"What was I supposed to do? Weezi's incessant calling—"

"Not him! Dwayne. That leech has been awarded temporary custody of Ivy? How did he pull that off when you have my Power of Attorney?"

"He's the child's legal father. I told you years ago that gigolo was going to be trouble. But I have to tell you, it could have been much worse."

"How—if a building fell on me?"

One of my biggest fears was if Ian, Ivy's bio-dad, popped up to make a claim for her too. Nah, I knew better than that. The last thing that deadbeat wanted was a teenager crampin' his bachelor lifestyle.

"Dwayne said something about jail? The police must realize this was just an accident?"

"I hate to remind you, but you were driving under the influence, Calysta."

"I feel bad enough, don't rub more salt in the wound. I know I made a colossal mistake but that doesn't make me a criminal."

"Unfortunately, that's not how the District Attorney's office sees it."

"The District Attorney's office?" I exclaimed, flinching from the pain across my chest. "The D.A. is getting involved in my little accident when the state is bankrupt and we have rapists and serial killers runnin' around?"

"Calysta, this is serious; you could have killed someone. The D.A. has caught a lot of flak for being lenient on celebrity DUI offenders in recent years. He wanted to make an example out of you but fortunately, with all my contacts downtown, I was able to head him off at the pass."

"Will I have to do some sort of community service like Naomi Campbell?"

"Community service will definitely be a part of the deal, but that comes in a bit later. You've got more pressing things to focus on."

"You're scaring me."

"You're gonna have to go through six weeks of drug counseling."

"Are you shittin' me?"

"'Fraid not."

"I don't have time for counseling. I have a career to rebuild."

"You're unemployable for now."

"Stop talkin' crazy."

"I'm serious, Calysta. There's no way around it. You're court-ordered to fulfill a six-week intensive residential drug treatment at a facility specializing in addiction. As soon as your doctor gives the okay, you'll be transported door-to-door to Tranquility Tudor in Malibu."

"There's no way I'm going to a stupid rehab. Besides, it's two streets up from my house and everyone will recognize me in the neighborhood. That place drives their rich clients around in those psychiatric-looking vans that have 'We Do It One Day at a Time' stamped on the back."

"It's either Tranquility Tudor or a year in jail," Sly said matter-of-factly.

"This can't be happening,"

"It's not all bad," Weezi reasoned. "As far as these types of places go, Tranquility Tudor is top shelf. It's the Waldorf-Astoria of detox clinics and where *all* the celebrities go. They've got a spa and everything. And guess what? There's a *huge* motion picture director who just checked in for the third time to dry out. Who knows, you might land a part in a film just rubbing elbows over chocolate mousse while sharing your strength, love, and hope."

"Do I look like Winehouse? I'm a substantial *actress*. I don't have time to sit around talking about my feelings with some has-been teen stars from *The Partridge Family*."

"We have your best interests at heart. Now, you get some beauty rest," Weezi began. "*Cliffhanger Weekly* and *Soap Suds Digest* are still talking about your comeback to *The Rich and the Ruthless*. You know what they say, you gotta be ready when opportunity strikes. Call me if you need anything."

I couldn't even muster enough strength to say *get out, you bum*. And as for Sly, though he'd saved the day keeping me out of the pokey, I didn't thank him too much. I knew he'd be sending along a fat bill to my accountant by the end of the week.

I reached over to the bedside table to get my BlackBerry, wanting to talk to Derrick. He'd know how to fix this, he always did. Too bad we'd broken up again shortly after I was fired.

He'd been ultra-understanding about my beef with Emmy and smoothed my ruffled feathers in more ways than one.

However, after I saw him in *The Globe* canoodling in the buff between two Brazilian bombshells on a beach in Rio while shooting his hunky Man of Prime Time calendar I had a nuclear meltdown.

I'd auto-dialed him demanding an explanation but only got a recording, "This number is no longer in service. Please check the number and try again later."

The sex god had played me like a fiddle and I reverted back to possessive ghetto-stalker mode, plotting to scale his security gate and Krazy Glue his front-door keyhole.

Derrick had attempted to call me when he got back home, but I made myself unavailable. It was torture not answering any of his three calls. Once again we were done, finished, kaput. And as gutted as I was, I moved on.

Now, scrolling down my contact list, I dialed Shannen instead. Sometimes a girl is a girl's best friend.

"Hello?" she asked on the first ring.

"Hey Shan, need your help."

Soap Stars' Marriage Hits the Skids!

SHOCKING BLIND ITEM: It looks like a real-life soap opera super-couple is currently in the throes of a Blissless Wedded Mess. We can't tell you which one, but a pair of married bubblers is this close to calling it quits, that is if they don't end up killing each other first! To think only a few short years ago these two lovebirds were on the covers of *Muscle & Fitness, Plumpers,* and *Soap Suds Digest*—not to mention receiving the most hits on YouTube talking about how they balanced love and bubbles—and are now inculpating each other over rumored affairs with hot Latino leading men (her) and lack of employment opportunities (him). Oh well, what's that they say, 'tis better to have loved a bubbler and lost than never to have loved at all?

The Diva

CHAPTER 24

Big Bear

*D*on't worry, Calysta," Shannen whispered into her phone. "On my way; I should be back in L.A. in a few hours."

"I thought we agreed no cell phones," Roger hypocritically snarled. Felicia's last words from a recent call were still fresh in his mind: "Don't worry, Roger, I'll fix Shannen's wagon. I'm going to write you into a front-burner *R&R* storyline if it's the last thing I do."

Stomping into the bathroom behind Shannen while stripping off his sweaty workout digs he heard, "Calysta, hold on a sec," as she hit Mute.

"Roger, it's Calysta; she's been in a serious accident."

"So?" he said, turning on the shower and stepping in.

"So she needs my help."

"We're not driving all the way back to L.A.!" he yelled. "Tell her to call *her* people."

"Roger, she's in the hospital!"

Roger and Shannen were at their vacation cabin in Big Bear, making use of it before the bank repossession, in yet another attempt on Shannen's part to find a pulse in their quickly flatlining marriage. The couple had agreed when they bought the rustic hideaway on Big Bear Lake that it was a place to unplug, unwind, and have lots of sex. That meant zero distractions; no television, no laptops, and absolutely no cell phones. Time proved that was easier for Roger than for Shannen. She still had a J-O-B and needed to stay in touch with the world outside their Big Bear bubble for auditions and script and schedule changes.

"It's going to be okay, Calysta, I'll see you before you know it," Shannen said with assurance. "And don't worry about Dwayne, we'll figure out a way to get Ivy back."

As she hung up, Roger asked, "Who's Dwayne?"

"Calysta's ex," she explained, heading to the bedroom closet to get her overnight bag. "Calysta was a little . . . impaired when she had her accident and now Dwayne is manipulating the situation to get custody of their daughter."

Nonchalantly stepping out of the shower and wrapping a towel around his soft waist, Roger said, "Sounds like a smart guy to me."

"What?" Shannen dropped her bag and zipped back to the bathroom for toiletries. "Roger, it's not like she's some bad mother. She made a mistake. Calysta loves Ivy."

"What, and you think the dad doesn't love his kid too? See, that's what's wrong with *you women*. You think just because you lie down and grunt out a kid, you get all the say. Sorry, doesn't work that way. You know, most guys don't even want ankle-biters, but you women always insist, naggin' us, 'I want a *baby,* my biological clock is *tickin'*,'" he whined, "and all we want is sex, a good football game, and a cold beer."

"Stop talking crazy. You don't even know all the facts."

"And you do? Sounds like you're just taking your loopy friend's word for it. You only like her anyway 'cause she defended you that one time Bonnie Blackburn jumped you in a fitting. I don't blame this guy for doing what he has to do to protect his kid. I've heard stories about that chick from Felicia. She sounds like a piece of work."

In all the years Shannen and Calysta had been friends, Calysta had socialized with played-out Roger only a few times. A graduate of the *theatre*, Roger believed Shannen's soap opera friends were beneath him, sadly ironic since he himself had been a bubbler until his low-rated half-hour soap *Obsessions* was mercifully canceled, and he hadn't been on a Broadway stage since *Cats* opened. (Roger had played Carbucketty for six months before being fired for shooting a spread in *Playgirl* on the side, while the show went on to have an eighteen-year run.)

"Felicia hates Calysta, I've already told you why," Shannen replied. "She's not a good judge of my friend's character, not by a long shot."

"Oh and I guess you are?" Roger said mockingly. "What, did you get a degree in psych from the same place you got your Acting for Dummies certification?"

Shannen looked down, reminding herself, *Roger is feeling emasculated since he lost his job. Most men's egos are intrinsically attached to their employment. When he speaks to you disrespectfully, try to exercise patience and let it roll off your back. It's his bruised pride, not the man you fell in love with, a way to gain back power with dominance.*

The words of Dr. Jordana Walker, the marriage counselor she had been seeing, on her own since Roger refused to go, came into Shannen's mind in time to prevent her from striking back.

"I don't have time for this, Roger, my friend needs me." Shannen darted back to the bedroom to finish packing.

"Where do you think you're going? You're the one who insisted we come up here for the weekend when I could've been back in L.A. auditioning." Roger's agent had dumped him after his soap was canceled.

He was obsessively combing the Web and *Back Stage* magazine for open calls.

"We'll come back next weekend. They're talking about putting Calysta in rehab."

"Good. She needs to dry out."

"You don't understand."

"You're right. I don't understand why you can make time for everyone else's needs except for your husband's!"

"That isn't true," Shannen protested, throwing things into her Kate Spade luggage. "Look, I'm going to go home to support Calysta and then I'll come right back, okay?"

"No, it's not okay." Roger ripped the bag out of her hand and threw it to the floor. "I bet if I was your hot little Puerto Rican leading man Javier you wouldn't be leaving, would you?"

"Don't start that again," Shannen warned. "And he's Mexican."

"Are you calling me a liar?" Roger confronted, as Shannen took a step back. "Bet you wouldn't leave to rescue your bloodsucking girlfriend if Mr. Latin America was standing in front of you."

Shannen was the consummate actress and played her role to the hilt, moving past her husband, calmly stating, "See, this is exactly what Felicia wants."

"Felicia? What the hell does she have to do with any of this? Don't blame *my* friend—"

"Your supposed friend only paired me with Javier to fuel your blind jealousy. She hoped we'd fight so you'd run to her for consolation. Why can't you see that?"

"That's a bunch of bull! Felicia's one of my oldest and best friends. I've known her since college and trust her with my life."

"Yeah and she's been in love with you since day one."

"Well at least someone is!"

"Okay, this is really getting us nowhere." Shannen sighed. "I'd hoped we could work on our marriage this weekend, but obviously that can't happen with you behaving like an irrational child, so I think you should stay, keep the car, and I'll call a service. Come back when you want, *if* you want!"

"Don't walk away from me!" Roger growled, grabbing Shannen around the waist, roughly ripping her blouse as he spun her around.

"Stop it, Roger!" she cried, terrified eyes wide in disbelief as he threw her like a rag doll onto the bed, his full weight on top of her, ignoring her desperate pleas. "Roger, stop! You're hurting me. Get off!"

"What? You only like your little *Mexican* screwing you now?"

Shannen gasped for air, smothered by Roger's unwanted and forceful beer-breath kisses as he reached down to unfasten her jeans, giving her enough opportunity to dislodge a knee and aim squarely for his groin.

"I'll kill you!" he threatened, doubled over moaning in pain as she sprang free, not wasting time, rushing to grab her bag.

"I swear, Roger, I don't know who you are anymore. I hate you! We're done!" she frantically screamed as she ran out the door.

Unhinged, Roger whispered, "We're done when I say we're done. And if I can't have you *no one* will."

CHAPTER 25

Tranquility Tudor

*T*hirteen hours, that's how long I slept, well past noon the next day. Unbelievable! My skin was so ashy I looked like I'd been rolled in flour, and my hair was a matted hot mess. The good news was the fog was finally lifting.

Since leaving *The Rich and the Ruthless* I'd been going through the motions, a toothpaste commercial here, a talk-show pilot there, but if the truth be told, ever since Ruby Stargazer fell off that dang yacht, it'd been me, Calysta Jeffries, treading water.

Burying my head into a brick the hospital called a pillow, I wished a psycho male nurse would slip into my room and plug me into a morphine drip so I could forget my overwhelming problems.

"Ms. Jeffries, you have a visitor," my nurse interrupted.

"Who is it?" I asked in a muffled voice, not bothering to look up.

If I had to see anyone I hoped it was Sly. We needed to talk about my daughter's custody.

"That'll be all, nurse." I knew that voice anywhere and pulled the blanket farther over my head. I could hear my overconfident, all-purpose agent/manager's expensive Italian shoes, which I no doubt paid for, clickety-clacking against the floor.

"Kitten," he said. "You look like a million bucks."

Ignoring his lie, I said, "Quit it, Weezi. You can't even see me and why are you here?"

"I'm acting as a family representative and escorting you to your temporary home in Malibu, and if you'd come out from under that blanket I'd like to—"

"Why didn't someone tell me I was leaving today for crissakes!" I interrupted, tearing the covers off my electricity-charged head.

"We tried. Couldn't wake you up."

"*Anyway*," I continued. "Who the hell is that?"

"Kelly Lava, Tranquility Tudor's celebrity sober coach and intake specialist. She's the designated driver so to speak."

"Are you friggin' crazy, bringing a stranger into my space, invading my privacy? I ain't goin' anywhere, Ms. Lava. Where I lay is where I stay, besides my doctor didn't say a doggone thing about me leaving St. John's today, so there," I announced, cutting my eyes at them both.

As if on cue, my physician, a Dr. Doug Ross lookalike, strode in to inform me, "Ms. Jeffries, you'll be officially discharged within the hour and placed into the professional and capable care of Tranquility Tudor, a reputable rehabilitation center. Good luck," he added before briskly walking out.

Didn't want to go back to an empty house any-o-way. Didn't have any pets, just one plant, but couldn't bear the thought of letting it die, a Bleeding Heart. It grew in Grandma Jones's backyard. I'd taken a pod before leaving Greenwood years earlier, repeated the same ritual when I fled to L.A. Couldn't ask my cleaning lady, Ifaka, to water it. I'd laid her off months ago, a luxury I could no longer afford.

"Fine, but I need to go home first to pack a few essentials: my detangler, my wide-tooth comb, my silk pillowcase, my do-rag, my Dax, my Crème de la Mer lotion, my tea tree toothpaste, my Massengill, my African Black soap, my Japanese loofah, my clay masque, stuff like that."

"I'm afraid that's not possible, Ms. Jeffries," the TT VIP staffer abruptly stated. "You heard the doctor. You've been court-ordered to commence treatment immediately once discharged from St. John's. No detours. No exceptions."

"It's for the best, Calysta," Weezi chimed in. "And don't worry about your stuff. Shannen's packin' away. What a friend."

"What are you talking about? She doesn't have keys to my house."

"She does now. I didn't want the bad press to get out of hand in case *R&R* ever wanted to invite you back, so I killed two birds with one stone and paid *the brass* a little visit. Good thing too. That P.R. nerd Needleman was a nervous wreck. Saw that Shannen bouncin' around while I was there—man, is she cute. She asked how you were and when I told her things were in the dumpster she didn't hesitate to get on board and help out."

"Weezi, where were you when you were sharing my life story with Shannen?"

"In the *R&R* office. Anyway I took the liberty of giving Dwayne Shannen's number. Oh, and I had to go through your purse to get your keys so he could get the rest of Ivy's things."

My skin crawled. It was bad enough that Weezi had weaseled his way onto the set and rifled through my purse but Dwayne in my house?

"So c'mon, Calysta, let's get you up and at 'em and make this the first day of your new sober life," Weezi said, walking out.

"Yeah, be right there, Dr. Phil."

With the help of a nurse and Ms. Lava, who looked like a butch ex-Marine, I got dressed.

As we all got on the elevator, looking like a motley crew, I worriedly asked Weezi, "Was there anyone else standing around?"

"Oh, yeah," he remembered. "As soon as Shannen left this slinky chick came outta nowhere, a real cougar. Said she was looking for new representation."

"Ohmagod, Weezi, what was her name?"

"Can't remember. There's so many people on that show."

"Try!"

"Okay, okay, take it easy already. Think she said Remy. Gave her my card. Gotta keep the business goin'. Don't worry, she's no competition."

I slumped deeper into the wheelchair and the next thing I knew I was being helped into the dreaded "We Do It One Day at a Time" van. I was mortified in every direction as Ms. Lava strapped me in and slammed the rolling door shut, before taking her place in the passenger seat adjacent to an enormous black driver. Wondering if this was the infamous *bottom* I'd heard about, I sobbed the whole way to Tranquility Tudor, realizing the wheels had definitely come off my wagon.

I was in desperate need of a drink and a Dramamine as we wound around and around up the side of a mountain for what seemed like an eternity. Weezi's incessant yammering on his cell phone was driving me and everyone else crazy when mercifully we arrived at two enormous gates, automatically parting to reveal a lush and palatial estate: a Mediterranean villa set against mountains dotted with California poppies and Alpine gold.

After we came to a stop, my motion sickness about to get the best of me, I was assisted over the pebbled piazza on liquid legs. The haunting cry of a hawk reminded me of fleeing the back porch of my childhood.

"Hello, Eunice," a man's voice said.

Eunice? I knew he wasn't talkin' to me.

"Weezi Abramowitz," came the reply, obnoxiously cutting in. "Calysta's representative and adviser. Thanks for helping me out with an alias for my client."

Now I *really* needed a drink.

"Pleasure. I'm Pat Quigley, founder and owner of Tranquility Tudor."

"Nice establishment you got here, real classy, top shelf. Nothin' but the best for my girl."

The director's face impressively covered his disapproval.

"Hello, Eunice, welcome to Tranquility Tudor," he began again.

I grunted something unintelligible, wishing I could give Weezi a piece of my mind.

"I hope you'll be comfortable here. Just let Kelly or myself know if you need anything and we'll do our very best to accommodate you." He smiled warmly before walking away.

The debonair rehab director must have had a past of his own. Somehow I couldn't believe this Sean Connery double was there out of the goodness of his heart; there had to be more to his humanity than running a sobriety clinic.

"Let's get you settled, Eunice. I understand you have badly bruised ribs," Kelly said, escorting me toward the villa, Weezi trailing behind.

Uniformed groundskeepers and kitchen staff scurried around unloading crates of fresh vegetables and other foodstuffs. The sprawling facility teetered precariously on the side of a cliff, and a huge chasm not unlike a moat lay between the rehab and the mountainside, making an escape into the wilderness virtually impossible.

A black sedan with tinted windows pulled into the tony compound and out bounded young, beautiful, rail-thin movie starlet Dolly Burke, covered head to toe in Isabel Marant, escorted by a TT sober coach.

As she breezed by in huge sunglasses, Weezi, unable to control himself, exclaimed, "Isn't that Dolly Burke?"

"Incorrigible," I muttered.

Kelly Lava whipped around. "Mr. Abramowitz, when you called Tranquility Tudor, I believe, six different times?"

Huh? I thought.

"Our staff thoroughly explained how our world-class ultra-exclusive facility is as much a program about anonymity as it is steeped in sobriety. If you can't show restraint we'll have to ban you from visiting the premises."

"Jeez, I'm sorry."

At the door, Kelly stepped between Weezi and me, handing him two sleek Tranquility Tudor folders and saying, "These are for any other clients you may have in need of our services. This is where you say good-bye, Mr. Abramowitz."

"But—"

"No buts. If you don't leave, you'll be trespassing. Rock!" she called.

Immediately, the TT van driver eclipsed Weezi, morphing into security. "Yeah man, gotta bounce."

"Okay, but if I could have another second with my client?"

Kelly arched an eyebrow then nodded.

"Hurry up," said Rock.

"Privately?"

"No," Kelly said, scowling.

"Okay, okay. Calysta, I hate to lay this on you right now, but I think you should consider selling your car . . . what's left of it, that is."

"My Jag?"

"Gas, insurance, a whole bunch of stuff. Plus, you're behind on a few bills."

"Thanks for puttin' me out on Front Street."

Couldn't believe he was asking me to give up one of the few things that gave me pleasure even though it was totaled. I'd worked damn hard for my '54 XK120 roadster, and now I'd have to sell it for parts? Never! I'd heard somethin' about all that surrenderin' mumbo-jumbo stuff but this was over the top. Still, I did have to ask myself, *you wanna live in a house or a crumpled car?*

"All right," I said reluctantly, too beat-up to fight back. "And while you're at it see what you can get for my emeralds."

Broke was not an option.

"Thatta girl. That's why we do business. You're stubborn but eventually listen to reason."

"Good-bye, Mr. Abramowitz," Kelly said pointedly, gesturing to a staffer. "Take Eunice to intake."

"Call me if you need anything, Calysta."

I was too pissed to turn around.

"Mr. Abramowitz! Her new name is Eunice," Kelly reminded him.

"Oh, yeah. Sorry. She's so not a Eunice. I'll get the hang of it though."

"If you secure more business for us, you'd receive an even bigger commission. And if *you* should ever need our services Mr. Quigley would extend a special discount."

"Cool!"

"No calls during the week and visitation is on Sunday, nine to three," she continued as Rock escorted Weezi to the van. "So as not to interrupt this vital rehabilitative process."

"But what if Calysta—I mean Eunice gets an audition?"

"Mr. Abramowitz, do you realize that if your client doesn't get the necessary treatment she needs there may be no next time?"

The van door slammed shut.

Concerned about the business transaction I thought I had just overheard, I shuffled through a side door and into the intake office. There I waited.

"Eunice, please have a seat," Kelly Lava said.

"When you stop callin' me that name. I don't need an alias."

"Fine. Suit yourself. Calysta, we need your credit card."

"What?"

"We need your credit card so we can complete processing."

"Wait a minute. How much is this place costin' me?"

"Didn't Mr. Abramowitz tell you?"

"No. How much?"

"Thirty-six thousand for six weeks."

"*Thirty-six thousand bucks?* Have you people gone and lost your minds? You better look like turnin' that druggy buggy around, I ain't stayin' nowhere for thirty-six K."

"Ms. Jeffries, need I remind you, you have been court-ordered? If you'd like to leave we can make arrangements for the sheriff to pick you up and escort you to jail, that's free. Furthermore, this isn't an outpatient facility. You'll be receiving equine therapy, top-notch medical attention, nutritionist, hypnosis, psychotherapy, Pilates, yoga, massage and spa privileges, shopping excursions, gourmet meals, and much, much more."

Hmm. That didn't sound too bad, actually.

I sat back down and handed over my AmEx Centurion, thinkin', *All this over two Xanax and a split of champs.* After payment, I was met by a voluptuous nurse whose uniform was unbuttoned one too many. She took my vitals, noticing my blood pressure was high, and administered a Klonopin.

Good, more sleep.

Shockingly, she took a Polaroid.

"What the hell is that for—blackmail? I paid in full."

"It's for our files. Don't worry, it's all confidential."

"Better be."

Kelly Lava stepped in. "Okay, Calysta, let's get you to your room."

The hallway walls were appointed with the 12 Steps like Stations of the Cross. Shuffling into the room I was horrified to see two adult-size Princess Barbie canopy beds with matching gold-speckled vanities. My bed was adorned with crystals, dream catchers, and an assortment of ruffled throw pillows.

"Are you kiddin'? I'm sharing a Barbie playset for thirty-six thousand dollars?"

"Calysta, if you're going to make any progress here you have to leave your ego at the door. And by the way, this is one of our premium suites. We've paired you up with Gretchen Gibson, who's been here for three months and is one of our model clients, to be a sort of mentor for you, show you the ropes. Now, you've just taken a Klonopin and you need to rest. We'll wake you for supper where you'll meet the TT *family.*" Kelly walked out, closing the door behind her.

The family? They better not slip me any Jim Jones juice while I'm here, I thought as I climbed into my toy bed.

The last thing I saw before falling asleep was the Serenity Prayer embroidered in big gold letters above me on the inside of the canopy. I began reciting, "God grant me the serenity to accept the things I cannot change, the courage to change the things I can andthewisdomto . . ."

CHAPTER 26

Dressing Room Rehearsal

*E*ntangled in a steamy embrace to the pulsing beat of Esperanza Spalding's "Samba em Prelúdio," heightened with a few drops of Spanish fly, Javier's body pressed Shannen's into the cushions of her dressing room sofa. It took her a few moments to hear her phone vibrating on the vanity.

"Mmph, Javier. Javier, I need to get my phone."

Method acting, her amorous lover responded with several kisses along her neck. They had been rehearsing a scripted love scene for an upcoming episode of *The Rich and the Ruthless.*

"Mmmm, no really, it could be important."

Shannen wiggled out from under Javier and grabbed the phone before it went to voice mail, quickly checking to see that it wasn't her husband. He'd been stalking her via cell since Big Bear and it was Hannibal

Lecter creepy. Calling randomly, breathing in her ear like a perverted crank caller.

Sometimes Shannen felt guilty about giving in to Javier's advances before she was actually divorced, but Roger's increasingly psychotic behavior, not to mention Javier's smoldering prowess, always allayed those feelings. It wasn't Roger, though, it was Calysta's pestering agent.

"Weezi?" Her voice was still breathless.

"Hey, Princess, how ya doin'?"

"Fine."

"Yes you are."

Rolling her eyes at his overly familiar comment, she knew he was fishin' for her commission, and was annoyed as hell that he'd interrupted her rehearsal with Javier, and how dare he not once mention Calysta.

Javier crossed over and slipped his arms around her itty bitty waist, nibbling on her ear, providing distraction as Shannen asked, "How's Calysta?"

"Excellent. Just dropped her off and it's swank; she loves it. Saw that starlet Dolly Burke out there too. But never mind all that, just wanted to remind you to drop off Calysta's stuff today and, you know, say hi."

"Mmm-hmm, I called her grandmother, Mrs. Jones . . . stop, honey."

"What's that?" asked Weezi hopefully.

"Nothing. I was saying Mrs. Jones is heading out by bus tomorrow, wouldn't let me get her a plane ticket."

"That's great, kid, everything's great."

"I was, uh, in the middle of running lines?"

"Oh, right. I'm sorry, pussycat."

"No worries. Already have Calysta's stuff in my car."

"You're such a pro. Love that you rehearse and everything. Probably have to leave the bags with security; there's a dragon out there running things. But no hurry, you're a gem to do it."

Shannen grimaced at his smarm, then with faux cheer said, "Oh, it's no trouble at all. I'd do anything for Calysta." She rushed on before he could add anything, "Thanks for calling. Bye!" She hung up on his *"Ciao, bella!"*

Swatting Javier's hands away to free herself, she whispered, "Baby, I have to go," grabbing her crumpled clothes from the floor.

"No go. Stay. More rehearsal," he said suggestively in an Antonio Banderas accent that weakened her knees, but she stood firm.

"I think we've nailed that scene." She smiled as she pulled her T-shirt over her head.

"Come, my *palomita*," he pleaded, kissing her hand and pulling her down onto the couch. "Have *comida* with me."

"I can't, I have to do something super important and super confidential, Javier."

He didn't inquire what that was, trying to suck her toes.

"Okay I'll tell you . . . and that tickles! Not a word to anyone. Calysta's checked into a rehab in Malibu."

"You bring my sexy back."

"Javier! Did you hear what I said?"

"You make me *caliente*."

"Okay, I really have to go."

Shannen jumped up, grabbed her purse, and left the room before being sidetracked, not noticing the hidden camera light blinking from the air vent.

CHAPTER 27

It Works If You Work It

By the light of a sole fringed lamp, I made out the silhouetted profile of my super-enhanced roommate, poured into skin-tight liquid pants and a tiny tank top that showed off her glittering diamond navel piercing.

Bleary-eyed, I noticed my luggage had magically appeared at the foot of the bed.

"Hi, my name is Gretchen," she chirped. Teased-out tresses framed what some might regard as circus makeup. "Time to get up, honey, it's dinner and we can't be late."

She helped me with my robe and slippers and I shuffled down the hallway to the table, where four strange pairs of eyes stared back at me. The fifth pair of this little "family" I already knew. It was coked-out, oversexed teen heartthrob Toby Gorman, my potential TV son-in-law from *the soap*. Ugh.

"Ohmagod, Calysta! What are you doing here? You too? Everybody, everybody, this is Calysta Jeffries! My future mother-in-law on *The Rich and the Ruthless*!"

"Hello, Calysta," everyone chorused, before holding hands to say grace.

As the lavish gourmet dishes were passed around, the residents introduced themselves, though most needed no introduction.

"Hello, Calysta, my name is Erroll." Erroll Cockfield was the legendary director Weezi had told me about. Also at the table was Dylan Finch, a popular heavy metal musician covered in tattoos and several piercings, and of course Dolly Burke, notoriously troubled Hollywood starlet who was as famous for crashing her car into tall inanimate objects as she was for her family-friendly blockbuster films.

Ambling through the door, Kelly Lava escorted yet another poor soul, an athlete of the football variety, into the intake office.

"Two more will check in tomorrow," Gretchen whispered. "There's usually ten at a time."

Man this is some racket, $36,000 times ten residents, every six weeks? Not bad. Maybe I'm in the wrong business.

"Calysta, do you want any?" Chad Brodure, a famous politician who I later found out was there for a gambling addiction, held out a dish of coq au vin.

I ate every bit of it hoping to get a tiny buzz from the extra helping of sherry sauce. As I dabbed the corners of my mouth with my linen napkin, Kelly Lava informed me, "Alcohol burns off, Calysta. You have dish duty."

"What?"

"Yeah, Calysta, you and me have dishes!" Gretchen chimed in. "Dolly clears the table, you wash, I dry, Chad puts them away, Erroll sweeps, and Toby and Dylan set up the coffee and dessert and light the fire for our bedtime sobriety share."

I feebly pushed away from the table and walked into the state-of-the-art stainless steel kitchen. "And why aren't we using the dishwasher?"

"Discipline," Kelly said.

As I ran the hot water, bad Greenwood, Mississippi, memories washing over me, I looked out the wide picture window and began planning my escape.

Gretchen was the appointed group leader of the evening meetings, pointing out how delicious the espresso and profiteroles were. Finally, the last person was introducing herself.

"Hi, my name is Dolly and I'm a druggie."

"Hi, Dolly," everyone sang in unison.

"Group, as you know we have a new member to add to our TT family and she'd like to introduce herself."

I would?

Gretchen looked at me expectantly.

It was the last thing I wanted to do.

"Calysta?"

"Nope."

"She's a little shy. Maybe tomorrow then."

Staring into the crackling fire, I sat in the corner of the overstuffed couch, listening to all the sensational *shares,* one topping the next, in disbelief that my life had spiraled this far out of control.

Once the hour-long meeting was over, and two grown men were in tears after explaining the unfortunate events that transpired with either business associates and/or family members while attempting to *make amends*, we all stood up and formed a circle. I listened as the others recited a memorized mantra that ended with, "It works if you *work* it."

Peeling off, I beelined it for my room followed by "Sweet dreams, Calysta," "Don't let the bedbugs bite," *"Bon soir, cherie"* from several of the glossy residents, as they went outside for a smoke.

"Don't forget, tomorrow's collage therapy. I'll be waking you bright and early at seven a.m. sharp, and make sure you read at least one chapter out of the Big Book before you fall sleep. I recommend 'My Bottle, My Resentments, and Me,' it's one of my favorites. And don't worry, I'll help you find a sponsor at one of our off-campus meetings too. I know everybody. TT always gets the best reserved seating," Gretchen added before lighting up a cigarette and walking outside to the blazing fire pit.

Ugh, they paired me with a sobriety zealot, and I thought Weezi said I was going to get some rest.

CHAPTER 28

Just Cut Your Pain Right on Out

After a sumptuous breakfast of freshly squeezed orange-mango juice, johnnycakes and sorghum, crawfish beignets, free-range poached eggs, and roast bacon, I knew I was gonna have to spend some quality time at TT's state-of-the-art gym if I didn't want to turn into a Chunk-a-Munka.

We all obediently did our designated chores before walking down to a shingled outbuilding and into the activity room for collage therapy. In large Times Roman lettering its sign read, Art Saves Lives.

Set up on a series of banquet tables with folding metal chairs on either side, there were bins of magazines, beads, ribbons, stickers, stamps, glitter, yarn, fabric and felt patches, and various other arts and crafts supplies, placed intermittently along the tables with baskets of Elmer's glue and safety scissors in between, an elementary schoolchild's paradise.

The art therapy teacher was a mellow black woman with long blond dreads. She introduced herself as Zima and encouraged us to check out her art, frequently showcased at the local health food store.

"Now class," she said, as though we were five, "today the focus of our collage is pain. I want you to feel free to take as many of these magazines as you wish, cut your pain right on out, and paste it on the foam board in front of you; a catharsis if you will. I want you to break off in pairs and make a conscientious effort to collaborate on this one, feel each other's distress. Addiction is a disease that makes one feel completely isolated. So, I want us all to focus on our teamwork skills."

"But Zima, didn't I hear Alcoholics Anonymous should be a selfish program?" Toby piped in.

"Yes . . . but this is different. So, since we only have one hour for art let's get down to business and leave the Big Book discovery reading for later. Everyone find a partner!"

"Hey, Calysta," Toby enthusiastically invited, "let's pair up!"

"All right, sure, I'll be back in a sec," I tossed, heading toward Pat Quigley, not thrilled since he'd blown my cover at dinner, but it was better than *chine collé*-ing it with Gretchen, who had proudly completed thirteen of the collage-catharsis boards.

As Pat poked his head in to make sure things were running smoothly I thought it might be a good opportunity to have a much-needed chat with him about my sleeping arrangement.

"Mr. Quigley, may I have a word?" I whispered *sotto voce*. "You said to come to you about anything."

"Yes of course, Calysta. What is it?"

"I appreciate and understand why you paired me with Gretchen, I really do, but—"

"C'mon Calysta, I need your help," Toby yelled out.

"Be right there," I replied with a forced smile before turning back. "You do realize she suffers from sleep apnea and that contraption is *so* loud?"

"Yes, it's been a problem in the past with other clients."

Hold up. Did he just say other clients?

"So, I was wondering if I could get a different room or roommate?"

"I'm afraid not. We took in three new clients since yesterday and we're at capacity. Why don't you look at this as an opportunity to exercise tolerance and acceptance?"

Nodding my head, I began chewing the fatty flesh on the inside of my cheek. Turning on my heels, I flip-flopped it back to the craft table and slid into my chair beside Toby. Erroll and his collage partner Chad were seated across from us.

"Hey, Calysta," Toby cheerfully greeted as he dexterously cut a marijuana leaf out of a *Rolling Stone*. "So glad you're here too. Always kinda thought of you as a mom, you know? Now that I think of it, isn't this what they call 'art imitating life'? Or is it 'life imitating art'? I don't know, whatever, we're here together. Isn't it cool?"

"Cool doesn't really come to mind."

"That's true, I guess. I did get in trouble last night."

"Why?" I asked, half-interested, flipping idly through a *Glamour* magazine.

"It was me and Dolly. She's so dope. We snuck out and went skinny-dipping in the pool around midnight; dude her tits are *so* big. Too bad we got totally busted. Now we've got extra bathroom duty for a week! They are *so strict* at this one."

"This one? Where else have you been?"

"Downey Jr.'s place. Dude, I had so much fun there, the girls were way hotter. They finally kicked me out, though. Oh yeah, and after Hazelden my parents got really pissed and did something radical, sending me to, and don't tell anyone, the Scientology rehab Narconon. Dude, there were more stars there than at the People's Choice Awards, couldn't believe it! But I got kicked out for smoking weed. Don't remember after that, but I've been in at least five different spots so far."

"So far? Since the Sudsys?" I was shocked, even if it *was* Toby.

"Yeah. Check *this* out," he said, sliding an open *Vanity Fair* toward me, pointing at a picture of what looked like an orgy in a bubble bath. "I gotta cut this out for my collage. Talk about recall! This club Amnesia in New York was one of my favorite hangouts. Man, did I have fun. I was up for three days straight there and ended up crashing in a 7-Eleven bathroom. I was so wasted; the police came, an ambulance, and everything. My parents even flew in from the Caribbean to bail me out." He shook his head, smiling at the memory.

Blinking slowly, I said, "Your parents must really care about you."

"Yeah, cool, huh? And they're divorced!"

"Yeah, cool."

"Ever since then they're always talking about me on *Cliffhanger Weekly*'s gossip page," Toby barreled on. "How I'm coming back to the show all the time. You know they're just pimpin' my fame to get my fanatical fans to buy their mags. Speaking of fans, Needleman tells me *R&R* had to use spillover for all my mail, but I never answer the stuff. I like to keep the base frothin' for more of the Toby-meister."

"Mm-hm."

"Yeah, I treat 'em like crap and they love me for it, especially the girls, it's amazing. Dude, I'm such a friggin' catch. I tell the babes not to call after eleven on Tuesdays and Thursdays; those are my nights off. I've got them *so* trained. But then again, I learned from the best."

"Who's that?"

"My man Derrick."

"Really?"

"Hey, Zima, gotta whiz like a racehorse."

"Go 'head. Keep the door open."

"Be right back, Calysta."

"Can't wait," I said dryly.

Erroll caught my eye and rolled his. Leaning forward, he said, "Poor you, working with that kid," under his breath.

"It was brief," I whispered. Half-amusing myself, I thought, *Maybe*

Weezi was right. If I could win over a big film director, my time in this place would be worth the investment.

"Calysta, right?"

"Right."

"Nice name."

"Thanks."

"Fairly new to Hollywood?"

"No, actually I've been in L.A. for fifteen years."

"You're kidding? How old are you?"

I went back to cutting out an ad for Moët.

"What have you been in, Calysta? I mean besides that show Toby mentioned?"

Holding on to politeness, I gave a stiff smile as I thought, *Can't believe after 3,120* R&R *episodes and more than two million words memorized I'm still a fresh face.*

Lifting my chin, I said, "I've been in several successful projects on stage and screen like *The Refined Politician* and *Dumb Bell.*"

"I must have missed those films."

"Maybe you saw me on cable. I was the face for 'Tweeze-it.'"

"No, I missed that too."

"The Butt-Blaster?"

"Afraid not."

"I was the lead in *Impatient Virgin* and *Purrr-fectly Eartha,* ran briefly in New York."

Returning to his foam board, Erroll said, "Guess I can't know everyone, but I'm surprised I missed that last production since I'm an avid theatergoer."

Glancing down, I noticed he'd cut and pasted an assortment of young blond actresses; noticeably, many of them were of the same ingénue. I cocked my head for a better peek; she seemed familiar though I couldn't quite put my finger on it.

Erroll grimaced, stabbing the photo with his index. "This broad.

This broad right here is the cause of all my pain. Stupid starlet was in *my* movie, a sixty-million-dollar Russell Crowe studio film I was directing. Took me fifteen years to get this friggin' picture on its feet. Little bitch couldn't remember her lines to save her life. Could-not-remember-her-lines," he ranted, raising his voice.

"Shhhh," Zima said as she wandered around the room gently plucking her kalimba, "let's keep it to a whisper. We only have twenty minutes left, so think about wrapping up your pain projects. I have to go check on Toby."

"She screwed up every bloody scene," Erroll ranted on. "We taped her lines on props, the fruit she was about to eat, on the floor, we tried everything! I thought maybe she couldn't read. Russell was so patient with her. But I lost my temper and had a Christian Bale meltdown. Someone filmed it, played it all over YouTube. Absolutely killed my career. Couldn't stop drinking."

"Wow, that's rough," I fake-sympathized.

"You don't know the half," he continued. "Mick even offered me a stay on his island but I was isolating and couldn't get on the friggin' jet. Damn casting directors! That bimbo had an absolute *shmuck* agent who kept reassuring me she'd shape up any day and that he got her an acting coach, turns out *he* was the friggin' coach. It was one disaster after another. Found out he doesn't even have a license to operate; a complete fraud. I wanted to sue but my attorney told me, 'Don't waste your money.'"

I knew he was talking about Weezi and was spared thinking up a response other than "Bummer," thanks to Toby returning to his seat.

"Sorry, Calysta, had the runs."

"TMI," I said, looking down at his hands then back at him.

"Oh man, I forgot. Be right back."

Gretchen was cutting into a *Soap Suds Digest* featuring the headline "Rich and the Ruthless Megashocker: Calysta Jeffries Is Out and Vivica A. Fox Is In."

My pulse surged.

"Gretchen, may I see that magazine before you cut any more?" I choked out.

"Don't you have enough magazines down there?"

In a staccato voice, I said, "It's just . . . there's something . . . on the front . . . I need . . . to read."

Pursing her lips, she said, "Okay, I guess," tossing it down the table. "But make it snappy. I want to finish my collage in time. There's a picture of Shelly Montenegro in there from *The Daring and the Damned* screaming that perfectly captures my inner suffering. I just love her."

Trying to quell my shaking hands, I flipped through the magazine until I found the article. It was short but deadly.

Execs at *The Rich and the Ruthless* confirmed today that Ruby Stargazer will be finding her way to shore soon, and none other than film star Vivica A. Fox has been hired to replace popular bubbler Calysta Jeffries. Co-Executive Producer Randall Roberts said, "Vivica has signed a six-week contract to come on as Ruby Stargazer to tie up some loose story ends. The WBC and *The Rich and the Ruthless* are thrilled with the casting. I know she'll make a wonderful addition to our #1 daytime show." *R&R* cast members were all smiles, as well. "I just adore Vivica," says Emmy Abernathy. "She's the best! A real pro." Jade, who plays Ruby's daughter, had this to say, "Like wow, we totally resemble!" It's unclear how Calysta Jeffries's many fans will react to this potential upset, but Ms. Fox assured us, "I love Calysta, we go way back. I know she won't mind if I take a stab at the role."

In disbelief, I read it three times. There was a picture beside it of Vivica, Ethan Walker clutching her, planting a kiss on her cheek.

My heart pumped. *Take a stab at the role? A real pro? A wonderful addition to the team?* How could they do this to me? I could forgive Vivica, since roles for black actresses were slim to none in Hollywood. But now I knew exactly what Dell Williams had meant when she said, "Honey, the suction sound you hear walking back to your dressing room will be nothin' but you pullin' those knives out your back."

The last straw was when I read on further that *R&R* was building Viv a new set.

"A *new* Ruby Stargazer set?" I screamed out loud, rising to my feet. "I stood in that dinky excuse of a living room and kitchenette for fifteen years, acting my ass off making it look like the Hearst *friggin'* Castle, chowin' down on plastic artichokes like they were gourmet Rachael Ray, and this is the thanks I get?"

I ripped the pages out of the magazine, tearing them to shreds before collapsing in my chair, hysterical.

"My *Digest*!" Gretchen hiccuped.

"Heavens, Calysta, calm down. What's all this about?" Erroll exclaimed, coming around the table to pat my hand.

"I know what's wrong," Toby said with a knowing look, wrapping his scrawny arm around my hot shoulders.

It was a few moments before I could get any words out and when I did they were, "*R&R*. Replacing? Ruby. Viv?" Toby was the only one who understood my cryptic gibbering, giving me a reassuring squeeze.

"Aw, Calysta, forget the soaps! You're bigger than them. Look at me, when I bounce outta here I have multiple offers to consider."

I sobbed louder.

By now everyone was standing around me offering words of comfort, except for Dolly, who sat snipping away at a picture of a rival starlet, hundreds of cuttings lying in front of her, clearly high on something.

"Okay, everyone," Zima's voice called out as she hung up her phone,

"I need you all to calm down and take your seats, I'll take care of Calysta." She clapped her hands, causing her bangles to chime, shooing everyone away.

Holding me firmly by the arm, she steered me into her office, shutting the door behind us.

I knew I needed to get a grip but a dam had broken. I was exorcising my pain, all right.

"Breathe, Calysta," Zima instructed. "Breathe in. Breathe out. Did someone say something to upset you?"

Still hyperventilating, I said, "Nooo. Hhhh . . . I'vvve . . . been . . . reeecaaast!"

"Excuse me?" Zima clearly didn't know who I was. In fact, she didn't know who any of us were. She only listened to NPR and watched heady programming like Link and Ovation.

"On my soap! Those bastards are recasting me!"

"Okay, Calysta, let's calm down. I think I understand what's causing your reaction, but whatever you did on TV doesn't really matter in the here and the now. We are in search of the truth. The present. The real."

"But I'm Ruby Stargazer! I created that character! Everything I do matters!"

Zima gave me a stern BML (black mamma look), the kind that reminded me of Grandma Jones. "If you don't calm down I'm going to send you back to your room."

Swallowing hard, embarrassed by my diva behavior, I said, "You know what? I think that'd be best."

"Fine then. But you'll have to make up your collage session. And I'll be reporting this to Kelly."

"Oh come on, Zima, between us sistahs can't you let this one slide?"

"'Us sistahs'? 'Let this one slide'? This ain't about you. Do you think just 'cause I'm black I'd risk *my* sobriety? *My* integrity? *My* spiritual foundation? My *job*, to cover for your ass? You have gone and lost your mind, girl. 'Cause the last time I did that I paid dearly for it."

I looked into Zima's midnight eyes and couldn't believe she'd gone from a Topanga Canyon hippie to a Chicago South Side gangsta in ten seconds flat.

"That's right, wasn't always a self-taught painter and collage therapist. See, I helped out one of my *sistahs* from the hood back in the day and I was the *dummy* who ended up holdin' the bag, literally. That's right, she talked me into robbing a dang bank to pay for our crack habit. Next thing I knew I was in a shared prison cell at Women's Reentry Center in cold-ass Maine lookin' out at freedom. And my *sistah-girlfriend* nevah came to visit me while I was doin' time either, not once. I don't break rules no more, you dig? I enforce 'em," she asserted, rockin' her head from side to side, dangly cowrie shell earrings brushing the sides of her neck. Zima continued, pursing her lips, "It's all about the KISS."

"Huh?"

"Keep It Simple, Stupid."

Put in check, I dragged my sorry butt back to the TT big house numb, digesting Zima's sobering message. You just never knew what someone else's bottom was or what they'd been luggin' around. Really didn't care for the journaling jazz all that much, but this was something I couldn't wait to write about.

Kelly Lava kept that from happening. Holding up a halting hand, she barked, "Calysta. I've just been notified about your disruptive episode in collage therapy. You'll have to do a double session with Zima next week and I think it would be best if you shared at tonight's off-site AA meeting. You clearly need to."

"Okay," I said dully.

"Also, I checked beds this morning and yours wasn't made up properly."

"Huh? I made my bed before breakfast."

"Military corners, Calysta. I took the bed apart so you can do it right. And remember, you need to be in the van no later than five o'clock sharp for the meeting. You'll want a good seat up front. As for our alum meeting tomorrow, be primped and prompt. TT always has a powerful speaker and I hope you get something out of it. I've been sober for eleven years and I still learn something new," she said with an air of superiority, resting her thumbs behind her oversize turquoise triangle belt buckle. Walking several steps away before stopping, she pivoted around, saying, "I forgot to give this to you the other day."

"Thanks." I took the already-opened envelope from her icy hand, heading to my room.

> *Hey, Calysta,*
>
> *Hope you're hanging in there, sweetie. Just wanted to let you know that I'm picking up your Grandma Jones this Saturday at the Hollywood Greyhound station. She's staying with me so don't worry for a sec. We'll be there on Sunday, bright and early, promise. Chin up. Fern secretly told me there's bags of fan mail for you in the WBC mailroom. I'll bring some when I visit. See you soon.*
>
>

xoxo,

Shannen
>

While my friend's note was comforting, I missed Ivy so much it hurt. And the thought of Grandma Jones seeing me in rehab was more than I could bear. All I could think about was how disappointed she must be in me. Unable to stem my tears, I let them flow.

CHAPTER 29

Sibling Rivalry

*A*uggie, the vote is *next week* and you keep canceling meetings with Mom and me! I can't *believe* you didn't fly out to Baltimore to visit Dad," Veronica fumed. "We're back home now so there's no excuse. And don't tell me you were too busy working, either. I checked the Burbank flight records, there's no business in Scottsdale."

"Okay, Nancy Drew, you caught me, now would you stop being such a nudge?" Auggie agitatedly paced. "I don't need to go to any meetings 'cause there's nothing to discuss. It's the twenty-first century, Dad's in the Stone Age, and selling is for the best."

"Best for whom?" Veronica tersely asked.

"Ronnie, don't be shortsighted. We gotta strike while the iron's hot. The WBC has an offer worth millions on the table for both shows; we'd be fools to pass it up. Plus, as an added incentive they'll cut us in on a percentage of foreign, which is more than they do for those idiot actors. The only one who was getting wise to it was Wolfe but we paid him off. Mom's putty in my hands. I can get her to change her mind. And as much as Dad's disappointed in me for flunking out of Duke, you don't need a college degree to figure this one out. Besides, who needs college when you're rich? Jobs are for losers. This is a dying industry, I say we jump ship before it sinks and untangle ourselves from those whiners. Let's face it, most of 'em should be working for Andy Gump or Homeland Security. Only one I ever cared for was that sexy Shannen Lassiter, now, she's good. The rest of those bums, if it weren't for Dad, couldn't get arrested in this town. Besides, I want to get into nightclub promotion or Formula One racing."

"Over my dead body will you sell Dad's legacy. I'll fight you *tooth and nail* now that my suspicions have been confirmed."

"Give me a break. You expect me to believe my baby sister, the one who cried if she broke a nail, *really* cares about the family business? Last I checked you and Mom were on your way to Milan for fashion week." He sneered. "You have no idea what it takes to run this operation. That's why Dad's got one foot in the grave right now. We've lived a whole different life, sis. We didn't inherit Mom's wealth and Dad's empire to be slaves to it. Dad wants us to live the privileged life we were born into. I have no intention of sitting up in his office taking meetings with that shmuck Randall, that lesbo Edith, and that hack Felicia. Dad knew how to work hard, growing up poor, but that's not our cross to bear. I'm rich and I'm ruthless—"

"You're disgusting is what you are. And I'm leaving. Consider yourself notified, the vote is next Wednesday; be there. We'll see how cocky you are once Calysta has her say."

"Must be that time of the mon—Calysta?"

"You heard me. Dad made her his proxy while he was in the hospital; she has the deciding vote. And I doubt she's your biggest fan."

"You're really reaching, Ronnie, if you expect me to believe that bull. I may have had my differences with Mom and Dad over the years, maybe they had to bail me out of jail once or twice for those DUIs, and I'm sure you want to throw those meaningless flings with Emmy and Jade in my face, and that one pregnancy, but let me remind you I'm Augustus Barringer the Third, heir apparent. Dad definitely would have discussed this proxy stuff with me first."

"Oh noble and powerful big brother, how wrong you are." She swept her Prada purse off the mahogany desk and faced him. "But hey, if you think I'm bluffing come see for yourself next week. What? Not going to open the door for your sister? Don't tell me you're letting our differences kill good breeding, even if you don't use it very often."

Auggie opened the door in thorny silence.

Veronica strode out of their father's corner office, leaving her brother tilted. He immediately picked up the phone.

"Hello?"

"It's Auggie. We need a face-to-face. Might have a *little problem*."

Edith forced herself to say through gritted teeth, "Sure, whatever you need, Auggie, but what's this *little problem* about?"

"Just be at Burbank airport at eleven."

"That doesn't give me much time. I have to—"

The phone went dead.

Three hours later, on his second hole of golf, Auggie's femme "caddies" Ginger and Sparkle attended to his every need as Edith, never having golfed in her life, stiffly walked across the green in her perfect ecru Nancy Lopez golf outfit, on a mission.

"Could've saved yourself a lot of trouble and used a golf cart," Auggie joked, his Ray-Bans dangling by an arm out of the corner of his mouth.

"Love walking, don't do enough of it in L.A." She was still smarting from the way Auggie dismissed her the moment she boarded the Barringer jet.

The horny heir apparent had disappeared into a back bedroom with his playmates for a private "golf lesson," never emerging until they landed. Feeling hijacked, furious that she was at the mercy of a moronic party boy until the soaps were hers, Edith had endured the high-pitched giggles and outrageous banter as she tried to focus on reading about the ripple effect the financial tsunami was having on daytime in the business section of the *Los Angeles Times*.

"Is this the nine iron?" Ginger asked now.

"No," Auggie corrected, "it's the driver, the wood."

"Wow. The *head* on this one is so big," Sparkle marveled.

"Yeah, the face is the area where you make contact with the ball," Auggie lectured. "And don't forget to check out the size of a club to hit that ideal sweet spot right in the middle."

"See, Ginger, size does matter." Sparkle giggled.

"Auggie, I'd *really* like to know what this is all about," Edith began, wringing her hands. "I couldn't help but notice you were preoccupied with your 'companions' on the plane. And that turbulence—"

"That wasn't turbulence," giggled Ginger.

"Wow, is this like your mom, Auggie?" asked Sparkle.

"I beg your pardon?"

"Just ignore them, Edie," Auggie said, sliding his sunglasses back on.

Her face tight, she asked, "Would you tell me what's going on?"

"The thing is, Ronnie and I had a fight this morning at the studio. She told me Dad made Calysta his proxy. Can you believe that?"

"Wanna Corona?" Ginger asked Edith.

Snubbing the bimbette, Edith said, "Don't tell me."

"She has the deciding vote at our family business meeting next week! Whether or not WBC gets control of the soaps."

"Calysta Jeffries has the deciding vote? When did that happen?"

"Just. Allegedly," he quickly added. "Still think my sister's pulling my leg. Don't see how Dad could've done something this moronic behind my back."

"Auggie, you don't see a lot of things," Edith said sharply. "I knew it was a mistake for you to ignore what Augustus was up to all these months. But you were too busy at that regatta in St. Barts."

"Dad's been sick forever, in the hospital, and is still on some kind of a drip at home, how much could he have been up to? Look, Veronica was probably bluffing, hoping I'd back down. She doesn't know *me* as well as I know *her*. Don't worry about it, Edie, I just wanted you to know what she said on the off chance it was true."

"And if it is, what's your B-plan?"

"Um, well then we talk to Calysta, right? Cut her in for a quarter mill, she'll be stoked and vote our way. You know, grew up dirt-poor . . . shit like that. My dad worked her real-life drama into her Stargazer storyline, real popular with the fans but everybody on the show hates her. Heard she had a breakdown or something and is at some rehab. She could probably use the cash. Plus I think she has a kid."

Edith glared at him, clenching her jaw. "I think I have a better understanding of Calysta Jeffries than you do. That nervy bitch is a troublemaker and she has some twisted loyalty to your father. Even with her misfortune I doubt very much she'll be an easy sell. You have no idea the balls I'm juggling in this chaotic financial climate. Unless *you* want to go talk to her yourself . . . ?"

"Naw, that's okay," Auggie scoffed. "I got balls of my own in the air."

"Is it time for your *driver* yet, Auggie?" Ginger purred, holding the club suggestively.

"I'm bored," Sparkle chimed in rereading an old Tiger text. "Let's go back to our suite."

Shooting daggers at the girls, Edith said, "I suggest we prioritize and pull Randall in now. He's such a power-hungry idiot he'll do anything to ensure the sale. We give him the right motivation, I'm sure he'll deliver. And when he secures Calysta's vote I'll reward him with control of *both* shows."

"*Both* shows? Really?"

"What do you care? You'll be long gone with Ginger and Sparkle."

"True."

"And if Randall doesn't succeed," she continued, fishing her phone out of her purse, "he's out on his ass. He can look for a job as show runner for *Barney* for all I care but he'll have absolutely no future with the WBC. That should light the proper fire under his ass."

"Cool with me." Auggie sighed.

She dialed, then snapped, "Fern, get me Randall now!"

"But how do you expect him to get her vote? Calysta hates him."

"I don't care *what* he has to do," Edith said dry-ice cold, "as long as it gets results."

Hey kids, I know you've all been worried sick about one of daytime's fave soap stars and that rumored revolving door; for good reason. And although The Diva has been splattered all over the Twitterverse and the tabloids (I'm still not mentioning names, suffering from selective amnesia) it's rumored that more than one of our bubblers are holed up in a posh celebrity sobriety mansion, spillin' their guts. If only we could all be there to "share." But wait! Seems I'm already too late, a known hater could be unfolding a deliberate Facebook firestorm in the very near future, revealing tawdry, sordid, and unspeakable secrets. Stay tuned!

The Diva

CHAPTER 30

Getting Even

*A*wakened by the cracking shrill of Gretchen warbling Barbra Streisand's "People, people who need people, are the luckiest people in the world," I couldn't have been unluckier as I played possum, spying my roommate, earphones and an MP3 player attached to her hip, oblivious to the world.

As I tried in vain to catch a few last precious Z's before sobriety boot camp began, the fragrant scent of fresh-brewed coffee, grilling rosemary sausage, and corn bread softened my reality. Through squinting eyes, I witnessed Gretchen in a high-sheen-pink-leopard-print-low-cut-dress and heels. Already in full makeup, she was sitting at her portable high-powered vanity mirror, Farrah Fawcett-ing her hair with a curling iron and singing, "No more hunger or thirst. But first be a person who needs people . . ."

Unable to take the Chinese water torture one second longer, I interrupted with a loud, exaggerated stretching yawn.

"Wow, you're such a deep sleeper," Gretchen remarked, pulling her earphones out.

"Yeah, once I *get* to sleep . . ." I replied, rubbing my eyes. "What's the occasion? Today your psych appointment?"

"No, silly, tonight's the alum meeting!"

"It's Friday already?"

"Yeah, and it's the most exciting day of the week here at TT. People come out of the woodwork for this meeting. Because it's a program of anonymity I can't tell you who the guests might be so don't ask, but lemme tell you, it's one long red carpet, just like going to the Oscars."

I couldn't believe this bored, rich housewife who'd *slipped* at least a dozen times on OxyContin had probably been up since six a.m. primping for an AA meeting.

"Why are you getting ready *now* when the meeting's tonight?"

"Because of the zinger of a day we have! There's our in-house meeting, hypnotherapy, lunch, nap, Big Book Study, role play discovery, snack, journaling and meditation at the Zen garden, and then our five-kilometer oceanside ride along the PCH bike path."

"All in your dress?" I asked incredulously.

"Well *yeah*, by the time we get back it'll be five, then we have dinner and you and I have *set-up* duty, we're serving crudités and green tea magic bars for dessert, my favorite! It takes me at least two hours to get ready, there just won't be enough time if I don't prepare now."

Leaning on my elbow, I rested my heavy head on my fist, utterly exhausted by the time she finished laying out the day's plan.

"Toodle-oo, see you at breakfast."

Gretchen was right, the day was nonstop. After role play, where Toby and Jerome were dealers, Erroll a cop, Gretchen and I family members, and Dolly an EMT, with Kelly presiding, we walked down to the Zen garden for our journaling. I had to admit, all this meditation and quiet time was starting to rattle some doors I'd thought were closed for good. I began thinking about approaching Grandma Jones with something I'd wanted to discuss with her for two decades but suppressed: our secret.

Dressed in comfortable CJ jeans, a Bob Marley T-shirt, and my Tims, I found the ride unexpectedly churned up a lot of musty feelings; hadn't been on a bike since my last day working for Winslow.

By the end of the day, I was looking forward to the alum meeting for no other reason than to sit in the cut of the couch to recover from the Tranquility Tudor decathlon.

Not understanding why I was anxious, I helped Gretchen set up the food station while the banjo clock ticked down. Dylan and Toby brought in wood to light the fireplace even though it was a bazillion degrees. And the rest of the TT'ers unfolded our all-purpose metal chairs, placing Big Books with pads and pencils on each seat.

Kelly breezed in to oversee the preparations before giving orders into her walkie talkie, "Everything looks good, Rock, open the gate."

Intermittently, an assortment of guests of all ages, some high profile, twenty in total, filed into the TT living room. I tried not to stare but my eyes widened in awe at the realization that our guest speaker was none other than celebrity pop idol and child TV star Bruce Skylark! I'd had a crush on him since I was a kid, he'd been on every cereal box in America. There was also Migg D., Flash Friklin, and singer Taylor Buckfield, and more kept streaming in.

The room swirled with industry chatter and fraternizing laughter; no doubt a few deals were being made. Bruce Skylark turned out to be surprisingly friendly; I felt my schoolgirl infatuation returning.

Feeling underdressed, I tiptoed off to my room to put on a dab of makeup and change out of my jeans before quietly returning to the meeting.

After formal introductions, Pat Quigley gently suggested, "All newcomers please stand and introduce yourselves. This is not to embarrass you but rather to acquaint you with the 'family' and possibly to pair you up with an excellent sponsor. Will all the willing sponsors raise your hands?"

Ugh. Was I really about to stand up and expose my secret? Did I have to say, "My name is Calysta Jeffries and I like poppin' 'n' swiggin' now and then for nerves?" One by one, I watched the new TT residents obediently stand and introduce themselves.

Palms sweating, it was my turn. Everyone was staring. I'd feign illness, dramatically fainting to the floor. Who'd challenge it? Everyone. Half the members were actors. Forget it.

"Calysta?" Pat encouraged.

Slowly I stood up, looking down at the sisal carpet, reciting, "I'm Beul, I mean Calysta Jeffries . . ."

"Just your first name," Pat reminded.

"Right. Calysta, pills and bubbles."

"Hell-ooo, Ca-lys-ta," the group said in unison, scaring me to death.

"Wonderful." He smiled. "I think that's everyone?"

"*Wait,*" a familiar voice drawled from the opposite side of the room, her face obstructed by a ficus. "I'm new."

"I'm sorry. And what's your name?" Pat asked.

"Gina. This is my very first meeting."

Everyone clapped as I leaned forward, straining to see if my worst fear was about to be realized.

"Keep coming back, Gina!" Gretchen cheered. "It works if you *work* it!"

"Gee, thanks, guys, I feel so special being a newcomer," she oozed, stepping forward.

What a skank. Emmy had scammed her way onto the property. Knowing she was up to no good, my mind raced. I could blow her cover and Rock would put her in a headlock until the cops came. Or maybe something less dramatic like quickly writing a note and passing it to Kelly? Or flying across the room, attacking her as I screamed, "This bitch is a fraud!" But then I'd risk being carted off for a 5150, an institutions hold invoked when a person displays erratic mental-health behavior or is a danger to themselves or others.

A look of satisfaction stole across Emmy's face while she stroked her Moo Roo feathered clutch as if it was her pet Pomapoo, hawkishly scanning the room.

Enthusiastically, Pat announced, "Okay, everybody, now it is my great pleasure to introduce an old friend and one of our esteemed alums, Bruce S, sober for twenty-two years. It's all yours, guy."

I couldn't hear a word Bruce was saying. Everything sounded as though it were under water. The presence of Emmy poisoned the evening just like everywhere she went and everything she touched. I didn't want to imagine why she was here.

Momentarily putting the unsettling thought out of my mind, I along with the others sat spellbound by Bruce's gripping share about his rock-bottom saga before he was brazenly interrupted by Emmy when she said, "That is un-friggin' believable. You did all *that* and lived? Wicked!"

"Shhh," Gretchen loudly hushed. "Don't ask questions until the share is over."

Unfazed, Bruce continued on about his hope, strength, and love. Moved as I was, I continued to be distracted, roving between his inspirational share and Emmy's tapping heel.

Following the meeting and touchy-feely good-byes, alums spilled into the outdoor patio covered by a canopy of scuppernong grapevines. Bruce gave me his number before leaving, saying, "Out of everyone in this bunch I know you can do this, Calysta. Use the digits and stay close."

Naturally, I was flattered, restraining myself from confessing I was a fan.

Eagle-eyed Kelly Lava came from behind, whispering, "Keep it all in perspective. Bruce doesn't give his number out to just anyone so don't abuse it. His kindness doesn't mean a date but that he *might* want to be your sponsor if he has time. Take it from me, I learned the hard way. And Dylan's running a fever, his tat's infected, so I need you to help Toby with cleanup."

"No problem," I said, noticing that sneaky minx Emmy had slipped out before I could confront her.

"Calysta," Toby said, plunging coffee mugs into the sink, "can you believe Emmy was here? I'm, like, blown away she's joining the program!"

"Toby, can you for once put two brain cells together? She's *not* in the program. She was spying. I wouldn't put anything past that twit now that she knows I'm here."

"What about me? She knows I'm here too now," he said, worried.

"Yeah, right. But she doesn't have an axe to grind with *you*." I sighed, emotionally spent.

"Whaddaya mean? How 'bout that time she went up to Randall's office and demanded I be blown up in the Fink laboratory so she didn't have to have me as a long-lost son? Nearly got me fired. Remember that?"

"Who could forget?"

"Yeah, and when that didn't work she claimed I was living in my dressing room on weekends dealing drugs, which was a boldfaced lie. Remember what she said in *Cliffhanger Weekly*?"

Emmy's quote was so famous all of daytime could recite it. Toby and I said it together over the soapsuds in the sink, "'I'm too firm, too fierce, too freakin' fabulous to have an older child. It's soap opera suicide for crissakes!'"

Though we both had a chuckle, I remembered it was Randall's kowtowing to Emmy's incessant needling that possessed him to have Felicia kick the gawdawful kiddy storyline to me. Maximizing on the worst, I slung Ruby Stargazer's fabulous French-manicured feet into the oh-so-not-glamorous stirrups at Whitehaven Hospital, screaming bloody murder while birthing Jade; it always took an *R&R* mom a whole week to birth one baby. That scene alone should've earned me a Sudsy. Providentially, Edith ultimately overrode Randall, making Toby Emmy's bastard son.

Sliding off yellow rubber gloves, I grimly thought, *That scurrilous Emmy was here for one reason and one reason only, revenge.*

Wow! Things are really heating up over at *The Bitch and the Ruthless* . . . I mean, *The Rich and the Ruthless.* I was just down at MOCA treating my favorite soap spy to lunch—you art snobs already know what that stands for but to the masses it's the Museum of Contemporary Art—and let me tell ya, there's something at that place for everyone. I found my new favorite quote there. It goes like this:

"It is not so much where my motivation comes from but rather how it manages to survive."
—Louise Bourgeois

Boy, ain't that the truth.

The Diva

CHAPTER 31

Two Ships Passing

Oh my Lord, what a trip!" Candelaria Jones exclaimed as she stag-gered off the Greyhound bus a little bedraggled with the help of the driver.

In a straw hat and a cardigan draped over her dress, she gripped her pocketbook and Samsonite with one hand, waving at friends she'd made on her journey with the other. "So long, Richardean! See you at tomor-rah's eight o'clock service."

"Mrs. Jones?" Shannen asked, waiting for her in Juicy sweats, Jordan slides, and shades.

"Lord have mercy, it's Dr. Justine Lashaway!" Candelaria exclaimed, dropping her suitcase with a thud, sweeping Shannen into a big bosom hug before stepping back to straighten her hat. "You didn't have to come all the way out here to get me but I thank you all the same. I just love you on the show, you're my favorite after Beulah."

Richardean and a few others skittered over to Candelaria for Shannen's autograph, before going on their way.

Catching her breath and picking up where they left off, Shannen asked, "Beulah?"

"Yeah, y'all call her by her stage name but her birth name is Beulah Espinetta Jones."

"Oh."

"Mm-hm."

"Okay. Well, why don't we go back to my house so you can rest?"

"I could really use some stretchin' out after bein' on that cramped bus for two days. Folks were real nice though. You just met my new friend Richardean. Oh now listen, before I forget, I need to go to church tomorrah morning before we go see Beulah. Can you take me?"

"Of course," Shannen asserted, picking up her suitcase and leading her to the car.

"Listen, sweet, do you have any Coca-Cola at your place?"

"Oh, yes, Mrs. Jones, quiet as it's kept, I drink at least one Diet Coke every day. I'm addicted to the stuff. Matter of fact, help yourself to one in my glove compartment."

"Your glove compartment?"

"Yeah, it's actually a cooler, neat, huh?" Steering with her left hand, Shannen leaned over and pressed the button, revealing an iced Diet Coke and a raw kombucha drink.

"As I live and breathe, I never would've guessed. But I don't need the whole can, I just need enough to sprinkle a few drops of my spirits of ammonia in. My stomach's a little sour."

"Spirits of what?"

With singsong laughter, Candelaria said, "Chile, that's old-school medicine. Yep, between my home remedies, iodine, spirits of ammonia, and my black salve Beulah was rarely sick a day in her life. Did she tell you she's allergic to hornet and bee stings, and so was her mother and so am I? I'm *nevah* caught without a little bottle of spirits of ammonia. But it's good for all sorts of other things too."

Arriving at Shannen's house in Tarzana, Candelaria let out an "Ooooo-wee, you sure do know how to live, Justine. I'm sorry, forgive me, pump-kin, I know your name is Shannen, but I've been watchin' you for so long as Justine it's habit."

"It's all right, Mrs. Jones, you can call me Justine all you want. Let's get you settled in your room."

"That sounds just fine, but I wanna keep askin' you questions. I've been worried sick about my Beulah and grandbaby Ivy. How's her spirits been?" Candelaria asked, following Shannen into a tastefully decorated guest bedroom.

"You mean is Calysta depressed? I'd have to say no."

"Hallelujah. Our whole Church of the Solid Rock prayer circle's been prayin' real hard for Beulah's recovery."

Sitting down on the bed, Shannen searched for the right words before saying, "Mrs. Jones, I have something to tell you."

"Well, c'mon, chile, I'm not gettin' any younger, let's hear it."

"She's worried you're ashamed of her being at a rehab. She told me you believed anything that needed to be fixed could be done through prayer."

"That's true, I did say that, but I also said, he who doesn't open his mouth don't get fed. I'm proud of my homespun gettin' help. Told her a long time ago to stay away from that devil water but she's a hard head and had to do things her way. She's gonna be right as rain when she gets outta where evah' she is and comes home to Greenwood for a spell to rest. That's what she needs, some Southern home cookin' and a good helpin' of church. Y'all too skinny out here any ole way, eat like birds. Back home, we call what she got 'nerves.'"

"Nerves?"

"Yep. I'm fixin' to put that to rest when I see her tomorrah. Yes 'n deedy. And my goodness what a green thumb you have, that's a beautiful Bleeding Heart you're growin' by the window."

"Actually I'm taking care of it for Calysta," Shannen said.

"Used to have a great big one in my backyard. Thing up and died on its own after Beulah left. Strangest thing."

A beat.

"Bet you're hungry," Shannen said, changing the subject. "I made a spinach salad for lunch."

"Thank you, sweet, but there you go again with that bird food. Darlin', in my neck of the woods, spinach is for cookin' and it's a side dish I serve with smothered pork chops. How 'bout you let me fix you some *real* food?" Candelaria offered, pulling off her sweater. "I wanna show you how much I appreciate you bein' a friend and watchin' over my Beulah. Can't thank you enough for your hospitality."

That same day, Randall reserved a Northwest Airlines flight for the nearest airport to Greenwood, a place he never imagined he'd visit to meet with an unlikely sort, Calysta's childhood friend.

Since receiving Edith's urgent phone call, he'd racked his brain for a way to force Calysta to surrender her vote.

He recalled cryptic, poorly written letters postmarked Greenwood, Mississippi, in which the sender claimed to be an old friend of Calysta's, revealing her true name was Beulah Espinetta Jones and that she had a *big* ugly secret. In all fifty-two letters, Seritta Turner solicited that she had *secrets for sale*. Of course Randall couldn't be bothered with kooky fan mail, especially since more than a million pieces were delivered to *The Rich and the Ruthless* every year. And for no pay college interns sifted through offensive letters, cards, edible gifts, and bad portraits, discarding whatever they thought would be a bubble-buster.

"Hey Ben," Randall had asked the PA late Friday night before leaving work, "remember those letters you showed me last year, from some wacky Mississippi chick threatening she had something on Calysta?"

"Sure do. I did what you told me and bundled them and put them in storage, but I was thinking shouldn't we give them to Calysta in case she wanted to hire a private dick."

"Better yet, give them to me," Randall had ordered. "I'll take care of them."

Seduced by the honey of power, having worked his way up from *The Rich and the Ruthless* mailroom and standing at the precipice of becoming the executive director of the number one soap opera in America and its sister show, *The Daring and the Damned,* Randall wasn't about to lose all he'd dreamed of and schemed for for years because of one vote.

Randall had shown tremendous promise as a visual artist in high school, winning a full scholarship to Kansas City Art Institute, where everything seemed perfect until his mother pulled him out of college in his junior year, citing that she couldn't afford him not working. Randall resentfully got a job to help support the rest of the family, which included two younger sisters.

Heartbroken, he had watched his future disintegrate before his eyes, working two years on a Harley-Davidson assembly line. Craving the life he'd been teased with at college, he'd do whatever it took to be rich and breathe that rarefied air once again.

Abandoning his mother and sisters for California, Randall had immediately landed a job in the WBC mailroom. Always power-hungry, he soon kicked and clawed his way up the correspondence ladder, meeting Alison when she came to collect packages her fans had sent. Unbeknownst to her, Randall had penned hundreds of letters and stuffed them into her mail bin. It was lust at first sight. Soon after, Randall was hired as a production assistant on *The Rich and the Ruthless* and Alison saw his potential, suggesting his promotion to Augustus every chance she got while getting others fired. Together, they made the perfect soap opera social climbers, woodchippin' anyone who got in their way.

Considering how close the duo had come to getting their sticky fly-paper hands on that dreamed-of title, First Couple of Daytime, Randall wasn't about to let a second chance get derailed, and certainly not by someone as trivial as Calysta Jeffries. She would have to be dealt with, as Edith said, "by any means necessary."

Taking a swig of Jack Daniel's from a flask in his desk, he smoothed out one of Seritta's letters with his fat palm, pressing it against his desk blotter. Rereading the correspondence, he thought, *Seritta could be a crack-pot or the key to my whole future.*

Calysta aka Beulah Espinetta Jones done some thangs. I got proof 4 $$$.

Seritta Turner

CHAPTER 32

Secrets of a Soap Opera Diva

After waking up early Sunday morning to catch a seven a.m. flight, Randall showered and threw on a gray Brooks Brothers suit while Alison watched from their custom king-size waterbed.

"How much do you think you'll have to pay this Seritta character? I mean what a loser," she said, revealing a freckled thigh suggestively.

"Shouldn't be more than five hundred," he said airily as he tightened the knot in his paisley Sid Mashburn necktie. "Calysta's so-called friend will take whatever I give her and like it."

"Randy, what do you think Calysta's secret *is*?"

"Who cares as long as it's something I can bribe her with? Seriously, Alison, we've got to make this stick or—"

"Or what?"

"We're pushin' sixty and daytime is drying up all around us. Starting over on another soap is *not* an option. This is our window and we're climbin' through it. It could mean everything for us."

"Don't worry, Randy, you'll dig up something juicy. I can smell it. Always knew that bitch was hiding something. I'm so sure of it I'm already planning a rockin' pre-victory party for you on Tuesday night. We're gonna get Calysta's vote and karaoke ourselves right into the WBC chips."

Randall spontaneously gave her a rare kiss good-bye.

Grabbing the tongue of his tie at the last second, Alison whispered breathily, "I'm feelin' kinda frisky this morning, Randy. Sure there's no time to squeeze in a little *stimulus package* action before you leave?"

"Gotta go, babe, or I'll miss my flight."

Shortly after one in the afternoon, Randall spotted his name in big, black hand-printed letters on a placard outside the airport. He'd contacted Pride-All Taxi Service to shuttle him from Greenville Airport to Greenwood, requesting they send a town car, but what awaited him was far from the sleek Hollywood Mercedes sedan he was accustomed to. Stunted and boxy, it looked as though it could've been an experimental hybrid.

In his Sunday best, accessorized with a thick gold rope chain with a large crucifix swinging at the bottom, the driver greeted Randall cheerfully, revealing a silver-capped bicuspid in the corner of his warm smile.

"Hello, Mr. Roberts, I'm your driver for today. Just call me Jacob," he said before opening the door.

Randall tentatively climbed into the odd-shaped car, settling back into the burgundy tufted seat to Muddy Waters's "The Blues Had a Baby and They Named It Rock and Roll" as they drove out of the country airport.

"Excuse me? Is this a custom car, Jacob?" Randall couldn't help asking.

"Why yes, sir, thank you for noticing. This is one of two family funeral limos Pride-All Taxi Service has in its rotation. Our company's been in business in Leflore County for over forty-seven years now," he said proudly.

Randall instantly got the heebie-jeebies.

Jacob kept up a steady stream of chatter, proudly pointing out historic and not-so-historic sights as they made the forty-five-minute drive to Greenwood.

"Now this place right here, got the best BBQ for miles. Wanna pull over?"

"No, thank you. My return flight is at five. Need to get in and out."

"What a shame you won't get to enjoy Greenwood to the fullest. It's a fine place, you should come back when you have more time, Mr. Roberts."

"I'll try to do that."

The car stopped in front of Seritta Turner's rundown trailer propped up on cement blocks. The front yard was spotted with chickweed and goosegrass, littered with broken toys, surrounded by a chain link fence, punctuated with a large satellite dish.

Jesus, I can probably get away with a couple hundred bucks, Randall thought.

"Here we be," announced Jacob, jumping out to open Randall's door. "Take your time, Mr. Roberts. I'll be right here waitin'."

Randall made his way past a rusted Buick station wagon filled to the gills with odds and ends, toward the Villager trailer, and up rickety steps to knock on the tin screen door.

"Y'all goin' to be lookin' at the end of a strap if you don't quit it!" There was a whack and then crying. "Didn't I tell y'all to stop? Now clean it up!"

A young black woman with a baby on her hip swung open the inner door, thumb in mouth, wearing jeans and a faded halter top, her hair braided back in thick cornrows, eyeballing Randall and saying, "You Roberts?" before reinserting her thumb.

"Yes, Randall Roberts, and you must be Seritta Turner?" He tried not to react to her thumb-sucking.

"Yeah, but everybody calls me Baby CiCi. C'mon in and take a load off." Randall followed her in stunned silence.

"Want somethin' to drink? I got Mountain Dew and grape drink."

"No thanks." A beat passed. "You're younger than I expected."

"That's 'cause the Seritta you're thinkin' of is my mamma. This here's my son T.I., named him after my favorite rapper." She lit up a Camel, swallowing the smoke.

"He's quite the charmer," Randall replied, barely seeing her son. "So CiCi, where's your mother? I called and made arrangements to meet with her today?"

"Actually, I'm the one you spoke to on the phone."

A look of shock washed over Randall.

"Yeah, I wrote all them letters. My mamma's at church still, she been 'saved' and whatnot."

Looking at her appraisingly, Randall replied, "I see."

The nicotine-stained windows struggled to provide sunlight as he took in the sparse décor of worn car seats, a couch, a La-Z-Boy recliner, an oversize flat screen, and a small mustard Formica table with four chairs.

"Have a seat, ain't nobody gonna bite," CiCi teased.

After pushing the Lucky Charms box to the side and wiping the drying spilled milk with a sponge, the evidence of breakfast, she popped open a Mountain Dew and took a swig, then licked her index finger preparing to count her food stamps with her baby on her lap.

"So," Randall coughed out, "what's this secret you have for sale?"

"Do I look stupid? You see me countin' food stamps. How much you payin' me first?"

Randall hadn't anticipated hardcore negotiating and was startled by her brazenness.

"I don't have all day either. I gotta clean up before Mamma gets home from church and you gotta be gone. So?"

"How's five sound?"

"*T'h*, best be talkin' 'bout five K and stop wastin' my time with any other nonsense."

"Five thousand! How about two?"

"You can't count? I said five, and·in a minute it's gonna be six."

"W-w-well, I don't have that kind of money on me right now."

"We gotta ATM in town."

"I can't take that much cash out all at once."

"Not my problem," CiCi said with finality and started to get up.

"Okay, okay. Wait a minute."

Shifting T.I. into his walker, she asked, "Well?"

"I have two. And Pride-All Taxi wants to be paid in cash."

"I don't care 'bout Jacob an' 'em. I'll take what you got in your wallet . . . and your watch, and you can stop by the ATM and pay Pride-All on your way back to the airport."

"This is a Yacht-Master II!" Randall sputtered. "It's worth way more than five grand!"

"Man, call it whatever you want, it's a Rolex to me, and my information is worth every penny."

Knowing she had him over a barrel, Randall reluctantly withdrew his leather billfold. "I'll give you the cash on the front end and my Rolex *if* you deliver."

"Please, I ain't even worried," CiCi said, closing her eyelids with much attitude, sucking her back teeth while holding out her hand as he peeled off twenty Benjamins.

Unable to take the stifling air any longer, Randall carefully suggested, "Why don't we sit outside?"

"Okay, but I already feel like I'm on blast with Jacob's hooptie parked out front. Damn funeral car. So we're gonna sit out back."

"Fine," he agreed, taking shallow breaths.

"Terrell, Pre'tentious, let's go! Oh and um, can you carry T.I. out while I get his bottle?"

"Ah, sure."

Awkwardly holding the toddler, Randall followed CiCi to a low wood bench balanced on two milk crates located next to a silver-painted propane tank. The rough-and-tumble five-year-old twins, a boy and a girl, ran off, one skillfully climbing a ladder to the slide while the other got on a swing.

"You kids better play right," CiCi warned as she fired up another cigarette next to the tank, causing Randall to tense up as he handed her the baby.

"I'ma tan those hides again if I hear y'all fussin'."

She offered Randall a smoke.

"No thanks, I'm a cigar man, so whaddya got for me?"

Leaning forward, CiCi reached into her back pocket and pulled out a faded *Greenwood Commonwealth* newspaper clipping, handing it to Randall.

The headline announced, "Community Stunned at Beloved Pastor's Untimely Death."

Quickly scanning the article, Randall read that Pastor Chester Winslow, "a pillar of Greenwood society," died due to mysterious circumstances. Below, there was a grainy picture of a young Calysta with an old, dark woman leaving a building. The caption stated,

> Beulah Espinetta Jones and her grandmother Candelaria Jones exiting Greenwood police station following questioning. The seventeen-year-old was the last to see Pastor Chester Winslow alive.

Randall held the clipping as if it was a priceless work of art. "May I keep this?"

"After you gimme that watch," CiCi aggressively reminded him, looking as if she could kick Randall's butt, baby and all.

"Of course, I'm a man of my word," he said, fondling his eighteen-karat diamond-faced timepiece. "So are you saying Calysta . . . I mean Beulah . . . had something to do with the pastor's death?"

"Man, can't you read? Dude was her daddy," she drawled, a cigarette dangling out of the corner of her mouth. "Nobody talks about nothin' 'round here in Greenwood, secrets so thick you can cut 'em with a knife, but everybody been knowin' Beulah's a stone-cold killah, poisoned the preacha'."

Randall's heart beat double time but he masked his excitement so as not to cause CiCi to ask for his Gucci loafers.

"See, Mrs. Jones had a side business," CiCi continued. "Everyone and I mean everyone, even the church folk, went to her for those old African root medicines she made. Some kind of voodoo mess, if you ask me."

"But if it's true," Randall interrupted, "why did Beulah kill her father?"

"If?" She exhaled perfect smoke rings that hung in the oppressive heat like angel halos while stomping out the butt beneath her rubber flip-flop. "Man, her daddy was scand-a-lous, that fool loved him some sanctuary sistahs. Most folks thought Winslow got what he deserved, so everyone just looked the other way when the po-po started snoopin' around. When the dust settled, Beulah bounced. Ain't been back since. She ain't no joke, I know that's right. Old-timers say she got the gift, the 'knowing.' Whatevah. You best catch that snake by the head so the rest is rope or you're gonna be one sorry Mr. Roberts."

"Oh, I don't believe in all that hocus-pocus."

"Well don't say I didn't tell you so."

She looked at the yard thoughtfully. "Yep, Beulah bought that swing set for the twins. Just 'cause she in Hollywood she think she all that, I don't think so. Yeah she makes payments on this property, so what?

That's chump change f'her. She shoulda' bought us a house. My mamma's so loyal to her, that don't mean I have to be. Shoot, I hate this place and I hate this town. Got dreams too, you know what I'm sayin'?"

Randall nodded his head, egging CiCi on.

"My sister ran off a long time ago, it's just me doin' all the cookin' and cleanin' lookin' after those brats. My life ain't my own. Tired of pullin' this goddamn weight." She pointed, saying, "They ain't mine. Ma had eight kids altogether, four of 'em in foster care right now. I ain't nevah gonna be like her, *gotta* break before I get caught up. B'sides, I'ma hundred-dolla woman, don't need no five-dolla man. Everybody 'round here my age got more than one kid and barely knowin' how to read. Don't know why you come all this way for this little bit of information, and I don't mean Beulah any harm, but this here secret is my sure-fire ticket out of Greenwood and in this life you eat what you kill."

Randall could relate. It was his song but a different tune.

A honk startled them.

"Mr. Roberts, need to get goin' to make your flight," Jacob called out.

Giving an "Okay!" in acknowledgment, Randall extended his hand to CiCi and said, "Thanks, you've been very helpful. But you still didn't answer my question. Why did Beulah kill her father?"

"Give me that watch and I'll tell you," she said, unclenching the baby's fist from around her hoop earring.

"Right," Randall said with a nervous laugh, unsnapping the safety latch, dropping the heavy Rolex into her waiting palm.

"She killed Winslow 'cause he killed her mamma."

"How?"

"Her mamma died giving birth to Beulah."

"You mean . . . ?"

"Yep."

"Wow. Well, like I said, you've been very helpful."

"You know, me and my mamma watch *The Rich and the Ruthless* every day. You think when I get outta here you can hook me up?"

"Sure, give me a call when you get to town."

"Don't act like you don't know me when I show up, now. And is Derrick Taylor as sexy as he seems?"

"Uh-huh," Randall replied, picking up momentum.

"And tell Emmy Abernathy I'm her biggest fan," she yelled out before returning to the comfort of sucking her thumb.

"Will do."

Jacob closed the car door as Randall exhaled, while CiCi plucked the cash out of her halter, marveling at her future.

"Jacob, do you know Candelaria Jones by any chance?" Randall asked as they pulled off.

"Know her? Why Miss Candelaria is a beloved pillar of this community, known her all my life."

"Does she live close by?"

"Sure does. She ain't around today though, I drove her myself to the Greyhound station out on Highway 82 a few days ago. She went to visit her granddaughter Beulah in Hollywood. You know she's a big-time actress out there on my favorite story, *The Rich and the Ruthless.*"

"You don't say? It's mine too. What a coincidence. Do you think we could drive by Mrs. Jones's place on our way back to the airport?"

"No problem. Miss Candy got herself a nice place out there on Money Road. And Beulah helped pay off that mortgage . . . girl's a *Jet* centerfold if I evah saw one. Greenwood sure is proud of her. But we ain't seen her for some time now 'cept for those tabloids. Matter of fact, just saw her face on the front of *Cliffhanger Weekly* at Piggly Wiggly. She workin' so daggone hard she done got herself in some kinda pickle out there in Hollywoodland."

"Pickle?" Randall asked innocently.

"Mm-hmm. You didn't hear it from me 'cause I ain't one to gossip, but Miss Candy told me she had to rush out there and help Beulah with some trouble she was havin' with her constitution, seems she has 'nerves.'"

"Really?" Randall smirked. "Hollywood can be so cruel."

"She just goin' a little too fast that's all, needs to slow down some. She done run over herself, poor thing. You know how young folk do."

Driving slowly along the Yazoo River before turning, Jacob pointed out Cottonlandia. "That's our museum and don't let the name fool ya either, it's not just about cotton, it has all kinds of art and native stuff. And up on the left? Church of the Solid Rock, that's where Pastor Winslow preached. And over there to your right is my barber and Pride-All Taxi Service," Jacob said with a big grin.

"Nice," Randall said, checking the time on a watch no longer there, only the evidence of a tan line.

"Here we are. This here is Miss Candy's house," announced Jacob, rolling to a stop in her driveway.

Her nosy neighbor Miss Whilemina was leaning out the window, forearms resting on a pillow just above a patch of climbing sweet peas.

"What you doin' 'round here, Jacob?"

"Afternoon, Miss Whilemina, just passin' through, this man wanted to see Miss Candy's place, that's all."

"Well she ain't here! And her property ain't for sale and neither is mine! You developers come 'round here all the time tryin' to steal our homes, talkin' mess! Make me sick . . ." She fussed as she grabbed her pillow and slammed the window shut.

Voulez-vous coucher-ing it back to the Greenville airport, compliments of Patti La Belle's pipes, Jacob said, "Sorry 'bout that, Mr. Roberts. She's a little sensitive. Times been tough on everyone, folks been losing their homes. People work real hard around here to own a patch of dirt. They get suspicious when strangers like you show up. Just last year a developer bought up a whole bunch of old houses, knocked 'em down, and sold the land for ten times what he paid!"

"Awful," Randall murmured.

"I hope Miss Whilemina didn't spoil your Greenwood visit any," Jacob added. "Folks is real friendly here. Wouldn't want you to go back with a bad taste in your mouth."

"Not at all," Randall reassured him, pulling the newspaper clipping out of his inside lapel pocket. "I can honestly say Greenwood was everything I'd hoped for."

CHAPTER 33

"To Get Somethin' You Never Had, You Gotta Do Somethin' You Never Did"

Shannen blissfully sang to country music star Heidi Newfield's "Johnny and June" before asking, "Did you sleep okay, Mrs. Jones?" as she popped four vitamins, swishing them back with half a bottle of Save the Glaciers water.

"Did I ever!" exclaimed Candelaria. "I don't mean to be nosy but why you takin' all them pills?"

"They're my vitamins!"

"Only gonna give you pricey pee. I could fix you some collards that'd do more than them pills could evah do. But to answer your question, I feel like new money! Slept like a baby, sure did, but do you think we could stop and put the top up before I lose my hat and wig and catch a death of cold?"

At the press of a button the convertible canopy of Shannen's VW Beetle automatically unfolded and locked into place.

"Now we're cookin' with gas! My word, I have nevah, times have really changed."

"Mrs. Jones, you are such a breath of fresh air and so much fun to have around. You remind me of my own grandmother."

"Do I?"

"Yes, you do. And thanks for inviting me to go to church. I had a *blast* singing with everybody and shaking Miss Richardean's tambourine. And I just loved the part when Pastor Barnabas said, 'Look at your neighbor and say, "Neighbor, I've been guilty of a few things."' I just loved that part. Who knew church could be so much fun?"

"Uh-huh."

"And when he said we're all like pencils. That we're made imperfect with the expectation of making mistakes and that's what the eraser is for? Wow! How genius was that? Then the pastor topped himself by saying, 'Just 'cause *we* break don't mean we should be tossed.'"

"Preach, Shannen. Bring it on home."

"'All we need is a little resharpenin'.' That part just about tore me to pieces. It's been a while, surprised the walls didn't fall in on me. My whole family's Evangelical, I'm the black sheep."

"Like I always say, 'If God's your copilot, it's time to switch seats.' Besides, I don't know how else I was gettin' to church today if you weren't takin' me, so thank *you*. But I must say when pastor invited folks to join the church family you sure did surprise me, tearin' off somethin' fierce up and down the aisle, runnin' around the sanctuary lookin' like the Holy Spirit had taken hold, speakin' in tongues before fallin' up on the altar steps. Whew, I was tired just lookin' at ya. I hope you know how serious tithin' is though."

Vrooming down the 101 freeway on a crystalline Sunday morning, Shannen and Candelaria were en route to Baldwin Hills to pick up Ivy from uptight Dwayne. He'd selfishly fabricated some sorry excuse for why Ivy couldn't attend the inspiring service.

"Calysta is really looking forward to seeing you and Ivy today, Mrs. Jones."

"Haven't seen my babies for a month of Sundays, not since Beulah came out to New Orleans three years ago to be queen of the Zulu Parade, that's the black Mardi Gras parade, you know. Dressed in a coconut top and grass skirt, covered head to toe in beads. Too bad her horse and buggy got pulled over by the *police* on St. Charles. Organizers didn't pull a permit that year. But my Beulah, bein' who I raised her to be, climbed down and walked the rest of the way. Sure did. We painted the town red, went over to that Harrah's Casino. Ooo-wee, that place is somethin' else . . . got a whole city inside, never had to leave the building once and you can eat all you can eat too. I like playin' the slots. Go to Biloxi every so often with the seniors at my church, helps me relax. But I hate that everything's electronic now. Miss that jingling sound of coins comin' down."

"Do you ever win?" Shannen asked.

"Never, chile, but I sure do enjoy myself."

"You should get Calysta to take you to Vegas. It's awesome! I got married at the Graceland Wedding Chapel there."

"Is that a fact?"

"Yes, ma'am," Shannen said wistfully.

"One thing's for sure, we won't be goin' to no Vegas on *this* trip," Candelaria said soberly. "And I didn't know you were married. Where's your husband?"

"Um, he's on a retreat . . . sort of . . . you know, trying to *find* himself? He should be coming home tomorrow. You'll meet him. He's going through a rough patch right now being out of work, he's a little grumpy."

"Honey, tell him he ain't alone. That's half the world right now. Speaking of finding things, when we gonna find this address for my grandbaby?"

"According to my GPS we should be there in five minutes."

"Your who?"

Giggling, Shannen said, "My navigation system; helps me get around L.A. and it beats the *Thomas Guide.* I'm sorry, Mrs. Jones, I don't really ever come over here so I'm a little turned around."

"Uh-huh. Oh, my goodness. What was that place we just passed that smelled so good?"

"I think it said M&M's. Wanna stop and get something?" Shannen asked politely, hoping Candelaria would say no, feeling out of place at the intersection of Crenshaw and Martin Luther King Boulevard.

"No, sweet pea, that's okay. I'm not gonna spoil my appetite. I'ma save it for my Beulah and Ivy this afternoon. Got some saltines and hard candy in my pocketbook and that should hold me just fine till then. Besides, fastin' causes all kinds of clarity. Matter of fact, I got me a *sign* in church this morning from the Holy Spirit, sure did. Ain't no question 'bout it. Me and Beulah's gonna have an understanding to-day! Pastor was right when he said,

> To get somethin' you never had, you have to do somethin' you never did. When God takes somethin' from your grasp, he's not punishing you, but merely opening your hands to receive somethin' better. God will never take you where His grace will not protect you.

"Amen!" Shannen said a little too loudly over the country western music.

"Everything's gonna be all right and that goes for you and your husband too," Candelaria declared as she began humming the closing hymn the lively choir sang earlier in church, "His Eye Is on the Sparrow."

CHAPTER 34

Listen, Son, We're Here to See My Girl

unning down the topiary-coiffed walkway, arms outstretched, Ivy exclaimed, "Mother Jones, Mother Jones, you're here!" She reached into the car window, wrapping her long caramel arms around her grandmother's neck, saying, "I've missed you *so* much."

"Missed you too, *skillet*, you just don't know. Look how tall you got and just as pretty like your mamma. Now hop in and buckle up. Shannen tells me we have quite a ride ahead of us."

"Morning, Shannen," Ivy said as she pecked her on the cheek before sliding into the backseat.

"Morning, Ivy, sorry you missed church. It was really good."

"Yeah, well what could I do? Dad said no."

"Least he coulda' done was come down to say hello instead of actin' like a simpleton, lookin' out behind the curtains. Forgave what he did to your mamma a long time ago, he's been a good daddy to you too."

The trio waited their turn as they inched closer to the wrought-iron Tranquility Tudor gate, decorated with colorful balloons, disarmingly inviting, giving the rehab a carnival atmosphere.

"May I help you?" asked Rock, wearing shades, holding a clipboard.

"Yes, my name is—" Shannen began.

Cutting her off, Candelaria released her seat belt, taking the bull by the horns, saying, "Listen, son, we're here to see my girl, Beulah Espinetta Jones. My name should be on that thing, Candelaria Jones . . . C-A-N-D-E-L-A-R-I-A Jones, this here is my great-grandbaby Ivy Jeffries, and beside me is Shannen Lassiter, she's a big star on *The Rich and the Ruthless* and a family friend . . . that's L-A-S-S—"

"That's okay, ma'am, you're all down here, but there's no Beulah Espinetta on my list."

"Maybe if you took them sunglasses off and checked again . . . I know I didn't come all this way to be told my Beulah ain't where she 'posed to be," Candelaria fumed.

"Mother Jones, I think I know what the problem is," Ivy interjected softly.

"Well speak up, chile, say somethin'."

"My mom's an actress—Calysta Jeffries?"

"Oh, yeah, yeah, yeah. Wow, 'Beulah,' you-all went *way* back on that one, huh?" He chuckled.

Candelaria stared back from under her hat, deadpan.

"Go right on in, ladies, parking's on your left and *no* picture taking. Turn off the music and you-all have a nice visit."

"And *you* have a blessed day," Candelaria said.

CHAPTER 35

Pam 'N' Paris

Suffering from insomnia, Roger surfed the Web for soft porn and Facebook friends, suckin' back brewskis and eatin' Cheetos, when a Celebutante Alert flashed for none other than Shannen Lassiter.

On his second six-pack since last night, Roger slammed his Sam Adams on the nightstand mid-sip and sat up, still in bed. The secluded camp, not known for its Internet expedience, caused him to tap his orange-dyed-fingertips on the keypad.

"What the . . . ?" His eyes went from two pissholes in snow to what resembled Jack Nicholson's in *The Shining.*

Shannen's sex video, already in a dead heat with Paris's bedroom romp hits, turned Roger's face purple with rage as he watched the thirty-second showcase. The lusty *grunt 'n' grind,* featured his wife whooping it up in her dressing room with her on-screen Latin lover, Javier de

L'Vasquez. The sudsy duo were oblivious to the micro-wire pinhole spy camera Felicia had arranged to be installed.

In a jealous outburst, Roger stood up butt naked on the bed, fists clenched, screaming at the top of his lungs, *"Noooooo!"* before whipping his laptop across the room, through the open sliding glass doors, and into Big Bear Lake.

HOLY SOAP OPERA CRUISE! Looking into my smudged crystal ball, I can see things haven't improved on the set of *The Rich and the Ruthless*. In fact, my behind-the-curtain spies tell me bubbles are bursting everywhere and things sadly are getting worse. Since a *Cliffhanger Weekly* scribe prematurely spilled the beans about an upcoming top-secret shocker storyline—Shannen Lassiter (Dr. Justine Lashaway) is preggers with Javier de L'Vasquez's baby—that may not be fiction, all press has been banned from the set. Blah blah blah, we know that won't last. I already have the scoop that an acting coach has been called in for Javier and Jade since *R&R* completely canned cue cards to save time and money. Boy oh boy, trouble is bubbling to the surface like an overflowing septic tank and this is only the tip of the shit.

The Diva

CHAPTER 36

The Visitation

"Calysta, no isolating in your room. Let's go. Guests are starting to arrive," Kelly Lava said as she did a sweep. Looking down at my bed, she remarked, "Nice corners."

"Thanks."

"Here."

"What's this for?"

"Random urine test. Don't freak out and don't forget to label the cup."

Balloons, a Jump O'Rama, popcorn machine, clowns, folksy fiddlers, and deafening cheery family banter were over-the-top overwhelming.

I hoped somewhere in among the yoga, the gourmet butternut squash soup, the upper intestinal herbal colonics, military corners, dish duty, meditation, Korean body splashes, equine and collage therapy, Big

Book studies, and even Gretchen's pep talks, I had fortified myself to face more than the music outside.

Looking in the mirror, sweeping my hair back in a ponytail, wearing no makeup, I whispered, "How did you get here?" before venturing out.

"This place is somethin' else," said Grandma Jones.

"You can say that again," agreed Shannen, staring in the opposite direction. "Ohmagod!"

"What?" asked Ivy. "Remember the rules, you're not supposed to get all starstruck or take pictures."

"I know, silly. It's just I think I know that man over there."

"I see a lot of folks over there and I got my eye out for one person and one person only and that would be Beulah," said no-nonsense Candelaria.

"Yes of course, Mrs. Jones, that was really insensitive of me. But I was thinking, you and Ivy should have a private moment with Calysta first . . . I mean Beulah. How about I meet up with you a little later? I'm sure she wouldn't mind."

Looping her arm through her grandmother's, Ivy said, "C'mon, Mother Jones," as they headed in the direction of the villa, weaving their way through the carnivalesque obstacle course.

"Mom, Mom!" shouted Ivy as she ran across the lawn, Grandma Jones snailing behind with her cane.

"Oh, baby."

After hugging for the longest, I felt a tapping on my shoulder and heard, "Mind if I get some of that sugah?"

Immediately, I fell into Grandma Jones's arms, tearing up. "I'm so sorry for causing all this trouble."

"Now don't start cryin' and carryin' on, Beulah. Everything's gonna be just fine, you watch and see."

For a nanosecond I forgot that was my real name, it had been so long since anyone had called me *Beulah*.

Grandma Jones knew how to hold on to a penny and was wearing the same Sunday dress she had from back in the day.

She wiped my tears with a fished-out Chantilly-scented Kleenex she always had in her pocketbook, as I asked, "Where's Shannen? Didn't she drive you-all over here?"

"Yes, but she thought she saw someone she knew," reported Ivy.

"Really?" Though I knew it must be Toby, more important business was at hand. The moment was too special to take an ounce of attention away from our precious family time.

"We don't have all day and can't be dilly-dallyin', we have serious talkin' to do," Grandma Jones reminded. "But first I need a bathroom and some food."

"Let's get you inside," I said.

As I wrapped my arm around Grandma's padded waist, supporting her, and Ivy wove her fingers into mine, I couldn't help but think back to that fateful evening long ago, me, just a year older than my daughter was now, standing in our Mississippi garden.

Shannen tentatively made her way toward a red-and-white-checked table where Jerome McDonald, onetime Baltimore Ravens superstar and the man she almost married, sat quietly, nursing a glass of juice.

"Jerome?"

He looked at her quizzically for a moment before jumping up, exclaiming, "Shan-Shan!"

Her heart lurched at the nickname; no one had called her that since they broke up six years ago.

"Jerome, what are you doing here . . . are you visiting a friend too?"

Stepping back, he smiled ruefully. "No. I'm afraid I've had a tough time of it since I was forced into early retirement because of my injury. Underestimated the steroids and painkillers."

Struggling to arrest familiar white-hot feelings, Shannen said, "I'm sorry to hear that, but you look like you're on the upswing now." Discreetly eyeing her old flame, Shannen noticed he wasn't at full strength, but his swarthy mug and football-toned body were just as she remembered, picture perfect.

"Yeah, actually this place has been pretty good for me. Detox was brutal but I'm starting to feel human again."

"That's good," she murmured, gazing up through long lashes.

He thoughtfully said, "Time's been good to you, Shan-Shan. You're even more beautiful than I remember. Took me the longest to get over you." He chuckled, sweeping her into a bone-crushing hug.

"I was head over heels in love with you too when I was young-*er.*"

Pushing a curl behind her ear, he said, "You're still young, honey."

"Hi, baby!" A woman's bubbly voice interrupted the reminiscing pair. Startled, Shannen stepped back.

"Oh hey, there you are," he said, giving the woman a nuzzle. "Honey, I want you to meet an old friend of mine, Shannen Lassiter. Shan, this is my wife, Jewel." Immediately disappointed, Shannen forced a smile. Like everyone else in the universe, she had never *really* let go of her first true love no matter how much time had passed. And no matter how sweet and kind his current in-your-face significant other was, she would always be the *enemy.*

The trophy wife was friendly but watchful as she extended a UES handshake, an enormous diamond flashing. "Hello, Shannen, it's nice to meet you. Are you in recovery too?"

"No! I mean, no, I'm here visiting a friend. In fact, I should go, she's waiting for me. Take care," she said, awkwardly waving good-bye at the couple.

"Bye, Shan-Shan," Jerome called after her as she made a speedy retreat, smacking into Toby Gorman in her haste.

"Shannen? No way! This is too cool! When did you check in? This is like one of those *R&R* BBQs where the whole cast is in one place. We're gonna have a blast! I'm stoked—"

"Toby, Toby, it's not what you think. I'm here to see Calysta."

"Oh yeah, she's here too. Dude, can you believe they have a cotton candy machine here? And the Jump O'Rama's the *bomb*!"

"Yeah, nice. Well, I should get over to Calysta. Take care, Toby."

"You look *hot*, Shannen, even walking away. Can't believe you came out here to visit Calysta and me! Anyone else from the show with you?"

"Uh, no."

"Well, tell everyone I said hi, and look for my featured interview on the 'Quitters' page of *Cliffhanger Weekly*, 'A Day in the Life of Rehab with Toby Gorman.' It's kinda weird 'cause I didn't really quit but whatever."

"I'll do that. Bye!" Shannen trotted away to find Calysta before she could run into any more familiar faces.

With the Pacific marine layer burning off, I stood on the veranda facing the flower-dotted mountainside, reflecting while Ivy and Grandma Jones got their lunch. The contrast of singed peaks in the distance, evidence of arson, was ever the reminder that evil was standin' right next to you watchin' the fire burn.

"Guess who?" a familiar voice asked, as two soft hands covered my eyes.

"Shannen!" I exclaimed, quickly turning around, embracing her.

"Calysta!"

After an exuberant love-fest, Shannen said, "Before I forget, here's your mail," pulling a small stack out of her shoulder bag. "And your Bleeding Heart's just fine."

"Thank you, Shan—"

"About the fan mail . . ."

"What about it?"

"There wasn't one piece. Fern swore me to secrecy, before spilling that Randall hired an intern to relabel it all for Alison's bin. Can you believe?"

"Actually, I can."

"And Ethan's having a conniption. He's so bummed the show's phasing him out. Working him like every two months. Put him on recurring."

"Mmm-mm."

"He's been asking for your number."

"Pff . . ."

"Wants to talk to you about—"

"No. Tried tellin' his Tomin' ass a long time ago. Even *Toby* got paid more than that brown-noser. Damn shame. All that tap-dancin' for nothin' and here I was tryin' to set it up for the next generation. What a joke."

Thumbing through bills and junk mail, I noticed an envelope addressed from Zylissa Pippin. "Zylissa? You mind?"

"Go 'head."

I ripped open the envelope and unfolded the letter. A check fell out.

Hey girl,

Know you haven't heard from me in a minute and probably thought I ran off with your cash. But I booked the Valtrex, and honey, I'm makin' beaucoup bucks. Here's ½. You'll get the rest when my resid comes in. Peace out.

XOZ

I smiled.

"Good news?"

"Yeah."

"So, how are you doing?"

"Girl, you know me. Doin' what I got to do to get by. Readin' more. Can you believe they won't let me watch Nancy Grace? What's goin' on with that crazy case?"

"Sorry, I'm a Cooper fan. But never mind all that," she said, noshing on a carrot stick. "I'd be having major panic attacks by now if I were locked up in this Taj Mahal. Want one?" she offered, extending the crudités.

"No thanks. Actually I feel like I'm on an imposed vacation. I've calmed down considerably having spent quality time 'becoming one with a horse,'" I said, making fun of the much-hyped equine therapy.

"That sounds *so* kinky."

"Trust me, it's not that exciting and has nothing to do with Catherine the Great."

Shannen's laughter was replaced with a pall of melancholy.

"What's wrong?"

"Nothing," she replied, biting her quivering bottom lip.

"Stop lying." Glancing to see that Ivy and Grandma Jones were settling in at a nearby table, I called out, "You-all start without us."

"But Mom—"

"Be right there, we both will."

As Grandma Jones began blessing the food I steered Shannen into a quiet corner. "Okay, we have a few minutes, talk to me."

Wiping her eyes with the heel of her hand, she quickly confessed, "I'm such a terrible friend. Here you're the one going through all this traumatic stuff and I'm the one crying like a big baby."

"Never mind all that."

"Roger's gone nuts. Felicia keeps giving me gratuitous sex scenes with Javier and I swear she's doing it on purpose. And to top it all off, I just ran into my first love and he's *married*."

"Oh honey," I comforted. "Not to be nosy, but who'd you run into?"

"Jerome McDonald. We were engaged and I called it off like an idiot, I think I told you."

"*That* Jerome? The football player you 'bout ran off with? I had no idea. Damn, girl, he's definitely the one who got away and *fine* as all get out. I heard his wife flew in on their private jet, they are load-*ed*."

Shannen sighed. "His wife has a rock the size of a baby's fist and all I have left from that relationship is a jersey and an autographed football. No glass slipper for this Cinderella, just mice."

"So Roger's still trippin', huh?"

"Things are so bad, Calysta. I mean, when 'At Home with a Soap Star' aired, Roger went ballistic! They'd featured me talking about my 'fabulous soap star lifestyle' but edited out every shot of him. And then *I* got all the criticism on Facebook, being compared to that Robin Givens and Mike Tyson interview with Barbara Walters. It was hell at home. We were sleeping in separate rooms and everything. I *told* Roger he should have taken that game-show host job when he had the chance but he stupidly said it was beneath him."

"Wow, I had no idea."

"Yeah, and I've barely been able to pay our mortgage. If I miss one more payment the house is going into foreclosure. Fans think soap stars are all rich and happy, leading lives right out of some Danielle Steel novel; if they only knew. Don't get me wrong, I feel grateful for the money I make, but by the time I pay the agent, the manager, the publicist, Roger's anger management therapist, the entertainment attorney, my personal trainer, and my psychic . . . heck, there's nothing left." She hyperventilated, beginning to hiccup.

"Okay, now now, take a deep breath and hold it while you count to twenty, then exhale; it always works."

Inhaling deeply, Shannen began, "I made a last-ditch effort to fix things at our *hiccup* cabin but it went horribly wrong I actually told Roger *hiccup* it was over but he keeps *hiccup* trying to reconcile." She went on, turning beet red, "I don't think it's going to happen but I agreed to talk to him tomorrow I blame Felicia for all this." She finally exhaled.

"See, it worked. Your hiccups are gone."

"Oh yeah," she acknowledged, continuing, "You know Felicia and Roger were friends in college."

I nodded.

"Well, when things started to go *really* south she came over all the time, insinuating herself into our lives like she was Sue Johanson. When Roger wouldn't confide in me anymore but could somehow express his feelings to *her*, I was *so* humiliated, knowing Felicia knew more about my life than I did."

"You think Miss 'Best Pal from College' wants to move into the 'More Than Friends' category?"

"I know it! Felicia sees Roger as 'the one that got away.' He told me once how she used to joke that if they weren't married by the time they turned forty she wanted the two of them to get hitched. You can just imagine how she felt when I came along and snagged him six months before his fortieth birthday. It wouldn't surprise me if she had a little blond voodoo doll that she pokes the hell out of every night."

Seeing where this was going, I said, "Felicia doesn't need a doll. All she has to do is poke her word processor."

"Exactly. Hence all the love scenes with Javier, which didn't even make sense. One minute I was with Wolfe and the next I was falling into a compost pile with Fink's gardener Pepe. It made my character look so slutty to fans and drove Roger straight over the edge. You should see all the hate mail I'm getting. Went from being Top Five in the Soap Polls to number one on *Cliffhanger Weekly*'s Losers List."

"Damn, I knew Felicia was vicious but to risk ratings? Does Roger know?"

"He didn't believe me, said I was being paranoid. He's one to talk. Anyway, I guess it doesn't really matter. I broke it off with Roger and broke down with Javier. He was so tender and attentive, and only too eager to blur the lines between real life and reel life."

"I'm glad *someone's* giving you some TLC," I said, walking toward the picnic table. "Now listen, promise as soon as I'm outta here we're going to fix some things and jet off to Jamaica for some much-needed R&R."

"Mom, is everything okay?" Ivy asked as we approached.

"Yeah, baby, just catchin' up. Sorry it's taken me so long."

"It's okay. Do you mind if I walk down to the stables with Shannen and let you and Mother Jones have some time together, alone?"

"But *we* haven't—"

"Mom." After a beat. "We have forever."

CHAPTER 37

Gotta Colt .45?

*S*tomping into a rustic Big Bear pawnshop that same afternoon, Roger Cabott startled the sleepy proprietor seated behind the counter. The name Shell was stitched above his shirt pocket, stuffed with leaky pens and eyeglasses.

"I need a *piece*," Roger growled.

"Uh, if you mean a gun what kind are you lookin' for?" Shell asked carefully, removing the pipe from his mouth.

"I don't know, something that shoots bullets I imagine," Roger said sarcastically. "Something I can get for *this*." Unballing his fist, he slammed his platinum and diamond ring down on the glass counter.

"Ohh-kay." Shell didn't want to ask his next question but felt he should. "What do you want to do with a firearm?"

"I might wanna go *hunting,* and I definitely need to protect myself and my honor."

"Protection for the home. NRA member I bet. Good. Town Hall meeting tomorrow night if you're interested. All right, let's see what we got. Rifles are over here."

"I didn't say anything about a rifle. I'm looking for a handgun."

Not saying a word, the storekeeper nodded, leading Roger past the enormous knife display, fishing equipment, and a Confederate flag collection. Roger pointed. "Gimme that one, yeah, that'll do the trick."

"Good choice. Colt .45 automatic, but you do understand this firearm isn't for hunting?"

"Yeah, yeah, yeah, I'll need some ammo too. Can you throw it in?"

"Sure. Need to see some ID though."

Roger slid his wallet across the counter and fifteen minutes later emerged with a gun and a box of Remingtons. Revving the engine, he peeled out heading due south, back to L.A. to pay his Internet "It Girl" wife a visit.

CHAPTER 38

What's Done in the Dark Will Come to Light

*U*nder the shade of trellised wisteria blossoms, we sat wondering how to start a conversation we'd avoided having for more than two decades.

"You sure they feedin' you enough here, Beulah? Look like a string bean."

"I've already gained three pounds, Grandma."

"Where—your earlobes?"

An awkward silence stood between us before Grandma Jones said, "Sure is high cotton. Real uppity. Wish I could've afforded a *breakdown*. Shoot, in my day us women never hearda' such a thing, and those that *did* we ain't never seen since."

"Wait," I interrupted. "Couldn't afford a breakdown?"

"Had kids to raise, mouths to feed, and jobs to get to, a lot of 'em in the field. We prayed for mercy and salvation and kept right on goin'. Had your mamma to care for, plus my job cleanin' at the Country Club, then you come along. God gave me the strength to raise you even though—"

"But Grandma, sounds like you're sayin' bein' in rehab's a luxury."

"Ain't it? Seems like an awful lotta money to be spendin' on self-control. 'Specially in these times."

Stemming my percolating frustration, I said, "But it's more than self-control. It's things built up inside that I kept a lid on from a long time ago."

"Oh, I don't want to hear all that *goobly-gob*. Prayer is the best medicine, all you gotta do is turn your life over to the Lord and *recognize* grace is 'favor' and you wouldn't have *any* success without *that*. The past is the past, dead and buried. Move on and get back on track, a new world's right around the corner."

Grandma was entitled to think she was right, but I wasn't about to let her off the hook and sweep our dark secret under the rug.

"No disrespect, but it ain't *goobly-gob*. It's the truth and I've been talkin' about it with my therapist here."

"Shhh," she said, looking around to make sure we were alone "Lower your voice, people hear you talkin' like that they're liable to think you're *special*. And what exactly have you been discussin' with a stranger anyway, Beulah?"

"Therapist."

"Same thing, answer the question."

"You know, our secret."

"What secret? I don't know about any secret. What the devil are you talkin' about?"

"Grandma," I said softly, taking her hand, "I know this must be as painful for you as it is for me, but if I'm gonna get any better I need for us to talk once and for all about what happened to my mamma, me, and what I did afterward. Remember what they say, 'We're only as sick as—'"

"Beulah Espinetta Jones, I didn't come all this way to listen to some foolishness."

"I'm afraid you're gonna have to," I insisted, shocking my grandmother, who'd reached for her cane, threatening to leave. "We can't keep pretending what happened in Greenwood is a figment of my imagination."

Stoic and tight-lipped, pocking her chin like an orange peel, she sat there just like I remembered as a girl returning home from my theatrical debut in the Pride-All taxi.

"As much as I've tried, Grandma, it's a promise I just can't keep. I want us to come clean with each other. And if you love me the way you say you do, you'll do that."

As she slowly released her cane, I sensed she might be ready to talk.

"You know, Beulah, everybody ready to jump on board when the goin's good, but the minute you down in the dust, who's there to pick you up? Look around, who's here? Me and Ivy. I worked my whole life and done the best with the hand I was dealt. Your great-grandma, God rest her soul, worked them cotton fields and when she was pregnant with me they sent her to squeeze cottonseed oil through Chinese hair. You come from strong stock, a long line of hardworkin', God-fearin' women, and for the life of me I don't know why you'd want to go and dig up the ugly past and spoil things now. We moved on from all that pain," she lamented.

"*You* moved on, Grandma, not me. I feel things, deep things, still."

"Just ask the Holy Ghost to help change you on the inside and you'll be able to let all that confusion and hatred go. See, I wrote down what the pastor said this mornin':

> To get somethin' you never had, you have to do some-
> thin' you never did. When God takes somethin' from

your grasp, he's not punishin' you, but openin' your
hands to receive somethin' better. He'll never take you
where His grace won't protect you.

"Here," she said, passing me the pamphlet.

Looking down at it, I said, "Grandma, there's two ways to interpret
this sermon. To me it says, I wouldn't be here if I wasn't supposed to be.
And long before Hollywood was even in the picture, you told me, 'If
ya keep doin' what you're doin' you're gonna keep gettin' what you get.'
Why did you send me to dust and make tea for Winslow, knowin' full
well what he was capable of?"

Silence.

"Grandma?"

"I've prayed for forgiveness, chile. Couldn't imagine him harmin'
my baby Maddie Mae while she was up there cleanin' for me."

"For you?" I got chill bumps.

"I fell ill . . . was on bed rest."

I'd only seen Grandma Jones cry once before.

"Nevah gave it a second thought sendin' her up to Winslow's in my
place. Didn't want him to hire somebody else."

"But when she came up pregnant?"

Silence.

"Grandma," I said pointedly, "weren't you suspicious when she came
up preg—"

"Yes! Yes, 'course I was. But folks didn't talk about such things back
then for fear of scandal. When I tried sayin' somethin' Winslow threatened to run me and your mamma outta town and where was we gonna
go?" She wept.

A hungry hawk circled above his next meal.

"Said he'd take care of you even though he nevah admitted to any
wrongdoin'. I made room in my heart and forgave him."

"Well I never did. What gave you the right?"

"Jesus. Jesus gave me the right. And Pastor Winslow made me a promise. Kept it every week."

"And do you know where that *promise* came from, Grandma?"

"Well . . . I-I . . . "

"I do. Caught that wolf passin' you that bloody promise in an envelope in the shed. Nevah said a word for fear of the tongue of your strap."

"What strap?" She questioned like every elder I knew, conveniently forgetting terrifying discipline over nothin'.

Storming on, I said, "But because you taught me to keep secrets, including poor Mamma bein' raped by that jackleg preachin' thug, I took matters into my own hands before he could do any more damage."

"Beulah, stop 'fore I . . ."

"What? Get a switch?"

"It wasn't 'cause I didn't believe Maddie Mae! You're upsettin' me with this gone by business."

But I couldn't stop. A dam had broken wide open.

"Figured if we repressed our secrets, they'd go away? Or is insanity my only option? Is that what you meant by me comin' from strong stock?"

"It was survivin'! I was consumed with guilt and blinded by fear. Yeah, I was weak and made mistakes and allowed myself to be swallowed up by sin, I admit that. Don't judge how I dealt with my grief, please don't. I lost my daughter, my *only* child, and knew no amount of prayin' was gonna bring her back but she gave me you, a miracle born outta tragedy, I can't lose you too, Beulah."

There was so much more I wanted to say but couldn't.

"Can't make what *was* no more 'cause I don't have the power to rewrite history but I do have the power to go forward with . . . with what we have . . . love for each other."

Emotionally spent, we watched as a pair of hummingbirds searched for nectar.

Ivy and Shannen headed our way, enjoying the fiddlers as they passed.

"Mom, the guy at the gate said we should start wrapping up our visit and we've barely had any time . . . Mother Jones, are you crying?"

"Happy tears, pumpkin, nothin' for you to worry your pretty little head about." Looking at me with a tender smile, she continued, "Your mamma and me had a lot of catchin' up to do and it's been a beautiful visit."

I could hear Rock in the background. "Okay folks, time to wrap it up. Visiting hours are over in a half hour."

After devoting the remaining time to Ivy, I walked my family to Shannen's Love Bug. I noticed her glancing in Jerome's direction as he lifted his son out of the Jump O'Rama and kissed his wife good-bye.

"You okay?" I asked Shannen.

"Yeah. Just not looking forward to tomorrow."

"If Roger starts any stuff just call the cops and get a restraining order against his crazy butt."

"I tried that once before, remember? It ended badly and I had to call in sick. On a brighter note, I'm going to surprise your grandma and take her to the set tomorrow. What do you think?"

"I think you're excellent. She's going to have the time of her life. Just wish I could be there too. Take lots of pictures and make sure she meets Wolfe and Maeve, and especially Willie, they're her favorites after you and me."

"Don't worry, we won't *miss a trick*," Shannen said with a wink, repeating an oft-used phrase she'd learned from Grandma Jones.

"You know, Shannen, I can count on one hand the true friends I have in this world and you're one of them."

Tearing up again and hugging me tightly, she said, "I'd better go or we'll never leave."

"Thanks for everything, I mean it."

Reaching in through the front window on the opposite side, I gave

Grandma Jones one last squeeze, breathing in her familiar talcum powder scent, whispering, "I love you," in her ear.

"We'll be back next week, Mom," Ivy said, planting a kiss on both my cheeks before getting in and buckling up.

"Be home for your birthday."

"Mom, you've told me three times already."

Veiled by tears, Shannen's VW became smaller and smaller as I waved good-bye, spontaneously curling my index and thumb into the shape of a small "C" measuring my family driving away. Once they were out of sight, the country western music fading, I repeated, "Traveling mercies . . . traveling mercies . . . traveling mercies . . ."

BLIND ITEM: What anally retentive muscle-head actor was seen in leather chaps making out with a colleague from *Our Lives to Contend* in Whispers Lounge, a gay men's S&M club near the Piers, before heading home to his frumpy wife and kids on Long Island? I'll never tell.

The Diva

CHAPTER 39

Knit One, Purl Two

On a full moonlit night, Phillip McQueen, clad in a smoking jacket, was in the throes of another whine-a-thon to his ever-under-standing wife, Pinkey, as he gave himself a facial.

"Can you believe Edith and Randall gave that blowhard Wolfe five shows a week, reducing my guarantee to a measly two? Using the excuse 'due to extreme soap opera anorexia we're asking everyone to take a fifteen percent pay cut.' The nerve of those imbeciles *emailing* me the news!"

"Just terrible, Phillip," his wife sympathized as she knitted one, purled two. "By the way, the show faxed your changes for tomorrow and I put them in your script binder."

"You know, if Augustus Barringer were still running things this wouldn't be happening," he hissed into the mirror, fondling his reflection. "Edith didn't even give me the common courtesy of a face-to-face meeting. Or at the very least have that Neanderthal Roberts deliver the horrid news in the privacy of my dressing room," he babbled, still looking at himself in the mirror. With a predilection for self-preservation, the obsessive stay-youthful-forever thespian dotted on caviar eye cream, continuing his facial.

"Just awful, how could *R&R* do that to you after all you've given them, the best years of your acting career."

Phillip turned, stone-faced, staring at her.

"I mean, *some* of your best years, honey," she recanted, looking over her bifocals.

Resuming his regimen, he said, "And I know Edith has told that ground-gripper Felicia to write me off the show. I can feel it. If anything happens to me . . . like if I fall into an icy Whitehaven pond and drown or fly off course in my upcoming hot air balloon expedition storyline, know it has everything to do with my contract negotiations with those WBC tightasses. Ever since I left my agent, Edith thinks she can Betsey Johnson all over me."

"Who's she?"

"Not important. If that prune wants to play hardball, I'll show her what a hardball feels like."

"What are you going to do, Phillip? Don't forget what they did to Maeve Fielding's love interest of twenty-two years, Ulysses St. Nick, when he asked for a raise."

"Pinkey, of course I remember, but when have I ever cowered to intimidation? If I have to I'll swallow my pride and rejoin the cast of *Our Lives to Contend*."

"*OLTC*? But that soap's number four in the ratings with a zero point nine audience participation."

"Who cares? This is *not* the time for soap opera discrimination. You like the lifestyle we live, don't you?"

"Yes, of course."

"And you want to keep Bert in private schools, right?"

"Yes, dear, but won't you be taking a huge pay cut if you go to *OLTC*?" she said, recovering dropped stitches.

"Don't worry about that. I'll handle our finances," Phillip stated coldly. "I can make up the difference going to Canada for personal appearances and selling my eight-by-tens and calendars. All I need from you is a show of domestic engineering unity."

"But that's one of the biggest things you said attracted you to me, that I'm a 'natural born penny-pincher.' I cut out coupons, shop at Costco, do the cooking and cleaning, volunteer for carpool so we don't have to pay a premium for school bus pickup—"

"Sorry, Pinkey, how insensitive of me. I don't know what I'd do without you."

Swishing back an Ambien, Phillip finally turned away from the mirror, switched off the bathroom light, and shuffled over to their four-poster oak bed, dropping to his knees.

After wrapping up an abbreviated Our Father and placing his velvet slippers beside the dust ruffle, he said, "I can't wait for tomorrow," as he slid between the 800-thread-count Egyptian sheets. He pecked Pinkey with a stingy kiss before placing an embroidered *R&R* eye mask over his baby blues.

"Good night, my darling."

"Good night, Phillip."

"Tomorrow I have those *insipid* pool scenes with Wolfe and that airhead Shannen on that hideous set they call a ranch. Of course casting will dust off Willie Turner and prop him up as the butler, and I'll have to listen to all his unbearable glory days with Ben Vereen on Broadway, and those redundant civil rights tales while he serves me the same warm near beer for hours. And why does he always have a damn facecloth hanging from his back pocket? Probably gang related. I hate Willie almost as much as I hate 'product placement'! And they only bring him back so he can keep his health benefits."

"But honey, doesn't Willie give you his Sudsy vote every year?"

"Pinkey!" Phillip said, irritated, pulling off his eye mask, sitting up. "Where did that come from? You're totally off topic. Are you even listening to me?"

"Every word, Phillip, every word," his browbeaten wife replied apologetically as he sank back down.

"Willie's voting for me has nothing to do with what I'm talking about right now. On top of everything else I have to navigate on the set tomorrow, I'll have to suck up to that idiotic director Julius, whom you know I despise with a passion, and deal with Alison's phoned-in performances."

"Is Julius still with the show?"

"Yes, unfortunately. That ex-cartoon director always underuses me, gives me the same friggin' blocking, planting me on a shitty chaise indefinitely like a glorified extra. I can see it now, Emmy running around half-naked in a thong, Wolfe strutting around like a Scandinavian peacock in a tacky Speedo, when everyone knows he wraps it in baby socks to make a bulge like that, Maeve's intolerable nicotine breath hacking away, contaminating everyone with her bronchitis, ruining my takes while I suffer in a floor-length terry cloth robe. The singular positive thing about tomorrow is that I won't have to deal with that *too hot to trot Hottentot*, Calysta Jeffries. Oh, gawd, why me?" Phillip said, replacing his eye mask.

"It's just four scenes, honey," Pinkey soothed.

"Don't remind me."

"Ready to run lines?" she asked hopefully, replacing her knitting needles with Phillip's *R&R*-embossed leather script binder conveniently poised on her nightstand.

"Go 'head."

"I'm going to start with your scenes with Wolfe, okay?" she confirmed, clearing her throat, dropping her voice three octaves, speaking with a generic European accent.

VIDAL

Vonderful day for a BBQ on the Vinn Hansen Ranch,

vouldn't you say, Fink?

"On second thought I'm going to pass on running lines tonight. I'm tired."

Pinkey's lollipop face dropped as she swapped the script out for her knitting, clearly disappointed. She looked forward to their nighttime routine, vicariously standing at the footlights of a Hollywood stage, momentarily a part of her husband's glamorous world in her own secret, secret way.

"I have a better idea," whispered Phillip.

Perking back up, Pinkey hoped it was what had been lacking in their marriage for months. "What's that, honey?"

Removing his eye mask, he slurred devilishly, "I'm going to conveniently get sick in the middle of taping tomorrow and see what that witch Edith and her henchman do then. They'd never expect Mr. Dependable to hold up shooting . . ."

Phillip drifted off to sleep leaving his worried wife knitting and purling another sweater for the upcoming *Rich and the Ruthless* Fan Club auction.

BLIND ITEM: Which longtime actor, who plays a part-time private dick on one of daytime's most popular soaps, causes the crew to routinely make bets on how many takes he'll need to get through just four contiguous lines of dialogue without a flub? One of the crew members was overheard telling that day's winner he should buy the bubbler a new rug with his earnings!

The Diva

CHAPTER 40

Speedos, Thongs, and Boas, Oh My!

(Vinn Hansen Ranch, poolside. We see Gina, Jade, Dove, Wilson, Lady Leslie, Rory, Justine, Pepe, the whole cast festively mulling around, a few extras frolicking in the pool with a beach ball—make it look like there's more than two feet of water. Don't talk to any extras and tell them to mime their conversations or we'll have to pay them)

VIDAL

Vonderful day for a BBQ on the Vinn Hansen Ranch, vouldn't you say, Fink?

BARRETT

Just dandy, Vidal.

VIDAL

(Gloating)

Even vith the skyrocketing price of veat, my international biscuit business is thriving. Sorry to hear you
had to fire vun hundred and fifty-two employees last
veek.

BARRETT

Actually . . .

JUSTINE

*(Heavy flirtation with Vidal, swiping him with her
voluptuous chest. Feature her bikini top. Keep wind
fans on high to give her a windswept look)*
Vidal, there you are. I have something red and juicy
to share with you.

VIDAL

Ah, my pet, my vision of loveliness. I am breathless
vith anticipation.

JUSTINE

*(Suggestively whips out a super-sized chocolate-
covered strawberry and puts it between her teeth)*
Bite it, Vidal. Bite it quick before Pepe spots us.

VIDAL

I'd share a chocolate-covered grasshopper if it vere
vith you.

BARRETT

(*Showing jealousy here. Remembering the history of
his recent and painful divorce with Justine*)
Hello, Justine.

JUSTINE

(*Not too mean*)
Barrett! What are *you* doing here?

VIDAL

I invited him.

JUSTINE

That's why I'll always love you, Vidal. You're so cool.
Barrett, where's your bathing suit, wonder-boy? It's a
pool party, not a Fink board meeting. I'm sure Vidal
wouldn't mind lending you his spare trunks, would ya,
Vidal?

VIDAL

Of course not, my svan, but I highly doubt Barrett
could fill my—

BARRETT

I came to enjoy the festivities, not to swim. I have my
own heated Olympic-sized pool, you'll recall, Justine,
at Fink Manor, the one you had the habit of skinny-
dipping in whenever I hosted an important business
meeting.

WILSON TURNER

Mr. Fink, here's your near beer jus' like you asked.

BARRETT

Thanks, Willie. And Vidal, thank you for the invitation. After all you didn't have to.

VIDAL

Yes, I know.

BARRETT

I'm pleased you don't harbor any ill will against me in light of the fact I was acquitted, found innocent of hiring a hit man to assassinate you at the Whitehaven Hospital Gala.

VIDAL

Vater under the bridge, my man, vater under the bridge. I'm not going to let a little sqvabble get in the vay of business. But I'd look over my shoulder every so often if I vere you.

JUSTINE

Yeah, Barrett, that's such old news. Don't be a bore. Loosen up and take that ascot off and go toast some marshmallows with Dove and Jade.

(Reminder: Lady Lovekin is considering selling off her Fink Enterprises stock and Vidal wants to buy it so he can own Barrett Fink and his shipping company. A lot of brown-nosing here)

VIDAL

Lady Leslie Lovekin, you are . . . you are . . . I
can't seem to find the vords. Ah‚yes, you are a cas-
cading vaterfall of loveliness.

LADY LESLIE

You're such an incorrigible charmer, Vidal. Hello, everyone.

(Adlib hellos)

LADY LESLIE

Lovely affair, Vidal, as usual you are the consummate
host, and I see no love has been lost between you and
your skanky ho ex-fiancée.

(As Justine licks a small piece of chocolate from
Vidal's mustache)

"*Cut!*" Julius screamed. "Maeve, darling, you cannot say 'skanky ho.'"

"Says who?" bit back Maeve. "I heard Strasser say it on *her* soap. Besides, what's the difference between 'skanky ho' and 'bitch' anyway?"

"The WBC network, that's what. We don't have to lower ourselves to
third-rate soap opera circus tricks. We're a hallmark channel and we're
number one."

"Whatever," Maeve mumbled.

"We'll leave it in this time. Let's pick it up with your line, Shannen.
Five, four, three, two, *go!*"

JUSTINE

Give it a rest, Lady Les. You're just jealous and wish
you could have some.

LADY LESLIE

(Ignoring Justine)

Barrett, I hadn't expected to see you of all people here at the ranch. By the way, I'm looking forward to the board meeting next week. I don't think I can hang on much longer to my fifty-one percent of Fink Enterprises with the market sinking the way it is.

BARRETT

Why don't we talk about this in priv—

LADY LESLIE

But since you're here and single again—

GINA

(Slinking over in a red thong bikini. Emphasize showing body shot.

Yeah, since you're here and single again—

"*Stop tape!*" screamed Phillip.

"What's the problem?" Julius inquired from the sound booth.

"Ask the script supervisor, if she's not filing her nails. Maeve keeps stepping all over the few lines I have, along with everyone else! And where's makeup? I need powder. I can feel myself shining."

"Oh, for crissakes, you petty pussy," spat Maeve. "I'd get on all fours, twirl around three times, and bark twice if it meant I didn't have to do this scene with you."

"Maeve, darling?" Julius purred.

"Yeah?" she responded, blowing fussy boa feathers away from her mouth.

"If you wouldn't mind, please, let's let Phillip get all of his lines out, every syllable, before you speak, okay, my love?"

"That's lunch, folks!" the stage manager announced.

"Damn it!" said Julius, slamming down his cowboy hat.

"Be camera ready in an hour. We'll pick up where we left off."

Shannen raced over to Candelaria, seated in a red director's chair next to Weezi, who'd invited himself. He'd explained he wanted to help Calysta's grandmother feel more comfortable, but Shannen knew he was just there to troll for future clients. She didn't care as long as he stayed out of her way.

"C'mon, Mrs. Jones, I want to introduce you to the gang before they go back to their dressing rooms. Hey everybody, wait! This is Calysta's grandmother, Candelaria Jones. She's visiting all the way from Mississippi."

"Hello, m'deah," said Ethan, badly tapping into Tyler Perry, lifting her off her feet.

"Oh, my," she squealed. "Dove Jordan, sakes alive!"

Almost to her dressing room, Emmy did an about-face, tearing a muffin top from a food display on her way back to the set.

"Remy, you're looking beautiful—" Weezi started.

"No thanks," she snapped, shooting him down before he could make a pitch. "And it's Emmy."

"I like you better than the first Dove," Grandma Jones gushed to Ethan. "And I think I'm the only one."

Dressed in ribbons and rainbows, wearing blue contact lenses, Jade extended one limp, fishlike hand while twirling her stubborn curly hair with the other, a nervous habit.

"Hi, I'm Jade, nice to meet you but I gotta go, I have an audition for a cartoon voiceover. Later."

"Wow, Mississippi? How *Gone with the Wind* exotic," said Emmy, stuffing the rest of the muffin top into her pie-hole, taking Jade's place.

"For heaven's sake, Gina Chiccetelli! My Beulah talks about you lots."

Beulah? Emmy thought. Though no one asked and Emmy definitely wanted to, everyone chalked it up to Candelaria being old.

Stepping in and chivalrously kissing her hand, nearly causing Candelaria to faint, Wolfe interrupted, "It's an absolute pleasure to meet such a grand and important lady. Calysta's told me such admirable things about you." Into her ear he whispered, "She vas the best actor on the show after me. I miss her terribly. Shall ve take a picture?"

"Oh, my word, Wolfe Hudson, you are too many things and this is much too much excitement for one person. You bet I want a picture! Everyone in Greenwood just loves you! Shannen would you be a honeybee and help me fish out my disposable? It's at the bottom of my pocketbook."

"You bet," she answered, spotting crabby pants Phillip trying to scurry off.

"Phillip!" she shouted. "Come get in the picture. It's for Calysta's grandmother."

Silently seething, he stomped back, saying under his breath, "Like I care. I hate Calysta generational-ly. Why is that old biddy visiting now?"

"Well if it isn't Barrett Fink. You rattlesnake, you. I've always hated your character. And I mean that in a good way. Are you as mean in real life as you are on the show?"

"No, of course not."

"'Cause honey, you be *playin'* that part."

Trying to stem his irritation and leaning down next to Candelaria's five-foot-nothing frame, he asked, "Did you know Calysta got killed off months and months ago?"

"'Course I do, but she'll be back. Just as sure as 'tick 'n' bite won't get no bunny beat from me.'"

What did she say? Phillip thought along with everyone else. *No doubt*

Mrs. Jones is the source of all those kooky adlibs Calysta frequently slid into my scenes, also known as "flayvah."

"See the apple hasn't fallen far from the tree, and I mean that in a *good way*. Well, let's get this picture before lunch is over," Phillip said smoothly.

"Oh, my stars! Is that who I think it is? Lord Jesus somebody tell me I ain't seein' a ghost. Wilson Turner, I just love you! You're my favorite! Been watchin' you since *Yesterday, Today and Maybe Tomorrow*. Can I get a picture, *please*?" Candelaria said coquettishly.

Basking in the rare acknowledgment, he gloated, "Step aside, folks. The lady wants a photo with *me*. Whatchaname, beautiful?"

"Candelaria."

"You can call me Willie."

"Oh, Willie, I just love you, I'm your biggest fan. Wait till I tell all the ladies in Greenwood, you just don't know."

Phillip roiled, incapable of understanding how the under-five-near-beer-serving actor could be popular with *any* demographic.

"Can I just say, your Calysta is an outstanding actress?"

"Why thank you, Willie."

"I tell her all the time, no matter what them writers give her, she always finds a way to put some 'pork chop' in a scene."

"What did he say?" whispered Phillip into Ethan's ear.

"Hell if I know."

"You sure are some kinda nice, Miss Candelaria. And I hope I make your front room wall," Wilson said flirtatiously, kissing her hand.

"Ah, Willie, you are such a stitch. I'ma blow this one up 'n' every-thing." She beamed.

"If you wouldn't mind, I have an interview waiting and—" attempted Phillip.

"I'm so sorry, Mr. Fink, to keep you waitin' but could you give me one more second so I can get a picture alone with my Wolfe? And then you can jump in with the rest of the cast."

A chorus of "No problem, Mrs. Jones" could be heard as the bubblers moved away from the pair, with the exception of Phillip, smarting from the snub.

Flash went the disposable.

Emmy noticed Alison heading back to her dressing room from craft service, the actors's trough, wearing high-waisted mom jeans and her Sarah Palin T-shirt—she just couldn't let it go—and sidled over to her, saying, "Alison, Calysta's grandma is visiting."

"So?" Refusing to be in today's pool scenes next to the bikini-clad youngsters, an intimidated and water retentive Alison, still bound in breast augmentation bandages, had been sulking in her dressing room.

"Wanna come over and be in the group shot?" Emmy asked.

Alison glared. "I'm not taking pictures today." She moved past with her plate of bagels and cream cheese.

"Is that for you and Randall?" Emmy pointedly asked.

"No, it's for me."

"*All* of it?"

"Yes."

"No wonder," Emmy scoffed, sashaying away in her mini set robe, leaving Alison staring down at the carbs.

As the group finished taking a barrage of pictures, Emmy interrupted, petting Candelaria's arm, "Grandma Jones . . . do you mind if I call you that . . . I just feel so close to you already, after being like a sister to Calysta. You know, I rushed to the hospital to be at her side as soon as I heard she was in that car wreck, but incredibly they wouldn't let me in. I'm so sorry she's in rehab. You simply have to tell me all about her troubled childhood."

Shannen narrowed her eyes. "Not now, Emmy. I'm showing Mrs. Jones around the set. Excuse us."

"I'll uh, catch up with you guys in a few," Weezi said, sizing up Javier.

"Whatever, Weezi," Shannen dismissed.

Throwing in the kitchen sink trying to sound black, Emmy put her hands on her hips and cocked one to the left, saying, "Yo Shannen, slow your roll, sistah, and stop bogartin' Ms. Jones. Tryin' to get acquainted is all, but that's *aight* . . . I ain't gonna sweat it 'cause I sho nuff gotta bounce . . . laytah, homie."

CHAPTER 41

The Rich and the Ruthless

*R*olling to a stop in her Bentley, Veronica pressed the security intercom button.

"Hello. May I help you?"

"It's Veronica Barringer, I have an appointment."

The gates swung open. The soap heiress drove forward and parked, immediately to be met with a firm handshake from Kelly Lava. "Welcome to Tranquility Tudor. If you'll follow me I have lunch set out."

"Thank you, but I just came to talk to Calysta Jeffries."

"I understand, Ms. Barringer, but there's a protocol we like to follow here at Tranquility Tudor. It's what sets us apart from the rest. Now if you please."

Kelly led her out to a sunny veranda. Rising as she approached, Pat Quigley said, "Ms. Barringer."

"Mr. Quigley, thank you for meeting with me on such short notice and on your day off."

"Don't mention it."

"Today we're serving black curry fluke carpaccio and jicama slaw with a green apple feuilleté for dessert," Kelly announced. "See what you would've been missing?"

"Lovely." Veronica sat, placing her hemstitched napkin in her lap.

"So, Mr. Quigley—"

"Call me Pat."

"Pat, I came to ask permission to discuss a personal matter with Calysta. And although my family is saddened by her predicament and this is a sensitive time for her, my ailing father insisted I deliver his highly confidential message in person. I'd be grateful if you'd assist me."

"Well, Ms. Barringer . . ." He paused, waiting for her to give him permission to use her first name; she didn't.

". . . where your concern for Calysta and loyalty to your father are admirable I couldn't possibly—"

Gracefully interrupting, Veronica continued, "I read that Tranquility Tudor has an endowment. My father would like to make an anonymous donation for a future client who might not otherwise be able to afford such a noble and illustrious establishment," she said, sliding a check across the table. "I also heard that in special cases you offer sober coaches to chaperone clients for off-site business."

"My, you've done your research."

"I don't like to waste time. Can that be arranged for Calysta? I need her at Oppenheimer and Berger Law Offices in Century City Wednesday morning at nine. I can't go into more detail."

Glancing at the check, he suavely said, "You're a very beautiful woman and your father's a very generous man. I never could resist beauty or generosity. *Salut,*" he toasted, holding up a sparkling lemonade. "Calysta should be back from collage therapy by the time we finish lunch. *Bon appetit!*"

★ ★ ★

"Haven't seen you in a while," Jay said to Roger Cabott as he pulled up to the WBC security gate.

"Yeah, been real busy these days. I'm here to see my wife."

"Sure, no problem."

"Jay, do you mind if I park in the back by the loading dock?"

"Suit yourself, Mr. Lassiter."

Roger bit his tongue and drove onto the lot.

"I'm going in, Anita," Emmy announced as the secretary cut her eyes at the bubble-trouble.

Before the door closed, Emmy purred, "Hi, Snuggle Bunny, I brought you a Starbucks and a Krispy Kreme."

The doughnut was a knockoff and she had recycled the cup, filling it with commissary java.

"I only have five minutes, Emmy."

"That's all we need, you naughty boy, let's get busy," she went on, dropping her robe and wiggling out of her thong. "I figured with everything going on, you could use a coffee break."

Four minutes later, she faked, "Wow, that was one for the record books. You still taking that Viagra?"

"Only for you, my little slut."

"I love when you talk dirty."

"So, Emmy, I have some news."

"Oh?" she said as she slipped back into her thong.

"I've decided to stick it out with Alison."

"What?" Emmy's eyes blazed. "You mean . . . stay together?"

"I've done more soul-searching than you could possib—"

"But what about *us*? *Our* future? You were gonna marry me and dump old crispy-crotch, you sonofabitch!"

That was before Alison told me she would fillet my dick if I ever left her, he thought.

"I'm sorry, but everything's changed. It's over."

"You piss-ant, you really think you can *do* me then *dump* me?"

"Uh, yeah, I do. Don't get me wrong, it's been a ton of fun, but you're D for done."

Emmy dropped to her knees. "But Randall, I'll do anything, anything. I'm begging you—"

"Get up, Emmy, don't degrade yourself any more than you have."

"I *hate* you," she snarled, baring her teeth like a rabid dog.

"And Emmy," Randall added, not raising his voice. "If you value your job you won't mention our little secret to anyone."

". . . and this is wardrobe, Mrs. Jones. This is where the entire *Rich and the Ruthless* archive is kept. Let me show you our humongous cast closet."

Candelaria, at a rare loss for words, followed along with a pep in her step. "Whoo, it's kinda tart in here."

"Yeah well, what are you gonna do? It's a big cast and producers had to cut back on dry cleaning to save money."

"What are you all doing in here?" The Pattern Cutter emerged from the back pulling two full racks of clothing. "Shannen, you don't have a fitting today."

"I know that, Penelope, I'm giving Mrs. Jones a tour."

"Mrs. Who?"

"Nice to meet you too. Isn't that Beulah's wedding dress and aren't these her clothes?" Candelaria asked.

"You mean Ruby Stargazer's dress. And yes, it is. She was such a headache to deal with, I'm happy to say I'm ridding the department of all her wardrobe, including the wedding dress. *R&R* is selling all her costumes to *Medical Clinic*. Good riddance! But to tell you the truth, we didn't get much money for it. Most of the clothes I bought on sale. She didn't deserve the designer labels like the rest of the cast."

"Well, Miss Penelope, Ruby Stargazer happens to be my granddaughter, and you oughta be ashamed of yourself. If you can't say somethin' nice 'bout somebody don't say nothin' at all. Shannen, let's go."

Shannen flashed her eyes at the Pattern Cutter, "Hmph."

As they left, Ben rushed in out of breath, Weezi trailing behind. "There you are, Shannen! Felicia wants to talk to you right away."

"But I only have thirty minutes left of break. Tell her I'll come see her after my scenes."

"No can do, she says it's urgent."

"I'll keep the tour going," Weezi volunteered smoothly, offering Candelaria his arm.

Holding the elevator doors open, Shannen said, "I'll catch up with you as soon as I'm done, Mrs. Jones."

"'Course, sugah."

Weezi bragged, "I'm the *only* representative Calysta's ever worked with. If you need anything, anything at all, don't hesitate to use my card," he said, handing one to her. "Let's head over to *The Daring and the Damned*."

Shannen shook her head as the doors closed.

"I hate you!"

As she knocked on Felicia's door, Shannen spied Emmy storming out of Randall's office, madder than hell, cinching her robe with her do slightly askew.

"Come in."

"Hi, Felicia, you wanted to see me?"

"Yes, have a seat. I know you're on your lunch break so I'm going to get right to the point. Unfortunately, the *R&R* blog is going crazy, fans have written in, and they absolutely hate the Justine/Pepe pairing. We can't afford to lose more audience, so I've decided to go with the storyline we were saving for Sweeps, and it's a sizzler, by the way, premium front-burner stuff."

Felicia stood up, coming around her desk to act out the scene. "You're upset, you find out Pepe is having an affair with Gina Chiccetelli, you get in your car after catching them in the sack, speed down Whitehaven Highway, around Fink Rotary, roaring onto Lovekin Lane, narrowly missing a bus, you crash into a light pole. It's going to be *so* dramatic. As a matter of fact, I'm already predicting you're going to get on the pre-nom list for a Sudsy with this scene."

"Um, Felicia? Not to sound ungrateful or anything, but it kinda sounds like Calysta's real-life accident."

"Well then, I guess it's in the universe. But where was I? Oh yes, you get into a fantastic diabolical car crash and flip three times before it explodes into a fiery blaze, the special effects are going to be off the charts. Then you go into a coma."

"And?"

"And that's it."

CHAPTER 42

You Shall Have Joy, or You Shall Have Power . . . You Shall Not Have Both

—RALPH WALDO EMERSON

*V*eronica, laid out in Kinder Aggugini, rose from the sofa in the common room to greet me as I entered with other TT residents.

"Veronica! Holy crap. This is unreal," Toby enthused.

"Toby, man, you gotta help put the stones back in the Zen garden," Rock interjected. "I keep tellin' you you can't use them for weights."

"Aw man—"

"Let's go," he reinforced. "Now."

"I'll see you at supper, Veronica, and don't let Rock fool ya, these people are dope."

"I heard someone was here to see me but I didn't expect it to be you. Please don't tell me—"

"No no no, don't worry, Calysta, Dad's still hanging in there but he *is* the reason I'm here to see you. Let's go somewhere more private."

I led her to TT's Quiet Room.

"Veronica, what's this all about?"

"Dad's resting comfortably at home with around-the-clock care. He asks about you quite a bit. He cares about you."

"Your father means a lot to me."

"I don't think he'd mind if I confided, when he was a little boy he lived in an orphanage until he was adopted. He prefers not to talk about that time in his life, but he admires determined people who work hard and rise from humble beginnings. And believe it or not, he saw a lot of himself in you. As you know, when a writer falls in love with an actor, they write not only for the character but for the person behind it, that's why he wrote so passionately for you."

I sat there, *full* and sad at the same time.

"He'd come home from work and say, 'Calysta did it again. She took my words and breathed life into them.' He was so tickled with your enthusiasm, you really honored my father doing that."

"It wasn't hard to do. He let me fly and do my thing in every direction."

"And he knows you've taken a lot of heat for that. Calysta, our family business is in crisis. We could lose control of *The Rich and the Ruthless* and *The Daring and the Damned* if we don't move quickly, and my father desperately needs your help. We all do, with the exception of my brother."

"What can *I* do?"

"Wednesday morning there's a very important vote that will determine the future of Barringer Dramatic Series. Auggie hates the business, he's been trying to get Dad to sell the soaps for years."

"For real?"

"For real. Anything that disturbs his golf game or partying, he wants nothing to do with. He's defiantly created an alliance with Edith and Randall to sell Dad's shows for millions. And where most people would jump at the opportunity, Dad's legacy is not for sale. Mother and I are voting against it. Dad, knowing he's in serious condition, called his attorney and asked me to give this to you."

"What is it?"

"Open it."

I slowly opened the padded envelope containing a black leather binder; the quality paper oozed rich. I read each page carefully before asking, "Is this what I think it is?"

"Yes, Dad wants you to be his proxy for Wednesday's meeting."

"Ohmygod, Veronica, are you serious? Why me?"

"Keep reading."

Opening a sealed envelope bearing my calligraphed name, I read:

My Dearest Calysta,

Thank you for all your get-well cards, the donation to Holly-grove, and the box of Godiva chocolates. They were as divine as you were thoughtful.

By the time you receive this letter, you'll have met with Veronica and know what an enormous favor I'm asking. And even as you, my dear, struggle with a different kind of illness, and hope all is on the upswing, there's no one I'd rather have cast my vote. You've given everything you possibly could to make our show a success and given me such infinite joy and inspiration, thus I want to show my appreciation. Where I could not buy you a Sudsy, I can give you power. These are uncertain times, but knowing the future of my shows rests in your capable hands gives me hope and a sense of satisfaction for what you've endured.

Finally, my attorney, Mason Oppenheimer, has made a special provision. If at any time you wish to reprise your role as Ruby Star-gazer it would be welcomed with open arms.

Affectionately,

Augustus Barringer

I looked up at Veronica bleary-eyed and said, "I'd be honored but how can I? I'm stuck here for five more weeks."

"Don't worry, I've made arrangements with Pat Quigley and he's sending a sober coach, Kelly Lava, to Century City with you. I'll send a car and there's already a business suit hanging in your room. My family thanks you in advance.

"Not a word to Toby," she said, hugging me good-bye, leaving me with a lot to process.

Nothing earth-shattering, but thought you kids would like to know cat hair was flying on the set of *The Rich and the Ruthless* last Wednesday. Soap snitch Emmy Abernathy (Gina Chiccetelli, *R&R*) reported that Maeve Fielding (Lady Leslie Lovekin, *R&R*) was smoking in her dressing room again, causing a firestorm of sailor-switchblade-swearing between the pair during the annual cast photo shoot.

Naturally, both muscled their way to the front row, smiling for the camera.

The Diva

CHAPTER 43

Show Business Is for Freaks and Strange Folks

Fizzing with anger, Shannen burst into her dressing room to find Grandma Jones eating the last bites of a cheeseburger.

"That Weezi is so nice. He went and got me lunch and everything," she said as Shannen slammed the door.

"I hate this show!" she spat.

"What happened? Last I saw you, you were as happy as a clam."

"Yeah, well, I'm not happy anymore, Mrs. Jones. That bit—"

"Watch your mouth, now. Slow down," Grandma Jones said, patting Shannen's arm.

"That creepy Felicia is up to her antics again, *sabotaging* my character!"

Grandma Jones sat transfixed, hanging on to every word while eating her French fries as though watching the soap itself.

"Go on," she encouraged.

"They're putting me in a coma!"

"How?"

"Well, according to Felicia, she's our head writer, the *R&R* blog is going nuts, the fans hate the JusPe pairing."

"Oh, what a shame. I liked you two together."

"And then she went on to say that *R&R* can't afford to lose any more audience, so the show's decided to go with the storyline they were saving for Sweeps, that's when . . . never mind. Anyway, she said, and I quote, I have to pinch my nose first to sound like her, 'It's a sizzler, by the way, premium front-burner stuff.'"

"Go on."

"Then she stood up and came around her desk and actually attempted to act out the scene. 'You're upset, you find out Pepe is having an affair with Gina Chiccetelli . . .'"

"Keep goin', this is gettin' good."

"After I catch Pepe and Gina in bed, and by the way I hate Emmy Abernathy, I get in a car, and I hate car scenes, they always look so fake with the fake scenery and two stagehands rocking the car back and forth and that faker-than-fake twirly light that makes it look like another fake car is passing in the opposite direction. I just *hate* it!"

"Oh, I wish you hadn't told me all that, Shannen. Kinda spoils it for me now. Anyway, I need to know what happens next?"

"Okay, I speed down Whitehaven Highway, around Fink Rotary and onto Lovekin Lane narrowly missing a bus, then crash into a light pole. Felicia lied, saying, 'It's going to be *so* dramatic.' Predicting I'd get a Sudsy nod. She's so nauseating. Anyway, I just had to tell her that the whole thing sounded like Calysta's real-life accident and you know what she said?"

Taking another French fry, Grandma Jones, eyes wide with anticipation, said, "No, chile. And don't leave me hangin'."

"'I guess it's in the universe.' That's what she said. Can you believe it? She stole a real-life chapter right out of Calysta's life and put it on the page. Just disgusting."

"I always said show business is for freaks and strange folk but let's get to the end."

"That witch told me I get into a fantastic diabolical car crash and flip three times—"

"Oh, my word, I've gotta call Whilemina and Odile right away."

"Wait, there's more, Mrs. Jones. And this is the kicker," said an unraveling Shannen. "The car explodes into a fiery blaze—"

"I don't think I can take much more," Candelaria said, falling back into the couch.

"It's just plain vicious. Maiming *me* of all people, wrapping me in miles of hideous gauze bandages like a mummy for weeks. You'd never know I was the one voted 'Most Beautiful' on the show by *Cliffhanger Weekly*."

"And . . ."

"And then I go into a coma."

Riveted, Grandma Jones asked, "For how long?"

"Indefinitely!"

"That don't sound too bad to me, layin' around collectin' a check."

"We're back," the stage manager shouted over the loudspeaker. "Wolfe, Emmy, Shannen, Ethan, Jade, Maeve, Javier, and all the extras. Item twenty-three, Vinn Hansen Ranch, be camera ready."

"Oh gawd, gotta get ready."

"Need any help?"

"No, it'll just take me a sec to fix my makeup and then we'll go back to the set."

"No, chile, I'm gonna sit right here, finish my fries, and watch the *story* on your TV."

"Are you sure?"

"I don't want to get in the way. Sorry you're not happy with what they're givin' you to do, but try to look at the glass half full instead of half empty, there are folks out there who would break their necks to be in your shoes."

"I guess, Mrs. Jones," Shannen said, finishing applying her mascara. "I'll try to look on the bright side, can't get any worse than this."

"Okay, everybody, let's get in the dinghy, places," the stage manager called.

"Um, cast, there's been a little change in plans," Julius announced, standing on the stage. "Alison's going to join us after all, so her lines are back in the script," he said to disgruntled actors.

In oversize Versace sunglasses, the soap diva shuffled onto the set looking like a whole bowl of crazy in her worn SpongeBob slippers, her strappy Rossi sandals dangling in one hand, stuffed into an Emilio Pucci one-piece and support hose without a wrap.

"Sorry, everybody, I had a colossal migraine."

"Alison, darling," Wolfe said, "I'm so happy you're feeling better now," then under his breath, "*Suit min pik, kælling.*"

"Besides, Phillip asked that we take the scene from the top to build momentum and so that he could get *all* his lines in this time," Julius added, throwing Phillip under the bus and dragging him.

"*For fanden da ogsa, dot pikfæs,*" Wolfe cursed in Danish.

"*Wah wah wah,*" Maeve poked.

"Why are we starting from the top again? I nailed that scene before lunch," Shannen complained. "What if my next take sucks and you use that one? It's not fair. Phillip, the only reason you want to take it from the top is because you want to figure out where you can *cry* in it. You're such a player hater."

Clapping his *R&R* script binder shut, Phillip barked, "If you people weren't so unprofessional, we would have been on to the next scene eons ago. But so many of you come to work unprepared; not knowing your lines, changing the tag, stepping on dialogue, adlibbing, coughing, showboating half-naked, taking up precious time getting tattoos covered. Not one of you could ever be in Connecticut summer stock. Let's go!"

"Vhy you pompous—" Wolfe began, stepping forward with balled fists.

"Okay, guys, come on, we've got a show to do," the stage manager said. "Five, four, three, two, *go!*"

VIDAL

Vonderful day for a BBQ on the Vinn Hansen Ranch, vouldn't you say, Fink?

BARRETT

Just dandy, Vidal.

VIDAL

　(Gloating)

Even vith the skyrocketing price of vheat, my international biscuit business is thriving. Sorry to hear you had to fire vun hundred and fifty-two employees last veek.

BARRETT

Actually, that's not—

JUSTINE

　(Heavy flirtation with Vidal, swiping him with her voluptuous chest. Feature her bikini top. Make sure fans are on high to give her a windswept look)

Vidal, there you are. I have something red and juicy
to share with you.

VIDAL

Ah, my pet, my vision of loveliness. I am breathless
vith anticipation.

RORY

You nympho, stay away from him, Vidal and I are getting back together.

JUSTINE

Don't worry, Rory, I'm with Pepe now.

RORY

Isn't he Barrett's gardener? Wow, Justine, you're really
slumming now. Why am I not surprised?

VIDAL

(Much innuendo)

Rory, my love, vhy don't you go lounge by the pool and
I'll be there in a moment to massage sunscreen into
your beautiful body?

RORY

(Melting)

I'll be waiting.

WILSON TURNER

Excuse me, Miss Rory. Here's your martini.

RORY

Thank you, Willie, you're right on time.

*(Rory walks away toward Lady Leslie Lovekin and
other guests around pool)*

VIDAL

(Turning back to Justine)

Now I believe you had something red and juicy for me?

JUSTINE

*(Suggestively whips out a super-size chocolate-
covered strawberry and puts it between her teeth)*

Bite it, Vidal. Bite it quick before Rory and Pepe see
us.

"*Bite this!*" Roger Cabott shrieked from across the room, firing a wild shot into the backdrop of the ranch set. Extras scrambled, running for their lives screaming. Holding the Colt .45 with two hands, he aimed it at Shannen.

"What the *hell*?" Turning to the script supervisor, Julius said, "I don't remember this being in the scene."

"It's not," she replied, putting down her nail file. "I'm calling security."

"You guys keep rolling those cameras out there, do you hear me?" Julius whispered into the headsets of the three trembling cameramen. "We might be able to use this in editing."

"Roger!" Shannen exclaimed.

"Nobody move!" he ordered. "Especially not you, my *palomita*," he said menacingly, with wild eyes and disheveled hair.

"Roger, p-p-put the gun down," she stammered.

"You've got some nerve telling me what to do," he said through clenched teeth, sweating through his green plaid shirt. "I saw the tape. I know all about your tryst with that *Mexican*."

Like 007, Wolfe stealthily made his way around the scenery hoping to take Roger by surprise. Ethan and Jade hid behind the rented ferns and ficus, while Alison ducked under a picnic table. Phillip ruthlessly pushed a slumped-over Maeve from behind the chaise to take her spot.

"*Que pasa,* Roger?" a bronzed, bare-chested Javier inquired. "You *loco*?" He bravely stepped in front of Shannen, defending her.

From behind the barbecue pit, Emmy called out, "Javier, don't. She's not worth it."

"You're an idiot, Javier," Roger slurred. "She doesn't care about you, all that gold-digger cares about is her next tennis bracelet like the rest of these broads. Now *move* or else I'll blow you away too."

"You guys are still rolling, right?" Julius whispered from the control booth. "Guys?"

Guns drawn, Jay and the rest of WBC security began carefully surrounding the set.

"Man, you had too much tequila," Javier said.

"Who do you think you're talkin' to, you worm? I'm a graduate of the *theater*, Yale. I know you *R&R* snobs thought I was beneath you because I was on *Obsessions,* always seated in the back at the Sudsys . . ." Pacing back and forth, Roger continued as security, now joined by LAPD, closed in. "But let me tell you somethin', I've been on Broadway in a Tony Award–winning show. How many of you can say you've done *that,* huh?"

Silence.

"That's what I thought! I know what it's like to do eight shows a week, performing to *throngs* of fans. You know why? Because I was the original Carbucketty in *Cats*! That's right! Me! Roger Cabott! I deserve *respect*!"

As Roger got ready to squeeze off a bullet, Wolfe heroically headbutted him from behind, knocking him out cold, sending him crashing to the floor.

Security flew in to apprehend a limp Roger, while Phillip rushed to Shannen, saying, "Are you all right?"

"No thanks to you," she said, trembling as she fell into Javier's arms.

Running from the sound booth as sirens sounded in the background, Julius asked the cameramen, "Did you get it all?"

"Yep," replied one.

Randall flew in. "Are you all right, my darling? I ran all the way from my office as fast as I could!"

"Oh, Randall!" Emmy called, thinking he'd seen the light. "I'm barely alive! Thank G—"

Randall dashed past her to Alison, sweeping her into his arms, instantly unleashing all Emmy's inner demons.

"Mr. Hudson, where did you learn to do that?" Jay asked.

"Yes, where did you learn to do that?" asked tabloid reporter Mitch Morelli, who'd been interviewing Shelly Montenegro across the lot on *The Daring and the Damned*.

"It vas nothing, I vas an amateur vrestler in the Old Country of Skagen, Denmark, and I hail from a long lineage of fearless Vikings."

"And Javier, man, that's what I call bravery," Jay added.

"You can say that again," said LAPD Officer Bodine, stepping in. "I'm going to personally report your heroism to the chief of police. You both deserve a Citation of Bravery. Javier, I never could've imagined that you of all people, a gangbanger from South Central with a rap sheet a mile long, would turn your life around like this. I'm proud of you, son. Ms. Lassiter, are you all right?"

"Yes, just a little rattled. I'm so glad no one got hurt."

"I'm afraid we're going to have to ask you some questions."

"Sure, no problem. Oh Javier, how can I ever thank you?"

"I can think of something, my *palomita*." He smiled as they relaxed into a deep chemical kiss.

WBC News reporters swarmed the set; more were on their way. Never shying from an opportunity to be in the media's glare, bubblers Emmy, Randall, Alison, Jade, Ethan, and Phillip were firmly planted in front of cameras, giving melodramatic interviews.

"It was the most horrid moment of my life!" Alison hyperventilated.

"Ohmagod, it was like totally *Blair Witch Project* scary," reported Jade. "Oh, and meet me in St. Louis for my personal appearance at Caleco's next Saturday at noon."

"Wow, dude, the whole thing was like so Pacino, super surreal. Roger must be on roids or something. What a nut job! It took like six security guards and half of LAPD to hold him down," embellished Ethan. "I'm sure you guys have worked up an appetite by now. You should go check out my new restaurant, Studs, in the valley," he finished with a cheesy smile into the camera.

"I just want to assure my Tweethearts that I'm fine," Emmy said emphatically to Mitch Morelli. "Have almost fifty thousand now, you know. I love being accessible and involved with my fans. Would've totally tweeted while I was a hostage but I had nowhere to keep my iPhone in this Ed Hardy string bikini." The human billboard continued, "This is an exclusive, I'm thinking about adopting . . . out of *Africa*!"

"Really?" Mitch asked.

"And did you catch me on *Big Love*?"

"As a matter of fact, I did. What happened? I reached for my popcorn and you were gone."

"That's so freakin' harsh, Mitch. I had a much bigger scene but those blockhead producers trimmed my lines."

"Emmy, I know this is a weird time, but while I have you here can I ask a few questions about those bitchy scenes between you and Justine?"

"Sure! Ask away."

"How difficult are they to do?"

"Would you believe those scenes are the hardest for me to pull off?

I really detest doing them. It turns me into a monster and takes me the rest of the night to settle down."

"But Emmy, you're masterful at them."

"Yeah well, I consider myself an escapist. That's why doing the soap is so natural and therapeutic for me. I can lose myself in an unbelievable character and save tons of cash not going to a shrink." Lowering her voice, she continued, "I work my issues out on the other actors in the scenes . . . it's brilliantly cathartic. After I get my soap fix I feel completely liberated and primed for the real world. That's why I get paid the big bucks, 'cause I've figured this whole thing out. Oh yeah, and I'm a *Method* actor, too. But seriously, I love Shannen, I really do. We're super tight. I even voted for her to get a Sudsy. She tries so hard. But as you know, I won . . . again. And every time Felicia writes for me to wind it up for those psychological mind-bending Gina/Justine scenes and those three cameras start rolling, I *bring* it."

"Thank you, Emmy. I better move on and see who else I can get a quick interview with."

"Who else? Are you joking? You've got me all to yourself. Who's to move on to?"

"You're right," Mitch said, trapped. "What was I thinking? Well, Emmy, there have been some nasty rumors circulating that maybe there's a little tension between you and Shannen. Is it true?"

"Oh for crissakes, that's the most ridiculous thing I've ever heard. I just told you, we're BFF soap buds." Emmy rambled off subject, "Last year, Edith Norman personally called to tell me I was the most popular actress in daytime drama after those scenes Shannen and I had fighting over Barrett, when I pushed her over the second-floor banister, do you remember those?"

"Who could forget? It'll go down in the soap opera hall of fame."

"Anyway, Edith Norman suggested I read about the *Gin-arrett* versus *Just-arrett* frenzy on the *R&R* blog to see who was more popular and I was absolutely shocked at what I read."

"What'd it say?"

"There was a whole culture of haters on the site that referred to me as a shrunken apple face and one of the chatters even insinuated that I was really a man. I was devastated and wished I could hire a private dick to find that person and throw acid in their face, just kidding. But what was *really* bad, was how many people thought I was sexier than Shannen. I mean, I know I *naturally* have a killer body and Shannen doesn't, she's had a little work done, but that doesn't make her chopped liver. Thank goodness she knows nothing about that mean blog. She's so fragile, you know? Especially with Roger going friggin' crazy, nearly killing us all. If she knew that this blog existed and that"—lowering her voice—"they called her a slutty whore, it would probably send her over the edge. Anyway, I just love her."

"Over here! Maeve Fielding's been shot!" the stage manager yelled.

"Ohmagawd. Sorry, Emmy, we have to end it here."

"Not yet. Maeve has ice for blood. She'll live."

"Hurry!"

"I just wish the fans would keep the show and our personal lives in perspective. My name is not Gina; it's Emmy. And Shannen, soon to be ex-Mrs. Roger Cabott, is not Justine Lashaway Fink. And one more thing," she said, staring into the lens. "To all the number one wannabes flockin' to the Golden State from NYC, stay off from my turf."

Running back into the booth, Jules directed, "Cue the organ music."

"Are you serious, Julius?" asked the sound technician.

"You heard me. Cue it! And call post, tell 'em to slap some slow motion on it before it goes to air."

The cast and extras stampeded across the loose sod to where Maeve had been pushed by Phillip earlier. The lifeless legend was wedged between the potted ficus and overturned plastic geraniums.

"Get an ambulance over here now!" the stage manager yelled.

Shedding hopeful tears, Phillip crouched down next to the EMT, asking, "Is she dead?"

* * *

After they finished being questioned by LAPD Shannen remembered. "Oh Javier," she cried, racing upstairs, "I left Mrs. Jones in my dressing room watching us on my monitor, she must be petrified."

Calling out, "Mrs. Jones, Mrs. Jones . . ." Shannen and Javier burst through the doorway, finding the room empty.

A note, scribbled on the back of a script page, was on the coffee table.

Shannen baby, Thanks for everything, but I gotta get outta here quick in a hurry. Things is dangerous round here. Weren't kiddin when they said California is the wild, wild west. Expectin an earthquake and got a dang shootout instead! Thought it was part of the scene at first, but your husband ain't on my story. That gun is real and so is them bullets and I have a lotta livin to do. Dont worry, always kept my bus ticket in my pocketbook and one of them nice guards called a cab to take me to the station. Like I said, show business is for freaks and strange folk. You can send my suitcase US Postal Ground. Thats what the $20 is for. Come visit anytime.

Have a blessed day—love,
Grandma Jones

CHAPTER 44

Malibu Field Trip

The next morning, I climbed into the "We Do It One Day at a Time" activity van with the TT gang for our weekly field trip. Destination? Über-expensive Malibu Country Mart.

With Rihanna and Justin warbling "Whyyouwannabringmedown" on the radio, Rock drove everyone off the compound, gossiping about the shootout on the *R&R* set the day before. The sensational news was splashed across the cover of every newspaper.

Erroll commented from behind the *L.A. Times,* "I can't believe you worked with these people, Calysta." The front page featured a large picture of Shannen, Javier, and Wolfe, the caption reading, "Heroically saving the day, Wolfe Hudson commented, 'It vas nothing . . . I'm a Viking.'"

"This Alison person sounds like an absolute loon," he continued, reading on before licking his pointer to flip the page, adding, "Oh, look, Dylan, there's a wonderful review on your new album."

Dylan, wearing a Nine Inch Nails T-shirt, always dozed off in the backseat the moment the sober buggy moved.

"This would never have happened on *The Daring and the Damned*," Gretchen chirped, reading over his shoulder.

"I'm just glad Shannen's okay," Jerome commented.

Earlier, I'd felt a weight had been lifted after talking with Grandma Jones and Veronica's visit yesterday; now all that was dampened by the shock of knowing Shannen's life had been threatened by that predator Roger. Thank goodness Wolfe and Javier were bubblers with balls and used them.

Kelly Lava spiraled around in the passenger seat, looking over her Ray-Bans, and ordered, "Okay, everybody, settle down. Dylan, do you have your seat belt on?"

"Uh-huh," he grunted.

"We're almost there and I want to make sure you're all clear on the buddy system. The strip mall is spread out, so everyone's only allowed in one section at a time and always with your TT buddy. Today's pairings are Gretchen/Calysta, Dylan/Dolly, Jerome/Erroll, and Chad, since Toby had to stay back on behavioral probation, you'll be accompanied by Rock."

"Great," he murmured disappointedly.

"Yay, Calysta, we're buddies!" Gretchen said, grabbing my arm excitedly. "We're going to have such a blast. This place is bananas, it has all the shopping you could possibly want and a Nobu, they have the best shrimp and lobster roll with spicy lemon sauce."

"I'm familiar," I said, still worried about anyone spotting me toolin' around in the TT druggie van or clumped together like kindergarten camp kids connected with a leash. For good measure, I pulled on my shades and tucked my chin.

Just as the door of Strutters Skin and Nail Care came within reach, I saw my neighbor, Kat, approaching me with shopping bags and her two squirming kids.

"Calysta, hi," she said politely. "Haven't seen you in spin class forever. How are you?"

"I'm fine, I've been working a lot lately."

"Calysta, don't drop behind," Kelly snapped.

Kat took in the motley crew ahead of me and arched an eyebrow. "You're not with *them*, are you?"

Cringing, I replied, "I'm doing some volunteer mentoring. Gotta go."

As I scampered away, Gretchen hooked her arm in mine, babbling, "After we get our pedis, and by the way I'm getting the deluxe silk-wrap airbrush French with rhinestone charms, we have to go into Malibu Shaman next door, they have the best crystals and dream catchers, and the metaphysical books are to die for. Of course we've gotta stop by the Makeup Hut, I'm all out of orgasm pink lip gloss. And Juicy just got new stuff in yesterday! Also, we just have to stop by John Varvatos and get something for Toby to cheer him up. And maybe something for my husband, even though I'm super mad at him right now, he says he's not bringing the kids to the next weekend."

Gretchen briefly took a breath to select her toe charms as I stepped up into the vibrating spa chair.

Erroll took the seat to my right while Gretchen, yammering away like a bell clapper, attempted to bookend me on the left. Mercifully, a nail technician stopped her, saying, "Sorry, ma'am, that chair's reserved," leading her next to Erroll.

"Great, now she'll be talking *my* ear off," he said out of the corner of his mouth.

I told the pedicurist, "Traditional, no polish," and blissfully slid my feet into the hot bubbling blue water, the spine of the chair massaging my tight back.

The creamy leather supported my head while I closed my eyes . . . forgetting.

"Hello, Beulah."

Startled, I stared face-to-face with reptilian Randall Roberts.

"What are you—"

"Such a unique name," he continued; then, waving away the nail technician, "Not now." He turned back to me. "Did you know in Hebrew it means 'married'? I see why you changed it. I paid a visit to your hometown this weekend, saw the sights. That Jacob at Pride-All is quite the tour guide. Saw Church of the Solid Rock, haunting. Even stopped by your grandma's place, quaint. And that neighbor Miss Whilemina sure is a busybody."

I was no longer able to feel the exotic lady buffing my heels; my pedicure went from pure pleasure to walkin' on hot coals.

"Speaking of your grandma, what's her name again? Ah yes, Candelaria. Spotted her holding court on set yesterday. Sweet lady, frail though, heard she ran off and left town after that unfortunate fiasco with Roger Cabott. Imagine that'd be enough excitement for any woman her age, what's she pushing eighty? Hope nothing else scares your grandmother into . . . say, a heart attack, with her high blood pressure and all," Randall wickedly whispered, never breaking eye contact. "Yeah, that Greenwood sure is charming. Gotta wonder how you turned out so corrupt?"

Grandma taught me "the best defense is no defense," so if you weren't sure you could win, keep your mouth shut.

Randall reached into his jacket for a newspaper clipping and extended it to me.

As I reached, he teased, "Now, now, not so fast. You already know what it says. Here's what we're going to do. There's an important vote tomorrow morning to change the balance of power of *The Rich and the Ruthless* and *The Daring and the Damned*, and I've learned that you're an integral part of it. It's in both our interests that you cast your vote to sell in my favor," he warned, refolding the paper. "I think you'll agree."

Leaning in closer, grinning like the Cheshire Cat, he said, "Tomorrow you *will* vote to sell Barringer Dramatic Series, making me king of the soap opera world, and in return, I won't spill the beans about this messy business with Pastor Winslow . . . I mean, your murdered daddy. Otherwise . . ."

I could only manage a small nod and concentrate on not flaring my nostrils.

"Sir? Are you ready?" the pixie technician asked.

"You know, on second thought, I don't think I'll get a service today. Give my friend here a manicure. I want her hands to look real pretty when she's strokin' that Montblanc tomorrow," Randall said cockily, throwing down a hundred-dollar bill. "Keep the change." He winked, walking out.

"Where do you think you're going, Calysta?" Kelly asked.

"My *buddy's* still gettin' charms glued on her big toes. I need some fresh air, the fumes are makin' me nauseous."

"Okay, but don't go far and come right back. I'm timing you."

Soon as I got outside I flew across the street to Howdy's Taqueria.

"What do you got pre-mixed?" I asked, out of breath and still shaking.

"We're running a special on margaritas," the hostess replied.

"Gimme a pitcher."

Seated at a nearby table with two empty carafes, toasting with drinks of their own, Dylan and Dolly laughed out loud, waving. "Ovah here, Calysta."

The van stank like a tequila distillery as Kelly furiously ripped us a new one. "I hope you all realize this sets you back to square one. I can't believe the blatant disregard you've displayed for the rest of the TT family. The fumes alone in this van could cause a relapse and TT would be held liable. I'm not naming any names, but when we get back I want urine from every person in this van. After supper, Mr. Quigley will discuss disciplinary action."

Looking over his shoulder to inhale my Jose Cuervo breath, Erroll whispered, "It's bad to admit, but I have such alcohol envy. Next time, take me with you."

Dylan and Dolly drunkenly giggled in the back ignoring Kelly's tirade, while the rest looked out the child-locked windows. Mad. I was scared to death Randall had somehow dredged up my past.

Self-sabotaged, I was marched to my room by moody Kelly, who didn't leave until I supplied her with a measured cup of wee-wee.

An hour later, there was a knock at the door.

"House of Ruby, come in."

Lying across my Barbie canopy bed three sheets to the wind, I stared upside-down at stone-faced Kelly Lava standing over me, who suddenly looked Chinese. I burst out laughing. Then laughed some more. I laughed so hard my face hurt. Then she went Linda Blair ballistic on me.

"We'll see how funny you think it is when you find yourself sitting at Tranquility Tudor tonight instead of going out to the Brentwood meeting with the others, forfeiting a stop at Starbucks. Reading chapters from the Big Book with Dolly, Dylan, and *me,* then journaling about what you've done and going to bed without snack!" she shouted, slamming the door behind her.

Through an oncoming migraine Randall's threat stuck like chewed gum on the bottom of a shoe. "You *will* vote to sell Barringer Dramatic Series, making me king of the soap opera world, and in return, I won't spill the beans . . ."

About to fall apart like a two-dollar suitcase, I reached for Augustus's letter under my mattress, clutching it like a lifeline and not having to open it to know what it said.

". . . the future of my shows rests in your capable hands . . ." I recited, slowly straightening my spine. After all, I'd only had four margaritas. I told myself *Get a grip, girl, show up and show out.* I would fix this and fix it tonight.

CHAPTER 45

The Daring . . .

*W*oozy but determined and Big Booked to death, I crawled out of my bedroom window in skips, dressed like a ninja, creeping low to the ground to avoid TT's prison camp lighting. Fueled with enough caffeine to kill a cow, I used my homegirl technique to scale the stucco wall, makin' a mad dash into a waiting Rover.

The bass rocked D's ride as he listened to Drake, the unmistakable scent of sinsemilla giving me an instant contact high.

"Thanks, D."

"Anytime, babe," he said with a broad dimpled smile. "But can a brotha get some sugah?"

Derrick didn't know I needed to plant that kiss more than he needed to receive it.

"Whew . . . nice." I exhaled. "D, honey, I kinda 'slipped' today, you know, snuck in a few cocktails and I'm, um, sort of on punishment at TT so I have to get back before they find me missin'."

"Don't worry, shortie, I gottchu," he said, chowin' down on a Lay's.

This may be a random thought for sure, but one worth sharing; I loved the way black men ate their chips, especially Derrick.

He knew how to put style into crunch, first snappin' the bag open, gently tossing the crumbs to the bottom. Then pluckin' out a fat chip, never lookin' down . . . piggybackin' his index and middle finger like spoonin' lovers, he placed a Salt 'n' Vinegar on the tip of his dexterous tongue, lettin' it rest there for a nanosecond like a meltin' snowflake before flirtatiously retractin' it . . . *crrrunchhh* between his African-white teeth. This was always a turn-on for me. He did this over and over till he got to the last. Selfish with his chips too. Better ask if you wanted that hand back.

With a mint-flavored toothpick parked in the corner of his mouth he asked, "Turn here, Calysta?"

"Huh?"

"Turn here?"

"Yeah, right," I covered.

I was trippin' comparing eating chips to sex. I should've been thinking about making amends to Derrick like I told Kelly I would earlier, when she grilled me on what badness I'd done in the past.

"Derrick, there's something I've been meaning to tell you."

"Lay it on me."

"Well, remember how I used to get when you'd flirt with the ladies while you were seein' me?"

"Oh, yeah."

"Well . . ."

"C'mon, girl. Can't be that bad."

"Okay, but first pinkie promise me you won't get mad."

"Pinkie promise."

"I'm the one who spray-painted '2-Timer' on your car."

"Think I didn't know? You're the *only* one who could've tagged my bronze rims with pink glitter spray paint."

"I'm sorry. Forgiven?"

"Like I could resist."

Winding up Benedict Canyon to Augustus Barringer's estate, I felt my heart race as I thought about seeing him and the vote tomorrow.

"I thought you mainly drank champagne."

Not wanting to tell him the truth, I said, "I've been feeling kinda lost not having much control over my life lately."

"Wanna take a detour?"

"Nah."

"You sure?"

"Yeah, got a lot on my mind."

"Okay, but don't say I didn't offer. Honeys been blowin' up my phone. Guess since money's tight, folks be lookin' for more economical recreation. Timin's a little off, though. Been on a chick *de-lite* diet for the past few. Break my fast for you, Calysta," he said, turning up Young Jeezy.

"Thanks, but my sex drive's on hold."

"Wow, okay. Already told 'em when I resurface I ain't takin' nobody out to Yang Chow's, just Roscoe's Chicken and Waffles. They say I can whet their appetite a different way, 'romance the D stone.' Yeeaaah baby, I am pop-u-lar. Keep tellin' 'em I'm ovah-extended as it is and they say that's a good thang. Had to scramble my digits . . . again."

Giving him a look, I asked, "Can we change the subject, and how 'bout some classical?"

"You got jokes."

"No, I'm serious. I've got a splittin' headache. Plus, I've been listenin' to Bach during collage therapy and it's kinda sooth—"

"Listen babe, I ain't no DJ, but I'm gonna break a brotha's habit and give you what you want. Got some old school tucked away, Barry White, little Marvin . . . whatchuwant? That's some classical shiz if you ask me."

"Any of it'll work. After the mess at *R&R*, I . . ."

"Yeah, what's up with that? I heard Maeve took some metal, is it true?"

"Yeah, that's what Shannen said."

"Daaamn."

"My grandma was visiting the set too and was so freaked she took a cab to the bus station by herself and headed back to Mississippi."

"A bus?"

"Yeah, she don't fly."

"Oh, she old school, they do it like that."

"Mm-hm, but I can't help worryin'. I better hear from her tomorrow."

"I think this is it," Derrick said, as we pulled up to an iron gate and a security guard.

"Good evening, may I help you?" the uniformed guard asked suspiciously.

Leaning over Derrick, I said in my best Anglo-Saxon voice, "Good evening, Scott, it's me, Calysta Jeffries, I'm here to see Mr. Barringer."

"Who?"

"Ruby Stargazer."

"Can you take off that hat?"

"No problem."

"Sure is! Where you been, girl? Everybody been missin' you on the story. Hold on, I'll be right back," he said, checking on a computer. "I'm sorry, Ms. Stargazer, but it doesn't look like the Barringers called with your name."

"I know, it's a surprise."

"Hey man, you know who she is," interrupted Derrick. "She been on the show for a million years, you know me too."

"I knew it, it *is* you . . . Dove Jordan, you are the *man*! You know since I got a job I haven't been able to keep up on the stories. Did you ever get off that deserted island after your plane crashed? My mamma loves you, can I get an autograph?"

"Uh, yeah, but I haven't been on the soap for like three years. I'm on *Pathological Murders* now."

"Oh yeah, my wife loves that detective show. Can I get two autographs?"

"If you open the gate I'll give you five on my way out."

"Okay, I guess, but I still have to call ahead, don't want any mess with the Barringers. Gotta let the butler know, otherwise he's liable to see you all and you know—"

"Man, come on," Derrick said impatiently.

"No, he's right, D. Remember what happened last year in Bel Air when that black doctor broke into his own house and the SWAT team tear-gassed him?"

"All right, go on up," Scott said. "And I'll be lookin' for them autographs."

The gate opened to a long tree-lined driveway, leading to the graceful Barringer estate, spread out over ten acres.

"Want me to go in with you?" Derrick asked.

"Would you?"

As we walked up to the carved mahogany doors, Derrick gave me a quick peck on the cheek and said, "Relax," before gripping the brass lion door knocker. The sound echoed throughout the Marquina marble foyer, where I'd stood many times over the past fifteen years on happier occasions.

The huge double doors swung open to reveal Max, Mr. Barringer's loyal butler.

"Good evening, Miss Jeffries, what a lovely surprise. You look so elegant all in black, but what on earth has brought you out so late?" he said with his British accent. "And you too, Mr. Taylor, I haven't seen you in years. Please come in."

Leading us into a dimly lit library, he offered, "May I get you something to drink?"

"Bitters and soda, thank you."

"Hennessy for me," said Derrick.

As Max turned to the full bar, I said, "I know this is completely unexpected and I don't have much time, but would it be possible to see Mr. B?"

"I'm sorry, Miss Jeffries, here's your drink, but Mr. Barringer's under the strictest of orders from his doctor to rest."

"Yes, I heard, but you must know this is very, very important. Otherwise, I wouldn't have taken the risk—I mean shown up unannounced," I said, downing the medicine in one gulp.

Handing Derrick a snifter, he stroked his goatee thoughtfully before saying, "All right, but we'll have to be quick and quiet about it. Follow me. I'm sorry, Mr. Taylor, but you'll have to wait here."

"No problem."

As we climbed the grand staircase, I asked, "Where's Mrs. Barringer?"

"At the Armand Hammer Museum fund-raiser with Veronica."

"I see. This won't take long."

Max knocked lightly on the door, a private nurse cracked it, and after he whispered into her ear, she let me in.

"I'll be back," he said. "The nurse has to stay in the room."

"Thank you."

"Mr. Barringer's been sleeping quite a bit," the nurse said. "But he showed wonderful improvement today."

"May I sit next to him?"

"Yes, but please be careful of his IV."

Mr. B's room had been turned into a private hospital suite. As much as I told myself I wouldn't, I got choked up seeing my mentor so frail and seemingly helpless. Typically tanned and toned, he was now almost translucent. I gently took his long cool hand, a hand that had written so many beautiful lines for so many, and began to stroke it.

I felt the slightest movement. His eyes half opened.

"Calysta?"

"Yes, Mr. Barringer."

The nurse checked his monitor before returning to her chair across the room where she was reading by the fireplace.

"Mr. B, I had to come see you."

Still with his sense of humor he whispered, "It's good to be seen, even like this. Veronica give you my message?"

"Yes, I'll be at your attorney's office first thing tomorrow."

His cloudy blue eyes locked on mine, and barely audibly, he said, "Don't cry, dear. I'm so proud. 'Can't buy your own instrument like a violinist. You must make it.' Heard that somewhere. You've done that. Daytime can dull ambition, but not you, you only got better. Never looked for a handout . . . always admired that; you deserve everything coming. I have something special but . . ."

He drifted off to sleep again. It was enough.

"Excuse me, Miss Jeffries," the nurse said, softly touching my shoulder. "I'm afraid you'll have to leave. Mr. Barringer needs his sleep."

I carefully placed Augustus's hand on the cashmere blanket before leaning in to kiss his forehead, whispering, "'Night, Mr. Barringer, love you," and departing with an aching heart.

"It was wonderful of you to visit Mr. Barringer under such difficult circumstances. If I may be so forward, you are a brave young lady, rare and loved by this family."

"Thank you, Max."

As Derrick and I made our way back to PCH toward Tranquility Tudor I thought, *I can bear any amount of trouble I might be in, in exchange for those few sacred moments with Augustus Barringer.*

BLIND ITEM: Which wild child younger lead actress got her leading man fired by claiming sexual harassment, even though they'd been banging each other's brains out for months? The bubblette in question recently quit her show, only to return six months later begging the brass to take her back. "Thanks but no thanks," said the show's top exec. Like Gimhongsok always says, "Fiction is logical compared to the truth."

The Diva

CHAPTER 46

. . . And the Damned

*W*ith twinkle lights in every jacaranda tree, a rented rotating spotlight sent crisscrossing beams shooting into the balmy night sky above the Roberts's gaudy McMansion. Synchronized swimmers entertained as the celebratory soap opera soiree got into full swing and Emmy strutted up the front steps, fashionably late in a skintight black mini.

A waiting party planner met her at the door, saying, "I'm sorry, Mrs. Roberts's has asked that no one enter the house. The event is around to the back."

"*I'm* going to have an event if I don't get in that house to use the powder room."

"The chemical toilets are to the left of the tent and have sinks."

In a huff, Emmy turned on her Luella heels and followed the other latecomers. Swinging her purse that held her tiny Pomapoo, its head sticking out with diamond-studded doggy barrettes, Emmy snatched a Cosmopolitan from a waiter, sneering down at the tray pass of pigs-in-a-blanket and tuna-on-a-Ritz, thinking, *Ewww, you can take trash out of the trailer park but you can't take trailer park out of the trash.*

Pinching a pig from the tray, she said to her Pomapoo as she fed it, "No matter how much money you have, class just can't be bought."

"You can say that again," said a suave Auggie Jr., dressed in comfortable khakis and Top-Siders.

"Oh hi, Auggie," she flirted. "And who's this?" She changed her tone, not trying to mask her disapproval.

"My friend Ginger. Ginger, Emmy, she's one of the stars on my show."

"Nice to meet you. Sorry, I don't watch soaps. Cheers!" she said, chugging down her drink.

Glaring, Emmy walked off, scouring the crowd for Randall.

With the band on break, rowdy daytime *R&R* and *D&D* crooners took turns on the karaoke machine. Willie Turner and Shelly Montenegro sang Captain and Tennille's "Love Will Keep Us Together" in the background, as high-pitched laughter and animated chatter filled the tent-covered tennis court, fog and bubble machines providing dramatic soapy atmosphere.

"Hey, Jade, wanna share some tuna?" Toby asked suggestively with dilated pupils.

"You are so mental, Toby, you know I'm strictly off surf 'n' turf and only eating fruits and veggies. Just got the alkaline and acidity in my system equalized. Besides, who knows how old that Bumblebee is? I'm sure it's been sitting in Alison's pantry for years. Did you know canned food is filled with chemicals and—"

An expressionless Edith began, "Well, well, well. What a surp—"

Inappropriately kissing her on the lips, Toby said, "Mmm, Edie, strawberry . . . you sexy mamma, good to see you too."

"Yeah, Toby called me after he was bounced from rehab tonight and I was like, wow, cool, let's celebrate and go to the party together," Jade added.

"So Edie, Roger went ballistic yesterday, huh?"

No reply.

"What a dickweed. But you know, I can see how something like that could happen. You get kicked off a show, you're unemployed, depressed, your wife's tonguin' other men in front of millions of people. A dude feels castrated. I can see how he could go postal."

Waving to an invisible friend, mouthing *Be right there,* Edith said, "I've gotta go, but it was good seeing you, Toby," and briskly walked away to join Daniel Needleman, the last person she wanted to talk to.

"My people will be in touch with your people!" Toby called after her, before hearing, "Yo, Toby, Jade, over here!"

As they hustled across to Auggie Jr., Jade said, "You know, Toby, it's hip to be tilted these days, just own it. Look at me, I'm bipolar!"

"Hey, guys," Auggie said. "Dude, when'd you get out?"

"Just now, and man could I use a joint. Know where I could get some weed?"

"Nah, no one's been able to find any good stuff since you've been off the scene."

"Yo, about my job—"

"Don't worry, got it covered."

The party raged to Michael Damian's "Rock On" and grew rowdier as more and more alcohol flowed. Ethan Walker, grandstanding, jumped into the pool with the synchronized swimmers, fully clothed, almost drowning.

Later, Dell Williams belted out the most mellifluous rendition of Aretha Franklin's "R.E.S.P.E.C.T.," mesmerizing everyone.

Receiving guests like Vito Corleone, Randall, dressed in a tux, puffed on a fat Cohiba, greeting well-wishers and sycophants. The women were pulled closer for congratulatory kisses with the exception of brown-nosing and sweaty Felicia Silverstein. He slipped the young nubiles some tongue while a plasticized Alison held court across the tent with a tabloid reporter.

Dell, still glowing from all the adulation, made her way through the crowd and said, "Congratulations, Randall."

"Thank you, Queenie," he said, unwittingly calling Dell by her character's name. She didn't sweat it and got to the gettin', saying what she had to say.

"I hope this means you'll consider giving me a storyline without an apron. I was thinkin' you could turn me into a ghost like Sydell, God knows she's had more air time off contract as a spirit than on."

"I'll take that into consideration, but something I can do right away is have Felicia write your singing into the show. I had no idea you were such a musical wizard. Maybe you could sing a spiritual or two during an upcoming funeral scene we're writing."

Wolfe held court with a small circle of rapt admirers including Fern, Julius, Penelope, and Ben, listening to the heroic details of yesterday's *R&R* debacle.

Determined, Emmy slunk through the intoxicated horde, a drunk Phillip McQueen screaming "Master of Puppets," fists raised, devil fingers pointing to heaven as Pinkey looked on like a matinee idol groupie. Ducking behind a dripping ice sculpture to avoid unwanted solicitations from Bonnie Blackburn, Emmy sidled up next to Randall, now toasting with Edith.

"I have a *special* kiss waiting for you," she whispered, tonguing his waxy ear.

"Okay, we rolling?" *Cliffhanger Weekly*'s senior reporter Chauncey Brown asked his one-man crew. The cameraman nodded.

"Here we are with super soap opera star, Sudsy Award winner Alison Fairchild Roberts, at her magnificent Holmby Hills home."

"Mansion," she corrected.

"I'm sorry, Alison, *mansion*, what was I thinking? Take two, we rolling?"

"Yep."

"Here we are with super soap opera star, Sudsy Award winner Alison Fairchild Roberts, the quintessential iconoclast of daytimelessness, with a splash of Marie Antoinette, at her magnificent Holmby Hills mansion along with the cast of *The Rich and the Ruthless* and *The Daring and the Damned*, and let me tell you, folks, anybody who's anybody is here! I've selected ten questions from our *Cliffhanger Weekly* blog and the fans want to know: 'What does it feel like to be a daytime diva on the number one soap opera?'"

Cloaked in Chanel borrowed from *R&R*, Alison was a diva who'd survived oversize shoulder pads, big hair, and scandal. She knew how to squeeze mileage out of a declining career, and had stood the test of time, preserving her allure though her detractors whispered she was in the autumn of her soap opera career.

She replied, "First of all, Chauncey, I want to thank you and *Cliffhanger Weekly* for my sixty-three covers. And to the fans, well, as a child star, starred in *Pinocchio,* I've been in the biz all my life and . . . what's the question again?"

"What does it feel like to be a daytime diva on the number one soap opera?"

"First let me say, *The Rich and the Ruthless* isn't just a job, it's a career move. When I began on the show I took for granted how lucky I was. But now I realize it's the best job in the world; luxurious, sexy . . . look at me," she said as she twirled, flipping her bleached hair over her shoulder, "but sometimes it can be absolute murder."

"Are you referring to the time you wrestled a writer to the floor when you disagreed with a Martian storyline? Or the time you became tipsy, impersonating Blondie at the annual *R&R* fan club luncheon, and belted out Anita Ward's 'Ring My Bell,' then lost your lunch on the front row?"

An irritated Alison coolly replied, "I was having a rough time then and I'd rather not turn back the page."

"Of course. Alison, I'm honored to be invited to this fabulous party for an exclusive interview. And I'm sure the fans want to know more about your beautiful home, I mean mansion, since this is the first time you've allowed press onto the property."

"Estate. Naturally my mansion is my sanctuary, and I put a premium on privacy. As you can imagine that's very difficult to achieve with all my fame."

"I've been told you have a lot of mirrors in your mansion."

"Not enough. Without mirrors, I'm dead. They reflect my soul."

"What a beautiful answer. Who's your favorite movie star and favorite soap star?"

"Domestically, it's between Chuck Norris and Andy Williams. Overseas it's Amitabh Bachchan hands down, he's so sexy."

Confused, Chauncey said, "I know who Chuck and Andy are but I'm not familiar with the other actor."

"Yes, well, I'm not surprised. As you know, two years ago I was invited to make a special guest appearance on the Indian soap opera *Kumkum*, and while I was doing press for MTV India I was introduced to one of the most famous Indian actors alive, a dead ringer for Al Pacino in the face. As for a favorite soap star, I like me."

"Of course, what a silly ques—"

"Wait, wait, stop tape!"

"Alison, what's wrong?"

"Lose your 'talk-back' quips. They're unimportant and totally throw off my spontaneity and momentum."

"Got it. Rolling?"

"Yep."

"Alison, being an icon in the soap world for three decades, do you find yourself jaded at all?"

"I'll rephrase the question. Do you mean do I get lonely at the top? You betcha!"

"I hate to bring this up, but with all the hype around Brangelina and Jennifer Aniston the fans want to know . . . "

"Go ahead."

"Is it true there was a secret romance between your husband and Emmy Abernathy?"

Fake laughing, Alison stated, "That's rubbish. Emmy is such an unremarkable creature. I heard the first time she ate lobster she tried to eat the shell, can you imagine? I'm sure she was very good as a hot dog concessionaire on Coney Island."

"Alison, whaddya have to say about *R&R*'s incredible shrinking cast and the cancellation of *Obsessions*? Plus, sensational rumors of turning *Medical Clinic* into a webisode series and *Our Lives to Contend* moving across country?"

"Let's just say, some people on my soap are this close"—pinching her index and thumb together—"to joining the soap opera graveyard. But don't worry, my loyal fans," she said, looking into the camera and tossing her head, "I'm not going anywhere."

"Alison, any comment on the recent fifteen percent pay cuts?"

"Next question."

"I know this is a very sensitive time for the cast of *R&R*, and all of daytime is saddened by what happened to Maeve Fielding, but can you tell us *anything* about the violent shooting on *The Rich and the Ruthless* set yesterday?"

Alison whipped out her signature crocodile tears.

"It was absolutely dreadful, I feared for my life. Naturally, my executive producer husband Randall Roberts heroically ran onto the set and took me into his arms, protecting me. As for Maeve, she has no one, poor thing. That's why I forged our mother/daughter relationship off the set. We're so close. I've organized a forty-day candlelight vigil." Having peaked but going on too long, Alison turned to look squarely into the camera again, advising, "I'll be curbside at Cedars-Sinai hospital tomorrow night from six to seven if anyone wants to join me."

"There've been reports that you're addicted to plastic surgery. Is it true that you've had over twenty-five procedures?"

Like a needle scratching across vinyl, Alison plucked another apple martini from a passing tray, took a sip, then answered, "Do I look like it?"

Chauncey wanted very badly to tell her that her lips were so uneven he had difficulty choosing which one to focus on. Was she so vainly detached from reality that she took credit for a rack as erect as the one on a Pussycat Doll? There was no right answer. Chauncy took a chance.

"Alison, you are by far the most preserved woman I've ever met in my entire life."

That was the end of the interview.

Turning to his cameraman, Chauncey asked, "Did you get it all?"

"Sorry, Chauncey, battery went dead three questions ago."

"That's okay, won't use more than two bites anyway. She's such a bitch."

Cloistered away in the upstairs gilded powder room, Emmy placed her cocktail and Louis Vuitton pooch pouch on the marble countertop before reapplying gobs of iridescent tickler peach lip gloss, dropping to her knees.

"Ready for this, Snuggle Bunny?" she impishly asked, looking up at Randall.

"Absolutely," he replied, eagerly unfastening his trousers. "But this has *got* to be the last time."

"Of course, I just thought since it's such a special occasion," she crooned, rocking back on her four-inch premium pumps, withdrawing. "If you want me to leave . . ."

"Are you crazy? You're already down there—ahhh . . . woooo . . . yayayaya . . . whoo-we-wow-zah!"

Frighteningly fast, Randall fell to the "R&R" mosaic-tiled floor with a thud, face contorted, eyes bulging, sweating profusely as Emmy slowly stood, leisurely plucking up a tissue, straddling her victim to dot her smeared lips.

"Emmy," Randall rasped.

"What's that, Snuggle Bunny? Are you trying to tell me it was good?"

"Whatdidyo—" he managed to whisper before his throat fully closed. Writhing, his legs spastically kicked out, his face turning purple.

Unsympathetic, Emmy looked into the gilded mirror, took the last sip of her Cosmopolitan, and swished and spat it out before reapplying lip gloss laced with a secret weapon Randall was deathly allergic to.

Looking beneath her, she icily appraised, "Here's what I did for you, you fat bastard, since you forgot. I gave you the best sex in your life and laughed at your boring jokes and put up with your stinkin' cigars and pretended to have orgasms. And that takes skill when all you have to work with is a tub of lard and a tiny dick. I was sympathetic about your dumb wife and all her drama and listened to your problems with Edith and obeyed you to the letter, making certain Calysta never got a Sudsy, and for what?" Emmy slid off the ring Randall had given her months earlier, having found out from her appraiser that the bauble was three sparkling carats of cubic zirconium trash. She dramatically hurled it into the toilet but it wouldn't flush—it was a floater.

"You broke your promise to me," she hissed at an unconscious Randall. "This is what happens when you stomp all over the *other* woman's ambitions."

Distantly, Javier, who had been treated to a hero's welcome earlier, could be heard serenading Shannen and the crowd with Luis Miguel's *"La Incondicional"* as Emmy yanked up Randall's Brooks Brothers trousers, not caring what got caught in them, grabbed her Pomapoo, and strolled casually out of the loo, tossing over her shoulder, "Now *that* was one for the record books."

"Hey, you guys, there's like ambulances and cop cars everywhere," a hysterical Ethan in borrowed clothes yelled.

Screeching "Roxanne" at the top of her lungs, Emmy was caught off guard when the karaoke machine went dead and shouts erupted from the front of the tent.

"Cool, it's never a *real* party till the cops show up or the firemen shut it down," Toby chimed in, grinning. "Let's get this mixer started!" he crowed, pulling Jade in the opposite direction to discuss which Nine Inch Nails duet to sing.

"I just heard Randall Roberts might be dead!" Ethan finished. Mob mentality taking over, buzzed bubblers and reporters herded toward the front of the house, trampling the azaleas and agapanthus. Randall was already being rolled out of the McMansion on a gurney toward a waiting ambulance when a nasal shriek could be heard.

"For gawd's sake, wait! Let me through!" Alison frantically slurred, zigzagging her way through the clustering crowd, before being stopped by an officer.

"How dare you. Take your skeevy hands off me," she demanded. "I'm Alison Fairchild Roberts, Rory Lovekin on the number one daytime soap, a Sudsy Award winner."

"You're who?"

"His wife for crissakes and I'm not going anywhere without me."

Wolfe, taking the reins once again, soap-opera-ish-ly vouched, "The voman is despicable, officer, but she speaks the truth."

"All right, let her on."

Alison was hoisted into the ambulance wearing a sheer silk blouse revealing her perfect 38 C's, but before the red doors closed, she added with arms outstretched like Evita Perón, "Don't cry for me . . ."

The EMT slammed the doors.

"What a nut job," the officer said to Wolfe.

"And *I* have to vork vith her."

As sirens were blaring down the driveway, and a satisfied Emmy looked on in sadistic amusement, Wilson Turner sighed to Bonnie Blackburn, "Looks like that's a definite wrap on the party and it was just heatin' up."

"This is way too much drama in forty-eight hours," Shannen said, clutching Javier.

"Man, talk about brilliant! Edie, you sly devil. One down, one to go," Auggie crooned to Edith, who was uncertain what had just happened.

As the amplified voices of Toby and Jade sang "The Hand That Feeds" in the background, Chauncey Brown said into the camera, "That was one of the most dramatic exits I've ever witnessed. And that, ladies and gentlemen, is why I love daytime television. You just can't write the script. This is Chauncey Brown reminding you, what happens off the set is stranger than fiction and where the *real* drama begins."

CHAPTER 47

Kicked to the Curb

Busted, I resignedly walked past Rock waiting at the TT gate and into Kelly Lava's office.

"Unbelievable," she started in, sounding like the worst nun in the world. "You're already on thin ice and now this?"

"There was something I needed to do."

"Oh yeah? I'll tell you what you need to do. March to your room and give me another urine sample, now!" barked the bossy sober coach.

"You people take so much pee it's a wonder this place don't float."

"You've been out of our watch, you bet your ass we wanna know what kind of trouble you've gotten into."

After practically strip-searching me, Kelly waited with one foot in the bathroom door until I placed the warm cup in her hand.

Hearing her footsteps fade away, Gretchen unwrapped a paper towel, saying, "She's such a pill. Saved you a chocolate-covered macaroon."

"Thanks, I'm fine," I said distractedly. "What's she thinking—I'm gonna water down my pee? Or that I went out to score?"

"Actually, yeah. It's happened. In fact, Toby just got kicked out for that very reason. Kelly ripped his autographed Jessica Simpson poster right off the wall and tore it to pieces. I didn't even get to say good-bye or give him his Varvatos gift."

Sighing, I collapsed onto my bed, folding my arms, locking my fingers behind my head, saying, "Gretchen, why do you keep coming back here? It's not workin' for you, and girl, you *work* it. How come you keep relapsing?"

Looking serious through heavily mascaraed lashes, she said, "The truth of the matter is, I slip on purpose. They take care of me, I have friends, and actually feel like I'm part of a family."

Frowning, I said, "But that's no way to live your life. You have everything a person could ever want; husband, home, kids, more money than you can spend. Why do you need this place?"

"My husband has offices in Hong Kong, Paris, London, Saudi Arabia . . . eleven countries in all. He's never home. Kids are in boarding school in Switzerland. He has at least two mistresses that I know of. Do you have any idea how lonely it is to live in a twenty-thousand-square-foot chateau by yourself? Servants don't count. When I go to rehab he comes home. I get his attention . . . for a little while . . . "

Somberly looking at Gretchen in a different light, I felt sorry for her as we chatted till one in the morning. We were about to turn out the lights and go to sleep when Kelly barged in.

"Get dressed!"

"What, why?"

"Just do it."

"What's going on, Kelly?" Gretchen asked.

"Mind your business."

Gretchen locked eyes with mine, both of us knowing this couldn't be good.

I followed Kelly into the cold TT office. Pat Quigley was waiting, drumming his fingers against the desk.

"Calysta, I'm going to get right to it," he began. "We're tremendously disappointed in you. I personally hoped you'd be a model client of ours and that TT could use you as a spokeperson for the facility but all that's out the window now."

I kept my trap shut.

"We know you were out smoking meth tonight."

"Meth? Are you on crack?"

"You heard us," Kelly said.

"I thought you were making such progress here at TT," Pat continued.

"Wait. What are you guys talking about?" I demanded.

"Kelly found traces of meth in your urine, and as you know, TT's policy is that we do *not* tolerate *any* drug use whatsoever. I'm sorry, you'll have to leave the premises immediately. A staffer will assist you with your packing."

"Bitch, you *framed* me."

"Save it for the stage. That innocent victim act won't help you here. Do you think you're the first to try to get away with this?"

"You wait, Lava! I'ma get Pookey 'n' them to kick your ass."

"Talk about self-aggrandizement and grandiose. This isn't an episode on your little soap opera. This is real life, sweetheart, no one peed in that cup tonight but you and I have a witness to prove it."

"Sorry, Calysta, you have to go," Pat said.

This can't be happening. It was worse than being voted off *Survivor.*

Unclipping her walkie-talkie, Kelly asked, "Yes, Rock?"

"I got that new *whiskey foxtrot* you told me to pick up and she's gonna be trouble. Still doin' drugs in the backseat. Ovah."

"Okay, just take the long way back, I'm wrapping up right now. Over."

Turning back to me, she said, "If you don't leave, we'll have no choice but to call the sheriff, who'll gladly cuff you and take you to jail for trespassing and violation of a court order. Do I have to remind you you've only done one week of a six-week program?"

"That said," Pat interrupted, "as a gesture of goodwill, I could make an arrangement for you to be released into the care of a family member or friend until you find another rehab facility in the next twenty-four hours."

"You-all are crazy; nothin' but greedy, scandalous pimps. You have this rehabbin' thing all tied up. I'm gonna go but I'll be back, and it won't be for equine therapy either, you can *believe* that. You're gonna wish you never knew me."

As I opened the door to leave, Kelly reminded me, "Don't disturb the residents, Calysta, we'd prefer if you left quietly." Not responding, I walked out of the office.

"What's going on?" a worried Gretchen asked, sitting up, sliding her sleep mask onto her forehead, flicking her sleep apnea machine off.

"Got kicked out for supposedly smokin' meth. Impossible. First of all that ain't my thing. Lava makes me sick," I explained, sucking my back teeth while pulling my Louis Vuitton out of the closet.

"Not again!" Gretchen said.

"I wouldn't stay here for all the tea in China," I said, angrily throwing my clothes into the luggage. "Wait a minute. What'd you mean 'not again'?"

Breaking down in tears, a distressed Gretchen pleaded, "Calysta, you're the best friend I have. Don't let them make you go *too*," leaping out of bed to hug me, feeling like all kinds of desperation.

"Ready?" Kelly said, stepping in.

"Gretchen, I'm dealing with a complicated situation right now, it's outta my control but it'll work itself out."

"Break it up," Kelly barked as she snapped open a black garbage bag, tossing my toiletries into it.

"I hate you, Kelly," Gretchen snarled. "You're always ruining the harmony around here. It's a wonder any of us are sober. Let me guess, dirty pee again so you can bring in another helpless soul to fill Calysta's bed and keep her thirty-six K for a one-week stay? You and Quigley are pathetic! I've been in and out of here enough to know a pattern when I see one, and I'm going to report you guys once and for all."

"Temper, temper," Kelly said. "Sure you don't need a sedative?"

I took in every last word that came out of Gretchen's mouth. I had her personal contact information and would definitely be in touch to pick her brain later.

White-knuckling her walkie-talkie, Kelly demanded, "Rock, where the hell are you? I need backup, stat!"

"Pullin' in right now."

"Well hurry the hell up. And secure the package."

And she thought she was talkin' in code.

"And tell the nurse I need a tranquilizer, Gretchen's flipping out again."

I watched TT's scheming unravel before my eyes as Kelly yelled, "Let's go, Calysta. Now!"

Hands on my hips, I said, "I ain't goin' nowhere without Gretchen."

"You're really pushing it."

Rock sailed in with a nurse.

"What's all the commotion about?" asked Erroll, peeking in. "It's upsetting the rest of the house."

"I'm sorry, Erroll," Kelly soothed. "But I'm not at liberty to discuss Calysta's expulsion. Please go back to your room and go to bed."

"Expulsion? Calysta? What a pity. Don't worry, I'll find you, dear," he called out, shuffling off in his Valentino slippers.

As Kelly pointed, saying, "*Her*," a scowling Rock, loaded for bear, charged toward me.

Kicking and screaming, with Gretchen on his back, we all slammed into my frilly Barbie bed, breaking it. It was déjà vu: my Soap Opera Wedding of the Century scene minus the cake.

I felt a prick in my side, the room tilted, and the next time I woke I was in Derrick Taylor's bed. There's a lot to be said for dream catchers.

CHAPTER 48

The Vote

W hat'd they give you?"

Derrick's deep sexy voice cut through the fog as I struggled to regain consciousness.

My mouth bone-dry, I was feeling drugged within an inch of my life, as his strong, familiar arms cradled me into his chest.

"C'mon, Calysta, today's a big day, wake up," Derrick said, kissing a glass of orange juice to my parched lips.

"How'd I get here?"

"After those folks knocked you out, and I mean you were out *cold*, they tried to call your emergency contact but Weezi's out of the country, so they called your lawyer Sly, and he called Dwayne, and Dwayne called Shannen, and she called me."

"It's nice to know I'm so loved."

"They shoulda called me from the get-go. No one had to ask *me* twice to go collect your fine behind, even though, and I ain't gonna lie, I was bizzy and Laquisha was pissed off," he finished, giving me a mischievous grin.

Too much information, I thought, but I had to admit, lookin' at Derrick's silky, chiseled bare chest was like medicine for whatever was ailing me. Hair in all the right places. No beady cuccah-bugs for him, uh-uh . . . this was a brutha so vain he permed his chest. With him sitting next to me on the bed, close enough for a snake to bite, and the top button of his Calvins unfastened, there were no words to describe this lothario other than I could drink him with a straw.

We do anything last night? Nah, though Derrick was too many things, he would nevah, nevah, nevah steal the cookie and ask for it later.

"Man, my head feels like a cement block."

"Been sleepin' there like you dead to the world. Bet this espresso will straighten you right out," Derrick said, passing me a mug. "Better drink this octane on the move too 'cause Veronica already hit me on the hip ten minutes ago, sayin' she was sendin' the car to pick you up in half an hour. Don't ask how she knew you were here. Sly musta called her."

Derrick *been* had Veronica's number tryin' to play it off. He wasn't foolin' me. Truth was the soap heiress was just as curious as the rest of us and wasn't gonna let wealth and society get in the way of a hot urban romance. And who could blame her, really? As discreet as the lusty pair were, everyone knew about their flash-in-the-pan Peninsula Hotel dalliance during his soap-a-licious back-in-the-day days.

"What car? Ohmagod, the vote!" Swinging my legs off the bed, I headed for his black-on-black granite *double-vé çe.*

Showered and having thrown on the suit Veronica left at TT earlier, I wolfed down toast, feeling almost human again.

"Looks like your ride is here, babe," Derrick said, stepping back from the balcony. "Wonder what happened to her last . . . never mind . . ."

"Walkin' me out?"

"Sure."

"Morning, ma'am," the chauffeur said as he tipped his hat and opened the door.

"Thank you, Derrick. I-I . . . just want you to . . ."

He gave me a deep French before saying, "That should hold ya till I 'catchupwitchu' later, superstar."

Sliding across the posh Bentley leather seat, I plucked a newspaper sandwiched between a *Variety* and the *Hollywood Reporter* from the driver's seatback. Attempting to take my mind off the Barringer vote, I scanned the front page of the weary *Los Angeles Times,* reading about President Obama's health-care overhaul, foreclosures, and the Ballet Nacional de Cuba appearing at Lincoln Center.

At the lower right-hand corner was a tiny blurb about Maeve Fielding. *Please turn to page E14 for more . . .* I flipped the pages, sidetracked by my horoscope, which read:

> An unexpected change will throw you off your stride today, but being a fearless Taurean you will quickly regain your balance. Be flexible and bend with the breeze. According to love planet Venus, there's an exotic romance coming your way if you put your strong charisma to use.

Page E14 had a *"To the Readers"* correction notice:

> On Tuesday, regrettably we incorrectly stated that soap opera legend Maeve Fielding was shot and killed on the set of *The Rich and the Ruthless* by former soap star Roger Cabott. Fortunately, Maeve Fielding is alive and recovering. In lieu of flowers, Ms. Fielding has asked

that donations be made to the Edgar Cayce Association for Research and Enlightenment, Inc. Comments are welcome at latimes.com/readersrep.

"Ms. Jeffries, did you happen to feel that tremor last night?"

"Tremor?"

"Yes, ma'am, it was pretty substantial."

"Guess I've gotten used to them." Cracking the tinted window, feeling the breeze against my face, I asked, "Haven't I seen you before?"

Looking into his rearview mirror, he answered, "Yes, Miss Jeffries, my name is Otto. Mr. Barringer's personal driver. We've not met formally but of course I know who *you* are. Mr. Barringer's favorite."

I smiled inside.

"Mr. B's going to be all right."

"I hadn't heard one way or the other."

"My intuition's never wrong."

"Music preference, Miss Jeffries?"

"Keep it where it's at, love classical."

We drove for twenty minutes.

"Here we are." He quickly crossed behind the sleek car, but I wasn't ready to venture out.

"Otto, would you please give me a few seconds?" I asked through the window.

"Yes, of course."

The window glided shut. I lowered the illuminated mirror above, checking my mascara, and thought about what Augustus had said, "All the people and situations of your life have only the meaning you give them . . . and when you change your thinking, you change your life, sometimes in seconds."

I knocked on the window to signal the driver.

The Century City Oppenheimer & Berger Law Offices were located on the thirty-second floor in a soaring glass luxury office building, on the corner of Avenue of the Stars and Constellation Boulevard.

As I stepped out of the upholstered elevator, my heels sank into the plush cream carpeting. Nervously, I smiled at the receptionist, who greeted me, "Hello, Ms. Jeffries, they're expecting you, you can go in."

"Calysta darling, we are ever so grateful you agreed to come," Katherine Barringer said in her lilting voice, giving me a warm hug, pecking me on both cheeks as I entered the wood-paneled office.

"Yes, thank you again, Calysta," Veronica added.

Auggie crossly cut his eyes and stayed in his seat, arms folded, watching me.

My heart pounded, keeping it together. I wondered what Randall had told him, if anything, about my past.

"Auggie, aren't you going to stand and greet Calysta?" Katherine asked.

"Stop treating me like I'm a child, Mother," he said, annoyed. "*She* has no business here. Dad has really lost it. This is ridiculous."

A distinguished man dressed in an immaculate pigeon gray suit entered the boardroom. "Good morning, Katherine, Veronica, Auggie."

"Make that Augustus," Auggie corrected. "I don't want *anyone* calling me Auggie Jr. anymore."

"Yes, fine. Ms. Jeffries, it's a pleasure to meet you. I'm Mason Oppenheimer, the Barringers' family and business attorney."

"Nice to meet you," I said, returning his firm handshake.

"Would you like coffee? Something from the buffet perhaps?"

"No, thank you. Couldn't eat a thing."

Mason led me around the burlwood boardroom table, seating me in a tufted leather chair, before taking his place.

"The necessary documents describing why we're here today have been distributed and received, and it is my esteemed privilege to serve the Barringer family as well as Barringer Dramatic Series." Mason calmly slid his diamond-cufflinked shirt, revealing the time to be exactly 9:05 a.m. on his Bulova. "I've been requested to call this meeting by Augustus Barringer, Katherine Barringer, and Veronica Barringer to carry out and shepherd the extraordinary and important proceedings at hand in swift and dignified fashion."

"You call this swift?" Auggie snickered. "Let's get down to business already."

"Yes, as I was saying, since we all have extremely demanding schedules, I won't unnecessarily delay the agenda."

I shakily took a sip of water, pre-poured in cut crystal on the table, and without glancing in his direction, felt Auggie's resentful stare.

"Today's meeting is to vote for the sale of Barringer Dramatic Series. In an unprecedented arrangement, Calysta Jeffries has been appointed proxy for Augustus Barringer Sr. and will be voting *ex parte*, on his behalf."

"Unprecedented, how about outrageous?" grumbled Auggie.

"Before we commence," Mason continued, "I would like to remind everyone that if a unanimous vote isn't reached, there need be only a majority shareholders' agreement."

Butting in, Auggie said in disgust, "Which means if Dad's foxy-proxy decides to vote the wrong way, it'll swing Barringer Dramatic Series away from the twenty-first century and into the edge of night, killing our chances of ever selling these shows for a competitive price. That is unless you want to come to your senses, Mom? Sis?"

A dignified Katherine said, "Auggie, please, let's get through this," while Veronica pursed her lips, fixing her brother with a frosty look.

The room crackled with tension as Mason Oppenheimer called for the vote to begin. "Please give a simple 'yea' to sell, 'nay' to hold, or 'abstain.' Mrs. Barringer?"

"Nay."

"Veronica?"

"Nay."

"Augustus Jr.?"

"Yea, obviously," he said, obnoxiously drumming his pen on the polished wood.

"Calysta Jeffries."

Stemming my nervousness, I swallowed hard, thinking of Grandma Jones and what it would do to her, the publicizing of the Greenwood scandal.

"-ay," I said softly.

Everyone leaned in.

"I'm sorry, Ms. Jeffries, I didn't hear you," Mason said. "Would you repeat your answer clearly?"

Facing the attorney and clearing my throat, I said, "Nay."

"What?" Auggie stood up, knocking his seat over, menacingly circling the table.

"Please compose yourself and sit down!" Mason reprimanded. "The final vote is in favor of keeping Barringer Dramatic Series family-owned."

"Thank God," Katherine said, blinking back tears.

"I'll need each of your signatures," Mason said, handing me his heavy Montblanc pen.

Snapping, Auggie yelled, "You're dead!"

"Auggie, that's enough!" cried Veronica.

"It's Augustus, you moron! You just made the biggest mistake of your life, Calysta! I'm going to crush you like a bug. I'm gonna make sure you *never* work in Hollywood again!"

"Mr. Barringer, if you don't—" Mason boomed.

"Are you guys friggin' kidding me? What about . . ." He stopped, checking himself, realizing he couldn't mention blackmail.

"Auggie, stop it!" Katherine pleaded, trying to calm her son down, as he pushed her away.

"How dare you," Veronica interceded, getting between them. "You're out of control and an embarrassment to the family."

"I'll say and do whatever I damn well please. And this isn't over!" Auggie shouted, as he was escorted out by security.

"Wow," I said.

"Katherine, are you all right? Veronica?" Mason asked, concerned.

"Understandably we're shaken," Mrs. Barringer responded. "But I'm more concerned about you, Calysta. Are you—"

"Oh I'm fine. Honestly, compared to what I've been through, this was a cakewalk, threats and all. Lemme sign those documents."

Standing with the Barringer women in the foyer, Mason warmly shook my hand reassuringly, saying, "Thank you, Calysta, you've done the right thing. I'll be in touch, Katherine. Good-bye, Veronica," before heading toward his office.

"I can't apologize enough for my son," Katherine repeated. "He doesn't understand."

"Mom, stop covering for him. He understands; he just doesn't care. Auggie's spoiled and selfish and has no respect for what you and Dad have given him. He thought he'd sell our family business out from under us and head off to Tahiti, but instead he got the shock of his life and so did Edith and the rest of those vipers. We've saved Dad's legacy and we're incredibly grateful to you, Calysta."

"Here's to chick power." I winked.

"But what was all that nonsense my bratty brother was babbling about?"

"I have no idea."

"My husband will be so relieved this is behind us." Katherine sighed. "We appreciate everything you've done, dear," she said, gently kissing me.

"It was an honor, Mrs. Barringer," I assured her.

Turning to Veronica, she said, "Now, let's talk about Hyannis this summer instead of going to Côte d'Azur. I think spending time at our camp on the Cape will do your father a world of good and we'll be close enough to his doctors should he need them. Besides, you can join us—"

"Mom, I guess you didn't hear the latest, it's going to be a crash course in international soap opera business affairs for me. *R&R* just picked up a licensing deal with the BBC and new affiliates in Sydney, Greece, and Nigeria and I've agreed to take those meetings."

"Isn't that a good thing? But about our summer—"

"Mom, we'll discuss everything on our way home. I need a few seconds with Calysta."

"Of course. Take care, Calysta." Katherine half-smiled, walking toward her chauffeur.

"My brother hates me. I wish we were in this together," Veronica sadly confided.

"Don't worry, things have a way of working themselves out. There's this old story about two wolves inside all of us. I don't remember it verbatim but it goes something like, 'One wolf is evil, angry, jealous, and lies. Has a chip on his shoulder and a big ego. The other is loving, peaceful, generous, and has faith.' Which one do you think will win?"

"Tell me."

"The one you feed. In other words, 'do you' and don't change. Look what this business has done to Randall and Edith, your own brother even."

"I know I keep saying it, but how can—"

"You already have," I cut in. "I'm glad I could repay your dad in some way."

"He's right, it's time I put that journalism degree to good use and get involved in the family business. As a matter of fact I've already penned the perfect scene to rescue you from that deserted island."

We shared a laugh.

"And I wouldn't worry about Edith and Felicia. Edith's going to have enough on her plate to keep her very busy for some time. And if I have my way, which I usually do," she said with a tricky smile, "Felicia won't be head scribe on *R&R* for much longer. She's doing hideous things with the characters; the cast and fans despise her for it. And I want to be the first to tell you, I'm following your lead and hiring a black writer. As for Randall"—she shrugged—"have you heard?"

"Heard what?"

"He collapsed at his party last night. It's a mystery what caused it but he's in a coma."

"A coma?" *Did he say anything to anyone first?*

"Yeah, apparently Alison rode with him in the ambulance," she added, hitching her purse higher on her shoulder.

"Veronica."

"Yes?"

"Don't be surprised if I take your dad up on that offer to return to the show. But first I have some family business to handle."

"I'll expect you when I see you. The car's all yours for the rest of the day."

"Thanks, you're a class act, Veronica."

"So are you."

Heading toward the Bentley, the warm California sun on my face, I thought, *This is definitely a brand-new day.*

FIVE WEEKS LATER

And so I will fly. Where there is nothing left, I fly. And you cannot tie me with your fear, your dislike, or your envy. You cannot hold me down at all. You can only watch as I throw open your mind's eye like a thick curtain, and shake free the dust to reflect the sunshine a thousand ways and ride every mote to its end, laughing that thrown-back laugh that I have, all the way to further than you can imagine. But I do not spurn you. I never spurn you. Come, you.

—R.W.A. Friend, "Faerie"

CHAPTER 49

The Abby Singer

*I*vy, Shannen, and I excitedly ran toward each other while Derrick coolly lagged behind, making his way with a sexy swagga causing a commotion at Betty Ford.

Embracing Ivy tightly, I said, "Happy birthday, baby, we're finally going home!"

"Sorry, Mom, about the emails and calls the last three weeks but Dad said if I didn't spend more time with him he wasn't going to let me go to Greenwood."

"Sweet pea, all that matters is that *I* get you on your seventeenth birthday with Grandma Jones."

"Let me get that for you," Derrick said, sweeping up my luggage.

"Got that orchid you sent. Bloomed forever. One woman even told me the longer a flower lasts sent from a lover the longer . . . anyway, you get it . . . "

For two seconds I thought I saw him blush, his deep Hershey dimples accenting a smile.

"Wow, Calysta, you look amazing," Shannen gushed. "I need to go to rehab if this is the payoff."

"Girl, you're crazy." I laughed, releasing Ivy to hug her. "Tell you one thing, feel better than I ever have."

After TT's crooked antics, Sly got me into Betty Ford, a respectable no-nonsense place with no equine therapy, no shopping, and no Korean body splashes.

Clean and clear, I was returning *home* with Ivy after a twenty-year absence, to spend time with Grandma Jones and the ghosts of Greenwood. To start my life over, I had to learn how to live it right, revisiting my past, and making amends, the first steps to a full recovery.

Randall was still in a coma and it seemed my secret was safe, while Veronica had taken over Felicia's position, demoting her to story coordinator. It still gnawed at me, weeks later, that Emmy had crashed Tranquility Tudor. *What is she going to do with what she learned?* I worried. *Or what has she done?*

"Jump in, ladies, we're on the clock," Derrick said, sliding his hand under my tush, helping me into his Rover.

"Fresh."

"You like it."

"You right." I smiled.

"You-all have a flight to catch and we have a mad drive so buckle up."

We were heading toward LAX with the Noisettes playing, when Ivy turned to me excitedly. "Mom, guess what?"

"What, babe?"

"I asked Dad to swing by our house the other day so I could pick up a few things for our trip and . . ." She made a drumroll sound, patting her hands on her lap.

"C'mon, don't keep me in suspense."

". . . the kitchen is finally done!"

"Don't joke, Ivy."

"I'm serious. I know that contractor guy was a nightmare but Derrick took the bull by the horns. It's beautiful. You're gonna love it."

"Wow, D, you did that for me?"

"Since we're sharing good news," Shannen chimed in, "they're finally taking that nasty trach out of my mouth and I can bury that sud-dud storyline. Thank gawd Veronica took over."

Listening to Shannen talk about her storyline as though it were real life, I wondered, had *I* sounded like that, so caught up in that bubble that I'd lost sight? Soap stuff was far, far away from my reality right now and I knew if I *ever* went back it would have to be much, much different. Veronica and Katherine Barringer had assured me it would be.

"Roger's still in the pokey, couldn't make bail, it's half a mill. On top of that Maeve's suing him. Javier and I are still going strong, he's taking me to the Latin Grammys, he's a presenter with Eva Longoria. And he's teaching me Spanish! Did you know *fruta bomba* means 'papaya' in English? How sexy is that? Oh, and I filed for divorce. Everything is so great again!" Pausing for a breath, she continued, "'Cept for one thing. My air show scenes were going to be wicked fantastic, but I was preempted by another stupid car chase. And last year the same thing happened to me over Wimbledon, remember? Best damn scenes all year, I was going to put them on my Sudsy reel for a pre-nom."

"I feel ya," Derrick said, chewin' on a toothpick. "Last week I was knocked off the air by Obama, but that's okay, he's cool beans and it *was* the presidential address 'n' all."

"Yeah, but least you get to go into syndication. Soap stars only get one shot to be seen outside of being exported, and that doesn't count."

"Right about that," I said.

"Why doesn't it count?" asked Ivy innocently.

Together, Derrick, Shannen, and I chimed in, "Three years behind and pennies on the dollah!"

We all fell out with laughter, diggin' the international exposure, just wantin' to get paid for it.

"Seriously, Shannen, I'm sorry you got preempted, but I couldn't be happier for you and Javier, and proud that you handled your business with your knucklehead soon-to-be-ex-husband."

Two and a half hours later, with Ivy napping on my shoulder, we pulled up to Northwest groovin' to "Can't Believe It."

"Wake up, honey. We're here."

A flagged skycap came running. "Ruby, Ruby Stargazer, when are you coming back? We miss you." The fans were always amazing no matter who they were or where they were from.

"Someday," I answered.

"Sir, you need to move your car," an officer warned.

Right on cue, Shannen flirtatiously asked, "Hi, officer, can you give me directions to Marina del Rey?"

"Derrick, you've been there for me through the good, the bad, and the ugly—"

"Don't stress. Trust, next time I see you—"

I finished, "I'ma lay some *hip woo wong* on *you*," smacking a heavenly kiss on him.

"Come on, you guys. Mom, this is so embarrassing."

"Thanks, officer, for being so patient. It's my dyslexia." Shannen smiled.

I crossed to give her a squeeze good-bye while Ivy threw her arms around Derrick. He pulled out a small wrapped box from his jacket pocket and said with a wink, "Don't open it till tonight, birthday girl."

"Okay, thanks, Derrick!" She giggled.

". . . and don't forget, when you get back, we're going to Jamaica," Shannen reminded me.

"I couldn't have done it without you, girl. We'll call you when we land," I said on the move, blowing a kiss, looping my arm through Ivy's.

"Let's go see Grandma."

CHAPTER 50

Done Run a Hundred Miles and Ended Up at My Own Front Door

A blood orange sun dipped behind distant pines as I steered the rent-a-car onto Money Road, now paved, and parked it in front of Grandma Jones's house. I was instantly flooded with memories, some good and others I'd rather forget.

"C'mon, Mom."

Miss Whilemina came barreling through the screen door and down the steps at us full throttle as we got out of the car.

"Goodness gracious, Beulah Espinetta Jones, get over here and give me a hug right now. And you too, little bits," she said, addressing Ivy, squeezing us.

"Oh, Miss Whilemina, you don't know how good it is to be back home."

"It's been too long," she half-criticized. "And look at *you*, Missy Anne," a name she called every girl under the age of eighteen. "Just as beautiful and a spittin' image of your mamma."

"Thank you, ma'am."

"Your grandma been showin' me pictures of you growin' up for years. But now I get to see you in the flesh. Y'all just in time for Saturday's Annual Greenwood Barbecue Cook-Off too! Always did have good timin', Beulah."

Grandma Jones bounded out next. "Sister Whilemina, you let my Beulah and great-grandbaby loose so they can come see me right this instant."

"I'll catch up with y'all later," Whilemina said, walking next door.

Ivy and I ran up the steps and fell into Grandma Jones's arms as she smothered us with a deep-bosomed hug, before ushering us in to the delicious aroma of baking cake. "Thank God that flying tin can stayed in the air long enough to get you both here safely. Don't know how they do it but I prayed for travelin' mercies and here you both are in one piece. God is good."

As soon as that screen door slammed shut I went back two decades: familiar scents and sounds washed over me as if time had stood still. The Mills Brothers' "Sleepy Time Gal" was playing on WOHT from Grandma's transistor radio in the kitchen, and the plastic-covered furniture was exactly where I remembered it, only more yellowed. She'd refused a new living room set, insisting, "Me and your grandpa bought this furniture after the Korean War. Besides it took me the longest to break in that doggone couch and pay off the layaway."

Licking her fingers, Ivy lapped up the last bits of Grandma Jones's butter-fried chicken while we finished catching up on how she'd made the honor roll in spite of the recent drama.

"Babygirl, there's plenty more chicken where that came from."

"Thank you, Mother Jones, but I'm full."

"Coulda fooled me. Hope you saved some room for your birthday cake. Beulah, you see this chile eat a bird like there's no tomorrah? Suck the marrow right out the bone like I do," she added, shaking her head pridefully.

"Didn't get it from me," I agreed as I took our dishes to the sink, the same plates I ate from as a child with a black and red rooster in the center.

"And why you wastin' that skin? Folks over in Africa starvin' to death. It's the very best part."

"I know, Grandma," I said, scraping what was left into the swill bucket.

Wiping the countertop, I looked down at a faded coffee can half full of bacon grease; so many memories.

"Anyone mind if I get some air?" I asked.

"Shoot, better go before it gets dark and starts pourin'. Storm's on its way, know that much. Besides, we got an important birthday to celebrate. Ain't that right, sugah?" she said, looking lovingly at Ivy.

"Yes, Mother Jones, and that cake smells good too."

"And Beulah."

"Yes, ma'am?"

"Greenwood ain't what it used to be. Things have changed 'round here and not all good."

"Don't worry, I won't be long."

Inexplicably, I felt suffocated and happy all at once. I needed to get to where I needed to go and it couldn't wait, not for one more second.

"'Course, sugah. Ivy's gonna help me with the dishes and then we're gonna get my secret paprika barbecue sauce ready so I can marinate the rest of this meat for the cook-off tomorrah. I know *you* can't cook, Beulah, so I need to pass on the tradition to my great-gran."

I lingered after walking out the door, listening to Grandma Jones say to Ivy, "I'm very proud of you. Know things ain't been easy, runnin' all over kingdom come. But you strong just like your mamma . . . like all us Jones women."

"Mother Jones, I wrote my last English paper on you."

"Shush your mouth, Ivy. You don't say."

"Yes, ma'am."

"I am just tickled."

Leaving them to each other, I stopped in front of our old persimmon tree, now considerably bigger, reminiscing about harvesting clusters of the fruit for Grandma's homemade chutney and pudding, before plucking a ripe chocolate tomato, dropping it into my messenger bag.

Grandma was right. Driving through town, I didn't recognize whole blocks. Stopping at a Piggly Wiggly where a farm had once been, I purchased flowers and headed to the local cemetery down on True Bible Way.

After parking the car, I picked my way around the mix of new and crumbling gravestones, most of them dotted with sprays of colorful plastic flowers, big in the South. Folks said, "Hmph, real blooms too expensive but plastic ones? Baby, you can't kill those things with a stick."

Easily remembering the plot where Mamma was buried, I slowly knelt, taking a moment before clearing away dead leaves.

"Hi, Mamma, it's Beulah."

As I closed my eyes, my fingers traced the mason's outline of my mother's name, Maddie Mae Jones. Tearing up, I placed the bouquet against the granite, a headstone I'd purchased with my first *Rich and the Ruthless* paycheck but had only seen in a photograph. Listening to the whistling wind, a drop of rain on my cheek, I said, "Not in vain, Mamma, not in vain," kissing the stone before walking back to the car.

As quickly as I started the engine, I stopped it. Walking with urgency, I headed to the far side of the cemetery in a trance. Distant thunder rumbled in the opaque sky, an eeriness taking hold, leaving me alone in the whispering cemetery. Passing the unkempt plots of a silent jury, my adrenaline surged as I got closer and closer to the overreaching leafless arms of a craggy oak tree marking my father's headstone. It read:

Calm on the bosom of our God,
Fair spirit, rest thee now!
E'en while with us thy footsteps trod,
His seal was on thy brow.
Dust to its narrow house beneath!
Soul to its place on high!
They that have seen thy look in death
No more may fear to die.

CHESTER ZACHARIAH WINSLOW
BELOVED PASTOR OF
CHURCH OF THE SOLID ROCK
BORN 1922
DIED 1989

A chill ran through me as I stood over him, now six feet under, unable to deceive the innocent. Mindlessly reaching into my bag, pulling out the velvety persimmon, I bit into it, spitting out the seeds before making my amends.

"Payback's a bitch, mother——" A clap of thunder boomed.

"Happy birthday, dear Ivy, happy birthday to you. Make a wish, baby," Grandma Jones, Whilemina, and I cried.

She tightly closed her eyes. Seventeen flickering candles danced, glowing in my daughter's bright full-of-life face.

Ivy was now the age I'd been when I left Greenwood for New York City with all my secrets. How dramatically different our lives were, and would be, I hoped. Still, a pang of concern lingered from when Ivy had asked, "You know, Mom, I've been thinking, maybe I'll try out for the school play this September. What do you think?"

It was the last thing I wanted her to do. All I could think of was the rejection and the madness, but one thing was for doggone sure, I wouldn't whip her for trying.

A soft smile broke across Ivy's face before she blew her secret into the flames.

Grandma Jones had made her signature cake: vanilla coconut frosting with lemon filling. A birthday confection she used to bake for me when I was a girl.

Excitedly opening Derrick's gift first, Ivy squealed over the newest iPod Touch gizmo he'd given her.

"Gimme that bow and the paper, I can recycle it," Miss Whilemina said. "Think that storm's gonna pass, Miss Candy," she added, folding the paper against her broad lap.

Next, Shannen's gift, a book of poetry with a journaling feature.

"Aww, sweet," Ivy said, quickly turning her attention to an old metal box with a key placed on the table. "What's this?"

"Open it and see," I said.

She turned the key and lifted the lid.

"They're beautiful." She glowed, pulling out the same strand of pearls Grandma Jones had given me two decades earlier.

"We want you to wear them in good health, Ivy, for all of us," Grandma Jones said, with tears in her eyes.

Hickory-smoke-filled air added to the atmosphere the following day as I reconnected with old friends and extended family who'd watched me grow up as sassy, stubborn Beulah Espinetta Jones. It was a time and a half at the Annual Greenwood Barbecue Cook-Off and as at most reunions, gossip took center stage. Between horseshoes, Double Dutch, dominoes, and the Electric Slide, we all ate more than our fair share of greens, mac 'n' cheese, potato salad, pulled pork, ribs, and BBQ chicken, not to mention peach cobbler and rhubarb pie.

"What's this?" I heard Ivy ask Miss Bessie, another longtime neighbor of Grandma Jones.

"That's monkey meat, chile," she said as she sipped on her sweet tea.

Ivy gasped and Miss Bessie chuckled. "It ain't monkey and it ain't meat, it's a candy made of coconut and molasses. Real good, here, try some."

"Beulah?" a quiet voice said from behind me.

Turning, I saw my childhood friend Seritta, looking half who she was, accompanied by a young woman with a toddler on her hip.

"Seritta!" I exclaimed as we hugged, rocking side to side. "Girl, it's been so long."

"You can say that again, but you haven't changed a bit, look just the same."

"You are *too* kind."

"No, it's true. I know *I* look different, been through some thangs. My pastor taught me how to fix it though and preached, 'Woke up one mornin', fell into a hole, stayed there awhile, climbed out and went about my business. Next day, I fell into that same daggone hole, stayed there awhile, climbed out and went about my business. But the *third* day I went down a different street.'"

"Amen to that."

"Yep, mm-hm, I needed to walk a different way, that's all." Seritta smiled. "I've missed you somethin' terrible, Beulah, but you *nevah* did forget where you come from. You been so good to us. Even though I'm still in that trailer, that trailer is my home and it kept most of my family together, thanks to you."

"Oh, Seritta, you're givin' me way too much credit."

"I ain't blowin' smoke. Got my twins with me, and CiCi, she gave me my first gran. Let me say this out loud, there's a big difference between motherin' and grandmotherin'. I can hug T.I. all day long, give him back to his mamma, and keep it movin'. Speakin' of family, I see Ivy over there lookin' pretty as a picture. How's Dwayne?"

"Girl, he's still butt broke, callin' himself a housesurgeon or some such foolishness."

Seritta snickered before turning serious, saying, "I know I've said it a thousand times in letters but let me say to your face, I am so grateful for our friendship. We may not have seen each other for a month of Sundays but it don't matter 'cause I always knew you were there for me, Beulah, just like I'd be there for you. Say hi, CiCi, and take that thumb outta ya mouth."

"Hi," she said, looking down.

"Nice to finally meet you, CiCi, your mom's told me so much about you, I feel like I already know you."

She nodded, her face inscrutable, saying, "Heard a lot about you, too."

As the night wound down, dressed in a handbrushed cotton nightie, I lay in my dimly lit room, stuffed to contentment on the same old bedroom cot my mother had slept on as a girl. A muggy breeze blew Grandma's homemade sheers, ushering in the scent of rain signaling another storm was brewing as I listened to Ivy, Grandma Jones, Miss Whilemina, and Seritta, laughing and talking trash while playing bid whist on the back porch, the lone irrepressible sound of a neighbor's harmonica echoing through the night.

"You forgot to pluck, Seritta," said Grandma Jones.

"Did not."

"Did too," sided Whilemina. "Don't be tryin' to cheat. *Ah-choo!* God bless me, everyone." All adlibbed blessings. "You just worried we got all these *books* and about to go downtown on ya." They all roared with laughter.

"Wanna go to Biloxi with me and Miss Odile next Friday, Whilemina?" Grandma Jones asked.

"If you payin', I ain't got no gamblin' money. But I'll tell you what we got plenty of, these doggone mosquitoes, tryin' to eat a person alive," she said as she slapped her leg. "Good thing you got this porch screened in when you did, Candy. Don't know how that man's out there blowin' that harmonica."

"'Cause mosquitoes only like sweet meat," Ivy chirped. "Ain't that right, Mother Jones?"

"That's right, babygirl."

Plucking up a card, Miss Whilemina asked, "Candelaria, did Beulah say when she was goin' back to the stories? It just ain't the same without her."

"And it ain't gonna be, there's only one Beulah. And she's as stubborn as she pleases. Got it in her head she ain't goin' back till *R&R* acts right, hires folks to do her hair and things."

"Shush your mouth, Candy . . . don't tell me that child's been doin' her own?" questioned Miss Odile.

"Mm-hm, says she tired of doin' everything herself plus act. To hear her tell it, they don't pay her like the others, either."

"Whaaaat? That's a doggone shame," said the ladies in chorus.

"I'ma stop watchin'," said Whilemina.

"I don't want to hear all that," Seritta insisted. "Just tell her to go back to *The Rich and the Ruthless*. Dove needs her."

"Tried to tell Beulah before all that mess happened, be grateful you got a job. But she fired back sayin', 'If you don't stand for somethin' you'll lie down for anything,' and ladies, that right there shut me up."

All eyes fell on Ivy, who said, "Don't look at me, I don't know, but I *will* say I hope Mamma doesn't go back."

"Beulah just needs to sit her butt right here in Greenwood for a spell," Grandma Jones added.

"Always did think that girl had too much moxie for her own good," Miss Whilemina quipped.

"Bet you sure like having your mamma home full-time, Ivy," said Seritta, fanning herself with her cards.

"Mamma's been working since I was born and it's different for both of us, but we're lovin' it."

"We won again, Candy," Miss Whilemina exclaimed.

"Whew, look at the time. Gotta get to bed. We got church tomorrah," said Grandma as Ivy gathered up the worn cards, slipping them back into their box.

"Yes indeed," said Miss Whilemina, "I need somethin' to cover my press till I get home. It's damp outside."

The Church of the Solid Rock would be packed for eight o'clock service tomorrow morning and we all were invited to Miss Whilemina's for Sunday dinner after. But I was bracing myself for more than over-size horsehair hats and a flat sermon. I'd have to prepare for old memories that would surely surface, sitting next to Grandma Jones under the carved pulpit where my father once preached his "buckle in the Bible Belt" service about fire and damnation.

Robed, standing six feet tall, broad-shouldered and barrel-chested, he had a furrowed brow and long wiry eyebrows that made him look more like an angry eagle about to take flight than any preacher.

Without conscious thought, I wove my fingers into a shape resembling a steeple, remembering the finger game and poem Grandma Jones had taught me so long ago. Pantomiming the motions, quietly whispering, "Here is the church, here is the steeple, open the doors and here's all the people . . ." I realized as much as things had changed they had stayed the same. I could run a hundred miles but would always end up at my own front door.

To the pitter patter of raindrops on our tin roof, Lalah Hathaway's sultry "Bad by Myself" ringtone jolted me out of my thoughts. Reflexively snatching my phone off the nightstand, I hoped it was Derrick. The small screen illuminated my expectant smile, reading, "i no wat u did 2 yr daddy, beulah."

Acknowledgments

The women who encouraged me to write and beyond . . .

Dottie, Kit, Esther, Sylvia, Laura, Barbara, Patty, Paulina, Rosa, Robs, Nancy, Kasi, Wyllisa, Aunt Ruthie, Vicki and all the laughs in Antigua—everyone in my foster family who taught me to never underestimate the importance of correspondence—my first writing lesson.

Inspiration

All my children, art, blueberries, Gustav Mahler, *the South*, ballet, orphans, India, butterflies, Malaga, flowers, vintage hats, Sarah Vaughan, photography, Elizabeth Catlett, old movies, Maria Callas, Paulo Coelho, sequoias, Augusta Savage, the fans—my husband and collaborator, Radcliffe Bailey, who tirelessly read, listened, and was my sole audience as I acted out the scenes in a lampshade and curtains, BIG KISS.

Special Thanks

To my literary agent, Irene Webb, who with boundless enthusiasm, humor, and warmth believed in the bubbles from the beginning. And Malaika Adero, vice president, senior editor—the most brilliant, supportive editor in the world.

Dear Malaika,

Your steady leadership and vision to see Secrets of a Soap Opera Diva *published is by far one of the greatest gifts ever bestowed upon me.*

Infinite thanks,
Victoria

To the incomparable Judith Curr, executive vice president and publisher of Atria Books, Todd Hunter, Alysha Bullock, Jae Song, Christine Saunders, Christine Lloreda, Kathleen Schmidt, Rachel Bostic, and all of the Atria/Simon & Schuster family, especially all the hands that print, bind, box, and unload my books everywhere, thank you from the bottom of my heart. May this only be the beginning.

Special, Special Thanks

To the remarkable Heather Lashaway, Manuela Hesslup, Linda Livingston, Derek Blanks, Christopher Hayes, Stephanie Wash, "Q," Nelson Branco, Amy Brownstein & Associates, and Jamey Giddons for your extraordinary generosity.

Daytime Divas

Ruby Dee, Margueritte Ray, Veronica Redd, Tonya Lee Williams, Debbie Morgan, Tamara Tunie, Vivica A. Fox, Tichina Arnold, Tonya Pinkins, Davetta Sherwood, Renee Jones, Rosalind Cash, Mary Alice Smith, Stephanie Williams, Renee Elise Goldsberry, Vanessa Bell Calloway, Nia Long, and Ellen Holly.

Memorial Regret

Norma Donaldson, Frank Pacelli, Greg York, and Michelle Thomas.

SECRETS
of a
SOAP OPERA

Diva

VICTORIA ROWELL

A Readers Club Guide

You were born in Portland, Maine and you were raised in foster care for eighteen years. Did your memoir of that experience—*The Women Who Raised Me*—influence this book? Describe how your childhood experiences have helped shape you into the star you are today.

Absolutely. The women who raised me were all independent, successful, and intrepid. They were out-of-box thinkers, whether a farmer in Maine or a ballet teacher in New York. Without question, I was shaped by the discipline of farming, which requires acute scheduling and order—from the planting to the harvest. It's labor intensive while at the same time the physicality earns you a hard-won result that is gratifying. That said, discipline is at the heart of all my success and my first discipline is being a farmer.

How much of this story is "fiction" and how much is "true"? Would you classify this story as fiction based on personal experiences, or personal experiences peppered with fiction?

I believe the best writing is informed by actual experiences. Though *Secrets of a Soap Opera Diva* is entirely fiction, I've starred on three different soap operas over a span of twenty years and would conclude my personal experiences layer and inspire all of my writing.

Why did you decide to write this story? Describe the journey from conception to publication.

I had the extraordinary privilege to work under the daytime drama scribe William J. Bell. Bill Bell was the kind of person who inspired me to do more than act. Where I'd been writing since a child, I was further motivated to put pen to paper for a soap opera novel in the late 90s because I believed there was a part of daytime drama that remained shrouded in secrecy to its fans, and an opportunity to engage people who'd never watched soap operas at all.

I began toying with a film script but decided I needed to write the book first. Where I'd accumulated considerable amounts of material for *Secrets of a Soap Opera Diva* over the years, it was writing my memoir that gave me the momentum to finish my novel. Interestingly enough, as demanding as it was being on a *New York Times* bestselling book tour, I was fueled by how *Secrets* took on a life of its own. I knew I was onto something when the book began waking me up in the morning and I worked on it sometimes thirteen hours a day, completing it while on the road. It took two years to shape and get it published.

Were any of the characters based on people you have known in your life? On yourself? Do you relate most to Calysta? Why or why not?

I will simply say that, much in the way that I fashion my characters on myself when I act I, too, use that technique in my novel. For instance, the legendary character Drucilla Winters on *The Young and the Restless* is a compilation of multiple people I grew up with. So my characters may not necessarily be informed by one person, but rather a composite of individuals.

Naturally, I relate to Calysta Jeffries on many levels, first and foremost her survivor spirit, indefatigable energy, and zeal for fashion.

How did you make the move from acting to writing? Are the two similar? Do you give more of yourself when you act or write, or are the two equal?

I don't look at it as a move as I never stopped writing. I was a writer before an actor and used that skill in editing countless scripts. In fact, I believe my writing skills enhanced my performances.

In my world they're synonymous. They're equal because I pour just as much energy into the words while sitting in a chair, as I would acting them physically. Both acting and writing come from the soul, and I have a physiological reaction whether I'm dancing, acting, or writing. It's a spiritual encounter.

Your novel depicts a part of stardom that we don't often see in popular culture; that is, those who are victimized by racism in their careers, such as Calysta. Was it important to you to present an alternative point of view?

I actually don't see Calysta as a victim. As is the case with many individuals who are courageous enough to attempt to change something that's antiquated, it's never popular and always met with pushback. It's easier to minimize Calysta's contributions than to recognize them because to recognize them would force change. Sadly, change costs money and forces an upending of one's comfort zone. Therefore, Calysta is emblematic of countless people around the world. Whether you're prejudiced against as a woman, handicapped, gay, black, or for creed, she represents the pursuit of closing the disparity therein. I hope my readers will come away from reading my tome, *Secrets of a Soap Opera Diva* with more than daytime drama.

Why did you decide to structure the story as part first person narrative, part gossip blog, and part screenplay? What effect do you think the structure has on the story overall?

I felt it was imperative for me to write in first person. Being one of the top fifty actresses in daytime television, my fans would have expected no less, as it's a staple in soap operas. I personally love reading books in first person. I'm immediately drawn into the story and instantly absorbed in what the narrator is sharing with me.

Given the virtual nature of the world today with twitter, facebook, blogs, etc. and their global reach of hundreds of millions daily, it goes without saying how instrumental anything viral is to the success of whatever you're advertising, be it clothes, music, TV/film, and namely books. It's where media is at today. As I'm a huge fan of twitter and facebook and am giving my novel its own twitter and website, www.secretsofasoapoperadiva.com, having a blog incorporated in the novel made all the sense in the world.

Over the past twenty years, in answering oodles of fan mail, one of the most sought after items from me is a signed script. With that in mind, knowing the fans love the idea of owning a script, feeling a script, and reading the intricacies of stage direction that's encapsulated in a script, I incorporated that element into my novel. I think the fans will really enjoy seeing the script pages . . . with my actual changes.

All that said, the rules of the literary game have changed for the most part. Meaning, as writers we have to, without compromising our story, consider all of the modern tools available to us to further connect with the world that wakes up to the Internet and goes to sleep to it.

What would you name as the major theme(s) of the novel? What do you hope readers will take away from the story?

Behind-the-scenes soap biz politics. Family. And love conquers all.

I hope my readers will come away from reading my tome, *Secrets of a Soap Opera Diva* with more than daytime drama.

Do you hope to break any stereotypes with this novel?

In a perfect world, yes. But I won't hold my breath. I'll just say, it won't be color television in my eyes until there's more diversification in front of the lens as well as behind it. In every area, directing, writing, producing, and all creative endeavors. There's an ocean of rich talent out there and I know how hard I've worked to attain success and be counted. What's tantamount in order to bring about change or make a difference; you have to stay in the race. That's why I'm a long-distance runner.

Who are you reading now? Who is your favorite author? What is next for you as a writer? As an actress?

I'm reading *Victoire: My Mother's Mother* by Maryse Condé, a book chock-full of imperishable magic and beauty.

It's hard to limit it to one for I have many, but I will say Barbara Kingsolver's in my top ten.

Next I have the sequel to *Secrets of a Soap Opera Diva* and a screen-play. Also, the *Secrets of a Soap Opera Diva* One Woman Show at the Southwest Arts Center in Atlanta, Georgia, June 4–6.